ONCE A THIEF

ALSO BY CHRISTOPHER REICH

ONCE A THIEF

A SIMON RISKE NOVEL

CHRISTOPHER REICH

MULHOLLAND
BOOKS

Little, Brown and Company
New York   Boston   London

Mulholland Books / Little, Brown and Company
Hachette Book Group
1290 Avenue of the Americas, New York, NY 10104
mulhollandbooks.com

First Edition: April 2022

Mulholland Books is an imprint of Little, Brown and Company, a division of Hachette Book Group, Inc. The Mulholland Books name and logo are trademarks of Hachette Book Group, Inc.

The publisher is not responsible for websites (or their content) that are not owned by the publisher.

The Hachette Speakers Bureau provides a wide range of authors for speaking events. To find out more, go to hachettespeakersbureau.com or call (866) 376-6591.

ISBN 9780316456098
LCCN 2021944055

10 9 8 7 6 5 4 3 2 1

MRQ-T

Printed in Canada

For Laura, with all my love

Part I

OUTSIDE

CHAPTER 1

He was late.

Carl Bildt locked the front door of the bank and set off at a brisk pace along the Via Nassa. At 7:15 in the evening, the narrow, cobblestone walk bristled with activity. Crowds of summer tourists window-shopped, ate gelato, and sipped iced tea. Most wore shorts and open shirts, their faces tanned by the August sun. Bildt paid them not the slightest attention. His mind was focused on a more important matter: staying alive one more day.

He continued through a covered galleria and across the Piazza della Riforma. He was a large man, fifty-five years old, tall and broad of beam, with a thick head of silver hair and a sailor's windburned complexion. As always, he was dressed as befitted a bank manager: tailored charcoal suit, white shirt, burgundy tie, his Bally lace-ups immaculately polished. He was a punctual man in a punctual country, and as he walked, he checked his watch repeatedly, as if hoping to find its hands frozen or, even better, moving in the wrong direction. Bildt frowned. No such luck.

He had made his decision. There was no turning back.

He came to Riva Giocondo Albertolli, the thoroughfare running adjacent to the lake. A moment to put on his sunglasses. A glance over his shoulder. Nothing there. He felt rather than saw them. He crossed the street and continued on. The water was alive with sailboats and pedalos, the ferry leaving a broad wake as it steamed away from the pier toward Caprino, then into Italy.

In fact, Bildt was a sailor himself, and one of no small accomplishment. At eighteen, he had embarked on a solo voyage around the world, just him and his cat, Tango, in a twenty-six-foot sloop. The trip took three years. He survived by the grace of God and a preternatural instinct for danger. Then, it was in the form of an ability to sniff out storms, knowing when to go at them and when to seek shelter in port. Today, it was in the ability to gauge his masters' trust, or perhaps, more importantly, their lack of it.

Once again it was time to seek shelter in port.

They'd promised him somewhere warm and near the sea. More than that, he didn't know.

A hundred meters farther on he reached the building behind the casino, on Piazza Indipendenza. He took the stairs to the underground lot. It was a measure of his anxiety that he hesitated before remotely unlocking his car, and again as he climbed behind the wheel and pressed the starter button. If Carl Bildt was an adventurous man, he was not an entirely honest one.

Since coming to Lugano, he had taken actions as manager of the bank that did not wholly conform to the Swiss legal code. He was not the first. His predecessor had done the same. Such practices, Bildt was told, were standard operating procedure. All part of the job. He enjoyed his generous salary and the lifestyle it afforded him. An expensive car, a beautiful home, vacations sailing aboard his yacht. He knew better than to ask questions.

Lately, however, things had changed. It was getting harder to do what was asked. The sums were too large, coming too often. A kind of untamed financial river, overflowing its banks, growing more swollen by the day. And he, Carl Bildt, alone was tasked with taming it, with guiding it to calmer channels in distant lands.

Others had noticed. Authorities had begun to ask questions. Diverting so much "water" could not be accomplished without drawing notice.

And so, his dilemma.

Bildt left the parking lot and guided his car west alongside the lake. The meeting was scheduled for 7:30 at the Villa Principe Leopoldo, the city's finest hotel, situated on parklike grounds on a hilltop over-looking the lake. The meeting would be no different from any other he conducted with clients several evenings each week. An aperitif, an exchange of pleasantries, then down to business. He would hand over a dossier with the most recent statement of accounts. Tonight, however, the dossier would contain something extra. There would be a flash drive attached holding the information he had promised. Information valuable enough to guarantee him a new life. Then Carl Gustav Bildt would vanish.

Gone in the blink of an eye.

Or rather, the click of a keystroke.

The light turned red. Bildt slowed the car, stopping in front of the art and culture museum. A pale man in a dark blazer stood at the curb. Despite having the right of way, he did not cross the street. He was looking at Bildt's car, at Bildt himself.

The light changed. Bildt accelerated too quickly, leaving behind a patch of rubber. Calm down, he told himself. Everything was all right. The man hadn't been looking at him. *Or had he?* Bildt turned on the stereo. A bit of music to ease the nerves. Bach. The prelude to the first cello suite.

Leaving the lakeside, Bildt turned onto the winding road that climbed to the Villa Principe Leopoldo. He was rewarded with a view across the lake, mountains rising steeply from its shores on every side, the water sweeping in a great azure crescent south into Italy. For a moment, transported by the music, the vista, he allowed himself to drift off…to float across the water, to imagine that he had not turned his back on his entire life, that he would not be a fugitive for the rest of his days.

A look in the rearview mirror. A car drew close behind him. An Audi. Black. Two men inside. There was something about them. Bildt accelerated, taking the turns too quickly. The Audi matched his speed. Another look in the mirror. It was them. He knew it.

He saw the construction site at the last moment. Barriers blocked the road. Behind them stood a backhoe and a pile of gravel. He swung the car hard to the right, narrowly missing the blockade. Bildt shot down a one-way road, cars parked on either side, apartment buildings blocking out the sun. Ahead, a Beetle was stopped at the intersection. He braked and came to a stop behind it. And the Audi? Gone.

Bildt sighed. Nerves. Everything was fine. Just fine. A laugh. Relief.

Ahead, the door of the car opened. A man exited, looked his way, and ran up the road.

Bildt studied him. Odd. Why was he leaving his car? A moment passed before Bildt noted the urgency in the man's stride. It was, he decided, as if the man were running for his life.

Bildt knew everything at once. The Audi. The construction site. The car blocking his path.

A trap.

Bildt threw his car into reverse. His foot slammed the gas pedal to the floor. His head turned to look over his shoulder. A way out. He must find a way out.

Too late.

At that instant, fifty kilos of Semtex plastic explosive expertly packed in the car parked next to him detonated. The force of the blast obliterated the automobile, launching it twenty feet into the sky and sending deadly scads of metal in every direction. The fireball enveloped Bildt, roasting him alive. A piece of steel, rectangular, as sharp as a razor, flew through the open window of his car. Traveling at a velocity of five hundred feet per second, it struck Bildt an inch above his shoulders and passed through his neck, severing his head.

In the last fiery seconds of his life, Carl Gustav Bildt had the unique and mercifully brief experience of viewing his own torso wedged in the shattered windshield of his car as his head sailed through the air.

CHAPTER 2

Yountville, California

Dez Hamilton was telling the story about how he found the one-hundred-million-dollar automobile.

"It was the smell that got me. Imagine…sitting in a barn for thirty years, a barn missing half its roof, one wall nothing but splinters. And this in the south of England, a mile from the coast. Owls, cormorants, gulls, you name it, shat all over it for years, winter, spring, summer, and fall. Think they call it 'guano' when there's that much of it. Like those rocks off the coast of Peru. An entire mountain of shit. You could have mined the stuff."

Hamilton paused to let his audience laugh along with him. He was sixty-something, a Londoner, a short, jolly toastmaster with tousled gray hair and rosy cheeks, dressed in the pink golf shirt he'd purchased at Pebble Beach Golf Links the day before. Desmond "Dez" Hamilton liked to say God had given him two gifts: how to hit a two-iron on a string and how to make gobs of money. Hamilton was in commodities. His company, Dreadnought Ltd., was the world's largest trader in precious metals.

It was three p.m. or thereabouts on a sun-drenched August afternoon in the Napa Valley. Hamilton, Simon Riske—Hamilton's automotive advisor and restoration expert—and an elegant French woman named Sylvie Bettencourt were seated in the private dining room of the French Laundry, the fabled three-star eatery. All were elevated by the after-effects of eating as fine a meal as there ever was, washed down by several bottles of equally fine wine, and polished to a sheen by several flutes of Champagne. What better way to celebrate the sale of the 1963 Ferrari 250 GTO. The price: 102 million dollars and zero cents. The highest sum ever paid for a motor vehicle.

"Anyhow," Hamilton, the seller, continued, gathering steam, "I had no idea what it was. Some kind of rotted, rusting hulk. Thought it was farm machinery, to be honest. Didn't want to go near it. Did I mention the smell?" A laugh to raise the roof. "You see, it turned out the barn came with the estate. Had to get out of London. Too much for an old man these days. Traffic alone, God forbid. Takes an hour to get from Highgate to Bond Street. For the price of a three-bedroom flat overlooking the Thames, I got a three-thousand-hectare estate that had once belonged to the king himself—Henry the Eighth, no less.

"So there this thing was. Left it there for a month. Anyone could have pinched it. Course they could have done the last thirty years. Nothing stopping 'em. Still, I was curious. Came back for another look. That's when I saw the tires, I mean the spokes. Thought to myself, 'Hmm, rum, very rum indeed.' The old instincts kicked in. Money. I could smell it.

"Next time I was at the club, I passed this man's garage"—a nod in Simon's direction—"*European Automotive Repair and Restoration*. Went inside. Told him I might have found something and asked if he might have a look-see. 'Bring your rubber gloves,' I told him. 'And your Wellingtons.' Next day, he drove down. Walked right to the hood and swiped off a load of bird shit and *voilà*! There it was. The badge. Yellow and black with a prancing stallion. *Ferrari*. Ten minutes later he had the entire car cleaned off. Still didn't know what I was looking at."

"I had to tell Dez what it was," said Simon.

"Called it 'the Holy Grail,'" said Hamilton. "I said, 'What do you mean? I'm not the religious sort. Is it a car or a relic?'"

"'Both,' I told him," said Simon, flushed and as happy as he'd been in months. "He didn't understand until I told him what it was worth."

"Nearly pissed myself," said Hamilton. "Excuse me, Sylvie."

"I might have done something more," said Sylvie Bettencourt, the lilt of her accent making her words that much more amusing.

"Knew I loved this woman," roared Dez Hamilton. "Not just 'cause of the size of her pocketbook or her big—"

"Dez!" said Simon. No more DP for him.

Simon Riske had come to Northern California a week earlier for Monterey Car Week, the annual seven-day celebration of everything in the motoring universe. There were races and lectures and auctions and, of course, the Concours d'Elegance, a gathering of the world's finest automobiles on the eighteenth fairway at Pebble Beach Golf Links.

Simon's arrival had been advertised in advance. The event catalogue sent to participants included an article discussing the discovery and subsequent restoration of the 1963 250 GTO, which it had named "the Lost Ferrari." It hinted that the car might be for sale and that a record price was expected. (The car was too coveted to be sold at auction. The wealthiest collectors made their bids in private, away from prying eyes.) Interested parties could find the car on display on the grounds of Quail Lodge.

There had been a sheikh, from the Al Maktoum ruling family of Dubai, who'd offered to take Simon into the desert for some falconry if he'd give his offer a favorable nudge. Bid: $80 million. A Swiss industrialist drawn all the way to California from his secret alpine lair who hadn't offered Simon anything except an icy glare and a few well-aimed clouds of smoke from his Cuban cigar. And a five-foot-tall Indian venture capitalist named Patel who'd made and lost a billion dollars on five separate occasions. Bid: $95 million.

In the end, though, there had been only one real bidder.

The woman seated across the table, whose ice-blue eyes held his gaze as if he were cuffed hand and foot.

Sylvie Bettencourt was sixty, maybe more, though she looked hardly a day older than he—white-blond hair cut to her shoulders, a sharp, inquisitive face. Too hard to be considered pretty, too proudly professional, but more attractive because of it. And yes, as Hamilton had pointed out, quite a figure.

Just as Simon was Dez Hamilton's agent in the sale, Bettencourt had acted in a similar capacity for a client who remained unnamed. Simon knew better than to ask who. He'd seen her over the years at auctions and concours and exhibitions. There was a time when she'd allowed herself to be outbid. Not any longer. Once Sylvie Bettencourt raised her hand, the sale was as good as done.

"But, Dez, tell us one more time why the car was deemed to be your property," Sylvie Bettencourt was saying. "It must have belonged to someone."

"Property of a chap in finance like me," said Hamilton, "except he was bent. Crooked. Owed the Inland Revenue millions. Hid the car in a friend's barn to keep it from being seized. Before things got sorted out, he topped himself. No heirs. Chap's estate paid off the back taxes. When I bought the property, the barn—and the car inside—came with it. Finders keepers. Mine to sell and yours to buy."

"Quite a story," said Sylvie Bettencourt.

"Couldn't make it up," said Hamilton with relish.

"Good for you," said Sylvie Bettencourt. "And good for me...or rather my client."

Simon might have added that the Ferrari, known by its chassis number, 3387, was the second of only thirty-six manufactured at the plant in Maranello, Italy. Designed by Sergio Scaglietti, the prototype tested by Stirling Moss, and powered by a Colombo V12 engine, it was a working thoroughbred that had achieved seventeen podiums, including a second place at the 1963 24 Hours of Le Mans. "GTO" for *gran turismo omologato*—grand touring homologated. Simon had never learned what that last word meant.

3387 was painted racing red—"Ferrari red"—and had been restored to look precisely as it had that hot June day at Le Mans in 1963, the number 24 painted in black figures on a round white field on either door.

Inside, the car was stripped down to its essentials: a skeleton of exposed metal; safety bars; quilted leather bucket seats; steel instrument panel crowded to bursting; a bulky five-speed gearbox rising from the center console, a bony stick shift protruding from its cavity; a large, sturdy wooden steering wheel (giant by today's standards), the trademark yellow and black badge at its center.

Simon considered it the finest Ferrari ever designed. But not to look at. No, to look at, it was a gorgeous mutt. The nose—long, low, and curvaceous—was borrowed from the Jaguar E-type, which had thrilled the car world a year before. The resemblance ended there. The 250 GTO was a fastback, meaning the roof sloped sharply in the rear to a vertically chopped-off tail. It was a raw-boned street fighter clad in a prince's armor. A magnificent deception. Not entirely dissimilar to Simon himself.

Riske was pushing forty and looked it. He was fit, tall enough, his black hair cut short and receding at the temples far too quickly. He had a broad, lean face, a worker's jaw, cheeks nearly always dark with stubble. His father was American, his mother French. From her, he got the beryl-green eyes that women seemed to adore. If he heard someone say, "My, what lovely eyes you have," one more time, he'd throw up. Actually, he'd smile and say, "Thank you." He prided himself on being a gentleman. It had not always been the case.

The door to the dining room opened. Servers entered bearing dessert. Or, this being the French Laundry, *desserts*. There was panna cotta laced with summer fruits, chocolate cake, donuts and coffee, other pastries with names Simon couldn't guess, vanilla ice cream. They ate in delighted silence, punctuated by the occasional sigh. *This is really too good.*

Hamilton produced a leather case from his pocket. "Cigar? Romeo y Julieta from Havana. Sylvie? Simon?"

"Thank you but no," said Sylvie Bettencourt, bemused. It wasn't every day she was offered a cigar.

"Not a smoker, Dez," said Simon.

"You're missing out, the both of you." Hamilton repaired to the outdoor patio.

Bettencourt slid her chair closer to Simon's. "I've seen you at these things now and again. I'm surprised we've never met."

"Last year at Sotheby's. Battersea Park. The 270 Spyder. Sixty-two million, was it?"

"A bargain at the price."

"You have a good eye."

"I have help. What do I know about cars?"

They shared a look. The answer was "A lot" and they both knew it.

"And you, Mr. Riske, purchased a 1972 Dino. Six million, no?"

Simon laughed, taken aback. "I wouldn't have expected you to pay attention to that lot. A little below your standard."

"I paid attention to you, Mr. Riske."

"I'm flattered."

"I'm sure you're used to it. A man like you must have many admirers."

"Uh…" Actually, no. Simon didn't receive enough compliments to have a quick rejoinder.

She placed a hand on his. A perfectly manicured nail ran back and forth. She leaned closer. She had a secret to share. "It's come to my attention that restoring automobiles is not your only profession," she said softly, as if others were close by and might hear. "You handle different kinds of work, more interesting assignments, shall we say. You discovered a team of thieves robbing the casino at Monaco. Something about a tussle in Paris involving a Saudi prince that you sorted out. And didn't I hear something about a stolen Monet you removed from a yacht while it was at sea? Don't look so surprised. I have eyes and ears everywhere, Mr. Riske. *Simon.* Maybe I've been watching you longer than just a year. Word is that you are a resourceful man."

"I'm not sure what you've heard, but really, I spend most of my time at the garage."

The eyes narrowed, looking hard at him. A smile. A shake of the head. She wasn't having it. "I'd enjoy discussing it further. Maybe this evening if you're free."

"I'm here to help Dez. But I'm happy to give you my card."

"Oh, I know where to find you. I don't get to London as often as I'd like. Come back to the hotel. Nicer to talk about these things away from prying eyes. In private."

Simon couldn't mistake the promise in her eyes. Of what? Misbehavior? How to respond? She was, after all, the same age, or near enough, as his mother.

And yet . . .

The door to the patio swung open. Sunlight flooded the room. A stranger entered. Medium height, broad shoulders, pale complexion, dark hair. He wore a black V-neck T-shirt that showed off arms too muscular to ignore. He stood still as the door closed behind him.

"Excuse me," said Simon. "This is a private lunch."

"You, Riske," the man said, advancing on him, hand extended, pointed at him like a gun. "Shut up."

CHAPTER 3

Vadim, what is it?" Sylvie Bettencourt sat up straight. "Is everything all right?"

"Him," said the stranger, taking up position above Simon. "He lied to us."

Simon pushed back his chair and stood. A look at the man. Dead blue eyes. High cheekbones tapering to a sharp jaw. Colorless lips. "Who is this?"

"Vadim, please," said Sylvie, with authority. "You're being rude." She addressed Simon with politesse. "Meet Vadim. My assistant in all matters."

Simon did not extend his hand. Vadim looked like a snake. Venomous, make no mistake.

By now, Dez Hamilton, hearing the commotion, had returned. Cigar jutting from a corner of his mouth, jaw clenched, he looked every inch the seasoned trader. He knew when a deal was going south. "What's this, Simon?"

No answer. Not yet. "Well?" said Simon to the others, sudden adversaries.

"The car," said Vadim. "He lied to us. Something's missing. The gearbox. It's not the original."

The gearbox. Simon was unsure whether he should allow himself a measure of relief. "Of course it's not," he said. "It's a long-distance racer. They go through two every competition. I built it myself according to the original specs. Is there a problem?"

"You're lying," said Vadim. "That's the problem."

Sylvie Bettencourt asked to speak with her assistant privately. The two moved to a corner of the dining room. It was impossible to ignore Vadim's urgent imprecations.

Dez Hamilton poured himself a flute of Champagne too quickly, quaffing it as it overflowed. "Pray," he said to Simon, "that you didn't screw me."

"Pardon me, Dez?"

"I need that money, lad. Every last penny."

"Gearboxes break," said Simon. "3387 was a race car. They probably changed gearboxes three times that first year at Le Mans. Or at Sebring or Daytona. Just like they change out brakes, rotors, and sparks."

Unmollified, Hamilton poured himself another glass. When in doubt, self-medicate. He was officially in the enemy camp.

Sylvie returned to the table. "First, let's all of us remain calm. I'm sure we can work through the problem."

"Damn right we can," said Hamilton.

"Yesterday evening I wired 102 million dollars to your account, Dez, as payment for a 1963 Ferrari 250 GTO, chassis 3387, certified by both of our inspection teams as 'highly original.'"

"The top mark given," said Simon.

The inspectors had come from Ferrari headquarters in Maranello, Italy. Both were career mechanics, more knowledgeable about Italian motorcars than any other person on the planet. Every part of the automobile was examined and judged for being original or as close to it as possible: engine, paint, coachwork, chassis, instrumentation. If the original part was impossible to restore, replacements were sourced from other models. Only then, if still unavailable, was Simon permitted to make his own replacement part. No certification process was more rigorous.

"Yet," Sylvie continued, "it has come to our attention that you did not choose to source the original gearbox."

"Like I said to Dez, it was most likely exchanged during a race. Gearboxes are interchangeable."

"So the original must be somewhere."

"Doubtful. Probably used for spare parts, melted down, or just on a junk heap."

"Not this one," said Sylvie. "Everyone knew this car was special, even then."

"Tell that to the mechanic in the pit when the gearshift snaps sixteen hours into a race," said Simon.

"Stop making excuses," said Vadim. "You didn't do your job and you know it."

Sylvie placed a hand on Vadim's arm. *Down boy.* "My buyer is a demanding man. He wants the original. He is an investor. He believes the value of the car will increase should it be found."

"He's not wrong. That's why my team scoured the world looking for it," said Simon. "Look, Madame Bettencourt...*Sylvie*...I spent fourteen months on this car. Believe me when I tell you that the gearbox cannot be found."

"The gearbox is out there," said Vadim. "The original. Someone has it."

"How do you know that?" said Simon.

"Someone contacted us," said Sylvie. "Someone we trust."

"Who?"

"A reliable source."

"Saying what?" demanded Simon. "That they have the gearbox? Nonsense."

"Not that they have it," said Sylvie. "Only that they've learned that someone else does."

"Does that someone have a name?"

"We're not at liberty to say."

Simon wasn't buying. "And this reliable source just happened to know you're in Pebble Beach buying 3387 when news about that very gearbox popped up?" He looked at Dez. "Come on, this is ridiculous."

"What are you angling for?" asked Hamilton, waving the cigar. "A refund? That it? Want to bargain us down? Forget about it. Too late. The papers are signed. The car's in your garage. The money is in my account. Deal done."

"But it isn't," said Sylvie, with painstaking authority. "It's my obligation to my client that I give credence to this report. And so it is your obligation, too."

"Bollocks," said Hamilton. "We don't have to do shite."

Vadim hit him. A shot to the side of the head. Dez Hamilton stumbled, then collapsed.

Simon grabbed Vadim by the shirt, shoving him against the wall. Suddenly, Simon's world was topsy-turvy. He collided with the floor, facedown, a knee in his back. A grunt and the pressure on his back abated.

Simon got to his feet, dazed and winded but ready for a fight. The knife in Vadim's hand cut short any ideas he had about retribution. It was a karambit, gleaming bare steel shaped like a crescent, only the short, very sharp blade visible.

"Here's how we will work out our differences," said Sylvie, unfazed by the spate of violence. "You have one week to find the gearbox. If you can't, you will wire me the sum of ten million dollars."

"Ten million?" said Hamilton. "Are you crazy?"

"Consider it ample motivation."

"What if your source was mistaken?" asked Simon.

"That's not possible," said Vadim.

A look at Hamilton. The Englishman was smart enough to keep his mouth shut.

"Should you refuse to comply," Sylvie continued, "or should you go to the authorities, which of course is your right, then other, more severe measures will be taken."

"Never," said Hamilton. "Not going to happen. Won't do—"

Vadim was on him in a flash, the blade pressed to his cheek, a hand wrapped around his windpipe.

"Please," said Hamilton.

A flick of the wrist. A gasp. Vadim stepped back. Slowly, the gash appeared on Hamilton's cheek. Two inches long. Deep.

"You were saying, Dez?" Sylvie asked nonchalantly.

"Nuh…nothing."

"Ah," said Sylvie. Right answer. "Vadim, give the man a napkin. We don't want to stain the carpet."

Hamilton pressed the napkin to his cheek.

"To be clear, the people I represent do not make threats. A threat implies that we are not going to get our way. As you know by now, I always get my way." Sylvie Bettencourt picked up her purse. She approached Simon on the way out. "I'm sure a man of your gifts will have no problem fulfilling our request. Seven days, then."

A moment later they were gone.

Dez Hamilton turned on Simon. "Just so we're clear, I don't threaten anyone either. You don't find the gearbox, it's you who's paying the ten million." He slumped into a chair. "And you can pick up the check while you're at it."

Chapter 4

Lugano, Switzerland

Anna Bildt stared at the wall of faces sitting, standing, hovering around her. A dozen or more officers crowded into the stuffy meeting room on the first floor of the Lugano *stazione di polizia*. Men and women, some in uniforms, others in suits. Local police, federal police, even Danish police. All had introduced themselves, but with so many names and organizations, Anna didn't remember any of them.

"Miss Bildt, when was the last time you spoke to your father?"

"When did you see him last?"

"Did he mention that he was in trouble?"

"Were you aware of him being involved in any illegal activities?"

For thirty minutes, the pack of them had hurled questions at her like grenades; red, anguished faces pressing her for answers she couldn't give. The problem was, Anna decided, as the last of her patience evaporated—water heating to steam—no one appeared to be in charge.

"*Basta!* Enough!" A new voice. Commanding, unimpeachable. A small, round man with a tonsure of black hair, dark-rimmed eyeglasses, and a professorial regard stepped forward. "Gentlemen, ladies, please. We are all of us anxious to learn whatever Miss Bildt can tell us about her father. If I may ask her questions on behalf of us all, I think we will proceed more efficiently. All of you may arrange private interviews later, if Miss Bildt is so willing."

Categorically, no, thought Anna, doing her best to keep a composed, cooperative expression on her face.

"My name is Hans-Peter Tell…no relation to William." A smile. *Sorry.* Anna wasn't buying. "I am the deputy director of the Federal Intelligence Service. I'm sure this must be overwhelming. Understand,

18

we have never had a car bombing in Switzerland. We are all of us upset, though nothing, of course, compared to your loss."

Anna wasn't sure if she was meant to answer. Of course it was overwhelming. Forty-eight hours ago she'd learned that her father had been blown to kingdom come by a car bomb…not in Baghdad, not in Beirut, but in Lugano, Switzerland. She'd left Copenhagen the next night and driven straight through, due south across Germany, crossing the Swiss border at Schaffhausen, then another three hours south past Zürich, finally, traversing the endless Gotthard Tunnel beneath the Alps. Sixteen hours, stopping only for gas and the toilet.

Arriving in Lugano, she'd traveled directly to the crime scene. The crater, the blown-out windows, the curtains waving like flags of surrender, the disarray and damage. If she hadn't seen it, she wouldn't have believed it.

"May I offer you something?" said Tell. "Coffee, tea, a sandwich?"

"Tea," said Anna. "Black. No sugar."

Tell fired off an order. An underling scurried from the room. "And so, Miss Bildt, may I inquire how you are feeling?"

Anna said she was fine, just tired.

She was a lithe, athletic woman, five feet nine inches tall, a devotee of CrossFit and matcha tea. Muscles instead of curves. Vegan, of course. She was twenty-nine years old, her thick, straight hair colored a thousand shades of summer wheat, shaved to the scalp on one side, cut to the shoulder on the other. A sleeve ran down her left arm, the artist a Māori girl she'd slept with long ago. Her blue eyes stood out against a bold suntan. She wore ripped up jeans and a red T-shirt that said, DON'T STAND THERE, DO SOMETHING.

One look and you knew her type. The iconoclast. The change agent. The one in the back of the room who questions the rules. Not quite a revolutionary but ready for the revolution.

At seventeen, Anna Bildt had quit school to work with Sea Shepherd, the global marine conservation organization, and spent three years crisscrossing the seven seas, in her father's wake, so to speak, hindering whaling in the western Pacific and the plundering of fisheries in the North Atlantic.

At twenty, she returned to terra firma and moved to Brazil, where she joined in the fight against Amazonian deforestation and the displacement of the Yanomami Indians. For her efforts, she received a ten-month sentence in a São Paulo prison. From there, it was back to Denmark.

She'd spent the last seven years skipping from one non-governmental organization, or NGO, to another, adding her voice to whatever cause engaged her. She was anti-fascist, anti-globalist, anti-everything. What the world needed, in Anna Bildt's opinion, was a nice strong dose of anarchy to shake things up. And when it came, she would be there ready and waiting, anxious to rearrange what was left when all the pieces fell out.

The tea arrived. Anna took a sip, nodding to Hans-Peter Tell that she was ready now. Please continue.

"So far, Miss Bildt, we have ascertained that you last spoke with your father this past Sunday, saw him two months ago for a sailing holiday in Sardinia, and he never gave any indication that he might be in trouble or that he feared for his life."

"That's correct."

"You are aware of his position?"

"He ran the Lugano branch of the Danske Bank."

"An important job, by any definition."

"If you say so."

"Did you know what his duties entailed?"

"We didn't discuss work."

"Never."

"Never."

Tell didn't like the answer. "Private bankers often meet wealthy, glamorous individuals, persons of merit and accomplishment. It would hardly be surprising if he wanted to share this with his only daughter."

"Isn't that against bank secrecy?"

"So is sharing information with a foreign government."

"Excuse me?"

"I'm only saying you do, in fact, know something about his job."

No, that's not what you're saying, Hans-Peter—no relation to William—Tell. You're saying that my father was not entirely an innocent victim. "Let me be absolutely clear with you and everyone in this room. I know nothing about his work. I have never heard him say the name of a single client.

I have no idea who might have wanted him dead. Now please, if I may, I'd like to go to our home."

"Of course," said Tell.

The roomful of law enforcement professionals erupted in a clamor. Questions ricocheted off the walls. English, German, Italian, Danish. Something was amiss.

Anna made her way out of the room—it was easier to leave a Coldplay concert—and down the corridor toward the stairs.

"Miss Bildt, one last thing."

Anna turned. It was Tell with several colleagues bunched at his shoulder.

"It would be helpful if we could examine your father's office at home, his bedroom, even. It is likely we'll find something to help our investigation."

"You want to search it?"

"Just to have a look."

Them. In her home. Picking through their belongings. The thought made her ill. "I don't want you in our house," said Anna. "Please respect my family's privacy."

"Perhaps another day."

"I don't think so."

"We can obtain a warrant," said Tell.

She was getting him upset. Good. "Go ahead. Get one. Until then, stay out."

Anna hurried from the police station before Tell could utter another word.

CHAPTER 5

London, England

Who is she?" asked Simon as he stormed into D'Artagnan Moore's office in the Lloyd's of London building.

"What? No 'Hello,' 'How have you been?,' 'Damn it, D'Art, have you lost a few pounds while I've been gone?'" Moore stood and came around his desk, hand outstretched.

Simon ignored it, offering an accusatory finger instead. "What have you got?"

Wednesday afternoon. Ten past four. Outside the windows of Moore's eleventh-floor office, a heavy rain fell. The Thames, barely a quarter mile distant, was obscured by cloud and mist, the pinnacles of Tower Bridge as fleeting as ghosts.

Simon had come directly from Heathrow. He'd managed an hour of sleep on the flight from San Francisco, if that. He'd spent the time scouring the results of the past years' most prestigious automobile auctions—Sotheby's, Bonhams, Christie's—making note of every vehicle purchased by Sylvie Bettencourt and forwarding the list to D'Art.

Cars needed insurance. Expensive cars needed lots of it. Firms that insured vehicles valued at over twenty million dollars were as few in number as the cars on the list. Most of them—the insurance agents, that is—were located on the several floors above and below where Simon was standing.

For the record, Sylvie Bettencourt had purchased six Ferraris, two Bugattis, and a Mercedes 300 SL Gullwing. All no doubt in perfect factory condition. Price paid for the lot: $220 million, including chassis number 3387.

"Simon, please take a seat." An order, not a suggestion. "I've had a look at the list."

"And?"

"The usual. Good news and bad news."

Simon fell onto the couch with an exaggerated sigh. He was tired and looked it. Dark rings beneath the eyes. Two days of stubble. Blazer wrinkled. Shirt decorated with tomato juice, courtesy of an overly friendly flight attendant. Oh, for the days of social distancing.

"Drink?"

"Make it a double," said Simon, though he wasn't sure if it would keep him going or knock him out.

Moore crossed to the beverage trolley, selected two cut-glass tumblers, and poured two fingers of alcohol in each. Single-malt scotch from a crystal decanter for himself and, for Simon, Jack Daniel's from a bottle kept at the back of the shelf.

"Health," said Moore, lifting his glass. He was a bear of a man, six feet five inches tall, three hundred pounds, a thick head of unruly hair, a huntsman's unrulier beard. As always, he was dressed in the finest Harris Tweed, with a tartan tie and a paisley handkerchief overflowing his breast pocket. Simon had known him since they were boys. They weren't friends. They were family.

"Health," said Simon.

Moore sat down in a quilted club chair and set his drink on a table beside him. "Good news first. It wasn't difficult to find out who wrote the policies on the cars you gave me. Inigo James upstairs handled three of the Ferraris. Patrice Labiche in our Paris offices handled the Bugattis. All of the policies were written in the name of various holding companies. Oakmark Investments registered in the Bahamas. Victor Holdings of the Caymans, others in Panama, Cyprus, Curaçao."

"Keeping the buyer's identity anonymous."

"Not a Christian name to be found."

"Do any of your colleagues know her personally?"

Moore shook his head. "Everything handled through her offices. Investissements Bettencourt, 5 Avenue Charles Floquet, Paris."

"Nice address," said Simon. If he wasn't mistaken, the building was situated somewhere on the Champ de Mars with a view of the Eiffel Tower. "So a dead end?"

D'Art raised an eyebrow. "Do you think so little of me?"

"I gave you nine cars. Where else is there to look?"

"Laterally."

"Meaning?"

"Why just cars?" suggested Moore. "A woman who buys one-hundred-million-dollar automobiles for her clients...mightn't she be charged with purchasing other repositories of wealth? I mean, that's what a car like that is. She didn't buy it for her client to drive, did she? It's a hard asset, something that can be counted on to hold its value, or, with any luck, increase it."

Simon saw where D'Art was going. "So why isn't she buying up art?" he suggested. "Van Goghs, Picassos...?"

"Maybe a Hockney watercolor for 113 million," said Moore, a little too convincingly.

"At?"

"Christie's in New York two months ago. By the way, the sale set a record."

Of course it did, thought Simon. "Real estate?"

"Funny you should ask. The old Leopold the Second estate on Cap Ferrat. One of the last undivided parcels on the Côte d'Azur."

"I know it." Simon also happened to know the previous owner: an Israeli tech magnate named Dov Dragan, last seen in his Bugatti Veyron somewhere along the Grande Corniche above Monaco.

"Scooped up for one hundred ninety million euros," said Moore.

"You've been doing your homework."

"Always looking for new clients," said Moore, without the least irony. And why shouldn't he? "I called around and gave my associates a brief description of Madame Bettencourt, as per your recounting."

"You didn't use my words?" Which were: "An ice-cold, sixty-year-old, blond you-know-what who could crush a man's nuts with her bare hands."

"I took a wild guess that there are not too many women like her, at least not brandishing bottomless checkbooks. Chap on the eighth floor wrote a policy covering some jewelry she recently picked up. A tiara and crown made for the czarina of Russia."

"Alexandra?"

"Further back. Catherine. Peter the Third's wife. Another colleague in Manhattan wrote paper on a condominium she purchased a while back."

"For an anonymous buyer?"

"That appears to be her M.O."

"Does anyone actually know anything about her? Married? Children? Significant other? She didn't just appear out of thin air. Someone has to know how she got her job."

"That's the bad news," said Moore. "Not a whisper. Pays her premiums on time, never balks at rate increases. What more is there to know? The model client. Oh, there is one thing. She has a nickname. 'The Collector.'"

"'The Collector,'" said Simon. "Fits. It's my turn to take a wild guess, and I'd say that the person or persons she is collecting for are not the same upstanding, law-abiding citizens as you and I. Desmond Hamilton wasn't the first person she'd threatened. Not by a long shot."

"Are you ready to tell me what this is all about?"

"You really want to know?" said Simon.

"I'm all ears."

"A gearbox."

Moore cocked his head, eyes narrowed in bewilderment. "What the hell is that?"

Chapter 6

London, England

Traffic to the shop was as bad as Simon could remember. He needed thirty minutes just to get out of the City, cross Blackfriars Bridge, and make it onto the A3. A distance of just over two miles. Maybe it was time to pick up and head to sunnier climes. Marbella, Nice, Rome, even. He'd liked the hill country outside Monterey, California, at least until Sylvie Bettencourt had gone and ruined it. The fact was, Simon could run his business from anywhere. Clients sent him cars from all over the globe. Buy a building. Bring in a team of mechanics. No one needed to put up with this annoyance.

Simon turned on the radio. The Police. "Message in a Bottle." Appropriate. Memories of knocking around the country house in Royal Tunbridge Wells. What was he…seven? Eight? Had just come to London…Saturday mornings, music blaring from his father's stereo. The Police. Springsteen. Aerosmith. But mostly, the banging rock of the 1970s. T. Rex, Bad Company, Zeppelin. Simon's taste in music came from his father, a legacy he treasured.

Traffic came to a halt. His hands tightened on the wheel. The light turned green. No one moved. Horns sounded. *Yeah, why?* Simon shouted silently, eyeing the car behind him. *What good is that going to do?* He looked at his hands, knuckles white. He relaxed his grip. *For that matter, what good is it holding on to the wheel like you're strangling your worst enemy?*

Simon caught sight of his eyes in the mirror. He didn't like who he saw looking back. Too soft. Too polished. *One of them.* He'd seen it coming. Maybe it was him getting older. Attaining a degree of success. Banking a few dollars. Somewhere along the line he'd lost sight of who he was. Where he was from. What he'd been through. It wasn't that he'd stopped caring. It was that he'd willed himself to forget.

It was the fiasco in the restaurant that had done it. He'd been bested. He didn't mean by Vadim, though he would not forget anytime soon being tossed onto his back as if he were a Cub Scout. It was her. It was Sylvie Bettencourt. She'd had him fooled. Hook, line, and sinker. He'd taken her at face value. Her looks, her demeanor, her presentation. Sylvie Bettencourt, buyer for the richest collectors in the world, class act.

Oh, Simon. Oh, buddy. She got you. Peel off the veneer, the clothes, the makeup, the charm—*"Word is that you are a resourceful man"*—and she was a hood. A stone-cold criminal.

And he'd missed it.

He hadn't had a clue.

A kid who'd grown up on the mean streets of Marseille, who'd begun stealing cars at sixteen, taking down payroll trucks a few years later, a made man in La Brise de Mer, the toughest outfit in the South of France, at eighteen. He'd failed to spot one of his own.

This whole thing was a wake-up call.

No more, he told himself. No more forgetting who he was, where he came from, what he'd done. He was still the renegade youth who gloried in emptying an AK-47 at an armored truck. Who could jack a car in thirty seconds. Who enjoyed hearing the snap of a ligament shearing when he fractured a man's knee.

He'd show Bettencourt.

She was right about one thing. He was a resourceful man.

Once a thief.

This wasn't his first repo job.

Twenty years earlier.

Marseille. A month from his nineteenth birthday. Salad days, then, even if he was already neck-deep in criminality—boosting cars, knocking off jewelry stores, administering beatings to enemies and to anyone he didn't like. Before the Monet and the Patek. Before the nonexistent gearbox.

Before all of them, there was Mercedes. Simon was surprised he didn't trip over the memory more often. Then again, no one liked to be reminded of the times when things might not have gone the way they wanted…*shouldn't have gone that way* by all rights.

For the record, Mercedes was a person, not an automobile. French, not German, with more than a trace of Corsican blood in her, which always complicates matters. Her full name was Mercedes Isabella Campobello, and she was the youngest daughter of Alberto Campobello. "Don Alberto" to Simon and all those whose forearms were emblazoned with the mark of La Brise de Mer, the criminal organization that ruled the shadier side of the sunny Riviera.

"Americano, vieni. Per favore."

An August day like this one, sunshine instead of rain, and windy, the sirocco blowing across the Mediterranean, depositing a fine wash of sand from the Algerian desert and, remarkably, the scent of oranges grown there. An urgent call. Come to Don Alberto's home. "Just you, Ledoux," which was the name he went by in those days, his mother's married name. "Not a word to anyone." An anxious drive to the pale stone villa outside Cassis, on a bluff overlooking the Calanque de Port-Miou.

"Americano, look at you! Sit, please."

It was Simon's nickname, referencing his mixed parentage, though Simon was as French as anyone who'd grown up in the 16th arrondissement of north Marseille.

"Don Alberto, an honor," said Simon, bowing his head.

The don waved away the formality. They were friends, after all. *Amici.* Family, too, in a Mediterranean sense of the word.

Simon sat down, shoulders pinned back, jaw raised, gaze rock-solid. It was a Sunday morning. By definition, he was still either drunk, stoned, or high from the night before. He had showered, put on a fresh set of clothes—his best jeans, an open-collared shirt, and a pair of Ferragamo loafers that had belonged to the husband of a woman he was seeing. Visine for the eyes. A shot of fernet for the gut. And two bumps of Bolivia's finest for his head.

Andiamo!

Don Alberto conducted his affairs beneath a sea-green canopy in his garden. He was a dapper, middle-aged man, dressed in white linen, silver haired, with a raptor's fierce nose, and its dark, all-seeing eyes, too. He sat at an aged wooden table on a bed of gravel adjacent to his *pétanque* court. His dog, Bella, a wire-haired mutt he'd rescued from a rival's farm in Corsica, lay at his feet. To look at, he was a successful businessman enjoying a summer morning out of doors—that is if you didn't pay attention to the bodyguard standing behind him, a pistol in his shoulder holster and a *lupara* cradled in his arms.

"A problem," said Don Alberto. "My daughter, Mercedes. I believe you know her."

Simon said he did and asked if she was well. In fact, many people knew Mercedes Campobello. More than a few looked like Simon. Dark haired, lean as a girder, eager to get into trouble.

"I haven't seen her in a month," Don Alberto continued. "No, no, don't worry. I know where she is. With the older Spado boy. Vicente. Shacked up in his hotel suite at the Negresco."

"I know him," said Simon. Thirty, an underboss in the family business. Not a thief like Simon. No smash-and-grabs for him. A businessman, or so he fancied himself. Sharp suits. Slim wristwatch. BMW in his garage. Simon called him a drug dealer.

"Who am I to tell her who she can see?" said Don Alberto. "She's always done what she wanted. If she likes Vicente Spado, good for her."

Simon nodded, but his expression let the don know his true opinion.

"But…" Don Alberto pursed his lips. "She has something of mine. Something I need returned to me. True, I gave it to her. A present for her eighteenth birthday, but now, with things as they are, I cannot allow her to keep it."

Ah, thought Simon. The car. A red Porsche. The bane of drivers up and down the *route nationale*. Don Alberto wanted Simon to repo the car before she drove it off the Moyenne Corniche. Easy enough.

Don Alberto pushed a photo into Simon's hand. "Take a look."

Simon held it up. Not the Porsche. A picture of Mercedes Campobello wearing a black dress, dark hair up, brown eyes staring invitingly into the camera.

"See it," said Don Alberto. "The coin around her neck. It was my mother's and her mother's before it. Their dearest possession. A treasure."

Simon studied the necklace. It was a gold twenty-franc piece hanging from a slim chain. Common enough. He could find a dozen like it in jewelry stores and pawnshops for a few thousand euros. "It's very nice," said Simon.

"Now look at this."

A second photograph, this one of a thin man, black hair, mustache, wearing a dark suit and blue dress shirt. A poser.

"Vicente Spado," said Simon.

"Look closer."

Simon took the photo. His stomach clenched. There was the coin…*around Spado's neck.* Ah, it had to be. Simon made an unpleasant noise.

"My sentiments exactly," said Don Alberto. "She gave it to him. A knife in my belly would hurt less."

Simon handed the photos back, his own belly growling, an envoy of bad things to come.

"I can't have it," said the don. "The disrespect. If my mother knew…" He placed the pictures facedown on the table. A sip of espresso. The hawk's gaze landed on Simon. "If you could return it to me."

"The coin?"

"You're good at this kind of thing, I'm told. You have a light touch."

Simon accepted the compliment with aplomb. Yes, he could lift a wallet, provided the mark was drunk. *But this?* All the same, he nodded confidently.

"Take your time. Maybe you come next Sunday? We'll have a nice lunch together, just you and me. *Famiglia.* Some carbonara, wine? So I can thank you."

"Of course, Don Alberto. Next Sunday."

"Eleven o'clock. Before it gets too hot. You do like carbonara, *Americano?*"

"My favorite."

"Say goodbye to Bella."

Simon muttered a few words as he left. Goodbye was not among them. It would be easier to steal the *Mona Lisa* from the Louvre than a chain from around Vicente Spado's neck.

Spado was easy to find. As Don Alberto had stated, he had taken up residence in a suite on the top floor of the Hotel Negresco, Nice's finest, on the eastern end of the Promenade des Anglais. First the good news. After two days, Simon had his schedule down pat. Spado left the hotel at nine in the morning, a few of his cronies in tow, and zipped around town in the BMW, venturing to Cannes, Antibes, Toulouse, never farther. Always back by six. A businessman indeed.

Now the bad news. Spado wore the coin religiously. Simon didn't need the don's photo to recognize it. He'd seen it close at hand, the last time as it was swinging wildly back and forth between Mercedes Campobello's pear-shaped breasts as she straddled him in the back room of a club in the Vieux-Port in Marseille. Even so, it didn't look half bad around Spado's neck.

Be that as it may, there would be no getting it during the day.

Nighttime was a different story.

Every evening at nine Spado left the hotel with Mercedes Campobello, accompanied by a rotating band of friends and hangers-on. It was their pleasure to make a tour of a half-dozen discothèques and clubs along the Côte d'Azur. Villefranche. Saint-Jean-Cap-Ferrat. Cap-d'Ail. Each night, however, ended at the same establishment twenty-odd kilometers up the coast in Monte Carlo. Jimmy'z.

So Jimmy'z, then.

Except they wouldn't let him in.

He arrived Wednesday at midnight. The club was located a block from the port. Nothing special to look at. A two-story commercial building. White tile façade. Neon sign. Red carpet. A couple of tall plants. Other than the line outside the door, there was little to indicate that it was among the glitziest nightclubs in France, owned by Régine, a red-haired force of nature who'd singlehandedly introduced the word "discothèque" into the lexicon of nearly every language around the world. Régine and her well-trained staff didn't like nineteen-year-old Simon Ledoux, no matter how alluring his flashing green eyes and rugged good looks. There was something of the *voyou*—the hoodlum— about him, and hoodlums were not welcome at Jimmy'z.

Thursday night Simon arrived wearing a suit he'd borrowed from a friend, Tino Coluzzi, who unfortunately was a little smaller than him. He'd cut his ponytail and gone in for some of the greasy stuff Spado used by the barrel. A shave. No rings on his fingers. The diamond stud in his ear, however, stayed.

No go.

The handshake with a hundred-euro note never came into play.

Friday night. Time running out. He arrived a little earlier, this time paying one of the older guys, Jojo Matta, to act as his chauffeur and ferry him to the entrance in his new Renault. Jojo held the door as Simon climbed out and walked to the head of the line. This time he even was able to speak to the doorman, palm him two hundred euros. The money was promptly and politely refused.

"Fuck off back to Marseille, *p'tit con*."

One of his homeboys. Just his luck. Simon made a note of the bouncer's face. *One day . . .*

It was then that Simon saw the Ferrari. A red 308 GTB. The driver was a troll: short, fat, probably a Russian by the diamond-encrusted Orthodox cross around his neck. His companion, however, was lithe, blond, and a looker. Quicker than a hiccup they were inside.

Saturday night. Now or never. He found a Ferrari parked behind the Carlton Hotel. A Testarossa. White, not red, but there was that thing about "beggars." The girl was named Sophie. A knockout to look at and thrilled to have an honest night out. Beyond that...well, for tonight, looks were all that mattered.

He arrived at a few minutes past eleven, so early that the velvet rope wasn't in place. Same bouncer. No line. Before the guy could say a word, Simon palmed him five hundred euros and a plastic vial. A look at the Ferrari, at Sophie, at Sophie's décolletage, not necessarily in that order.

"Go ahead."

Simon was in.

Vicente Spado and Mercedes Campobello arrived at two a.m. From his vantage point at the bar in the rear of the club, Simon watched as they were led to a vacant table, one with a snotty little placard reading RESERVED. Four others joined them. Bottles were brought. Grey Goose, Dom, Perrier. A hand went up. Spado snapped his fingers. A tureen of caviar arrived in a moment, the waiters kowtowing as if Spado were the King of Siam. It was, to be honest, impressive. Maybe dealing drugs wasn't such a bad option after all.

Simon ordered a beer and, for Sophie, a gin and tonic. Another fifty euros. He was five beers in already. The problem was that he was too nervous to just sit and wait without taking a sip. If he wasn't drunk, he was definitely tipsy. There was only so much booze a one-hundred-fifty-eight-pound frame could hold.

His plan required two things: first, that Vicente Spado liked to dance. And second, that Sophie did what he'd taught her.

There was movement at the table…Simon rose off his stool. Maybe? The dance floor was packed, colored spotlights dashing here and there. No. Two of the women headed to the ladies' room.

It was critical Mercedes not see him, at least not until he was ready to move. She wasn't the quiet type. He was counting on the fact that his conduct—not entirely gentlemanly, it was true—had not left him in her better graces.

And then, like that, they were up, making their way onto the dance floor, Spado cutting a path to the center, shoulder lowered, Mercedes following close behind, hand in his.

"Wanna dance?" he said to Sophie.

"Now? I don't really like this song."

"Now." Simon gripped her hand and made his way onto the floor, taking his time until he and Sophie were beside Spado and Mercedes Campobello. Simon stepped closer, too close, nudging her. She looked his way, a moment to recognize him before returning her attention to Spado. Simon stayed close, purposely edging into her space, keeping his eyes on Sophie. Another bump, hip to hip. In his mind, he counted the seconds until she reacted. Mercedes was not what one might call "reserved."

"*Salut,*" he said when their eyes met.

"You. Jerk."

A word in her ear. "I've missed you."

"Leave," said Mercedes. "I don't want to see you."

"I just got here."

Simon glanced at Sophie, giving her a nod. She slipped in front of Vicente Spado, giving him her attention. Too blond, too buxom, she was impossible to ignore. She wore a crimson silk scarf around her neck and dashed it off, running it between her hands before draping it around Spado's neck. Who was Vicente to mind? Jimmy'z was that kind of place. Sophie sidled closer to him, still running the scarf back and forth, pressing her chest against him, overdoing it, but by then it was too late.

Enough was enough.

Mercedes transferred her ire from Simon to Vicente Spado. No violence. Not even a hint. A cold smile and some determined footwork to reclaim her place with Spado. Sophie let go of the scarf. Simon stepped in, looked Spado in the eye, and, in the time it took to whisk the scarf off his neck and return it to Sophie, unclasped the chain and slipped the coin—the don's precious family heirloom—from his neck.

Mission completed.

The only thing left to do was to leave as quickly as possible. But Simon was nineteen, full of himself, and as the bouncer had correctly noted the night before, *un petit voyou,* a little hoodlum.

"Nice piece," he said to Spado, meaning Mercedes. "If you can handle her. I don't think so."

As expected, mayhem. Spado threw a punch. Simon threw a harder one. He was skinny, but what was there was muscle. Spado was taller, probably stronger. Simon was crazier. The taste of his own blood turned him into a mad dog. Spado didn't stand a chance.

Memories.

An hour later, rain falling harder, Simon parked in the lot behind his shop. All these years later, maybe he still was *un petit voyou.* A little hoodlum. Why shy away from it?

He ran to the back door, getting soaked on the way. He threw open the door. The garage was dark, no sign of a living soul. The boys had picked the wrong day to play hooky. What was it, six o'clock? Everyone taking a half day? "Hello? Where is everyone? Lucy? Harry? Taking a half day?"

He ran a hand along the back wall, searching for the light switch. He was not amused. They wanted to play games. Fine. He'd show them how to play games. He heard a giggle. The overhead lights came to life.

Music blared from a boom box. Was it…disco? *Celebrate good times, come on!* His team popped up from behind the cars, some holding balloons, others blowing kazoos, popping confetti. As a group, they advanced toward him. "The hundred-million-dollar man!" "Congrats!" "You did it!" Shouts all around. Merriment.

A feminine figure in a gray coverall, baseball cap pushed back to reveal a pretty, insouciant face, approached. Lucy Brown pushed her way through the throng. "Very impressive, Mr. Riske. Everyone's talking about it." A kiss on the cheek.

Simon looked past her, to the jubilant regards, the cheery faces. "Turn it off," he said.

"Excuse me?" asked Lucy.

"Turn it off," said Simon, loudly. Then to the others: "Turn off the damn music. Friggin' hate disco."

"Simon, stop," said Lucy, her hands on his chest. "This is a party. For you. For the big sale. Everyone's so proud."

Simon looked at the young woman, his protégée, so to speak. "I don't want a party," he said. "I'll say when it's time to celebrate." A last wave of the hands. "Off!"

Someone killed the music. The mechanics backed away. Confused looks. Disappointment.

"You been drinking?" said Lucy.

"Long flight," said Simon.

"Well, we want to have a bit of fun, too."

"Today's not the day."

"But, the deal—"

"Isn't done yet," said Simon.

Lucy took a step back. "It isn't?"

"We screwed up."

"How…why?"

"In my office. Ten minutes. I need a list of all of our mechanical suppliers. Everyone we've worked with in the past. And I mean everyone. Got it?"

Lucy nodded.

Three months earlier, Lucy Brown had been involved in an automobile accident near Antibes, France, the passenger in a car struck by a drunk driver. Her injuries included a fractured skull, fractured ribs, and a broken leg. Simon, who'd been driving the car, had escaped with a partially dislocated shoulder and a bump on his forehead. After a long convalescence, Lucy had returned to work a different person. Gone was the playful, irreverent party girl who'd refused to grow up. In her place was a pensive, serious, melancholy woman. Even her accent had changed. She'd moved from the East End to Mayfair.

"And bring Harry," Simon added.

He shot his men a last look, then walked to his office. *A party. What were they thinking?*

At the moment, six vehicles were undergoing full restoration, and three, partials. All were Ferraris, dating from 1960 to 1990. Recently, he'd begun accepting Testarossas, after a rapid increase in their value over the past year. Two vehicles sat unattended at one side of the floor—a '73 Daytona Spyder and a '78 Berlinetta. Together the cars represented an outlay of six million dollars. His savings. It was the first time he had bought a car on spec—that is, with the goal of renovating it and selling it for a higher price. The cost of repairing the chassis, ordering new coachwork, painting, plus the man-hours of labor would come out of his own pocket. If the market held, he stood to double his money in a few years' time.

If the two cars weren't enough of a burden on his liquidity, he'd recently installed a new paint studio at a cost of eighty thousand pounds. Along with the new hardware, he'd purchased enough barrels of paint, solvent, and thinner to reach the roof. He was strapped, and now he had the gearbox to think about. He was not a man who could stand to lose ten million dollars.

Simon entered his office, leaving the door open, and crossed to his desk. Sitting, he dug out a box of Altoids and popped two into his mouth, crunching them with his molars for maximum effect. He opened his laptop and brought up a list of creditors. *Follow the money.* He flagged all those businesses that sold any type of automotive part and printed a copy. Finished, he took off his jacket and tossed his phone onto the desk.

"What's this about our suppliers?" Harry Mason trundled into the office, all piss and vinegar. He was a five-foot-seven-inch, red-haired

Irish bantamweight who lived for two things: soccer and automobiles. Specifically, the Arsenal Football Club and Ferraris.

"I need a gearbox," said Simon. "From 3387. The original."

"I thought she was out the door."

"We missed something."

"There is no gearbox," protested Mason. "Tore the original out at Le Mans in '63."

"The buyer thinks differently."

"The Frenchie? What does she know?"

"Enough."

"Tell her to toss off. We've already been to that circus."

"No can do," said Simon. "Call everyone we do business with and everyone we don't. Someone is spreading word on the grapevine that the original gearbox is still around. If that's the case, someone will be anxious to tell us, especially after news of the sale hits the streets."

"They'll want a pretty penny," said Lucy.

"I don't care what it costs," said Simon. "Jump on it."

"Why is this so important?" asked Lucy. "You're not back from the States for five minutes and you're up in arms about a gearbox."

"Just find it." She didn't need to know the details. It was his mistake, his pressure to bear.

"Correct me if I'm wrong," said Harry, "but we looked over hell's half acre for that gearbox."

"We have to look some more," said Simon.

"You're still not telling us why," said Lucy.

A dozen responses crowded Simon's mouth, none of them polite. "Lucy, Harry, please," he said. "Let's get busy and see if we can dredge this thing up."

Lucy gave him a very un-Lucy-like look and, arms crossed, left the office. Muttering, Harry followed her.

Simon leaned back in his chair. He was thinking of who he knew in Maranello, at the Ferrari factory, someone from whom he could beg, borrow, or steal some old casting iron. "Old" as in circa 1961. He didn't need much—just enough to fashion another gearbox, something with Enzo's fingerprints.

The phone rang. Simon snapped it off his desk. "Dez, how are you?"

"Having a force-ten nervous breakdown. Can't drive a city block without wondering who might be following me. It's not a nice feeling."

"We're looking, Dez."

"Not the answer I wanted."

"Give it time."

For a stretch, Hamilton said nothing.

"Dez?"

"Tell me this, Simon. What if you're right? What if there isn't an original? Eh, lad? What then? You got ten million hanging about? 'Cause right now I don't. And I'll tell you something else. She wasn't joking. That woman was as serious as a heart attack."

The line went dead.

Simon stared at the phone, then picked up his list of suppliers and began calling. By now, the name "3387" was known throughout the Ferrari universe. It was not, after all, a large universe. He placed one call after another, asking if somehow someone had missed the original when he'd called the first time around, a year back. Time and again, the answer came back, "No."

It was nearly eight p.m. when Harry Mason ventured back into Simon's office. So far, he'd had no luck. He didn't expect things to change. Even so, he'd keep trying. If Simon thought there was one chance in a thousand of locating that gearbox, Mason was determined to find it.

"Simon, you there?"

Not receiving an answer, Mason entered the office. The long, low-ceilinged room was lit only by the lamp on Simon's desk. There was a Wurlitzer jukebox against one wall and a leather couch beside it. Boxes overflowing with papers were stacked here and there. Glossy hardcover photo books showing every Ferrari ever made fought for space on the coffee table.

"Simon?"

He heard a faint buzzing noise from the corner. He took a step closer. Simon had left his phone on his desk. Not like him. It also wasn't like him to leave the shop without a word.

Mason checked the reception, then crossed the work floor. The mechanics had left an hour ago. A single overhead light burned. He snaked through the vehicles, tapping on the door to the men's loo. "Simon?" No answer. Then he continued to the rear exit.

The rain had finally stopped. Harry jumped to avoid the puddles on his way through the parking lot. Two cars remained. His own Audi and Simon's VW Golf.

Harry returned to his office, gathered his belongings, wrapping his Arsenal FC scarf around his neck before turning off the lights. He made sure the front door was locked, then headed out the back, activating the alarm and pulling down the shuttered steel door.

There he paused, ear turned to the wind. The night was quiet. He took a step toward his car when his ear caught the sound of wheels rolling slowly over a gravelly road.

A Ford entered the alley and pulled to the side of the road. It took Harry a moment to realize that it was Simon in the passenger seat. He couldn't make out the driver. Dark hair, brown skin…or was it the shadows? Whoever it was, it was clear that the two were in a heated conversation.

Harry stepped out of the light, unsettled that he was witnessing something he probably shouldn't. For ten minutes, the two sat in the car. Harry could hear raised voices, see Simon gesticulating angrily. Then the driver, whoever he was, made a U-turn and drove back down the alley.

Harry hurried to his car. All the way home he didn't know whether he should mention to Simon that he'd seen him.

CHAPTER 7

P apa."

The words died on Anna's tongue as she opened the door to her family home. It was a large, freestanding chalet built in the Italian tradition. Steep roof, window boxes, carved balconies. Fifty meters separated the house from neighbors on either side. A tall hedge surrounded the property. She paused at the threshold, uncertain of her new obligations. For years Anna had kept her distance from her father. Her mother had died when she was fifteen. Sepsis, after an acute attack of appendicitis. Taken ill and dead the same afternoon.

And now he was gone, too.

Two suitcases stood at the foot of the stairs. By their heft, it was clear that they were fully packed. She picked one up. Fifty pounds. The other weighed the same. A long trip, then. But where to? Papa was a sailor, by definition a light packer.

Anna's next discovery lay on the kitchen counter. An envelope addressed to "Letitia," her father's housekeeper of a dozen years. Offering an apology, Anna opened it. A short, handwritten note, but that was for later. First, Anna counted the money folded neatly inside. Twenty one-thousand Swiss-franc notes. A generous bonus and not yet Christmas. The note read:

My dearest Letitia,

It is necessary that I leave. I will not be back. I will miss you.

Carl

Terse, even for a Dane. But that was her father.

Anna replaced the letter in the envelope along with the money. Five minutes at home and already two surprises. Her father had intended to flee the country and had been carrying on an affair with his housekeeper. She didn't know which concerned her more.

Anna turned. She could see the front door, still ajar, and beyond it, her world. Leave now and she might spare herself further unpleasantries. Wouldn't it be better to preserve the image she had of her father? Why tarnish the few nice memories she possessed? No, she thought, suddenly feeling very grown up. What was life but a collection of unpleasantries? A smorgasbord, even, to borrow from her Scandinavian cousins.

Upstairs.

Her father's bedroom was a mess. Shirts, sweaters, socks, and underwear littered the bed, the floor, the dresser. The bathroom was more orderly, if only because he'd taken every last item. All that remained was a used razor, a few short black hairs caught in the blades—*Letitia?*—a bottle of Rexona shower gel, and an empty bottle of Halcion, a strong sedative. How long had her father, the lifelong advocate of muesli and Vita Parcours, needed sleeping pills?

To the study, her father's home office. Blinds drawn. Rolladen lowered. The dim room had the feeling of a fortress under siege. Anna eased herself into his old sea captain's chair, scooting back from the desk. Drawing a breath, she tried the top drawer. Unlocked. Surprise number three: a pistol. Semiautomatic. Stainless steel. Compact. She picked it up. At once, she could feel that it was loaded. She dropped the magazine. Twelve bullets plus one in the chamber. In Brazil, she'd learned to fire handguns. Police there had a way of making protesters disappear. She was no expert, but she could load, aim, and fire.

Not Papa.

He despised guns. Even on the open ocean, where anything might happen, and keeping a rifle or pistol was common practice, he had refused. A flare gun only. And a few knives to clean fish. Nothing more.

Beneath the pistol, another letter, this one addressed to "Anna Christina."

Dearest Anna,

Please forgive me. I

The note ended there. What to make of it? A farewell letter? Or, given its placement, something darker. A suicide note. Did it matter? Her father, Carl Bildt, had been leaving his home, his work, his entire life, without telling anyone, and going... well, *away.* Anna had the feeling far away. She also had the feeling he hadn't planned on coming back.

She remembered Tell's suggestion that her father may have been giving information to a foreign government. Was that why he was killed? Papa had revealed information about his clients to law enforcement. His clients found out and took the necessary steps. It made sense.

Anna's search of the remaining drawers did nothing to change her opinion. She found little of interest, except a package of flash drives— one missing—a pocket timetable for the Italian ferry line departing from Genoa to Corsica and Sardinia, and her father's old scaling knife, which she remembered him keeping on his boat at Porto Cervo, his real boat, the *Serafina,* a thirty-seven-foot yacht he had sailed around the Mediterranean for three weeks every summer.

So many questions.

Papa, why were you running away? What did you do to make people want to kill you? Bad people. The father she knew was not someone targeted by a car bomb. Yet his death was no accident. It was a premeditated, sophisticated, and intricately planned out act of violence.

Premeditated.

Sophisticated.

Intricately planned.

The three descriptors launched her into action.

All these years Anna had dedicated herself to helping others, pursuing one cause or another. The results were often fleeting and hard to measure. Now, in the course of a few days, all that had changed. Now Anna had a cause of her own, more personal than she would have wished but hers nonetheless. She thought of Tell, of all the harried, impersonal, self-serving faces surrounding him. *No.*

The decision struck her like a slap in the face.

No. No. No.

She could not trust the police. And why should she? She was more capable. More motivated. More invested.

She would do it herself.

Anna Bildt would find her father's killer.

Chapter 8

Simon reached for his phone after the fourth ring. "Yeah, I mean, hello…good morning."

"It's almost nine o'clock," said Lucy Brown. "Where are you?"

With an effort, Simon sat up. A look at his watch: 8:55. "Since when are you the boss?"

"Trying to be helpful."

"Did you find the gearbox?"

"Harry's still looking."

"Help him."

"I'm finishing the coachwork on the red Daytona. The owner is flying in from Dubai next week."

"That can wait."

"But—"

"Get on it."

"Wanker."

"What was that?"

"Just a cough. Sorry."

Simon rolled out of bed and hit the button for the drapes. A sunny day. He walked to the window. Not a cloud in the sky. An omen?

A stop in the bathroom. Brush teeth. Splash cold water on his face. To the kitchen. First things first. A mug of hot tea, cream, stevia. He was hungry. He stole three eggs from the fridge. Butter. Sprig of dill. Mixing bowl. He heated a nonstick pan. Hot, but not too. Whisk the eggs. In they go. Flip after three minutes. One more time. *Et voilà!*

Simon ate his omelette standing, while checking messages on his phone. Every inquiry he'd made had come back negative. He hadn't expected differently. The original gearbox belonging to chassis 3387 could not be found because it no longer existed. He had no right to feel dismayed.

He placed his plate in the sink, then called Harry. "Anything?"

"No joy."

"Who's left?"

"Schneider Autowerk in Baden-Baden and Gary Bobalik with Top Gun in the States. You?"

"Nada."

"You going to tell us why this is so important?"

"No." Simon ended the call and returned to the bedroom. He needed to call Dez Hamilton and start making plans to hide him away until he could settle matters with Sylvie Bettencourt. The solution? Money, what else? Renegotiate the price. Throw them a million or two. Or five. The thought raised his hackles. First, though, he wanted to touch base with his contacts at Scotland Yard. If Bettencourt engaged in extortion on a regular basis, word would have spread.

Simon stripped and went into the bathroom. He turned the shower handle fully to the right. Let the water get as cold as possible—45 degrees. Several slow, deep breaths, then under the water. That first moment. The secret was not to gasp, to concentrate on your breathing. Slow, steady. The shock passed. He counted to sixty, then turned the handle to the left. The water grew hot, then hotter, needles turning his skin pink, then red, and redder still. When he could no longer stand it, he adjusted the temperature to lukewarm. Soap, shampoo, shave. Total time: six minutes.

Simon toweled off, noting in the mirror that he'd put on a few pounds while in California. Too many good meals. Too many bottles of cab. Too much expensive booze. He could still make out the ridges in his stomach, but only just. It was not the time to be getting soft.

As punishment, he knocked out twenty pull-ups on the bar hanging from the ceiling of his walk-in closet. Then fifty push-ups, with a three-minute plank added on for good measure. Pain is only weakness leaving the body.

He dressed in a navy-blue suit, white open-collar shirt. Police attire.

He rolled up a necktie, also navy-blue, and stuffed it in his pocket in case he'd be speaking with a commissioner or higher. A brush to arrange his hair. A splash of cologne: *4711*—the original.

Get at it.

He heard the phone ping on the kitchen counter. Incoming text. Maybe a lead? He pulled on a pair of loafers and forced himself to walk slowly.

#neverletemseeyousweat #hopespringseternal #triumphofhopeover-reason

And?

The message was from JHawleyCars and read:

Heard you're looking for something. Don't bother. You're SOL.

Jack Hawley? Really.

Jack Hawley was as close to an enemy as Simon had in the business. A former race car driver—a Formula Three champion before he decided he liked tippling more than hoisting trophies—Hawley owned a shop in Lambeth. The world of automotive restoration was a zero-sum game. There were only so many vintage European sports cars in need of restoration at any one time. Fewer still if you counted only those from Italy—Ferrari, Lamborghini, Maserati—along with the occasional French Bugatti. If any one firm had suffered when Simon entered the business, it was Jack Hawley's Italian Motorsport Restoration. No better proof of its declining fortunes than the southbound journey of its premises from Highgate to Kensington to Lambeth, where it currently could be found occupying a storefront on the Brixton high street.

It was impossible to say that Simon had stolen Hawley's business, only that Simon's had thrived while Hawley's contracted. The last he'd heard, Jack Hawley had stopped restoring cars altogether and was simply a broker, helping collectors buy and sell their inventories.

Simon regarded the message, slipping the phone into his pocket as he made his way downstairs. *SOL.* Shit out of luck? What was that supposed to mean?

He took the last few stairs and threw open the door to the work floor much too forcefully. All heads turned. Simon ignored them, making a beeline for his office. In the time it took to cross the floor, it had come to him. The world was suddenly a brighter place. He banged on Harry Mason's door.

"Meeting. Now." He saw Lucy. "You too."

"Fab," she said.

"Cut it."

Simon dropped into his chair as the two hurried in.

"Is Jack Hawley on your list?"

Lucy said no.

Harry shook his head. "Quit restoring, didn't he?"

"He sent me a note saying he'd heard I was looking for something and that I was SOL. Shit out of luck."

"Sounds like Hawley," said Harry.

"Which means he knows we're looking for the gearbox, and for some reason we aren't going to get our hands on it."

"Because it's nowhere to be found," said Lucy. "It's gone."

"That's what I thought at first," said Simon. "But why would Hawley reach out to tell me there's no gearbox?"

"Not sure I follow," said Mason.

"If there were no gearbox, Jack Hawley wouldn't know anything about me wanting it, one way or the other. Like you said, he's not in the trade anymore. He's never had anything to do with 3387. No one has for the past thirty years."

"So?"

"So…Hawley reached out because he knows for a fact that the gearbox does exist…It's out there…but for some reason, we are 'shit out of luck,' meaning someone doesn't want us to get it."

"Hawley always was a prick," said Mason. "Remember what happened last time you saw him."

"I'd rather not," said Lucy.

The time in question was a ritzy cocktail party thrown by Pirelli, the Italian tire manufacturer. Simon had attended, with Harry, Lucy, and several other of his workers. Hawley had paid a little too much attention to Lucy. He was the "handsy" sort. Lucy protested. Hawley persisted. Simon stepped in. End of story.

"What are you going to do?" she asked.

Simon weighed his options. Calling Hawley was out, as was emailing.

He needed an answer quickly, a guaranteed way to know if Hawley was telling the truth. "Pay him a visit, I suppose. Harry, maybe you should come with me. You know. Backup."

"You're on your own, lad. He'd pick me up like a lawn gnome and chuck me through the window."

"I'm sure it won't come to that," said Simon.

The looks on Harry's and Lucy's faces said otherwise.

CHAPTER 9

Lugano, Switzerland

Her first task: a phone call.

A business card with a number in Bern. Federal Intelligence Service. Looking at the card, Anna noticed that her hand was shaking. What was she doing calling the chief of a country's security service?

"Fräulein Bildt, so nice to hear from you," said Hans-Peter Tell. "Have you changed your mind about allowing us to view your home?"

Nothing like a bossy, authoritative male to get her back up. "Good afternoon, Mr. Tell," she said, her unease instantly gone. "In fact, I'm calling to ask a question."

"Please."

"Can you tell me if you've discovered the license plates belonging to the car used to kill my father?"

"May I ask why you wish to know?"

"I intend to find who did this."

"You?" Was that a snicker? Tell had missed his calling in the diplomatic corps.

"Why not?"

"It's my understanding you work for an NGO in Copenhagen. Something to do with wildlife preservation."

In the space of a minute, Anna had learned not only that Hans-Peter Tell had programmed her number into his phone without her giving it to him but also that he knew her place of employment. What else, then? She must assume Tell had taken additional measures. Had he hacked her phone? Her laptop?

"You haven't answered my question."

"Fräulein, the individual you seek, or individuals, are violent, dangerous, and, I dare say, highly trained criminals."

Premeditated. Sophisticated. Intricately planned.

"I know this. I am not stupid."

"Anything but, it seems. Still, we must take your safety into account."

"I can look after myself, thank you."

"Miss Bildt—"

"Have you found the license plates? The vehicle identification number would be even better."

"No plates. The VIN was removed from the engine block. There, so you don't think I'm being dismissive."

"And on the dashboard or doorframe?"

"Nothing was found. In fact, some of my colleagues suspect the license plates were removed prior to the incident."

"I doubt that," said Anna. "A car missing its plates could draw police attention."

"My thoughts exactly," admitted Tell. "Maybe you missed your calling."

"You haven't looked hard enough," said Anna.

"I can assure you we have."

"Thank you, Mr. Tell."

Anna parked as close to the blast site as allowed. Days after the attack, there remained a significant law enforcement presence. Security tape cordoned off either end of the Via Montalbano. Policemen stood guard at crowd-control barriers. Anna approached, signaling to a policeman. She explained that it was her father who had been killed and asked if she might come closer. A beseeching smile, her hands clasped in prayer. *Per favore.* The answer was a resolute, and very un-Latin, "No."

Anna moved away from the barriers, determined to get the clearest view possible. The first time she'd come she'd been in too much shock to feel anything but overwhelmed, emotionally and physically. It was not an exaggeration to say that she'd felt as if struck by the blast herself. Now, with the benefit of a few days' distance, she was able to examine the site dispassionately. An observer, not a victim.

There was not much to see. With their customary meticulousness, the Swiss had not so much cleaned up the site as sterilized it. The Via Montalbano was a one-way street, with parking spaces on both sides. Apartment buildings four and five stories in height crowded its length, partially blocking the sun, and lending the road a claustrophobic feel.

To Anna's eye, a license plate had four places to go. To the north end of the street and beyond. To the south end. Or into one of the apartments overlooking the site. A count of the windows gave the approximate number of residences as sixty on one side and eighty on the other. Nearly all were missing their windows. Many were boarded up; others kept their blinds or curtains drawn. It was, she decided, a miracle that no one else had been killed.

Intricately planned.

Whoever had engineered her father's murder had been keen to avoid innocent casualties. Was the term "collateral damage"?

Anna started by searching the area to the south. She walked along the Via Montalbano five hundred meters. No apartments here, just one- and two-story commercial buildings. She kept her eyes to the ground, moving down one side of the street, then up the other. Not only was she unable to find even the smallest fragment of car, pavement, building— or anything hit, displaced, or destroyed by the explosion—she was hard-pressed to find so much as a dead leaf. It was as if the authorities had run a giant vacuum cleaner over every square inch of ground. She wished she had less reason to be impressed.

A search in the opposite direction proved no more fruitful. Anna was quickly losing her patience. Just how far could a license plate fly?

A look to the apartment buildings. Too late to start now; besides, she was tired and irritable. In no mood to knock on doors, put on her most ingratiating smile, and kindly ask if a license plate had flown through anyone's window. And to be honest, what were the odds?

Anna banished her pessimism. There was another way.

Chatterbell.

Chatterbell.

It was Anna's secret weapon, her everywoman's superpower.

Chatterbell was an investigative journalism website that solicited open-source intelligence from both professionals and private citizens—

anyone, anyplace—to solve a wide variety of crimes. Put simply, it asked for help from any person who felt inclined to give it. The crimes ranged from large to small: actions committed in war zones, human rights abuses, the activities of organized criminals in every part of the world. And now, finding her father's murderers. Yes, she'd decided there was more than one. How could there not be?

About the name: "Chatterbell" came from an old folktale about a group of mice living in a flour mill who gather together to figure out a way to keep from being eaten by a mean, ravenous cat, or *chat* in Old Norman. They decide to hang a bell around the cat's neck so they can hear whenever he is near. And so, one of them must sneak out and place the bell around the cat while he's sleeping. And there's the problem. None of them is brave enough to try. And so, one by one they are all eaten.

In a sense, Chatterbell was what she needed to hang a bell around the neck of the mean, ravenous cat who had eaten her father.

Anna logged on to the Chatterbell website and created a new project file. First her name: "Danish Seekr." Then a name for the file: "The Murder of Carl Bildt." Then she defined the criminal act—a two-paragraph description of her father's death, including date, location (along with precise GPS coordinates as given by her phone's map), time—both local and Greenwich Mean Time. To this, she added photos of the blast site and links to all publicly available reportage: newspaper articles, television clips, and the portion of the police reports released to the public.

She provided no directions about how to proceed, no instructions for all to follow. The beauty of Chatterbell and open-source investigation was, to paraphrase Martin Luther, that every man was his own cop. It was up to the individual to decide how, when, and what to contribute.

Founded by Alan Endicott, an Englishman living in a Leicester suburb, Chatterbell experienced its first success in 2015 when it proved that the Syrian army was using cluster bombs and chemical weapons against insurgents in its civil war. A year later, Endicott turned his attention to Malaysia Airlines flight MH17, shot down July 17, 2014, by an anti-aircraft missile over Eastern Ukraine while en route from Amsterdam to Kuala Lumpur. All 298 souls aboard perished. Russia, engaged in a conflict with Ukraine at the time, claimed the Ukrainians shot it down. The Ukrainians claimed it was the Russians.

Endicott, with the help of hundreds of volunteer investigators, collected images from local webcams, obtained eyewitness accounts, trawled social media, and scoured news reports to gather evidence about who, how, and why MH17 was shot down. Thirty days later, he had incontrovertible proof that a pro-Russian rebel unit was responsible and the missile launcher had been supplied and likely operated by members of the Russian army's 53rd Anti-Aircraft Brigade. Not only the rebels but the soldiers involved: officers, enlisted men, names, ranks, and serial numbers.

In 2018, a Dutch-led Joint Investigation Team confirmed their findings. Trials commenced and remained ongoing.

Since then, Chatterbell had grown into a formidable investigative force. It had identified mass murderers in Sudan and rooted out gangsters in Naples. It had tracked illegal arms shipments in Libya and found kidnap victims in Belarus.

Anna's first objective was to identify the car used to blow her father to kingdom come. Identify the car and she had a good chance of identifying its owner. News reports had specified the car as a Volkswagen Polo. No license plate number or vehicle registration number was given. If the police had either, they were not sharing the information. One by one, Anna scoured every photograph of the blast site. Many showed the bent and twisted frame of the car. Two of the doors were missing, as was the hatchback, all detached from the chassis by the force of the explosion.

In the project file, she typed:

Eyewitnesses? License plate needed of car packed with explosives! Webcams?

She hit the SEND button. Immediately, the file appeared on the Chatterbell site. It was as simple as that.

All she could do now was cross her fingers and wait.

It was up to people she'd never met and probably never would—total strangers—to help.

Or not.

Chapter 10

Before Simon could visit Jack Hawley, he had other, equally pressing business to attend to. Eleven a.m. found him in a café around the corner from Thames House, headquarters of the British domestic security service, officially known as MI5. He was seated at a table in the rear of the room. With him was a tall, gangly man with disheveled black hair, pale blue eyes, and a prominent Adam's apple. An English Ichabod Crane, if Crane had taken a First in mathematics from Cambridge University. In fact, his name was Nigel Cleak and he headed MI5's Financial Investigations Unit.

"So, Sylvie Bettencourt," said Cleak, setting down a steaming cup of tea. "You don't say."

"Name ring a bell?"

"I seem to hear a tinkle. She pops up on our radar from time to time. Tax authority, actually. All those high-value purchases. The Inland Revenue want to make sure they get their cut."

Cleak could have taken a job at any one of the city's better banks or private equity funds. For reasons that spoke for themselves, he had chosen to put his skills to use in the service of his country. Instead of driving a Mercedes and keeping a weekend home in the Cotswolds, he was the proud holder of an Oyster card—key to London's public transport system—and kept a three-room flat in Stepney. The two men had worked together on numerous cases over the past years. Simon considered him a friend.

"She play ball?"

"Cagey. Let's say she does her best to minimize her liabilities."

"So why are you involved?"

"You know us. We like to snoop. A foreigner buying up British real estate…*repeatedly*. Artwork, cars, collectibles. Year after year. We get curious."

"What's her nationality?"

"For the record, French, but she also holds Canadian and Cypriot passports."

"Can you have three?"

"Come now, Simon. You of all people should know that you can have anything you want if you're willing to pay enough money."

"How many years, by the way?"

"The file on her goes back to the nineties."

"Thirty years?"

"She does take good care of herself. She must be over sixty by now."

Simon smiled to himself. Cleak was discreetly letting him know that he kept close enough tabs on Sylvie Bettencourt to comment on her appearance. "She started young, then."

"Lived here in London for a bit—'88 to '95, I think it was."

Simon's father had moved to England in 1988. Simon was what— seven or eight years old—when they'd taken a small house in Royal Tunbridge Wells, a historical resort town fifty miles south of central London. His father, Anthony Riske, had run a commodities trading company, a branch of a larger operation he'd started in the States. London was to be the base for an expansion across Europe. For a while, all was well. There was a nanny, good schools, vacations. His father owned a few sports cars—yes, a Ferrari; no, not the '63 250 GTO. Simon still remembered the drives they took through the countryside. His first taste of speed, of danger. A taste he coveted to this day.

And then…*then something happened.* His father's business collapsed. There were whispers of impropriety. More than that, thought Simon, though he'd been too young to recollect the details. The end came with astonishing rapidity. Investigators appeared in the house. Cars confiscated. Furniture carted away. All without explanation, at least to Simon.

There was no explanation either for his father's suicide. Simon found him hanging from a beam in the barn early one Sunday morning. There was no note. That was the hardest part. *Why?* All these years later, Simon still had no answer.

One day . . .

"Think it was in '92 we first gave her a look," Cleak continued.

"At?"

"What she does now, if on a smaller scale. 'Collecting.'"

"For?"

"We'll come to that."

"And this latest incident…this threat against Dez Hamilton. Has she hurt people in the past?"

"Maybe, maybe not." Cleak leaned closer, his voice a shade softer. "Banker in town was roughed up not too long ago. Worked at a competitor of your former employer." He named a prominent bank. "Handled her accounts, or that's what we believe. Bank secrecy. You know."

"What happened?" asked Simon.

"Accident, at least officially. Broke his legs."

"Both?"

"Said he fell while doing odd jobs around the house." Cleak frowned. No one believed a word of it. "First time I'd heard of anyone snapping their tibias at precisely the same spot while trying to hang a painting. Compound fractures. Nasty business."

"And unofficially?"

"Someone wanted to make sure he kept quiet."

"Sylvie Bettencourt?"

"Ah, Simon, you do like your questions."

"I like answers better."

"Piece of luck. Someone in town I know who might help us," said Cleak. "As a matter of fact, she happens to share our interests. Ah, here she is now." Cleak raised a hand in greeting. Simon stood as an attractive Black woman dressed in business attire swept into the café. She carried a leather satchel slung over her shoulder and had the bearing of someone accustomed to being in command.

"Nigel, good morning. Look at you," she said, setting the satchel on the floor, gifting him with a kiss on each cheek.

American, thought Simon. Mid-Atlantic accent. If he didn't know better, he'd say attorney, banker, corporate exec. A woman most definitely on the way up.

"Nessa Kenyon, meet Simon Riske."

Kenyon extended a hand. Her grip was dry and firm as she looked him squarely in the eye. "Mr. Riske, a pleasure."

"Simon, please."

"Call me Nessa." She moved her satchel between her calves as she sat. Her hair was cut short, neatly styled. Eyes sparkling like pale agate. She had an athlete's lean build. And yes, more than attractive.

"Nessa's with FinCEN," said Cleak. "Financial Crimes Enforcement Network."

Kenyon slipped Simon her card. It read: "Special Agent, Global Investigations." And there in the corner, the seal of the United States Treasury.

"I know FinCEN," said Simon.

The Financial Crimes Enforcement Network was a discreet but powerful arm of the United States government charged with safeguarding the country's financial system. Their principal duties included combatting money laundering and monetary fraud and impeding terrorist finance.

The server returned. Kenyon ordered a cappuccino and a chocolate croissant. A woman with a sweet tooth, thought Simon. He ordered a tea, Earl Grey. They chitchatted for a while. She was from Virginia, had served in the army, a captain in signals intelligence, then earned her MBA at UVA before joining the government. Her cappuccino and his tea arrived, along with a fresh pour for Cleak. Kenyon allowed herself a bite of her croissant before beginning.

"If anyone has their phones on, please turn them off. If you wouldn't mind, hand them to me. You too, Nigel. This satchel functions as a Faraday bag. Nothing gets in. Nothing gets out. We wouldn't want anyone listening to what we have to say, would we, gentlemen?"

Simon and Cleak complied. Phones in the bag. Kenyon offered a nod of the head to say thank you. She took care to zip it up properly. So then. Time to talk.

"Sylvie Marie Bettencourt," she began. "Why are you interested?"

"I had a run-in with her in California last week. Sold her a car. Thought the deal was done. Turns out it wasn't."

"I saw that somewhere," said Kenyon.

"Really?" As far as Simon knew, the transaction hadn't been reported to the media. Of course, there were rumors in the trade…if you were in the trade…or if for some reason you were already paying attention to Sylvie Bettencourt.

"What happened?" she asked.

"One of her thugs, a guy named Vadim, put the hurt on my client, Desmond Hamilton, and threatened to do worse."

"Did you go to the police?"

"In the States?" Simon shook his head. "Wouldn't have solved our problem. Tell me, should we be worried?"

"The short answer is yes," said Kenyon.

"The long answer?"

"That I can't give you."

"Because?"

Kenyon spread her hands. The great wall of silence.

"Because you're investigating her," suggested Simon.

"I can neither confirm nor deny who we are or are not investigating."

"She's laundering money," Simon continued, with a look at Cleak.

Kenyon's expression indicated he might be correct. "Neither confirm nor deny."

"For whom?" asked Simon, then: "I know, 'Neither confirm nor deny.'"

A patient smile. This was how the game had to be played.

"Someone—person, organization, country—with lots of money," Simon continued. "Hundreds of millions. Someone who has too much cash sitting in too many banks and who is willing to over-pay for hard assets. Someone whose money isn't safe sitting in his or her own country." He thought long and hard. "Iran. Revolutionary Guard?"

Kenyon said nothing. Then, a discreet shake of the head. Wrong.

"Nigeria?" suggested Simon. Another oil-rich country known for endemic corruption.

Another shake of the head. Strike two.

A drug lord? Simon didn't think so. If Bettencourt was laundering money for one of the cartels, he'd be having this talk with an agent of the Drug Enforcement Administration. He looked at Kenyon. If she was, in fact, leading an investigation into Sylvie Bettencourt, why was she here in London? Why not France, where Bettencourt kept her offices? A pithy saying making the rounds came to mind…something about "the Russian city sometimes known as London."

So Russia…the big bad bear.

It made sense. Bettencourt could be laundering money for one of the oligarchs, or several of them. Given the scope of the purchases she made, he had to believe it was the latter.

"Russia," he said. "She's cleaning up money coming out of Russia."

"Told you he was a clever boots," said Cleak.

"Sylvie Bettencourt's Russian?" Simon shot Cleak a look. "I thought she was French, no?"

"The GRU prefers to recruit its officers from home," said Kenyon.

GRU. Russia's military intelligence agency. "You're shitting me," said Simon. "Excuse me, you're kidding, right? Bettencourt is a Russian intelligence agent? A spy?"

"Not any longer, of course," said Kenyon. "But once…years ago. They're not all thugs with daggers hidden in their trench coats. Back then—we're talking late eighties—she was on Gorbachev's team. It was the era of Glasnost and Perestroika. The Soviet Union was opening up. Restructuring its economy. The goal was to transform industry to make it competitive with the West. The best way was to privatize state-owned operations. Tractor factories. Bus factories. Lightbulb factories. Let's not get started with natural resources. Almost all were run to some extent, or at least overseen, by the KGB. The Committee for State Security—the Sword and the Shield—the GRU's bigger, stronger brother, and, importantly, its archrival. Anyway, the KGB saw this coming—privatization, I mean. Made it happen, actually. The generals arranged to buy out individual factories for a fraction of their worth—a tenth, a hundredth, even—then turned around and sold shares to international investors for a huge profit. One tractor plant in the Urals was valued at less than its annual profit but sold for its annual revenues, one thousand times that amount. This was not the type of 'restructuring' Mr. Gorbachev had had in mind. This was rape and pillage."

"What did he do?" asked Simon.

"Not a damned thing," said Kenyon. "His own people had beaten him to the punch. Russian intelligence put agents into the field to help move the money overseas. Out of Russia. Sylvie Bettencourt was one of the first."

"Which is when she came on to our radar," said Cleak.

"In '92?" asked Simon.

"Correct," said Cleak. "The U.S. was still the 'main adversary.' London was their first choice as a Western financial capital to park their money."

"And Switzerland?" asked Simon.

"You can't have as much fun on the Bahnhofstrasse as you can in Covent Garden," said Cleak. "No Stringfellows in Zürich."

"And Bettencourt?"

"Sent here under deep cover. Handled out of the embassy. Instead of fighting corruption, she was secretly finding shady English enterprises to help launder her countrymen's money. Plenty of English banks wouldn't touch it with a ten-foot pole."

"Who could blame them?" said Kenyon. "No one knew the source of the money. Drug dealers, corrupt officials, arms dealers, organized crime. All of them, probably. Taking their money is like providing fuel for the fire, allowing them to grow bigger and stronger."

"Was she ever arrested?"

"The consensus was better to tag and follow than arrest, deport, and start all over again."

"Lots of firms welcomed the investment," said Kenyon. "They didn't see it as laundering. They didn't even know what laundering was. To them, it was free money."

"Russians had a steep learning curve," said Cleak. "They couldn't pop into a W. H. Smith and pick up a copy of *Capitalism for Dummies*. It took them a while to get the hang of it. But by and by, they learned."

"It didn't help that the KGB began to partner with the larger organized crime families," said Kenyon. "The Solntsevo Brotherhood in Moscow. The Tambov Gang in St. Petersburg. The *vory v zakone* everywhere—thieves for life. All of the groups that had been loan-sharking for decades. They taught the KGB how to apply those principles abroad."

Cleak nodded. "All too many English businessmen made the mistake of going into business with them. There was a rash of murders, most unsolved."

Kenyon continued: "Year by year, the sums coming out of Russia, and now the independent states—Ukraine, Belarus, all the 'stans—grew larger."

"Think of a busted hydrant," said Cleak. "By '98, we were looking at upwards of twenty billion a year fleeing from the former Soviet Union and searching the globe for a safe home."

"It's only gotten worse since," said Kenyon. "We've identified fifty billion dollars' worth of investments made in the States as being of illegal, or at the least dubious, provenance. Office buildings bought by holding companies domiciled in the Dutch Antilles. Tracts of land in our largest cities purchased by anonymous foreign entities. Estates, artwork, any hard asset you can think of."

"Cars," suggested Simon.

"Especially Italian ones," said Kenyon, raising her cup of cappuccino, eyes on Simon.

"So," he said, leaning across the table. "Where does Sylvie Bettencourt figure in all this?"

"Our guess," said Kenyon, "right smack-dab in the middle."

"Well then," said Nigel Cleak. "Maybe this isn't such a coincidence."

"Maybe not," said Simon.

Chapter 11

London, England

The name of Jack Hawley's shop on the Brixton high street was painted in large red letters across a plateglass window: ITALIAN MOTORSPORT RESTORATION. Unfortunately, the paint had chipped and the glass itself was coated with a film of exhaust from the passing traffic. Not quite the impression one might like to give the owner of a multi-million-dollar automobile. But who was Simon to say?

He knocked twice on the wall as he entered. "Hello, you there, Hawley?"

"Come in, come in. Be right there." The voice was bluff and hearty, and matched the man who bounded from the back of the store. Hawley was a big man, and grown bigger since Simon had last seen him. Horizontally, if not vertically. How had he ever been able to fit into a race car? He was still handsome enough, blond, square jawed; a man who looked you in the eye as he gripped your hand. "Simon Riske...To what do I owe the pleasure?"

"Three guesses."

Hawley made no show of feigned ignorance. He'd issued a challenge and the challenge had been met. "Sit down, mate. Fancy a tea? Something stronger?"

It was apparent that Hawley had gotten an early start on the day's festivities. "What are you having?"

"A bit of good cheer. Celebrating. See what's in the front room?"

Simon glanced over his shoulder at a red Ferrari, a 1964 275, if he wasn't mistaken. "You buying or selling?"

"Selling. For a client outside of Bath. Asked me to give it a little spit and polish before."

"Congrats. That's a nice piece of business."

Hawley opened a sideboard and retrieved a bottle of VSOP brandy. He poured two glasses, handing one to Simon. "You got my message."

"I was hoping you could point me in the right direction."

"The possibility had come to mind."

"I take it you know who has the gearbox."

"I didn't say that."

"Jack, come on, maybe I can do something for you."

"Now that you mention it…"

Simon spread his arms wide. *Happy to be of assistance.*

"Lucy, she still work with you?"

"Full-time. Just promoted her. Good kid."

"Get me a date, then."

"Pardon?"

"A date. A rendezvous. A tête-à-tête."

"Jack, you're older than me. She's in her twenties."

"So?"

"You do remember the cocktail party?"

"You gave me a black eye."

"You'd had a few too many."

"And I apologized. Now, what do you say?"

"Bad idea, Jack."

"What are you, her father? Or are you dipping your wick in that? You are, aren't you?"

With difficulty, Simon kept a pleasant demeanor. "Let's not be vulgar. I'm here to find out who has the gearbox for 3387."

"You are a smooth operator, Riske. Not going to get it out of me that easily."

Simon had known all along it was about money. "How much? A thousand quid?"

"Don't insult me. Word on the street is you sold that vehicle for a hundred mil. A record. How 'bout the seller shoots me a mil?"

"A million dollars…for a gearbox? I can get a replica for fifty grand."

"Not dollars, pounds sterling. Cash. Go to the bank now." Hawley made a show of checking his watch. "Still have time. I'll wait."

"And for that I get the gearbox, too, or just the name."

"Just the name, mate. Like I said, you're *S-O-L*. Someone doesn't want you to get your hands on it. Up to you to change their mind."

"How do I know you're telling me the truth?"

"Look out there."

Simon turned to examine the Ferrari. Of course. The RM Sotheby's auction. Two years ago, almost to the day. Opening bid of $20 million. Simon had been there for another reason: a repo job. Not a car, a watch—belonging, not coincidentally, to the man who'd bought the Ferrari in Jack Hawley's showroom that night, and who had, in fact, been wearing the watch on his left wrist at the time. His name was Boris Blatt. He was a well-known and lowly regarded Russian oligarch who'd left Moscow ten years earlier and brought his operations lock, stock, and barrel to London.

But Blatt wasn't anywhere near Bath. He was in Wakefield, doing a ten-year stretch. "Porridge," the British called prison time. Simon wasn't sure what the Russians called it.

"Ten thousand *pounds*. Take it or leave it."

"Not a chance, posh boy. A million or nothing." Hawley finished his brandy. "And the date with Miss Brown."

What was it about people like Hawley? It was as if they wanted to bring the hammer down on themselves. "Let me ask you a question first," said Simon, his commitment to a calm, collegial demeanor herewith discarded. "Why did you say I was SOL?"

"You surprised to learn that I'm not the only one who doesn't care for you?"

"The list is long and colorful. So what did I do to earn your client's dislike?"

"Nuff said."

"And he refuses to sell me the gearbox?"

"Over his dead body," said Hawley, with delight. "His words."

"He told you that."

"Face-to-face."

Simon shot another glance at the automobile. Had a car of that pedigree changed hands, Simon would have taken note, particularly as he had a personal connection to it. He could only assume then that Boris

Blatt still owned it. And, therefore, that it was Blatt who had consigned it to Hawley to sell.

"Older gentleman? Foreigner? Thick accent. *Toks like ziss.* White hair, hooded eyes, on the shorter side. Pushing seventy?"

Hawley shifted in his chair, a hand darting to his cheek. "No. Not my chap."

A lie and a bad one. But how could Hawley's client be Blatt when Blatt was in prison?

And yet…there, not twenty feet away, was the car Blatt had purchased for twenty-five million dollars at the Sotheby's auction two years ago. Cue Sherlock Holmes: "When you have eliminated all which is impossible, then whatever remains, however improbable, must be the truth."

Simon poured himself another measure of brandy. "Cheers," he said, and drank it in one go. "We're done here."

Hawley shot out of his chair as if launched. "You're leaving?"

"Nice seeing you, Jack."

As Simon strode toward the front door, Hawley rushed to catch up. "You don't want to know who has the gearbox?"

"You told me."

Hawley put a hand on Simon's jacket, clenching the lapel in his fist. "You takin' the piss?"

Simon regarded the bunched fist, the bespoke suit from Richard Anderson of Savile Row, wrinkled and probably stained. "His name is Boris Blatt. A Russian oligarch who came to London ten years ago. He bought that car at auction in Battersea Park two years ago. I was there."

Hawley released his grip, bouncing on his back heel. A smile of self-satisfaction. "Wrong, wrong, wrong. His name is Gerstmann. He's German, not Russian."

Gerstmann. A new name. Now Simon knew more clearly what had happened. "One last chance. Where is he?"

"Sorry, mate."

Simon slugged Hawley. One blow, where the jaw meets the ear. Hawley dropped like a sack of potatoes. Simon did nothing to arrest his fall.

Kneeling, he ran a hand over Hawley's jacket, finding the phone, slipping it from his pocket. He activated it and held it in front of Hawley's face. Nothing doing. Next, he took Hawley's hand and, with difficulty, managed to place his thumb on the screen. Bingo.

Simon accessed the Maps app and checked recent history for driving directions. Several addresses in the London area—Maida Vale, Greenwich, Hampstead Heath—and that was all. No mention of Bath or any other spot in Somerset. He checked emails for something from Blatt. Nothing.

An idea came to him. He tossed the phone onto Hawley's chest and walked into the showroom. The Ferrari was unlocked. He slid into the passenger seat and opened a glove box the size of a pack of cough drops. A single paper inside, protected by laminate. *What do we have here?* Vehicle registration. Owner: Boris Abrahamovich Blatt. Address: Ditchfield, 1 Clarendon Lane, Swainswick, Somerset.

He returned the registration to the glove box.

He wasn't sure who was the more careless: Blatt or Her Majesty's Government. He was fairly certain that you were supposed to destroy all identification papers when a bad guy entered Witness Protection.

CHAPTER 12

Beverly Hills, California

Sylvie Bettencourt was riding north on Canon Drive. She had rented a convertible—what else does one do in sunny Southern California?—and gazed up at the endless row of palm trees lining the street.

"But what kind of palms are they, Vadim?" she asked, a hand on her sunglasses to shield the glare.

"How should I know? Do I look like a gardener?"

"Testy, aren't we?"

"He's asking questions. I don't like it."

"Wouldn't you?" Sylvie knew all about this. Her insurance brokers had contacted her, informing her that an American with ties to Lloyd's of London was making inquiries.

"Something about him," said Vadim. "We have to keep an eye on him."

"All I care about is that he gets us what we asked him to. Michael will not be pleased otherwise."

"Michael," said Vadim, as if chewing on something bitter. "When is he ever pleased?"

Sylvie put a hand on Vadim's arm. *Calm down now.* "Not at all like the palms in Cyprus or Grand Canary," she said. "I wonder if they're native. Did you know that the eucalyptus trees we see everywhere were brought in from Australia during the gold rush?"

"That so?" said Vadim. "I'll be sure to make a note of it."

It was Sylvie Bettencourt's first time in Los Angeles. It was her practice to read up on the places she visited both for work and for pleasure. History, politics, geography. She didn't like it when others knew more about a subject than she did. This, in addition to the research she did for her clients' investments. Art, jewelry, real estate, and, of course, automobiles. Somehow she'd missed out on the stratospheric rise in the price of collectible Italian sports cars. The name Ferrari was first and foremost on her list of future purchases.

She thought of Riske. She'd read up on him, too. Quite the achiever. Father dead when he was just a boy. A suicide, and that with the parents already divorced. Sent to live with the mother in France. By all accounts, not a warm and loving household. From there, a descent into the world of organized crime. Marseille was a hotbed of criminal activity. "Le Milieu," they called the French underworld. Age nineteen, shot in a gun battle with police during a failed attempt to rob an armored car. She wouldn't fault him on ambition. A stint in prison. Les Baumettes, no less. As bad or worse than the prisons in her own country. Rumor of a hit carried out for a *capo* while inside. Years in solitary. Then rebirth. A real-life renaissance. A degree from the London School of Economics. Graduate work in France. A job at a posh bank in London. Nothing short of a miracle.

But Sylvie didn't believe in miracles.

How? Why? The closer she looked, the more questions she had. Part of her felt as if she'd known him all her life. Another part, as if she didn't know him at all. Maybe that was what attracted her to him: the mystery at his core. Or maybe it was that they were alike, the two of them. Liars. Deceivers. Chameleons.

There was no doubting one thing: Simon Riske got the job done.

Vadim would be upset if he learned she'd offered him a job. Very upset indeed. He was jealous by nature.

"I don't like it," said Vadim. "He's not like the others."

"You didn't have a problem with him the other day."

"Maybe," said Vadim. "He didn't see me coming. Or should I say 'us.' Didn't know what he was up against."

"Worried? That's not like you."

"Just saying. Better keep an eye on that one."

"That's why I have you at my side. To make sure I stay safe and sound. Once we get the gearbox, you can decide what to do about Mr. Riske."

Vadim steered the car across Sunset Boulevard and past the Beverly Hills Hotel. They wound through the residential drives north of Sunset and made their way east toward Hollywood. It was a picture-postcard day. Blue sky, gentle breeze. Maybe she'd finally found the place to retire. Get a face-lift, Botox, a forty-year-old boyfriend, and she'd fit right in. A smile to say, *As if.* Too many people. Too many prying eyes. Too public. When she retired, it would be to somewhere far away. Bali, a ranch in the Argentinian wine country, an island in the Caribbean, preferably her own. A place where she could live peacefully and free from the ghosts of her past. Somewhere she could see them coming.

Speaking of which… a glance over her shoulder, a longer look in the side-view mirror. No, nothing there. To the best of her knowledge, they were alone—that is to say, not being followed. Of late, it was an ever-present concern. Which reminded her, she needed a refill on her Xanax.

"There it is." Sylvie pointed to a sign for Loma Vista Drive. "Right here. The address is 840. The agent's waiting for us. Gates are open."

Vadim turned, driving down a well-manicured road, homes on either side. No, not homes. Mansions. Estates worthy of a prince. Each on a lot nearly a city block long. "What's his name?"

"Pahlavi. Persian. Like the shah."

"Who?"

"Never mind," said Sylvie.

Vadim guided the car through the scrolled gates at 840 Loma Vista, down a curving drive beside rolling lawns, mature trees, to the neoclassical residence. Doric columns worthy of a Greek temple. It reminded her of the Acropolis—no, something else, something closer to home. The Hermitage in St. Petersburg.

Sylvie had the sales brochure on her lap. Twelve bedrooms, forty thousand square feet, tennis court, pool, guesthouse, on five acres. The billionaire owner of Amazon had snapped up the place next door. Michael's kind of neighborhood, not that he would ever set foot on the property. Asking price: $55 million.

Manoush Pahlavi, thirties, trim, smiling, arms spread wide in welcome, stood at the front door. A few minutes exchanging pleasantries, then a tour of the property. Sylvie, though, had already made up her mind. Prime real estate north of Sunset Boulevard in the Beverly Hills zip code was desirable by default. Large historical parcels, no matter their price, were too precious to pass up. Still, it was her job to perform due diligence, so to speak.

She listened attentively as Pahlavi described the ornate dining room, the private home theater and projection room including the latest digital projector, the professional-grade kitchen. She was more interested in the panic room, large enough to hold an entire football team, with its own gun locker, kitchen, generator, water supply, and air-filtration system. Landscaping ran ten thousand a month. Water four thousand. Not that such sums would trouble a qualified buyer.

"It's evident that the asking price is justified," said Pahlavi when they'd returned to the front door.

"Fifty million," said Sylvie.

"Fifty-two," said Pahlavi.

"Done. All cash. Closing in thirty days."

The realtor's eyes blinked excitedly. "May I ask the name of your client?"

"You may not," said Vadim.

"A foreign buyer," said Sylvie. "The family prefers to remain anonymous. All documents will be made out in the name of a holding company registered in Liechtenstein."

Pahlavi nodded. It wasn't the first residence he'd sold to an anonymous foreigner. "I'll need to confirm with my client."

"Be back to me by four. We're looking at other properties. Time is a factor."

"I think I can manage it."

"One last thing," said Sylvie—here she switched to Farsi, a language she'd picked up long ago. She wanted to establish a bond between them before asking a favor. "I'd like to purchase all the furnishings."

"There are no furnishings," said Pahlavi.

"Five million should cover it," she continued, as if she hadn't heard a word. "I expect you to take your usual commission on this type of arrangement. Shall we say five percent?"

"That should be fine."

Sylvie handed him a business card with her banking information. "I'll wire the funds under separate cover upon closing. Lovely, then."

Pahlavi considered the arrangement in the blink of an eye. There was a word for it in Persian. *Baksheesh*. Aboveboard or not, he was not about to throw away two hundred fifty thousand dollars cash. Not with the economy the way it was.

"Of course, Mrs. Bettencourt. It shouldn't be a problem."

"Call me Sylvie."

"Sylvie."

"Wonderful, and Manoush…I will have this property."

The remainder of the afternoon passed in a whirl. Sotheby's for a private sale of a Van Gogh. One of his *Sunflowers*. Not the best, but not bad for eighty million. The painting to be crated and sent to Geneva Free Port. On to Bulgari. An estate sale. A diamond necklace designed by Carl Fabergé. One hundred fifty carats. Hardly a bargain at twenty million dollars, but it was for immediate use. To be shipped to her offices in Paris, and then onward, destination TBD. Apparently Michael had a new girlfriend.

By six, she was back in the lounge of The Peninsula hotel, enjoying a martini. Tallying the day's activity. Total monies spent: one hundred fifty-seven million dollars and five shekels.

Not bad for a day's work.

Only eight hundred million more to go for the month.

CHAPTER 13

Simon was back in the shop by four. Entering his office, he locked the door and slid behind his desk, then placed a call to an old friend. Her name was Detective Chief Inspector Felicity Worth of the Metropolitan Police Homicide and Major Crime Command. It was DCI Worth who'd handled the government's case against Boris Blatt. The charges had been racketeering, extortion, money laundering, kidnapping, and battery with the intent to do grave bodily harm. And those were just the ones Simon could remember.

"One question," said Simon when Felicity Worth answered. "Where is Boris Blatt?"

"Simon, this you?"

"Where is he, Felicity? Where's Blatt? I need to know."

"Wherever do you think he is?" said Worth, as if the question were meant to be a joke.

"That's not an answer."

"He got ten years and you know it. Sent up to Wakefield. Convicted on all counts, thanks to you."

It was Simon who had provided Scotland Yard with Boris Blatt's SIM card—the memory chip that holds a cellphone's information. Mail, photos, texts, browsing history, passwords, the works. But that was another story.

"That's not an answer either," he said.

"Simon, please. Why are you calling me out of the blue asking about Boris Blatt? He's done and dusted. Out of sight, out of mind. The citizens of London thank you again."

"You could have at least told me. I mean, seeing that I was the one who put him away. The man is a gangster."

There was a pause. "He hasn't—?"

"Not yet," said Simon. "Somerset…you relocated him to Somerset. You gave him back his money."

A longer pause. Simon could hear her negotiating a crowded hallway before slamming a door. Then an anguished whisper. "How in God's name do you know this? All of this is strictly, strictly confidential."

"No one finked, Felicity."

"Then what?"

"I ran into one of his friends. Actually, a colleague of mine in the trade."

"I'm not sure I follow."

"Blatt couldn't keep his mouth shut."

There was a commotion outside Simon's office. Raised voices. Lucy shouting at someone to stop, then: "You can't go in there! Hey!"

A fist banged on the door. "Mr. Riske. Police. Open up."

Simon stood. He had an inkling what this might be about. "Felicity, listen, I can't talk right now."

"What is it?" said Worth. "What's going on over there?"

Simon unlocked the door. A squad of uniformed police pushed past him. With them was Jack Hawley. His face bruised, jaw swollen as large as a grapefruit.

"Do me a favor," said Simon, phone held close to his mouth. "Meet me at the Wimbledon Police Station in an hour."

"Whatever for?"

"I'm going to be visiting there for a bit."

"Simon, what's going on?"

"I'll tell you everything there." Simon hung up, then gave his attention to the police. "Afternoon, gentlemen. What seems to be the problem?"

The ranking policeman—a sergeant, by his collar tabs—addressed him face-to-face. "Mr. Riske. You're under arrest for the battery of Mr. John J. Hawley."

"No assault?"

"He says you hit him without warning," said the sergeant. "Assault's the part that comes before. You know, when you threaten him."

Hawley pushed his way closer. "Think you could come in, knock me around, and walk back out? Did ya?"

Simon ignored him as Lucy and Harry Mason rushed in, crowding the police.

"What's this about?" demanded Lucy. "What have you done?"

"It doesn't concern you. Don't worry. Everything will be fine."

She began to cry. "What's the matter with you? I got better. You got worse. Why are you acting this way?"

Harry put an arm around her shoulder, but she was inconsolable.

"Ready?" said the sergeant. "We'll charge you formally at the station. Shouldn't take too long."

Simon said he understood. "Cuffs?"

"Will they be necessary?"

Simon shook his head and gathered his wallet and keys.

Hawley followed him, insisting on standing too close, enjoying the entire circus too much. "And all for nothing. Still don't know where to get your blasted gearbox." A hearty laugh. "Wish I could see you in the clink."

"Not going to happen." Simon hit him again. Same place. Same result.

The cuffs hurt more than he remembered.

It had been a while since Simon was inside a police station. To his eye, the Wimbledon station was cleaner, better organized, and almost too quiet. He was treated respectfully and given tea and a biscuit. It was a far cry from the first time he saw the inside of a jail cell. The *commissariat* on La Canebière in Marseille. The charge: armed robbery. The cops there had known and disliked him, and hadn't hesitated to demonstrate their lack of affection. Instead of tea and biscuits, he'd received a liberal dose of corporal punishment. To be more specific, they'd beat the hell out of him.

Good treatment or bad, Simon despised every minute inside the station. Two hours is a blink of an eye as far as police custody goes, but it was two hours too long. He didn't regret his actions. Hawley would never have told him where Blatt lived, and his requests for payments had been beyond outrageous. He'd deserved a licking just for asking about Lucy.

Felicity Worth was waiting in the front hall when Simon was released. "Mr. Riske…the man who knows too much."

"DCI Worth…if you weren't a woman, you'd be next on my list to drop."

Felicity Worth ignored the barb. She was fifty, gray haired, and sturdy, her nearly thirty years on the force visible in every line and wrinkle on her face. She'd come from her office on Great Smith Street and was dressed in a worn, gray two-piece and maroon blouse, her credentials still hanging from her breast pocket.

"I think you've had enough trouble for one day," she said.

"I think you're right." He gave her a hug. "Thanks for coming."

"Think I wouldn't?"

"Not for a second," said Simon. "How's George?"

"A love, as ever. Has a bit of arthritis, but that's to be expected at his age."

"What is he, five? Six?"

"Seven! Getting on for a French bulldog."

They stepped outside. The night was warm. The station was close enough to the All England Lawn Tennis and Croquet Club that they could hear the grunts and shouts of players and the sounds of well-hit tennis balls coming from the nearest courts.

"Need a lift?" asked Worth.

"Your ride bulletproof?"

"We're keeping an eye on him," she answered.

Her tone was too confident for Simon's taste. "Don't!" he said, moving a step closer. "He isn't the one who's going to put a bullet into my head. He isn't the one who's going to shove a six-inch shiv into my gut. He isn't the one who's going to coat my doorknob with some kind of radioactive poison. You know that. He'll have one of his goons do his dirty work. One phone call. That's all it takes."

"Granted," said Worth, all too knowingly. "These things get messy."

"Define 'things.'"

"You know. Witness Protection."

"I thought you resettled criminals in Ipswich or Grimsby, the Shetland Islands. Somewhere off the beaten track. But Somerset? I bet he's living on a ten-hectare estate with his own private racetrack. You gave him back his twenty-five-million-dollar Ferrari."

"We never took it from him in the first place. Blatt paid a five-million-pound fine and received his sentence from the court."

"How long before he started singing?"

"He was cooperating the entire time. He did a few months for show and so we could keep him safe."

"You never breathed a word," said Simon. "Good on you."

"If it makes you feel better, you were part of the deal. Your continued health and well-being, that is. Strictly hands off. Then and now."

"I can't tell you how much safer I feel."

They reached Worth's Vauxhall. "Now it's your turn," said Felicity Worth, climbing behind the wheel. Simon got in. She drove him back to his shop, finding an open spot near the front entry. Along the way, he laid out the story, at least as far as it stood. He left out the part about meeting Nigel Cleak and Nessa Kenyon, and Sylvie Bettencourt's ties to Russia. That was something for MI5, not the London Metropolitan Police.

"A gearbox," said Worth, not quite able to bring herself to believe it.

"Blatt couldn't keep his mouth shut."

"You think he knew you'd find out?"

"Of course he knew. At the least, he wanted to gloat. He had something I wanted. He wasn't going to let me have it."

"I'll have a word with his controller."

"Not on your life," said Simon.

"Pardon me?"

"I don't want Boris Blatt to think I know anything about him or the gearbox. That's the last thing I need, him looking over his shoulder."

"Is that the only reason?"

"Excuse me?"

Worth chose her words carefully. "You aren't going to…"

"To what?"

"You know damn well."

"Me? I wouldn't know where to begin."

Worth looked at him askance. She wasn't having it. "Don't let Blatt's men catch you. Out here, we can help you. Step foot on his property, you're fair game. He's got a whole corps of uglies with him. They're just waiting for something to do…or someone to do it to."

Simon climbed out of the car. "I hope it was worth it," he said. "What you got out of him."

Worth didn't reply. Her expression gave Simon the answer. Yes, it was. Very much so.

"Thanks for the lift," he said.

"Don't call me from Somerset."

"Now, DCI Worth, why would I be going anywhere near there?"

CHAPTER 14

Simon wasn't going to Somerset. At least not for a day or two. First, he was going to 123 Great Smith Street, not coincidentally the site of DCI Felicity Worth's office.

Parking a block from the Embankment, he walked the streets of Westminster, head down, hands in his pockets. It was past midnight, a light rain falling. A few people were still out. Couples walking arm in arm. Tourists, heads tilted to the sky, taking in the grandeur of Westminster Abbey and Big Ben, awash in history. What was a little rain to keep them from walking in the footsteps of Cromwell and Churchill and Henry VIII? Few, however, moved with his evident intent. He was not interested in Whitehall or the Churchill War Rooms. He was a man with somewhere to go. A descendant of Guy Fawkes and Bill Sikes. A man with evil on his mind. A thief on his way to work.

The red-brick building at 123 Great Smith Street was four stories tall, with white-paned windows and a black lacquer door, standing cheek by jowl with others looking just like it. There was no polished brass plaque bearing the name of the organization occupying it. Just an old-fashioned doorbell and a very modern keycard reader. The building was anonymous, and so were the members of the London Metropolitan Police who worked inside it.

Simon walked to the front door and placed the plain white keycard he had borrowed from Felicity Worth's outside jacket pocket against the reader. The door buzzed much too loudly. A lock released. Simon pushed open the door and entered a darkened alcove. A second reader requiring a higher access. Again the keycard. This time the lock was quieter.

He was in. He stood there for a minute, as still as a post, listening. No voices. No footsteps. No LaserJet hard at work. Silence. The building was deserted.

Simon ran the stairs to the third floor and advanced to the last door on the left. DCI Felicity Worth's office was locked. With good reason. This building was home to the Met's Homicide and Major Crime Command. Too many criminals to count would love to get their hands on the information that was routinely traded between its officers.

Simon knew the premises intimately. Two years earlier, after handing over the SIM card from Boris Blatt's phone, he had assisted Felicity Worth, and a team of investigators and government barristers, in building a case against the exiled Russian oligarch. For months he'd visited Worth on a weekly basis.

No keycard reader here. An old-fashioned Imperial lock. He produced a set of picks, selected two, then wet them on his tongue. The flatter pick—the "tension wrench"—went into the bottom of the lock. A gentle turn to the right. There. Now the lock was prepped, the tumblers ready to fire. The slimmer, needle-shaped pick slid into the narrower crevice above it. It was the upper pick that tipped the spring-loaded tumblers.

A breath. Eyes closed. All feeling in his fingertips. *Gently, gently.* One…then the next…and—

Footsteps.

Simon froze.

Once more. Ascending the stairs. Slow. Plodding. A man, probably overweight.

Simon recommenced his efforts. One tumbler to go. He held his breath, calmed himself, jiggled the pick every so lightly. He could feel the tumbler, needed to raise it just a bit…

A cough. Loud. Much too close. Then a voice: "Doris, that you?"

A phone call.

Simon lost his touch. The tumblers fell back. He freed the picks, stood tall. Which way to go? Farther down the hall or toward the stairs…toward whoever was there talking on the phone? His instinct urged him to retreat into the darkness. He disobeyed it. Better to be nearer the stairwell. If discovered, he would retain some element of surprise. He might even get past the man without being seen.

Simon retraced his steps, trying one door, another. Both locked. Four offices, the last two barely a foot from the stairwell, and so no good to him.

"What do you mean he won't come to the house? Does he expect us to bring it to the shop? Does he know it weighs sixty pounds? Course he does, lazy sod."

Simon could see the man's shadow at the end of the hall. There was movement. Part of a dark uniform, a key ring hanging from a heavy belt. The man took a step. There he stood, ten paces away, back turned to Simon. Close enough for Simon to note that his billy club was chipped and to see the operating lights of his radio.

The next door was locked, too.

Simon turned. One left. He crossed the hall. Heel to toe. *Church mice, Simon. Church mice.* God help him if the floor creaked. Then what? Run like hell? What else?

He placed his hand on the knob. A gentle twist to the right. *Please.*

No resistance. Firmer now. The door opened.

Simon was inside. He'd never closed a door more carefully.

It was one thirty when Simon took a seat at Felicity Worth's desk.

The guard had vanished. The lock had put up scant resistance. Simon keyed the prompt on her computer and crossed his fingers that she had not changed the password. He hadn't planned for this day. He was observant by nature. A man in his line of work did not forget the password to a senior police official's computer.

Six letters. Two numerals. George15. There was a reason he'd asked about her dog.

He hit RETURN. Password Incorrect.

He had forgotten the password to a senior police official's computer.

No, not forgotten it, he realized too late. Forgotten to type all of it. Six letters. Two numerals. And a symbol. The most common were a hashtag or an exclamation mark. Neither would do for someone named "Worth." She would choose something far more apt. A pound sign. And so he typed:

George15£.

He hit RETURN. The screen flickered. He was in.

A moment to congratulate himself. He'd known it all along.

Now the hard part.

Simon accessed all records of cases closed. The list ran to hundreds of pages—all court docket numbers. He typed Blatt's name into the query bar. Nothing. Worth and her colleagues were more thorough about this than the car registration. Next, Simon typed in the name Jack Hawley had blurted. Gerstmann. A pane appeared showing an eleven-digit case number.

Proof positive of the old saw: "Three people can keep a secret so long as two of them are dead." *Thank you, Jack.*

Simon double-clicked on the link.

A moment later, he was reading a scanned copy of *Her Majesty's Government v. Boris Blatt.* The file ran to a thousand pages. A look at the contents. First, Blatt's crimes, a thorough accounting thereof. Money laundering, mail fraud, wire fraud, assault, the list went on and on. Somewhere in the list, "kidnapping," "battery with intent to inflict grave bodily harm," and "homicide."

The second half of Blatt's file was devoted to testimony given against others. There were too many names to count. One, however, stood out. Andrei Borisovich Blatt, age twenty-eight. Blatt's son. Despite the time and place, Simon could not stop himself from reading further.

In a court of law, Boris Blatt had provided evidence against his son, swearing that he had witnessed him give an order to have bodily harm done to another and to have sanctioned a bribe to a member of British law enforcement.

There was low and there was low. Then there was selling out your own blood to save your skin.

Simon inserted a thumb drive into the desktop's CPU. God bless the Met's obsolete IT system. Then again, twenty years old was brand-new when it came to Scotland Yard. Simon tapped his foot while waiting for the upload to be completed. Done.

He neither saw nor heard anyone on his way out.

Five minutes later, Simon was walking along the Embankment on his way back to his car.

Step one. Complete.

CHAPTER 15

Côte d'Azur, France

Eight hundred fifty miles to the southeast, at Le Perroquet Bleu on the Rue Sainte-Martine in Juan-les-Pins, it was closing time. Waiters in white aprons gathered in a corner comparing tips, sharing the evening's war stories. Young *commis* cleared the tables. Cutlery loaded into the high-pressure washer. Tablecloths in one bag for dry cleaning. Two of them swept the floor; bread crumbs, frites, clamshells, and, if they were lucky, money...a two-euro coin, maybe a twenty-euro note. More than that they had to turn in to *le patron*. A pall of blue smoke hung from the ceiling, drifting among the decorative fishing nets and stuffed blowfish and nautical paintings, mixing with the scent of garlic and butter and pommes frites.

Jojo Matta, chef and proprietor of Le Perroquet Bleu, lit a cigarette and threw a towel over his shoulder. A good night, not great. Ninety-six covers. Turned the place two and a half times. The problem was the clientele. Too many locals and not enough tourists. Too many orders of bouillabaisse and moules-frites, not enough for caviar and Dom, followed by filet mignon and langoustine. In short, not enough Russians.

So...closing time, but hardly closed.

A half dozen of his friends sat around the dining room, talking loudly, glaring at their phones, all of them smoking. To look at, they were family. Dark hair, swarthy complexions, open-collared shirts, gold chains, flashy wristwatches. If you looked closer, you'd see that all carried a tattoo on their forearms. A ship's anchor held by a grinning skeleton amid crashing waves. Most carried a few extra pounds around the middle, too. And why not? Life was short. Enjoy!

"Encore une pression!" called one of them, Pierrot. A new guy fresh from the hill country. Good with a knife. Lousy shot. A big talker. Not a big producer...*but he promised.*

"It's not water," said Jojo. "Five euros in the plate." He poured a beer from the tap and set it on the table.

"Merci, mon vieux."

Jojo brushed him on the head. *Fuckin' kids.* "Mauro, hear about the rental in Cap Ferrat? Family from South Africa. Parking lot kings of Johannesburg. The wife, she likes diamonds."

"You don't say. Put a man on them. Next time they go out, we go in."

"Hear that, Pierrot?" said Jojo. "Now you have something to do. I want you in front of that place day and night. And don't park in that red Simca of yours. Get something that blends in."

Jojo Matta was a gifted chef and an average crook. Like all those present, he was also a member of a criminal enterprise whose turf ran from the Côte d'Azur to the Bouches-du-Rhône, practically the entire southern coast of France. More specifically, Jojo was a *capo* in La Brise de Mer, the Corsican crime family that ruled Marseille, responsible for drug trafficking, prostitution, protection, and the occasional armed robbery. Jewelry and jewelry stores were Jojo's specialty. He had the same tattoo on his arm. These days, his sixtieth birthday in the rearview mirror, he preferred working on his tan—a wondrous shade of chestnut brown—overseeing Le Perroquet Bleu, and drumming up new recipes for his loup de mer and barramundi. Jojo knew everyone and everyone knew Jojo.

"*Patron*...phone call." A waiter held the restaurant phone in his hand.

"We're closed."

"Someone named Ledoux. He says, 'Answer your phone, *connard.*' He made me say that."

"Ledoux?" At the sound of the name, Jojo's night went from average to awful. Once Ledoux had been one of them, a made man at eighteen, an animal with an AK-47 practically grafted onto his hands, his specialty taking down armored cars. His nickname was "the American." These days he went by Riske. Simon Riske. Jojo despised him.

"What do you want, Ledoux?" said Jojo, after taking the phone and hiding in an alcove.

"Maurice Petrov."

"What about him?" Petrov was a Bulgarian arms dealer who'd set up shop in Fréjus, just west of Antibes, a few years ago. He didn't mix with the locals. He did his business in Africa, occasionally the Middle East.

"I need to place an order."

"You? Planning on taking over a country?" Jojo laughed mockingly. In truth, however, he wouldn't put it past Riske or Ledoux or whatever he wanted to call himself.

"Not hardly. In fact, I only need a couple of things."

Jojo found a piece of paper and wrote down the short list. "You getting back in the game, Ledoux? A little old-fashioned arson? An insurance job, that it?"

"Mind your own business," said Ledoux. "Oh, and one other thing. I need you to bring it to me."

"You're here? In town?" Jojo cringed. He didn't want the boys to know he was still doing business with Ledoux. There was an unwritten rule against that kind of thing.

"London. I'll send a plane. Let's say tomorrow at two. Nice airport."

"You kidding me? It's high season. I can't leave."

"Pay is five thousand. I'll put you up for the night at the Dorchester. Dinner at Restaurant Gordon Ramsay. Be a good boy and I'll arrange a tour of the kitchen."

Wasn't it just like Ledoux to know that Ramsay was his favorite chef? Practically an idol. "Ten thousand," said Jojo. "If Petrov has what you want."

"*If?* He has a warehouse full. Don't you watch the news?"

"I'll call you in the morning to confirm."

"Just get it, Jojo," said Ledoux. "I'll owe you one."

"You…owe me?" Jojo felt a bit of his old mean self. "Ledoux, I'm not going to forget."

Jojo Matta hung up the phone. Maybe it wasn't such a bad night after all.

CHAPTER 16

London, England

Jack Hawley woke with a start. He had time to gasp and blink his eyes before his head began to throb. Hungover again. A cautious glance out the window. Rain. But of course.

In the kitchen, he made himself a cup of tea—loads of sugar, thank you—fried an egg, and tossed it onto a piece of burnt toast. He ate standing at the counter. Three bites. Done. He wiped his mouth with the tail of his T-shirt. Always a gentleman. A shower, a shave, and a shit and he felt almost human.

He dressed for work in a pale gray suit and his least wrinkled shirt. A necktie could wait. His shoes begged for a shine. Tomorrow. He promised. A brief struggle with a hairbrush yielded no discernible improvement. Why mess with perfection? *And screw you, madam, if you don't like it.*

Hawley arrived at his store a few minutes after nine. Chamois rag in hand, he wiped down the Ferrari from stem to stern, then opened the door and dropped into the driver's seat. Heaven! With due reverence, he placed his hands on the steering wheel. Not only did the car look like new, it also smelled as if it had just rolled out of the factory. The odometer read 2,360 kilometers. How, he wondered, had someone resisted the urge to drive this beautiful machine?

He'd gotten the call from Gerstmann, or Blatt, or whatever his name was, two weeks earlier, asking that he travel to an estate in Somerset. "I'm interested in selling one of my cars. I'd like you to take a look. See what needs to be done. Tell me what I might get for it."

When Blatt told him the model—a 1964 275—he'd nearly fallen out of his chair. The car was legendary. Riske wasn't the only one present at the Sotheby's auction two years before. Since then, the car's value had doubled.

"May I ask how you selected me?"

"You restored one of my friend's cars a few years ago. Igor Shvets. He said you did a decent job of it."

Hawley sat a little straighter at the memory. Once, not so very long ago, he had been a gifted restorer. The equal of Riske, to be sure. It was the damned drink that did him in. Demon rum. Jack Hawley vowed then and there to stop. He'd taken his last drink.

And so…a second chance.

Do this right and anything was possible.

Hawley studied the interior coachwork, looking for cracks in the leather, scratches on the dashboard, blemishes on the instrumentation. Anything that might require his attention. It was evident that Blatt had treated the car with care. In fact, Hawley couldn't find a thing that needed to be done. He climbed out, closing the door softly. For the umpteenth time, he did a "walkaround." *Aha!* A scratch on the right rear panel. A closer look. Or was it the light?

In his office, Hawley set about making a list of buyers. Only so many people were able to spend fifty million dollars on an automobile. The vast majority were active collectors. It was exceedingly rare, if not unheard of, for a first-time buyer to pay such an astronomical sum. Hawley's focus was sharpened by the fact that should he not find a buyer, Blatt would most likely put the car up at auction and roll the dice. Not going to happen, swore Hawley. Not on his watch.

"Shall we discuss your commission?"

Fourteen days earlier. Hawley and Blatt were standing inside Blatt's spacious garage on his estate outside Bath. Poured concrete floor. Overhead lights. As brightly lit as a West End stage. Actually, "garage" was the wrong word. "Hangar" was more appropriate. Besides the '64 Ferrari, Hawley counted twenty-two other vehicles. Ferraris, Lamborghinis, Porsches, Mercedes, even an old Williams Formula One race car that had been driven by Alain Prost, the year he won his fourth world championship.

Hawley wondered why Blatt was selling this one—the prize of the collection—but knew better than to ask. Everyone had their reasons. The usual fee was between five and fifteen percent of the sales price. Given the amount the car could expect to fetch, however, Hawley made an adjustment.

"Two and a half percent," he said. Even at that reduced tariff, he stood to earn somewhere between one and two million dollars. The thought made his bollocks tingle.

"Flat two percent," said Blatt. "To fifty million. Higher than that and I'll give you five percent. How does that sound?"

"Fair enough," said Hawley.

An hour later, the Ferrari was on a trailer on its way to Hawley's London showroom.

Hawley's phone interrupted his greedy reverie. The caller ID was blocked. The telltale sign of a wealthy individual. He answered straightaway. "Italian Motorsport Restoration."

"*Allô, Monsieur Hawley, s'il vous plaît.*" A Frog. Pompous as hell.

"Speaking."

"Yes, hello. My name is Antoine Pechels de Saint-Sardens. I have watched you racing in the past. Formula Three championship at Silverstone. Was it '98? You won."

"Actually, it was '97," said Hawley, revising his opinion of the caller. "My last year on the circuit."

"Magnificent. I often wondered what happened afterward."

"Injury," said Hawley, offering his stock response. "Spinal cord. One more crash and the docs told me I would spend the rest of my life in a chair."

"A shame."

Not exactly the truth, but it did in a pinch. "Life, but one carries on."

"Indeed. And so, to my call. I have a piece of business that requires your attention. My brother, Marcel, has recently passed away. He has left me several of his cars. I was hoping you might appraise them."

"Do you know offhand what make of automobile, maybe the years and models?"

"His Renault."

"A Renault?" Hawley didn't bother hiding his disappointment. Didn't they have Carmax in France?

"It is quite new. Very nice. Black, of course. You know, Marcel."

As Antoine Pechels continued, Hawley typed the man's name into the search bar…or as close as he could see fit. The screen lit up with hits. The first read, BILLIONAIRE ANTOINE PECHELS DE SAINT-SARDENS…Hawley didn't need to read any further.

"You said your brother left you several cars," said Hawley.

"Yes, the others are his Italian cars. Marcel, he was a collector. My interest in motorsport died not long after you retired."

"What kind?"

"The usual. Maserati, Ferrari, some others. He has so many."

"Ten? Twenty?"

"At least twenty. I lost count years ago."

By now, all trace of Hawley's hangover had vanished. His heart beat as fast as if he were back behind the wheel of his race car. One day to appraise each car. A fee of five thousand euros a day. He was looking at a hundred grand easy. He typed in the name of Pechels's brother. Was it Marcel? An article in French. MARCEL PECHELS EST MORT. A photo accompanied the article, showing a slim, dark-haired man standing in front of a fleet of sports cars. Hawley wiped his mouth. The mother lode.

"All of Marcel's colleagues from the trade have been contacting me," said Antoine Pechels. "All claim to be experts. I trust none of them. I prefer an independent party."

"A wise idea, Mr. Pechels, if I do say so."

"I thought as much. So, when can you come?"

"Excuse me?"

"How about tomorrow? Better yet, if you can make it this evening, I can offer you a very nice dinner. You will stay at my château, of course. Tomorrow we can begin."

Hawley was taken aback by the suggestion. Tomorrow? His eye fell on an agenda that a friend had given him for Christmas last year. The cellophane wrap had yet to be removed. "I may be able to free up my schedule. Let me see."

"Of course."

"There is the matter of compensation."

"Name your price. I know, at least, that you will be fair and honest. In addition, I will need someone to oversee the sale, perhaps to arrange an auction."

"An auction?"

"Unless you think that is a bad idea?"

"No, no. It would be a pleasure."

"It is settled, then. I will email you my address. I'm just outside of Paris. Shall I wire you the money for your travel?"

"That won't be necessary," said Hawley.

"But I insist on reimbursing you."

"That's good of you," said Hawley. "I'll check the Eurostar schedule. If I manage to wrap up my business earlier than expected, I may be able to catch the two p.m. train."

"Are you sure? I don't want to impose."

"I'll do my best."

"I will have my driver meet you at the Gare du Nord. He will have a sign with your name."

Hawley ended the call a few minutes later. *Name his fee. Arrange an auction. At least twenty vintage Italian motorcars.* He leaned back in his chair and whooped. First Blatt, now Pechels. It was his lucky day.

Hawley jumped up and made a beeline for the cabinet. The occasion called for a drink. He poured himself a generous measure of brandy. He didn't pause for a moment as he drank it down.

He would stop tomorrow. He promised.

Five miles to the west, in the suburb of Southfields, Simon Riske hung up the phone.

Step two. Complete.

CHAPTER 17

Khimki, Russia

In the city of Khimki, in north Moscow Oblast, a twenty-story skyscraper stands alone amid the flat industrial plane and is visible from miles away, unique because of its darkly hued blue glass exterior and odd geometric shape. It is called "the Tower." To the uneducated eye, the Tower appears to be one more office building, not dissimilar to hundreds of others throughout Moscow, home to lawyers and bankers and the moneyed class of grifter that had thrived since the red revolutionary banner was replaced by the white, blue, and red tricolor, and capitalism, not communism, had become the law of the land.

In fact, the Tower was anything but.

The Tower belonged to the government—more specifically, the military—and it housed one of the most powerful weapons in the country's armory. Not a gun or a bomb or anything designed to slay the enemy. Something different. A weapon that relied on a resource Russia produced in abundance to achieve its ends. Brainpower. The men and (very few) women who occupied the top ten floors of the Tower formed the nucleus of Unit 29155 of the GRU, Russia's military intelligence agency. And it was Unit 29155's job to hack into the closely guarded inner sanctums of its enemies and wreak havoc in any and every way it saw fit.

Over the years, under aliases like "Sandworm," "Hades," and "Voodoo Bear," Unit 29155 had brought down the power grid of the capital of Ukraine, Kyiv; broken into the servers of the United States Democratic National Committee and released tens of thousands of emails to the unsuspecting public; destroyed the IT infrastructure of the 2018 Winter

Olympics in South Korea; and knocked the entire Saudi oil industry off-line for a week.

The newest member of the unit arrived for work promptly. Lieutenant Grigori Novalev, twenty-two years of age, slight of stature, bearded and bespectacled and dressed in civilian clothing, showed his ID to the security guard and took an elevator to the tenth floor. There wasn't the least thing military about him. So much the better.

A math prodigy, Novalev had studied at MIT before he was fourteen, graduated from Moscow State University with a doctorate in computer science at twenty, and at twenty-one completed his military training at the St. Petersburg Naval Institute. More important than all of that, at least for Unit 29155's concerns, he had been a hacker since he stopped nursing from his mother's teat. The man was diabolical.

It was August. Election season in the United States was in full swing. Grigori—or Grisha, as his friends called him—was devoting his efforts to gaining control of the Pentagon's servers. His goal was a new and top-secret nuclear propulsion system—purportedly already in the U.S. arsenal—that increased the velocity of ballistic missiles by a factor of ten. A missile equipped with such a propulsion system could be fired from a Los Angeles–class attack submarine parked off the Finnish coast and hit the Kremlin in seven minutes.

Novalev was getting close, very close.

At 10:42 a.m., the alarm on his laptop sounded. It was not an alarm he could ignore. Grisha saved his work on his military-issue desktop, picked up his laptop, and headed into the break room. No ping-pong tables here, no espresso machines or lovely masseuses wondering if he might need a quick neck rub to ease his tension. Not even a refrigerator with free beverages. Just a table from IKEA, four chairs, and a vending machine selling Red Bull.

Grisha sat and opened the laptop. A look at the notification. He winced. Someone or something had stumbled over one of his tripwires. A look over his shoulder to make sure he was alone. He tapped in his password. This was personal, not professional. Up came the details.

Chatterbell. But of course.

Someone using the handle "Danish Seekr" was asking questions about a car bomb that had exploded in Switzerland several days earlier.

Grisha reviewed the thread, following Danish Seekr's progress. License plates, a car dealer, even a photograph of an assailant. These amateurs. They had no idea what they were getting themselves into.

A few taps of the keys and he had a name. Anna Bildt. A few more taps and he had her particulars: Facebook page, Instagram account, email addresses with Gmail and YouSee, a Danish Internet provider, and finally, a picture. Of course, she had to be beautiful. A pity.

Anna Christina Bildt. The name rang a bell.

Grisha closed the laptop. It was almost eleven. Time for his first Red Bull. He drank half, then lit a cigarette. A last look at the photograph. An insincere "Sorry, babe, but there's nothing I can do."

He made a phone call.

She answered on the second ring. *"Allô?"* That French voice. Hard to believe she was Russian. Let alone his mother.

"Hello, Mama. I have some bad news."

CHAPTER 18

London, England

Jack Hawley's showroom on the Brixton high street in Lambeth stood in the middle of the block, sandwiched between a pizza parlor and a children's clothing store. The River Thames, Westminster, and Mayfair, all, were four miles away as the crow flies; Hawley's Italian Motorsport Restoration, however, was closer to Brixton Hill, a neighborhood more famous for stealing cars than paying upwards of fifty million dollars for one.

Simon walked slowly along the opposite side of the road, his West Ham cap pulled low, as he sipped a cup of black coffee. Anyone seen with a vanilla latte in this part of town was begging for trouble. That counted for women, too. It was his third circuit up and down the block. The red '64 Ferrari sat like a landed shark behind the showroom window. In fact, Simon decided, the car was safer in Lambeth than on Bond Street. A casual car thief would have no idea what to do with it. You didn't dump a car like that at a local chop shop. You couldn't drive it to Folkestone and stick it on a freighter to West Africa. The car was safe by virtue of its unique status.

Well…almost safe.

Another circuit of the block. Still no sign of Hawley. Good old Jack had emailed Antoine Pechels stating that he would be on the 14:12 Eurostar to Paris, arriving at 16:28. Pechels inquired if a rack of venison would be satisfactory for dinner. Hawley, bless his soul, replied that he was a pescatarian, and was there any "trout amandine" to be had? Hawley was in luck. There was.

*   *   *

It had been a busy morning.

Jojo Matta got back to him at nine. Green light. Maurice Petrov had Simon's order in stock. He was more than happy to help out his friends in La Brise and offered a price of one thousand euros a unit. Simon made a call and dispatched a Cessna Citation business jet to Nice to ferry Jojo and his cargo to London. It was harder arranging a face-to-face with Gordon Ramsay, and required the divine intervention of D'Artagnan Moore, who knew someone who knew someone who insured the restaurant. Only then did Simon leave his shop and commence his surveillance of Jack Hawley.

At 1:42 by Simon's watch, the door to Hawley's showroom opened. Hawley emerged, looking almost put together. Natty suit, pale blue shirt, briefcase in one hand. He locked the door and lowered the protective steel curtain over the showroom window, kneeling to attach a Master Lock. He stood and Simon noted that the man's fly was open. Poor bastard.

Simon followed him to the corner and looked on as Hawley hailed a cab. He was going to be hard pressed if he wanted to make it to St. Pancras by 2:12. Simon gave him a fifty-fifty chance. The next train left at four. Would Hawley wait at the station or turn around and come back, maybe forgo his trout amandine and catch the first train in the morning? Angered, Simon crossed the street and headed for Hawley's shop. He was furious that so much should depend on a drunk. Hawley could fuck up a...Well, you know what he could fuck up.

Simon continued past the store to the end of the block, turned right, then turned again up the alley that backed Hawley's store. Formerly, the address had served as a motor scooter dealership. A sectional steel curtain the width of the store ran from ceiling to ground. He saw no way to open it from the outside. The only way in was from the front. It was unwise to pick a lock on a busy street at two in the afternoon. Simon was sure that Hawley's neighbors knew him. Community policing had brought this part of Lambeth back from the dead. Still, this wasn't Simon's first visit to Hawley's shop. He hadn't returned without a plan.

He retraced his steps along the alley, phone to his ear, halting abruptly to double-check that he was not using his own. A Samsung, not his iPhone. He hit the speed dial. A woman answered. "Yes."

"Nothing doing," said Simon. "He left the place locked up tight. You ready?"

"Do you need to ask?"

"Professional courtesy."

"Are you?"

"Ha. Ha."

"Take up position. Stand by."

"Roger that."

"My, you do learn fast." The call ended.

Simon could imagine the woman's prim, satisfied smile. In fact, he could imagine more than that. He'd teach her. He reached the corner of St. Saviour's and Brixton. A look in both directions. He saw nothing out of the ordinary—but then he wouldn't, would he?—and continued on toward Hawley's store. He was ten paces away when he heard a screech of tires behind him, a car braking hard and, he knew, too late. He spun, looking back toward the intersection in time to see a small black MINI Cooper barrel through a red light and plow into the passenger side of a white panel van. Glass shattered. Metal shrieked. And then the wallop. It sounded louder than anything he'd heard. A horn blared, stuck. Above it, a man's voice cried out for help.

Around Simon, foot traffic halted. Every pedestrian turned toward the accident, attention focused on the entangled cars. Already, several men and women had rushed into the street, anxious to be of assistance. A siren began to wail. Police. *So soon?*

Simon walked to Hawley's shop. Two locks secured the front door. Deftly, he slipped on a pair of gloves. In one hand, he held a slim metallic canister containing a compressed difluoroethane-based freezing agent. He placed its nozzle to each lock and sprayed a burst. The chemical froze the metal at a temperature of $-13°F$, the locks turning as brittle as ice. Simon produced a small stainless-steel hammer from his pocket. Three hard knocks. The tumblers inside shattered. The door burst open.

He slipped inside, closing the door behind him. He continued to the back entrance and hit the button to raise the sectional door. He popped his head into the alley. A navy-blue Ford was parked at the designated spot. A slim arm extended from the window. A hand signal. All clear. Jack Hawley had made the train. By the time he arrived in Paris and discovered that no one was there to pick him up, that, in fact, the real Antoine Pechels de Saint-Sardens was currently at his family estate in Biarritz, it would be too late.

Simon made his way to Hawley's office. The keys to the Ferrari were in the top drawer of Hawley's desk. Easy enough. He slid into the driver's seat of the car and started the engine, goosing the accelerator for the hell of it. No sweeter sound. He checked the instruments.

A problem.

The needle on the fuel gauge rested at zero. Simon's heart sank. How could he have forgotten? He snapped his nail against the glass. Nothing. This was not happening. One more time. The needle jumped. A quarter tank. Four gallons. Range: fifty miles, maybe sixty. Salvation.

He backed the car into the alley, then drove in the direction of the Ford, which turned left onto St. Saviour's. A mile farther on, the Ford peeled off. Two hoots of the horn for good luck.

Ten minutes later, Simon was on the M1 headed north to Luton Airport. He could get gas on the way.

Jojo Matta's plane had better be on time.

CHAPTER 19

New York City

Friday was Los Angeles.

Saturday was New York.

Sylvie Bettencourt climbed out of the limousine at the corner of 54th and Fifth, hoisting her bag onto her shoulder. August in Midtown Manhattan. Heat, humidity, and a palette of smells and odors, one more awful than the next. A look to the sky told her their destination: a seventy-five-story steel-and-glass residential tower nearing completion halfway along the block. A wooden wall painted with renderings of the finished building surrounded the structure, aptly named "675 Fifth." No points for creativity, mused Sylvie. Then again, it was anonymity she was after.

Vadim in tow, she walked briskly down the street. She made sure to keep her eyes on the sidewalk. The city's infrastructure was in free fall. Potholes scarred every road, cracks in the pavement big enough to fall through, tunnels under repair. To the naked eye, New York looked more like the capital of a third world country than the financial dynamo of the civilized world.

"Anonymity," she whispered to herself, a look of distaste souring her features. "Wouldn't that be nice."

She was replaying the fiasco in London a few years back. It had begun with a luxury residence named 1 Park, situated fittingly at 1 Park Lane on the southeastern corner of Hyde Park, a brand-new fifteen-story building wedged between the Lanesborough Hotel and the InterContinental. The developer had advertised it as the most expensive residence ever built in the English capital. He knew his clientele. It was exactly that kind of hyperbole that appealed to a certain class of buyer, Michael among them.

As instructed, Sylvie had negotiated to purchase two of the residences (each took up an entire floor). Nonresident foreign ownership was permissible but required an endless amount of paperwork and wrangling with the British tax authorities. When the arguing ended and the smoke cleared, she had paid three hundred million pounds for the two top floors of 1 Park. On to the next piece of business.

Not so fast.

At just this time a foreign businessman living in London, Oleg Orlov, a Russian fertilizer magnate, was arrested and charged with a slew of crimes, including racketeering and money laundering. Prior to the arrest, Orlov had boasted publicly about his purchase of a home in "the most expensive residence ever built in the London capital." Alarm bells sounded. The press smelled a story, or, better yet, a scandal. Was London real estate a prime repository for organized criminals' ill-gotten gains? What other crooks might be living in 1 Park?

A cry went up for greater transparency in property transactions, especially those involving foreigners, and, more importantly, nonresident foreigners. Bills were introduced on the floor of the House of Commons, calling for a repeal of laws allowing anonymous corporations and holding companies to purchase real estate in the United Kingdom. In time, the developer of 1 Park was compelled to reveal the names of his buyers. All the residences except for two, those of an American pop singer and a Japanese software magnate, were owned by LLCs—limited liability corporations—which, in turn, belonged to holding companies domiciled in the world's most famous tax havens: the Cayman Islands, Netherlands Antilles, even Vanuatu. Not a family surname to be found on a document anywhere.

The battle raged for months. Government officials hammered at the bulwark of companies hiding the identity of the true owner of the fourteenth and fifteenth floors of 1 Park. It was, as Sylvie had made sure in advance, an impossible task—a matryoshka doll with one shell company inside the next, and the next. Moreover, a campaign was initiated behind the scenes, quietly reminding UK lawmakers of the tens of millions of pounds' worth of taxes paid by foreign owners. And the contributions made by these foreign owners to the election campaigns of certain lawmakers hailing from the London metropolitan area.

In time, the hue and cry for greater transparency faded. Did it really matter who owned these properties? What counted was that they paid their taxes and supported the British economy. Just like that, opinion changed. When all was said and done, the public was none the wiser about the identity of Sylvie Bettencourt's client.

But it had been close.

And now Sylvie was about to step into the lobby of another building seemingly designed and constructed exclusively for foreign buyers.

A look over her shoulder. A pain in her stomach, sharp as a dagger. Two men in dark suits stood fifty paces behind her. Surely they'd been outside The Mark earlier.

"Vadim, dear, are we being followed?"

Vadim caught sight of the men. "Not sure."

"Well, I am."

"Americans?"

"Look at them." Wasn't it obvious? The cheekbones, the shoulders, the crew cuts. "You know who."

A rotund, dark-haired man held the door. No tour of the premises this time. What was the point? The final twenty stories were still under construction. Instead, a meeting in the conference room. Present were Sylvie's attorneys, a team of three from the white-shoe firm of Powell, Pine, and Sanders. Across the table was a larger team from the developer's side. There wasn't a soul interested in how the finished units might look. Two bedrooms or three, an en-suite master bath, professional-grade kitchen. No one gave a damn. This was about a foreign entity parking money in the United States of America, still the safest refuge in the world.

Discussion quickly got down to price. Attorneys on both sides earned their thousand-dollar-an-hour fees. It took three hours for an agreement to be reached. Ninety million dollars for three of the top twenty floors (the exact locations to be allocated at a later date). A contract was drawn up. A deposit of twenty-five million dollars to be made this day to the developer's bank account.

And afterward, a more intimate exchange. Sylvie and the developer alone, a brief tête-à-tête, an agreement made in hushed tones, something far better than sex, a cashier's check duly presented to Sylvie in the amount of five million dollars.

It was nearly three p.m. by the time she and Vadim were back on the street. Sylvie knew from experience that Vadim had friends in the city. Interesting friends. She informed him that he was henceforth released from service for the evening.

"Meet me downstairs at six tomorrow morning," she said. "Wheels up by eight thirty. Don't be late, and don't come smelling like a speakeasy."

Vadim made his exit, promising to comply. There was no missing the glint in his eye. God knew where he was off to.

Sylvie waited until he was out of sight, then retraced her steps to Fifth Avenue. She did not see either of the men she suspected were following her. No matter. She must assume she was under surveillance. It didn't matter by whom. She walked to 58th Street, entered the Plaza Hotel, continuing past the Palm Court restaurant, exiting the hotel on Central Park South, where she hailed a cab.

"Madison and 70th, please."

The ride took six minutes. Sylvie had the cash fare ready and climbed from the cab as it came to a halt. Traffic was light. She crossed Madison against the light, then walked two blocks to Park. Another cab, this time going south.

"Saks, please."

She sat back, ignoring the small monitor embedded in the front seat playing short clips. Discreetly, she glanced behind her. No men jumping into cabs to give chase, in dark suits or otherwise. Still, it was too soon to allow herself to feel safe. A minimum of six legs. You never forgot the training no matter how many years had passed.

Never.

CHAPTER 20

Moscow, Russia

How old had she been when they found her? Thirteen? Fourteen? The era of Brezhnev and Gromyko, of Nixon and Kissinger. The Cold War burning its hottest. But to her, to little Sveta, it was a wondrous time. The blossom of youth. The first stabs of desire. The strange and not quite believable promise of all that beauty might bring. One day she had been a gangly twelve-year-old—knobby knees, dangling arms, dreadfully flat-chested. And her face: nose too large, eyes too wide, the grotesque lips, and her mouth with its tendency to hang open at all the wrong moments. The boys at school had a name for her. The Catfish. All she was missing were whiskers.

And then, in the course of a season, from winter to spring, she grew into a woman. She added four inches to her height. Despite her skimpy diet, she put on weight, and in all the right places: hips, derriere, breasts. She stopped walking like a drunken stork and learned (almost) unconsciously to sway her hips and thrust out her chest. Her features, for so long at odds with one another, blended into harmonious union. Her mother, God rest her soul, purchased Western makeup for her at the black-market shop on Tverskaya Ulitsa, a block from the Hotel Metropol, where all the foreign tourists stayed when visiting Moscow. And one day a special gift: a lace brassiere made by Christian Dior. How such a transformation could be wrought in so short a time she did not understand to this day. Back then she could only thank God, or the modern Soviet state.

The boys no longer called her Catfish but now Svetlana. It was a woman's name, and with it came a woman's obligations. She basked in their attention, their vulgar stares, their vile catcalls, their

101

suggestive gestures. Even their wolf whistles sounded to her starved ears like a Rachmaninoff concerto. In return, she perfected her finest scowl. They were Vronskys all, false idols, wanting sex in return for what? Nothing. Nothing at all. Her rebellious heart yearned for only one: Yuri Zhivago, sweetheart of her dreams since she'd fallen under Pasternak's spell. Kind, compassionate, committed. A soulful lover. A frequent visitor to her dreams. She would settle for nothing less.

But others were watching, too. Older men. Government men. They were not drawn to her beauty. At least not at first. It was her intellect that attracted their attention. No one earned better marks than Svetlana Alexandrovna Makarova, not at the Gorky Lyceum. She excelled in all subjects but was top of the class in mathematics, science, and, as important, ideology. She knew Marx better than Marx himself. To hear such a beautiful child discourse on dialectical materialism was to make Lenin himself cry. Added to this, she had languages. French and German she spoke fluently. English not yet, but only because it was not emphasized. Still, it was recognized: she had the gift.

It was a woman who came to the door. Alexandra Turischeva, as refined and cultured a woman as Svetlana had ever seen, let alone met. Her attire was Western, from head to toe. Her hair dyed a wondrous blond and tied in a French-style chignon. When she smiled, she revealed perfectly straight teeth a shade of white no Russian could ever hope to possess. She was a vision.

And the vision had a proposition. Would Svetlana Alexandrovna like to attend a special school for special young people? Not a Komsomol camp, nor a getaway for Young Pioneers. Not a grind house for mathematical prodigies. This was something different. Something that would forever alter her life. It was only then that Miss Alexandra, as she had asked to be addressed, handed Sylvie her calling card.

Major Alexandra Turischeva

Division 16 / Education

Glavnoye Razvedyvatelnoye Upravlenie

(Organization of the Main Intelligence Unit)

A glance between them. The GRU was not the KGB, the Committee for State Security. It was army. Military intelligence. The KGB's ugly stepsister. But Miss Alexandra was no one's ugly stepsister. On the contrary, she looked like royalty. A latter-day czarina. And this czarina wanted Svetlana.

The answer was yes. Yes, yes, yes. The details would follow later. Where, when, how long. At that moment, all Svetlana knew was that her world had suddenly and miraculously changed. It had undergone as violent an uprising as the October Revolution, which had installed the Bolsheviks in place of the Romanovs. The state had decided, in its infinite wisdom, that she, Svetlana, merited a future. Perhaps one in which she would wear only Western clothing and dye her hair a wondrous shade of blond and, dare she hope, travel to other countries.

The school, if it had a name, was called The Institute. It was not located in Moscow, as her family had hoped, but five hundred miles to the east on the banks of the mighty Volga, in Kazan. Svetlana would attend from September to January and from February to August. Twice a year she would visit home for a two-week holiday. A stern schedule, but there was much to be done.

From the age of fourteen to twenty-one, The Institute was her home. For the most part, it was like any boarding school, if more rigorous. Classes were offered five and a half days a week. The usual subjects with an emphasis on languages and a larger than usual dose of ideology. This last, to counter a class not taught in other Soviet schools: Current Events.

Once a week her class gathered in an auditorium to watch reports from England, France, Germany, and, yes, America. The BBC, Télévision Française 1, ARD, and, Svetlana's favorite, CBS, in the U.S., with a man named Walter Cronkite. Stories about a war in Vietnam, labor strikes in England, famine in Africa, but also about unrest in Prague, and a group of men in her own Russia called "dissidents." Among them, a man named Sakharov, a physicist, who was calling for greater freedoms at home, liberalizing emigration, negotiating with the Americans on everything from limiting nuclear weapons to entering into trade agreements.

None of this had she ever seen or read about. It was as if a curtain had been opened, and for the first time she was allowed to see the world in all its true colors.

Nearly fifty years later, the memory made Svetlana shiver. Nothing, she recognized, was more powerful than the truth.

And then, in her fourth year, a change. No longer did she board in the school's drab concrete dormitories, masterpieces of Soviet construction—crooked windows, faulty plumbing, spotty heat, and that was the good building. In the fall of her seventeenth year, she was moved with the other members of her class, fifty-seven in all, boys and girls, to a compound an hour's drive away. From afar, it looked like a camp... *that kind of camp. A gulag.* Tall fences topped with razor wire ran as far as the eye could see. Once through the gate and past the armed guards, another barrier: a concrete wall five meters high. To the last man, Svetlana and her fellow students were frightened. But the barriers were not for preventing students from escaping. On the contrary, once a student set foot inside the compound, few chose to leave. No, the wall and fences were to keep people out. Not spies, per se, but Russians. Ordinary Soviet citizens. Far more dangerous.

It was called Versailles, and Versailles was their first exposure to the outside world, ironically while a thousand miles from the nearest border. The one-thousand-hectare compound was divided into four discrete areas. There was Bond Street, the Kurfürstendamm, Madison Avenue, and the Left Bank. Students lived in a university quarter unto itself. Svetlana was given a modest apartment to live in, a studio not far different from those in Mayfair, the Upper West Side, or the 7th arrondissement. She continued her schooling, but the nature of her subjects had changed. In place of math and science and literature, there was dining, cooking, shopping, and colloquial conversation.

Once more at the top of her class, Svetlana was permitted to choose her zone of concentration. The U.S., England, Germany, or France. To say the choice would determine the rest of her life was an understatement. It would define her entirely.

Germany was too close to home and she didn't care for the food. The U.S. was too far. To choose the U.S. rendered one suspect, in and of itself. France, perhaps. The culture, the finery, but *Madame Bovary? Non, merci.* In the end, she chose England. Her accent was unrivaled. She enjoyed

English television programs, particularly comedies. Mostly, though, she chose England because she was a teenager and her favorite band— yes, she was encouraged to listen to Western music—was English. The Police. In her dreams, Sting had taken the place of Yuri Zhivago.

And so, to Bond Street. Not one street but four city blocks, in layout and architecture, identical to a midsized British city. There was a post office, a grocery store (Sainsbury's), a bank (Barclays), a café, a bookstore (Foyles), and everything else one might expect to find in "Blighty." Professional actors pretended to be real Englishmen and women. Shopkeepers, waitresses, policemen, ordinary folk on the street. Svetlana spent one day a week there learning a specific commercial or social interaction. How to make a bank deposit. How to ask the butcher for a roast. How to mail a package to a foreign country.

At home, she used only English products: Tate & Lyle, Yorkshire Gold tea, and Camay soap. She was even made to learn how to prepare a proper English fry-up: toast (burnt), eggs, beans, and the most godawful bacon. The goal was to turn her into an Englishwoman, head to toe. In dress, comportment, attitude, and upbringing.

And always there was language instruction, the coaching on idioms, the care and refinement of pronunciation, the practice to recognize different regional accents: Yorkshire vs. Liverpool vs. Midlands vs. Welsh. The work was never-ending.

On her eighteenth birthday, the focus of instruction changed again. She was a grown woman, mature in every way—Svetlana, perhaps, more than her peers. And so she was taught what could be expected of a woman her age. And what more would be expected of a secret agent trained by and working for the Soviet GRU living under deep cover in a hostile foreign country.

The instruction was at all times professional, delivered dryly and dispassionately, with the occasional smile to let the students know they were all human. And yes, goodness, some of this really was quite embarrassing. No examples required. A goes into B or C or D. No acts were forced. Coercion was not necessary for a proud daughter of the Rodina. Her virginity was her gift to the Party. Svetlana participated as actively as she was able. Her professors were no stand-ins for Sting. If anything, she was forced to develop an active imagination.

Concurrently, she began her training in the dark arts of espionage. Making dead drops and spotting tails, grooming a source, the finer points of blackmail and extortion. And finally, liquidation—the use of a dagger, stiletto, garrote, and pistol—though it was promised such acts would not be required of her.

Years passed. Training, training, more training. As always, Svetlana excelled in all of her subjects. She even enjoyed them.

And then her time at Versailles was at an end. After seven years in Kazan, her schooling was over. One last hurdle. The "exit interview" with the director, Pyotr Gruskov. Forty, handsome, a former Olympian, a wrestler, the GRU's finest. Who else would be given command of the service's crown jewel? But there were rumors, too.

Nine p.m. The director's personal quarters. Only the most ardent believer would not question the time or the place. Svetlana dressed in her new officer's uniform, freshly pressed, the creases so sharp they could slit a Slav's throat; her hair washed, braided, and tucked into her cap. Not a trace of makeup.

At the appointed hour, she knocked on the director's door. An aide admitted her to a grand living room. "Please wait. The director will be with you shortly. Oh, and you may take off your cap."

Of the interview, Svetlana remembered nothing. She emerged bruised, battered, her new uniform torn. A changed woman. In the morning, she was bleeding. She was discharged from the hospital five days later.

Everyone look, Svetlana Alexandrovna is fine. Prettier than ever and eager to take up her first posting.

Ironically, her treatment only amplified her devotion to the state. It was the state that employed her. The state that promoted her. The state that defined her in every way. The state was the one constant on which she could depend. A rock.

But loyalty remains blind only so long. Over time, shame, introspection, the constant attack on one's self-esteem, conspire to open one's eyes.

In loyalty's place, something new. Something equally consuming. A cri de coeur.

Revenge.

Not just against those who had wronged her.

Against everyone.

Chapter 21

New York City

Sylvie instructed the driver to stop at the store's 50th Street entrance. As they pulled to the curb, she handed him a ten-dollar bill and told him to keep the change. Inside Saks, she headed for the escalators at the rear of the ground floor. She rode to the fourth floor—womenswear. She walked to a far corner, ducking into an employees-only area.

"Ma'am! Excuse me!" A woman her age—Helene, according to her name tag—approached. "Customers aren't allowed here."

"I'm terribly sorry," said Sylvie, hand to her chest, breathing rapidly. "There's a strange gentleman who seems to be following me. I thought I might find an elevator here. I apologize if it's any trouble."

Helene appraised Sylvie. Her look said it was not the first she'd heard of strange gentleman stalkers. "Follow me, ma'am. And please, it's I who should apologize."

Sylvie rode the elevator to the ground floor and left the department store through the employees' entrance. Another cab. A hop on the subway. Four stops. Change lines. She was a spy all over again.

Thirty minutes later, she was back aboveground at the corner of 77th and Lexington. She ducked into a café and ordered coffee, taking a seat where she could see out the front window. Fifteen minutes passed.

She was clean.

One last cab.

"Where to?"

"Madison and 68th."

It was only a half mile, but Sylvie had walked enough for one day. The driver was displeased. Another measly fare. Three minutes later, Sylvie stood in the foyer of a modern office building, purposefully anonymous, reading the occupants' directory. Her destination was on the sixth floor. Bank Julius Baer. A representative office of the esteemed Swiss private bank. She emerged from the building a short time later, five million dollars better off than when she'd entered.

From there, a quick walk around the corner and down the block to a townhouse with a red and white bicolor flag flying above the front door. A bronze plate next to the entry read: CONSULATE OF INDONESIA.

Sylvie rang the bell.

A distinguished, dark-skinned man in a three-piece suit answered the door. "Ah, Madame Bettencourt," he said. "We've been expecting you."

Across the street, a few doors down, a small, elderly man, grayer than gray, shook his head. "Odd choice," he said to himself, removing his pince-nez and polishing the lenses with his handkerchief. Indonesia was hot, crowded, and, to his point of view, uncivilized. Even Bali wasn't what it used to be. Or so he'd heard. He would have thought Singapore or Dubai, or even New York, more in line with Madame Bettencourt's luxurious predilections. Then again, what did he know? Mother Russia had always offered him everything he desired.

The old man replaced his glasses, then tugged at the pockets of his vest. It was too hot to be wearing a black suit, but he wore nothing else while on the job. With a sigh, he set off toward Central Park. The afternoon's exertions had left him famished. He wanted a hot dog— a Sabrett, preferably with mustard and sauerkraut, *spasibo bolshoye*. A bottle of his favorite Moskovskaya waited in his hotel. He would need a drink as he wrote his report. Given the scope of the woman's crimes, maybe the entire bottle.

His name was Ivan Ilyich Borzoi. For fifty-one years he had worked in the office of the Moscow prosecutor general, rising to the post of deputy chief, an accomplishment of which he was justifiably proud. Two words had followed Borzoi throughout his career: "dogged" and "incorruptible." No one fought as hard to win a case. No one was more honest. This latter trait had not always proven a boon companion. There was a reason so talented a litigator had retired a deputy chief.

His reward came upon retirement. A call from a distinguished government office. A new job for Deputy Chief Prosecutor General I. I. Borzoi, if he cared to accept it. Doing what? Why, doing what he had always done: bringing criminals to justice. His pay would be triple what it had been. He would have access to any resources he might need. A bottomless expense account, if he was so inclined. His employer, however, was not the state but a private citizen. A musician, of all things. A cellist. About more than that, Borzoi knew better than to ask.

A car waited at the corner of Fifth and 70th. Three men sat inside, his pavement artists, talented beyond measure. "Get in, boss. It's hot."

"You go on. I prefer to walk." Borzoi waved the car onward. It took him one hour to reach the hotel on 42nd Street. On the way, he passed no fewer than five hot dog carts. He didn't notice one of them. He was thinking of Svetlana Alexandrovna Makarova, or Sylvie Bettencourt, as she'd recast herself. He was getting close…*oh, so close.* If he had his way, she would not escape to Indonesia or to Singapore or to anywhere else. He had a different home in mind for her. A place reserved for criminals of the worst stripe.

A cold, damp cell in the basement of the Lubyanka.

Chapter 22

Luton Airport, thirty-five miles north of London, England

The Cessna Citation ferrying Jojo Matta from Nice, France, was on final approach as Simon drove onto the tarmac. He watched the jet land, waiting for it to taxi to the end of the runway and begin its slow return to the terminal. Two uniformed officials from Border Force stood nearby, clipboards, handheld document scanners, walkie-talkies at the ready. Simon left the car and gave them a wave.

"You him?" one said. Red hair, wide around the middle.

"I am him."

"We had a nice chat with your friends," said the other, meaning quite the opposite. A woman, though he knew it only by her voice. Grimes was her name.

"I'm glad you got along," said Simon.

"Still don't think it's right," said Grimes.

"Well, thank you anyway."

"That's what you Yanks always say." Grimes didn't like it. Not a bit.

"That's what she said, too," added Red.

Simon didn't ask for clarification. He knew the identity of all parties involved.

The two officers stood aside as the jet came to a halt. The engines spooled down. The front door opened outward. A steward extended the staircase. A very tan, very svelte man, silver hair, peered from the doorway. Simon waved to Jojo Matta. *Come down. Nothing to worry about.*

Jojo scanned the tarmac, not pleased to see the uniformed officials standing next to Simon.

Simon waved again, more forcefully. Jojo descended the stairs, a black athletics bag hanging from a shoulder.

"Show them your passport," said Simon, speaking French.

"And the bag?" Jojo was not wrong to be frightened. Smuggling military-grade explosives into a foreign country carried a minimum sentence of ten years.

"Excuse me, sir, do you have anything to declare?" asked Red.

"Me?"

"It looks as if all you have is a change of clothing and some toiletries. Am I correct?"

Jojo nodded uncertainly. "Clothes," he said. "That's all."

It was Grimes's turn. "Passport or EU identity card, please."

Jojo handed the woman his passport. Her eyes flitted from Jojo to Simon to Red, then back to Jojo. "Welcome to the UK, Mr. Puccini. Giacomo Puccini."

The officials returned to their vehicle, muttering amongst themselves.

"Puccini?" The Jojo Matta Simon knew liked strip clubs, orange Fanta soda, Gitanes cigarettes, and hearty vins du table. But opera? Well…good on him.

Jojo shrugged. "It was the only name I could think of when I got the fake."

"Let's go." Simon took the bag from Jojo. It was heavier than expected. How were soldiers supposed to lug this stuff around? He led the way to the car.

"Yours?" asked Jojo, his hand stopped a few inches from the door.

"Temporarily."

"Putain." Jojo slid into the car. "You going to let me drive it?"

"Not a chance," said Simon.

Inside, he unzipped the bag. Two rectangular boxes, a foot long, half again as wide and deep. Markings in Cyrillic. "Danger," "lethal," "high explosive." Simon's Russian was better than ever.

He handed Jojo an envelope containing ten thousand euros. Jojo counted the money, then looked at Simon. "What about Ramsay?"

CHAPTER 23

Lugano, Switzerland

Someone was outside the house.

Seated at her father's desk, working through the postings on the Chatterbell site, Anna froze. A shadowy figure passed outside the window. A man, not especially tall, moving slowly, head turned to brazenly peer inside. It was nine o'clock, night overtaking dusk, the silhouette of Monte San Salvatore no more than a jagged line. While she had difficulty seeing outside, she knew the man—whoever he was—had no such problem seeing in. She might as well have had a spotlight trained on her.

And then he was gone.

Anna switched off the lamp and opened the top drawer. A glimmer of silver. A crosshatched grip. She shivered. It was a small gun, compact, with an abbreviated muzzle and a narrow beam. Her fingers closed around the butt and she lifted it out of the drawer.

Brazil. São Paulo. Years earlier. The last time she'd picked up a pistol with the belief that her life was in danger. So cold...a dull, terrible weight. There was only one reason to hold a gun. To fire it. To kill another living thing.

At the time, she had been implementing a clean water project in the city's favelas, the giant patch of slum dwellings that served as home to four million souls. It was really just a matter of plumbing, laying pipes into the neighborhoods from the main reservoir. There was certainly no lack of water. Not in Brazil. The police had other ideas. Water was politics, and politics meant crime. They called Anna and her colleagues communists, rabble rousers, revolutionaries. They came only at night— a secret police unit, Os Cavalheiros (The Gentlemen). One by one, the unit arrested or shot or killed them off. First the Brazilians, then the

112

Europeans. Some fled the country. Not Anna. She was awake when they entered her building. She heard their jackboots climbing the stairs, their raised voices, some of them drunk. *Brazen,* like the man outside her window. They shot instead of knocking. She shot back. Afterward, they laughed as they threw her into the paddy wagon. How was it possible to miss from so close a distance? Then they beat her.

Not tonight.

Tonight she wouldn't miss.

Anna slid out of the chair and hurried into the hall. Had she locked the front door? The back? What about the sliding doors in the living room? And who the hell was he?

Not a friend. A friend comes to the door. If not a friend, then the other thing.

Anna chambered a round.

From the start, it had been an eventful day.

The first response to her posting on the Chatterbell site had come from an "A.Spinozza." No text. Just a photograph with a time stamp in the lower right-hand corner. A street, cars parked on both sides. A construction site at the far end. The subject of the photo, however, was the sun setting behind a blue-green range of mountains. The kind of picture tourists take every day of every year. The time: 19:13. The date: this past Monday.

It took Anna a moment to realize that this was the Via Montalbano. And, more importantly, that the photograph had been snapped minutes before the explosion killed her father. She zoomed in on the line of parked cars. The third on the right was a navy-blue Volkswagen. She couldn't be sure of the model, but it might be a Polo, the vehicle used to carry the bomb. More than half of the front license plate was visible. At the top left, the red and white Swiss shield, and next to it, the letters G and maybe R. Below them, the numbers 6-1-1…and possibly a 0 or a 6.

It was then she noticed something else.

The silhouette of a person in the front seat.

She had him. She had the killer.

Anna downloaded the photo and went to work clarifying the image.

It was no good. No matter how she manipulated it—zooming in, minimizing noise, varying exposure—she was unable to sharpen the pixels anywhere near enough to actually see what the individual...*the murderer*...looked like.

Frustrated, she cropped the photo, superimposed the outline of a square around the blurred figure, and reposted it to the website.

Need help identifying person inside the car. Anyone??

On to the license plate.

Anna cropped the original photo a second time, zooming in on the VW's front plate. Once more, she uploaded it.

This is the vehicle that was detonated to kill my father. How can I figure out the exact license plate number? Owner?

Responses filtered in over the course of the day.
From MondoDave:

Plate is from canton of Graubünden. Car most likely sold there.

From EgonZ:

Dealer can give you identity of buyer.

Several others echoed the belief that the car had most likely been bought off a lot in the canton of Graubünden, as indicated by the letters *GR* on the license plate. Anna went a step further. It was her belief that the car had been bought recently, probably just days before the attack. Why? Because that's what she would have done.

Graubünden was the largest and easternmost canton of Switzerland. It was a mountainous region, best known for the resorts of Davos, St. Moritz, and the scenic Engadin Valley. A check of the map showed only one city of any size: Chur, population some thirty-five thousand, thirteen goats, and one alphorn. Chur, it turned out, had two car dealerships: one for Škoda, a Czech car company, the other for Volkswagen and SEAT.

Anna called the VW dealership and requested the used car department. Her policy was to be honest and forthright. Chatterbell was about transparency. The truth shall win out.

She explained to the salesperson who she was and that she was hoping to learn if he had recently sold a navy-blue VW Polo, license plate GR 6110…or 6116—apologies, that was all she had. Given the Swiss propensity for confidentiality—it was in their DNA, wasn't it?—she didn't expect to get an answer. Times change. As Darwin might say, the environment demanded genetic modifications. Secrecy was no longer a trait imperative for survival.

The salesperson, a man named Freddy Hold, informed her that, yes, a navy-blue VW Polo with a similar license plate had been sold just a few days earlier. In fact, the day before her father was killed. His cooperation ended there. No matter her persistence, he refused to reveal the name of the buyer. Anna had no time to be discouraged. The giraffe didn't grow a long neck overnight. Besides, she wasn't done with Hold yet.

She looked up Mr. Freddy Hold of Chur on social media. She found him on the big three: FB, IG, and LI—Facebook, Instagram, and LinkedIn. She followed him on each and sent a private message, asking if they might communicate off the site. She was open to meeting in person. Tomorrow, perhaps? She left her email and phone.

The afternoon passed with no more postings and no word from the car dealer. Waiting was the hardest part.

She had only just sat down after dinner to check the site when she saw the man.

Anna ran to the front door, found it unlocked, and threw the bolt. To her horror, she realized that none of the doors were locked. It was her habit to come and go freely. She hadn't thought twice about it. She turned, hesitating, undecided if she should go first to the living room or to the kitchen. The living room was closer…for her and for him.

One step before she caught the sound of the kitchen door closing. Voices. Not one man but two.

Anna raised the pistol, her thumb brushing the safety, making sure it was off. Slowly, she advanced down the hall. Not scared, not really. She'd spent her life moving toward challenges, not running away. She inclined her head, trying to catch the hushed conversation. She recognized the language, if not the exact words. Russian.

A figure appeared at the end of the corridor. A blond man, black turtleneck, dark trousers. Framed by the kitchen light, he presented an easy target. "Hey," she shouted. "What do you want?"

"Anna," the man answered, as if happy to see her. "Hi, there! I'm a friend of your father."

"Who are you?"

"I'm sorry about Carl's death. Just terrible."

Not Russian. English spoken like an American. "Why are you here?"

"For you," said the man, advancing toward her, step by step. "To see if you are all right. Now, please, put down the gun. We don't want any accidents."

"I asked you your name," said Anna, her arm extended in front of her, pistol pointed at the man's chest.

"Paul."

"Where's your friend, Paul?"

"What friend?"

"I heard another voice…when you came in. You were speaking Russian."

"Russian?" Paul laughed. *Impossible!* "I don't think so."

It was a forced laugh. She knew he was lying. Anna pressed her finger more tightly against the trigger. "You just said 'we don't want any accidents.' Who's 'we'?"

"Did I?" The smile on Paul's face faded. He shook his head. *Surely she was mistaken.* He stood halfway down the hall, five steps away. Only then did she see the gun hanging at his side, pressed to his leg. A silver cannon. In a flash, he raised the pistol.

Anna fired, once, twice, the report, the recoil, causing her to blink madly. Paul crashed against the wall. She turned and ran. Another shot, louder still. Wood splintered from the wall above her shoulder. Now she was scared.

Anna ran into the dining room. Another man turned, surprised. *Yes,*

Paul, you said, "we." He was smaller, darker, also with a pistol. She was upon him before she could slow, before she thought to shoot him. She lowered a shoulder, drove into his chest. They fell to the floor, the man dropping the gun, fighting to wrap his arms around her. Anna rolled free, jumped to her feet, kicked at him wildly, striking a blow to his cheek. She raised the pistol, met his eyes. No…she couldn't bring herself to fire.

Up the stairs. A look behind her. Paul was at the bottommost stair. He fired and she felt something cut the air above her head.

Down the hall to her bedroom. She threw the door closed, pushed her dresser against it. Breathing hard, maybe hyperventilating. She gave them a few moments to follow, heard their agitated voices—yes, Russian—then fired through the door. Her last shots.

A scream. "*Nyet!* Fuck!" Those words she understood.

To the window. Locked. She took hold of the latch and twisted it to the left. Nothing. The window had been closed so long it had fused shut.

A shoulder slammed into the door. The dresser budged. Anna struck the heel of her palm against the latch. The seal broke. She opened the window, threw a leg over the sill. Ten feet to the lawn.

"Anna! Please! You have to listen to us. We want to help."

Anna threw her other leg over the sill and lowered herself until her arms were outstretched. She dropped, rolled to one side, and stood, heart racing—*What to do? Where to go?*—then scurried to the corner of the house. A black Audi four-door blocked her old, battered Saab. What did it matter? She didn't have her car keys. She didn't have anything except her phone.

She sprinted in the opposite direction, never looking back, hoisting herself over the wall at the far side of the property, then across a field of tall summer grass, through an orchard, her house no longer in sight. She came to a road and stopped. Far-off headlights approached. *Them?*

Anna retreated into the grass and lay down. The car sped past. She didn't look to see if it was them. The shock of what had happened arrived gradually. She began to shake. A sob escaped. She cried, but not for long. It was over. She was safe. Crying would do her no good.

And so . . .

The phone's map showed the road ran east to Lugano and northwest toward Locarno. Not far was a highway south to Italy. She knew of only one place to go. There was a train station in Bellinzona twenty kilometers away.

Anna stood. A moment to wipe her nose, clear her head. She was good.

Keeping to the side of the road, sure to remain away from the highway lights, she began to jog.

CHAPTER 24

Somerset, England

Like all grand English estates, this one had a name: Ditchfield. Situated on fifty rolling hectares of Somerset countryside five miles north of Bath, the estate's house was first built in 1748, the home of Lord Micah Amberton, hero of the Battle of Culloden. Since then, it had been torn down, rebuilt, and renovated too many times to count. Today, Ditchfield boasted a two-hundred-room Georgian-style residence built from local limestone, a conservatory, a rose garden, a tennis court, a pool, and stables. Its current owner was no hero, unless one counted extraordinary valor in saving his own skin. He wasn't English either. He was Russian. His name was Boris Blatt.

Not that Simon Riske could see the country home as he approached the entrance to the estate. An unmarked police car stood watch in a lay-by a hundred meters from the gatehouse. A lone occupant. Blatt's babysitter. If the policeman took note of the red sports car flying past, Simon couldn't tell. The same Ferrari had left Ditchfield two weeks earlier. It was Simon's free pass.

The gatehouse was unoccupied, except for a closed-circuit television camera and a speaker. Simon rang the buzzer.

"Who is it?" A rough male voice. Definitely not Jeeves. Maybe *Jeeveski.*

"Simon Riske. I'm an old friend."

A minute passed, the longest minute Simon had endured in recent memory.

"Riske… What is it?" New voice but from the same country. Simon wagered it was the master of the house.

"Open the gate, Blatt. I'm not getting any younger."

"What are you driving…Is that…Is that my—?"

"It is. Now open the gate." When in doubt, be brash. Who can argue with a fifty-million-dollar automobile?

The gate opened inward. A leisurely drive over hill and dell, through a white birch forest, past bubbling brooks and winding streams. The England of yore. The trees fell away. The road widened, and there, Ditchfield House. A squatter, uglier cousin to Highclere Castle, but impressive all the same. Simon was quick to spot a new building farther down the road. White metal walls, a long, peaked roof. He'd seen enough similar structures to know it was the hangar where Blatt kept his cars.

He drove past the house's main entrance, stopping in the hard gravel forecourt fronting the hangar.

Wait, he told himself as a line of men streamed out of the main door and hurried in his direction. Four of them wore tracksuits and had identical haircuts—more or less no hair at all. The fifth was short, wide around the middle, and wore slacks and an open-collared shirt. He carried a wineglass in his hand.

Simon allowed them to encircle the car before getting out.

"Riske," said the short, round one. It wasn't a question. More like *How dare you?*

"Blatt."

The Russian had aged since Simon had last seen him. Deeper lines. Whiter hair. He'd lost none of his swagger, though. He was a vain, vicious gamecock. There would be no underestimating him.

"I don't need to ask how you found me," said Blatt.

Simon handed him the registration. "You left this in the glove box. I guess the Driver and Vehicle Licensing Agency didn't get the memo about your new identity. Mr. Gerstmann, is it?"

Blatt flinched, as if struck. "And Hawley?"

"In France. Don't blame him. His mouth is only a little bigger than yours."

"So that's the reason for your visit…a bloody gearbox?"

"Did you think it was a social call?" Simon studied Blatt's thugs. Even licensed bodyguards were not permitted to carry firearms in the United Kingdom. He doubted, however, that any of these gave a damn about a license. He didn't see any telltale bulges, no grips extending from the tracksuits. He wasn't sure whether to take that as a compliment or an insult.

"Demanding buyer," he said. "Wants everything original."

"For a hundred million, I would too." Blatt took a sip of wine, washed it around his mouth. "Do I know him?"

"Possibly. For now, the buyer wants to remain anonymous. I'm sure word will leak out soon enough."

Blatt brushed his hand across the car's hood. "What do you think I can get for this one?"

"Ask Jack Hawley."

"He says fifty. You?"

"My advice: wait a year. Market's only going higher." Simon spread his hands. A man with an exciting opportunity. "Tell you what. I'll give you a hundred thousand dollars for the gearbox. We shake hands. Everyone goes home friends."

"That easy?"

"Why not? What are you going to do with it?"

"Just having it," said Blatt, with relish, "and knowing that your buyer doesn't, is enough."

"That's not very sporting of you."

"Russians have long memories. It comes from our suffering history. I haven't forgotten about the watch. You made a fool of me."

Ah . . . the watch. Of course. "Debatable," said Simon.

"How's this? Get me back the original Patek Philippe and I'll be more than happy to give you the gearbox."

"Steal it, you mean?"

"You did it once."

"That wasn't theft. That was recovery. You stole it first."

"Semantics."

"I have another idea: let's trade."

"Trade?"

"The car for the gearbox," said Simon.

"I'm confused. Both belong to me already. What could you possibly have to trade?"

"I'll let you think on that."

"You seek to intimidate me?" said Blatt, in full Blatt mode. "Look around you. Do I look like I'm easily frightened?"

"Four bodyguards. I'm surprised you haven't soiled your pants already."

"You have a high opinion of yourself."

"When in low company, I do."

"Watch yourself."

Simon leaned into the car and took out a manila envelope stamped NEW SCOTLAND YARD. Blatt handed the wineglass to one of his thugs. Warily, he withdrew the papers inside and skimmed the contents. His countenance darkened.

"Not today, not tomorrow," said Simon. "But if we don't come to an agreement, every one of the people you gave sworn testimony against will know your new name, where you live, and what you said about them."

"I give you the gearbox and you refrain from sharing any of this?"

"That's the deal."

Blatt found the idea humorous. "Release that information and DCI Worth will have you in irons by day's end."

"I'll take my chances."

"You're forgetting something," said Blatt. "You're on my ground. No one is here to help you. You might as well be in Russia." A few choice words to his men delivered in his native language. Laughs all around. Simon was a dead duck, if his Russian hadn't failed him.

Out came the pistol. A Glock. Of course, the most expensive model. The smallest of the bodyguards held it casually at his side.

"You're going to shoot me?" said Simon.

"Why not? We've already established I'm not very sporting."

"That's why I have these. Russian, I believe." Simon freed two incendiary hand grenades from his belt. One thousand euros each, courtesy of Maurice Petrov, Bulgarian arms dealer, friend of La Brise de Mer, the grenades delivered to English soil by one Jojo Matta, *capo* in said organization.

"*Granata,*" shouted one of the bodyguards.

Two of the men stepped forward. Two, in the opposite direction.

"Stop," said Blatt. "You wouldn't."

"You can make this go away with one word."

"You're going to kill us all," said Blatt. "For a gearbox. I think not."

"You misunderstand me," said Simon. "I'm not going to kill us. I'm going to kill your car."

"Never," said Blatt. "I know you. You are a connoisseur. You love the car more than I do."

"Last chance."

Blatt fired off an order. The men moved in, one stepping in front of his armed colleague as the man raised the weapon.

Simon pulled the pins with his teeth, tossing one, then the other, into the car's open window.

Blatt's men betrayed their excellent military training. Each threw himself to the ground, not one giving Blatt a passing glance. The oligarch remained rooted to the spot, confused, slow to comprehend what he had witnessed. Simon threw himself at the diminutive Russian, knocking him to the ground.

Two more seconds. An eternity.

The grenades exploded one on top of the other, powerful, muffled blasts. Flames shot from the open cockpit. The windows shattered and flew in a thousand pieces high into the air. The gasoline tank ignited, a third explosion, louder than the others. The car itself seemed to levitate off the ground.

Rolling off Blatt, Simon pushed himself to one knee. He'd traded the grenades for a T-7 taser, essentially a pistol but with darts carrying strong electric charges. He jumped to his feet and ran toward Blatt's bodyguards, still stunned, ill prepared. He shot a dart into each man. Twenty thousand volts at five amperes. It was the amps that did the heavy lifting. Still, the charge wasn't enough to fully incapacitate two of them. Simon struck them as they rose. A heel to the jaw. A flat palm to the temple. Done.

He hauled Blatt to his feet. "Where is it?"

The Russian wavered, dazed. His mouth worked, but no words came out.

Simon shook him. "Where?"

"In the garage. The mechanics' bay."

"Show me." Simon slid his phone from his pocket. "Harry. Bring the truck. Just look for the burning car."

"You didn't!" said Harry Mason, who had been briefed on the evening's festivities.

"Think positive, Harry. Maybe we'll be the ones who get to restore it this time."

But one look at the Ferrari—engulfed in flames, chassis bent out of shape—and Simon knew there would be no such chance. The '64 275 was off to the Ferrari graveyard in the sky. *Addio, bella!*

The gearbox weighed eighty pounds.

Simon gave instructions as Blatt and Mason carried it from the mechanics' bay to the van.

Outside, Blatt stood next to his flaming car. "You cost me fifty million dollars. You think I'm going to forget."

"At least," said Simon. "More if you'd waited."

Blatt loosed a string of Russian invectives, with a few f-bombs thrown in for international goodwill.

"Remember the terms of your deal," said Simon. "Anything happens to me and DCI Worth sends you back to jail…if your business associates don't get you first. You and me…this is forgotten."

"Never," said Blatt.

"Win some, lose some," said Simon. "The important thing is that you live to fight another day."

"Riske…I won't forget. You're a dead man."

CHAPTER 25

Tel Aviv, Israel

The SON Group
Transcript / Cellular Communication #766
Subject: S. Riske. Device: 0044-71-xxxx-xx89
Correspondent: Confidential / Client XY776KR
Time: GMT 23:11. Date: 23-8-20XX
Duration: 4'45"

Simon Riske (SR): Guess what I found?

Client XY77 (C-77): Mr. Riske. A pleasant surprise.

SR: How did you know?

C-77: Know what?

SR: That it was out there. In never-never land.

C-77: Are you upset?

SR: Personally, no. Professionally, let's say my ego is bruised.

C-77: Men and their egos.

SR: Well?

C-77: Professionally, it is my job to know such things. I didn't get to where I am by being lazy. My client wanted the original. I made sure he got it. Details, Mr. Riske. Details.

SR: Where do you want it sent?

C-77: (Address of freight forwarding firm, London.)

SR: Lay off Dez Hamilton. We're done.

C-77: I keep my word. You should know that by now.

SR: Where's 3387?

C-77: In a safe place.

SR: Where no one will ever see it again.

C-77: Don't be dramatic. It's an investment. My client is allowing it to mature. Like the Dom Pérignon we enjoyed together.

SR: I'll bet you have an entire free port filled with his things.

C-77: Whose things?

SR: Your boss's.

C-77: Who says I only have one?

SR: Is the Hockney there, too? The czarina's tiara?

C-77: It's a car, Mr. Riske. Not a Da Vinci.

SR: *De gustibus...*

C-77: Latin? You?

SR: *De gustibus non est disputandum.* My father taught me. It means, you like Da Vinci, I like something else.

C-77: I know what it means. You continue to surprise.

SR: This is the last time. I promise.

C-77: My offer stands.

SR: Offer?

C-77: To come work for me.

SR: Oh, that. Lady...Mrs. Bettencourt...*Sylvie*...whatever your name really is...you are something else.

C-77: I do hope so.

SR: You still haven't told me.

C-77: Come to work for me and I'll share all my secrets with you.

SR: I'm only interested in one.

C-77: Do tell.

SR: Is Blatt one of you?

C-77: Pardon me?

SR: You see, I have my secrets, too. So tell me, do you two go back to the old days? You know, before the Iron Curtain fell. Schoolmates in the GRU academy? Rivals, I'm guessing.

C-77: (Prolonged silence.) Be careful, Mr. Riske.

SR: *Do svidaniya,* Madame Bettencourt.

END TRANSMISSION

CHAPTER 26

London, England

I may have gone too far."

Simon set the phone down on the kitchen counter. It was after eleven. A light rain fell, drumming against the windows.

"What did she say?"

"Not her words. Her tone."

"And before, when you told her you'd found it." Special Agent Nessa Kenyon removed her blazer and hung it on the back of a chair. "Was she happy?"

"Not sure she does happy," said Simon. "I would say 'content.' She got her way."

"She always gets her way."

"Have you heard anything about Blatt?"

"No. Nothing."

"I don't like it."

"Why?"

"If it were me, I'd be screaming bloody murder. Guy comes in, torches my car, threatens to blow my cover—"

"Don't forget the gearbox."

"Takes my gearbox," Simon added. "First thing I do is call my handler."

"Point taken."

"These guys—billionaires, straight, crooked, in between—I know them. They don't think like us. Sure, he got arrested, but look how? Blatt's convinced it wasn't his fault. Some two-bit mechanic steals his SIM card, gives it to the cops. All a big mistake. Blatt cuts a deal and a year later is back in clover. You should see his place. The one thing that life has taught him is that the rules don't apply."

"Which has you worried because…?"

"Maybe he thinks he can break his agreement, that he has so much left to give Scotland Yard, MI5, whoever, that they can't touch him no matter what he does."

"Break his agreement in what way?"

"Comes after me."

"He's under constant surveillance. Wherever he goes, he has to clear it with Worth. They put a tail on him the second he leaves Ditchfield."

"Come on, Nessa. Guys like him never get their hands dirty. Sure, Blatt has plenty of enemies, but he has plenty of friends, too." Simon offered her a bottle of pinot grigio.

"Have anything stronger?"

"Name your poison."

"You know what I like."

Simon retrieved a bottle of Jack Daniel's. A woman after his own heart. He poured a generous measure for each of them. They touched glasses.

"Know what Novichok is?"

"Vaguely."

"Vaguely…it's a nerve agent. Like sarin or VX but stronger. Someone puts a few drops in your coffee or tea, leaves a residue on a doorknob, suddenly you stop breathing, slip into a coma. If you don't die, you end up with permanent organ damage—liver transplant, dialysis for life, maybe a vegetable."

"How awful."

"Russians love the stuff. It's like the borscht of poisons."

"Don't be dramatic."

"You didn't just lose a man fifty million dollars."

"He deserved it—you said so."

"You tell him. Maybe he'll take it better from a pretty face."

"So what do you think he'll do?"

"I don't know." The picture of Blatt's face was fresh in his mind. He'd never seen a man as furious. "Believe me, he's going to do something."

Simon picked the phone up off the counter. He ran a finger over his throat. Kenyon nodded. She retrieved the Faraday bag and Simon dropped the phone inside.

"We good?" he mouthed.

Kenyon zipped the bag tight. "Working hours are officially over."

Simon put his arms around her, kissed her.

"I've been waiting for that," she said.

"You think Nigel believed it?"

"What?"

With care, Simon unbuttoned her blouse. "That we'd never met."

"Why wouldn't he?" said Nessa, her breath catching. "Does it matter? He played his part."

"Now it's my turn," said Simon.

"For what?"

"To pretend we've never met."

"Why?"

Simon undid her brassiere. Always his favorite part.

"First time is always the most exciting."

CHAPTER 27

Paris, France

Gentlemen, shall we get started? We have a lot to cover. I know how things are when I'm gone. Boys will be boys. Half of you look like you're still hungover from Saturday night. We are in France. May I suggest wine, not vodka?"

Laughs all around. The boss was back. All business, but not without a sense of humor.

Sylvie Bettencourt surveyed the executives seated around the conference table. All men, forty-ish, dressed in dark suits, clean shaven—stubble against regulation, a firing offense. All with hands on the blotter before them. A bottle of mineral water—Perrier, *mais bien sûr*—and a glass for each, though no one took a sip during the meeting. This was her show and she demanded their complete attention.

It was Monday. The scheduled time for the weekly team meeting, referred to as "the crucible." Come prepared or else. Madame Bettencourt was an unforgiving master.

Sylvie stood at the head of the table. She was dressed soberly—dark blazer, cream-colored blouse, a form-fitting skirt sure to touch her knee—as befitted the head of an investment company, even one as unique as Investissements Bettencourt. The trip to the States had been about spending. The beating heart of her business, however, was the opposite: collecting. For all the fancy trappings—the luxurious offices on the Avenue Charles Floquet, the private jet travel to every corner of the globe, the designer clothing, and the unlimited expenses—she was nothing more than a hood. A glorified mobster. Pay up or suffer the consequences.

It was Sylvie Bettencourt's job to make sure her clients paid protection. "Protection" defined as a minimum of five percent of their gross revenues. Six percent was preferred. Those who paid ten were granted apostolic status. They could do no wrong.

In return, her clients were allowed to conduct their businesses as they saw fit. No government interference. All decisions up to them. Oh, an additional perk: they were allowed to continue drawing breath on God's green earth. *Ahem,* not to put too fine a point on things.

"Monsieur Renaud, will you start things off for us?"

Renaud's "space," to use the investment banker's vernacular, was the Russian oil and gas sector.

The man stood. Pale, earnest, faceless. Another MBA from another top-tier institution. The Rodina turned them out like widgets. "Kamchatka Oil reports revenues of two billion euros for this last month. So far, they have wired eighty-six million euros into the designated accounts."

Sylvie frowned. Less than four and a half percent of revenues. Unacceptable. "And the rest?"

"Due by the first of September," said Renaud. Of course, it wasn't his real name. Every man seated at the table was working in France on a false passport.

"Is Litvak playing games?"

"His accounts receivable are up fifteen percent. An aftereffect of the pandemic."

"You know what we think of excuses, Monsieur Renaud? Please convey the same to Chairman Litvak."

A crisp nod of the head.

"Next?

"Siberco Natural Gas."

And so the meeting went on for three hours. Oil, gas, timber, aluminum, rare earth minerals. It was Michelet—in charge of gold and silver—who raised the problem.

"Lugano has gone dark. Our client needs a new conduit for their payments."

Sylvie leaned forward, concerned. "What seems to be the problem?"

"Danske Bank. Our liaison is no longer at his post."

"Explain."

"Carl Bildt, the bank manager, was killed last week. A car bomb. We must consider the institution compromised."

"I read something about that," said Sylvie. "Another of Mr. Bildt's clients must have been less than satisfied. Why didn't you know about this?"

"Bildt performed his work flawlessly. So much so, we doubled our deposits with him over the last year. I did run it past you."

"I remember. Still, if there was a problem with Bildt, you should have known. Do the police have any idea who killed him?"

"Not that I'm aware."

"It doesn't sound to me like you're aware of very much at all, Mr. Michelet. Perhaps you should consider finding another line of work. I've heard there are numerous openings in the salt extraction field. How do you feel about dark, tight spaces deep underground?"

"I don't like them."

"I imagine not. Consider yourself warned."

Sylvie closed the meeting. Lunch was waiting in her office afterward. Steak-frites from Le Relais de l'Entrecôte. A glass of Pétrus.

Vadim watched as she ate, not speaking.

Finished, she placed her knife and fork on the plate, laid her folded napkin atop them, then said: "About Danske Bank and that bastard Carl Bildt. Are we tied off?"

"We missed the daughter."

"We have her address, her photograph. I'm not sure I understand."

"She was armed."

"And we weren't?"

"Of course, but—"

Sylvie raised a hand. She wasn't interested in buts. "Where is she now?"

Vadim didn't answer, his pale skin growing paler. A vein at his temple grew visible. "Based on what Grisha found, we believe she's going to Chur."

"For what purpose?" Sylvie asked, then quickly, "No. I don't want to know. Bildt, Danske Bank, now the daughter… It is your concern. Given what's transpired, I think it best to bring her in."

"Alive?"

"To Shangri-la. If she was armed, she may have been in closer contact with her father than we knew."

"Helping him?"

"I don't know. That, in itself, is enough. I want you to take charge of matters. It is our lives that are at stake."

"A bit dramatic, Mother."

"You think so? Read this. From him." Sylvie turned her monitor on its swivel. A new email from the man referred to only as "the Cellist." It read: Re: June report. Discrepancy in receipts valued at twenty-two million euros per IG. Please explain.

IG meant "inspector general," which meant that dreadful little man Borzoi.

"Twenty-two million was our take last month," she said.

"Bildt?"

"Who else could have told him?"

"What will you do?"

"I will 'explain,' as I've done many times before."

"And Borzoi?"

"We will deal with Borzoi in due time. First things first. Bring me Miss Bildt."

Vadim left the office.

Sylvie stood and left her desk. A long look out the window. The Eiffel Tower. The Champ de Mars. How many apartments had she purchased for Michael on Boulevard Haussmann alone? And elsewhere? Manhattan, Madrid, Buenos Aires. It wasn't easy work. Hundreds of holding companies to be set up. An army of bankers, fiduciaries, accountants, and attorneys to recruit. The supervision of endless flows of money, in and out, in and out, always muddying the trail, imposing as many legal barriers between each destination as possible until even the most dogged investigator would give up. Had to give up. No one had the time or the resources. All to create an invisible Silk Road to allow the free, untethered transfer of monies across the globe. Free, untethered, and, most importantly, unnoticed.

Sylvie found a cigarette, lit it with her Swarovski lighter, puffed furiously. Just to buy the so-called Lost Ferrari, the wretched chassis 3387, had required weeks of effort. First, she must move the funds from the general account, then to another and another, from one bank to the next. Transfers of one hundred million dollars raise flags. Red ones.

She had already received multiple queries from the American financial authorities about the provenance of the one hundred million dollars. Her response: *"Speak to my attorneys."*

But she had done it. She had faultlessly executed every step, placed every foot correctly. No tracks could be found alerting anyone as to where the money originally came from and to whom it truly belonged.

And now this? Questions from the Cellist and his attack dog about a twenty-two-million-euro discrepancy. And similar queries last month and the month before.

Why this lack of trust? This questioning of her loyalty? This slap in the face over what amounted to crumbs?

Sylvie stubbed out her cigarette. Vile habit.

It was Borzoi. That quiet, old, relentless little bastard. The last honest man sent to regulate an enterprise that was, by its very definition, dishonest. The irony! Delicious, if only she weren't the brunt of it.

Sylvie drew a breath, calming herself. And so?

The plan.

The time had come now. To wait any longer was to risk everything.

Still, there was a problem. She needed help. The last steps were beyond her capabilities. She didn't need another brilliant MBA or a corrupt policeman or a bent politician. She didn't need Vadim either. She needed a cleverer sort. Someone accustomed to planning a crime. Someone gifted.

She needed a thief.

CHAPTER 28

London, England

So you better now, yeah?"

Lucy stood in the doorway to Simon's office, cap tipped back, wrench in hand.

"Better? How?" Simon was engaged in a rare bout of straightening up. He had far too many coffee table books, the kind that weighed five pounds, with pages so sharp you could slit your wrists, and they lay scattered all too haphazardly.

"You found it," said Lucy. "The gearbox. Everyone's happy again."

"I didn't realize I was unhappy."

"Well, not unhappy exactly but uptight."

"Is that right?" He turned his attention to the Wurlitzer jukebox. It was a 1956 original, the kind with a window where you could see the 45s being selected, and with push buttons A, B, C, and D and numbers from 1 to 25. The jukebox had come with the place, the property of the garage's former occupant, a crooked accountant who ran a night-club to launder his gains. "This thing still works," he said. "At least I think so. Songs are terrible. Air Supply. Milli Vanilli. Right Said Fred. Really?"

"You were driving us all crazy," Lucy continued. "Barking out one order after the next." She advanced a step, lowering her voice, talking like an American. "'Check all suppliers. Now!'"

"Did I? You're imagining things."

"You having me on?"

Simon stopped what he was doing and focused his attention on Lucy. She'd been growing increasingly brittle these last weeks. He was surprised she hadn't acted out like she used to. Coming into work late or with a hangover. Taking her sweet time on paint detail. Generally being churlish. "Come in. Shut the door. Take a seat."

Lucy closed the door. "On the couch?"

"Couch is fine."

Lucy removed her cap and sat, her hands folded in her lap. "Harry wanted to kill you."

"That's just Harry," said Simon, dropping down beside her.

"All right, then I wanted to kill you. You're not supposed to be getting arrested."

"Is that what this visit is about?"

Lucy nodded.

Simon considered this. "Now, that I didn't anticipate."

"You knocked Jack Hawley out. What did you think would happen? 'Actions have consequences.' Isn't that what you always say?"

"He wasn't cooperating. At least the first time."

"And the second?"

"He deserved it."

"The police were there," protested Lucy.

"So they were."

"Simon…you're supposed to be a role model."

"Says who?"

"I mean, aren't you?"

"You're getting a little old for that," said Simon. "Needing someone to look up to all the time. You've been here how long? Three years? Four? You've seen how I do things, right and wrong. You know what I do outside the office."

"You're bloody brilliant," said Lucy, then a pause. Self-reflection. Something he'd never seen in her. "But no, you're right. I am getting a little old to keep you on some kind of a pedestal. Getting harder not to see the cracks."

"What happened to 'bloody brilliant'?"

"You've changed. You're not acting like yourself." Lucy shrugged dramatically. "Maybe it is me. Maybe I'm not the same. Not after the accident."

"I'm sorry. I nearly got you killed."

"Stop with that! It was an accident. The other driver was drunk."

"You shouldn't have been there."

"Of course I should have. Without me you couldn't have gotten the painting off the boat. You said so yourself. Besides, I like helping you. What I mean is, it was my decision. Like it's my decision to sit you down and ask you what's the matter."

"Ask me?"

"Something's up. You're not...*you*. You haven't been for some time."

Simon leaned back, head tilted to the ceiling. A sigh. This had gone entirely too far. He returned his gaze to Lucy. "You finished?"

Lucy nodded.

"Sure?" asked Simon, with an edge.

"It's just that we're worried."

"About what? Afraid you're not going to get paid?"

"No...I mean, *what*?"

"That I might somehow jeopardize your job. That it?"

Lucy shook her head. "Not at all...We're worried about you."

"Don't be," said Simon, angered. "You don't have my permission."

"We're just—"

Simon stood. "I apologize if hitting Jack Hawley knocked me down a level in your esteem."

"It's not that."

"Then what? Go find someone else to look up to...anybody. I hereby resign my post."

Instead of losing her composure, Lucy bit her lip, eyeing him dispassionately. "I'm not buying into your bullshit," she said, much too maturely. "This little act, whatever it is, whatever you're trying to pull...no, just no. This isn't about me. It's about you."

Simon came closer, having none of it. "I'm your boss. I pay your salary. That's all you have to worry about."

Lucy got to her feet. "Why are you talking like this?"

"Like what?"

"Like a royal arsehole."

"Get used to it."

"You're cruel."

Simon spun and headed to his desk. "We're done here."

Lucy walked to the door. "Simon."

He ignored her, busying himself with arranging papers.

"Simon!"

He looked up, met her forceful gaze. It had happened. She'd finally grown up. "What?"

"I know you."

Chapter 29

London, England

Fittingly, lunch was at the Royal Automobile Club in Pall Mall across the street from St. James Square. White tablecloths. Plush carpets. High ceilings. Waiters in crisp waistcoats. Badges from automobile clubs around the world decorating the walls.

"You still won't tell me where you found it?" Dez Hamilton was back to his old self: cheeks ruddy, countenance lively, the picture of good humor. No golf shirt today. Today was business attire. Tailored black suit, gray vest, a mother-of-pearl stickpin in his silver silk tie.

"Need-to-know," said Simon.

"I bloody well need to know," said Dez, signaling for another bottle of wine. A Latour '64. He was celebrating, if Simon wasn't. "Load off my shoulders, tell you that. I'm not the sort who can go around with a pack of bloodhounds at his heels."

Hamilton ordered roast beef for the both of them. Extra au jus on the side, "if it wouldn't be too much trouble." He had forgotten all about his threat to make Simon pay Sylvie Bettencourt's extortionate demand. Bygones were bygones. He hadn't forgotten about her, though.

"Who is she, anyway? Some gangster's moll?"

"Something like that," said Simon. "You can ask her next time you see her."

"Not bloody likely," roared Hamilton. "I'll keep my distance, thank you very much. That muscle of hers—what was his name?"

"Vadim."

"Yes, Vadim. Scary chap. Got the better of you, didn't he?"

Simon ignored the question. He wasn't the one with five stitches in his cheek and a bandage to cover it. With care, he folded his napkin and set it on the table. "Have to run, Dez. Busy day."

"But we haven't eaten."

Simon stood. "Afternoon."

"Hold on there," said Hamilton, napkin raised in protest. "You still haven't told me where you found it."

Simon left the restaurant with a check for two million dollars in his pocket. Commission for the sale of 3387. Hamilton was old-school. Direct deposit was no fun. He liked to see the look on a man's face when he paid him an obscene amount of money.

And who could blame him, thought Simon as he strolled through St. James Park. Dez was Dez. If he ever needed another car restored, Simon would politely but firmly refer him elsewhere. Maybe throw Jack Hawley a bone. Then again…

He crossed the grass, carving a line through the groups seated here and there, having picnic lunches, throwing back a few beers. It was that kind of day. The stint of rainy weather had been shoved off stage by a high-pressure system parked over the Baltic Sea. The forecast called for blue skies and abundant sunshine across the United Kingdom.

Simon spotted an empty bench, sat down. It was, he admitted, a weight off his shoulders, too.

"Hello, Harry," he said, placing a call to the shop. "It's a beautiful day. What say we give everyone the afternoon off?"

"What for? We're behind on the projects for the sultan of what-do-you-call-it, and we haven't even started on your new ones."

"They can wait."

"The cars aren't going to restore themselves."

"Harry, we're celebrating. Dez got paid. We got paid. Life is good. I don't want to see a single face in the shop when I get home. Understood?"

"The entire afternoon?"

"It's two o'clock."

"Exactly," said Mason.

"Be careful, Harry. I just might give everyone tomorrow off, too."

"You wouldn't!"

"And I don't want to see your jolly smiling mug either."

"It wouldn't be smiling. I'll tell you that for nothing."

"And Harry…"

"Now what?"

"Look in your top drawer."

"Must I?" A sigh. A stubborn drawer opened. The sound of papers being shuffled. "What?…Manager's box? Arsenal versus Liverpool…Simon!"

"You smiling now?" asked Simon. "Seats that good you might even be able to rustle up a date."

"I'm taking my boy."

"But he—"

"That's right. The lad's mad for Liverpool. Thinks that German coach is the second coming. Imagine his face when Arsenal give them the drubbing they deserve."

Simon ended the call to Harry's delighted chuckling.

"Do you think he had it all along?" asked D'Artagnan Moore.

The old ship's clock on the bookshelf rang four bells. The sun was well over the yardarm. Moore marked the occasion by pouring himself a generous tumbler of single malt, this one with a name more unpronounceable than the last, and even harder to spell. Simon refrained from joining him, keeping to a sparkling mineral water with a healthy chunk of lime.

"Blatt?" said Simon. "He's been in the car game a long time. Most probably he'd come across the gearbox a while ago. When he spotted my name alongside the Lost Ferrari, he remembered it, saw it as a way to get even."

"One would think he'd have better things to do."

"Than eke out a little revenge? A Russian? Might as well tell him to give up vodka."

"Worried?"

"Not *if* he comes at me but *when*."

"I'd rather have thought it might be one of my colleagues in the building. They won't be keen on paying out a twenty-five-million-dollar claim."

"Tell 'em to take a ticket and stand in line."

"And Madame Bettencourt?"

"What about her?"

"No thank-you note?"

Simon remembered the ice in her voice when he'd last spoken with her. "Not exactly."

Moore lifted his glass. "Here's to 'All's well that ends well.'"

"Something like that." Simon finished the mineral water, taking a moment to gnaw on the lime. He considered telling D'Art what he'd heard about Sylvie Bettencourt, that once she'd been a trained Russian intelligence agent—*Who knows? She might still be one*—and that her purchases were made on behalf of Russian beneficiaries. Better to keep mum. "Schtum," as they said. What D'Art didn't know couldn't come back to hurt him.

"I picked up two new cars recently," said Simon. "Need to get some paper on them."

"Value?"

"Currently? Let's say three million each."

Moore shook his head in disbelief. He'd never been able to understand why grown, seemingly intelligent men and women would spend so much money on glorified tin cans with fancy motors. On the other hand, he himself thought nothing of dropping a thousand dollars on a bottle of wine. "I'll tell Inigo James upstairs. He'll be happy to write the policies."

"Sooner rather than later."

"Noted."

"So." Simon rapped his knuckles on the coffee table. "What's next up on the docket?"

"Well, well," said Moore, with alacrity. "Who's this eager young man seated before me?"

"I'm on a roll. Let's see if I can keep it going."

Moore raised an eyebrow. An idea. "Now that you mention it, I might have something."

Simon smiled to himself as Moore rose and, with both hands, picked up a fat dossier from the corner of his desk. *"Might?"*

With ceremony, Moore dropped the dossier onto the table. "Something right up your alley."

"Not a car?"

"Enough of those."

"Painting? Sculpture?"

"Strike two."

"I give up."

"You'll never imagine. A—"

Simon's phone rang. He checked the caller. A London number: Fire Brigade. He turned away and answered. "Yes?"

"Mr. Riske? Proprietor of European Automotive Repair and Restoration. Kimber Road."

"Speaking."

"Well, sir, I'm afraid we have some bad news."

Simon hung up a few seconds later.

"What is it?" asked D'Art. "You look as if you've seen a ghost."

"Come on," said Simon. "We have to go."

CHAPTER 30

London, England

Simon saw the smoke as soon as they crossed Latchmere Road, three miles from the shop. A great ominous cloud, liverish brown, portentous, rising into the sky. It was over. He'd lost everything.

D'Art tugged at his beard, eyes etched with worry. "Sorry, lad."

"Just get me there. Quick."

Fire engulfed the building. Flames shot from transoms on every side. And with the fire, smoke. Coils of it, smelling of oil and petroleum, and most sharply of paint thinner. Emergency vehicles blocked the road. Simon counted six hoses dousing the building, four manned by firefighters on the ground, two aimed down at the roof from ladders extended to their fullest.

Simon jumped from the car and ran to a uniformed policewoman. "This is my building."

"Right this way, sir."

The policewoman guided him through a throng of first responders—firefighters, EMTs, police. "This is Group Commander Graves."

"You Riske?" Graves—slim, earnest, with cropped gray hair—was enveloped in his fireman's jacket.

"Anyone hurt?" asked Simon.

"Not that we know. By the time we arrived, it was an inferno. We advanced as far inside as we could and called out. No one responded. Is someone missing?"

"I don't know. I'd given my guys the afternoon off. If someone had been inside the shop, they'd have noticed the fire, raised the alarm."

"There's that, then," said Graves. "A spot of luck."

"Yes, well…" Simon wasn't so sure. He ran a hand over his mouth, numb, not yet able to process everything that the fire meant, the ways it would change his life, none for the better. "What happened?"

"Explosion. Witnesses said it sounded like a bomb. Did you have a gasoline tank inside…you know, to fuel the vehicles?"

"No."

"Then must be all the paint and thinner you use."

"We store flammable liquids in a safety locker. We don't keep anything out overnight."

Graves appeared skeptical. Something had caused the place to go up. "We'll have an answer once we've tamed the fire and everything cools down. Send in an investigator. It may be a while."

Simon found D'Art at the edge of the crowd and relayed the information given to him by Group Commander Graves.

"Explosion?" said Moore. "What do you have in there?"

"Plenty, but everything flammable is kept under lock and key. It doesn't make sense."

There came a terrible, keening sound, the sound of metal under duress. Sparks erupted from the top of the building. Something inside fell to the ground, so heavy Simon could feel it.

"Roof's going!" shouted Graves. "All ladders pull back."

Moore put a hand on Simon's shoulder, guiding him away from the masses. "We do insure you," he said. "You'll rebuild better than ever."

"You're forgetting the two I bought on spec," said Simon. "The ones I asked you to write some paper on."

"Remind me of the value."

"Three apiece."

"Which leaves you?"

Simon shook his head. Even with the check from Hamilton, he was still four mil down. On top of that, there was the cost to rebuild, the loss of business for a year, maybe longer. Broke? Nearly.

The two walked farther from the hive of firefighters and policemen, away from the smoke and heat. Simon looked toward the rear of the building. The lot was empty, save one vehicle. A silver Audi. His heart jumped. Always someone who doesn't do what they're supposed to. He called Harry Mason's phone. No answer.

"What is it?" asked D'Art, sensing the change in Simon's bearing.

Simon pushed past Moore and rushed to a squad of firefighters, oxygen tanks on their backs, axes in hand, faces darkened with soot. "My shop manager may be inside."

"We looked, mate," said one of the firefighters. "No one there."

"Look again. Older man. Seventy. This tall."

"You're sure?"

"His car's here. He can't go far without it. I called his phone. He didn't answer."

The fireman's face hardened. Time to step up. "Know your way around?"

"I can show you," said Simon, setting off toward the rear entry, the sectional door that rose to let vehicles in and out of the shop.

The fireman caught up to him, grabbing his shoulders, forcing him to a halt. "No chance of that," he said. "Tell me. I'll go in."

Simon drew a breath, gathering himself, aware that every second that passed was a second Harry needed. He thought of how to describe the floor layout. Mechanics' bay to the left, dynamometer room to the right, the paint studio, not to mention the positioning of the cars on the floor. There was no way…

"Oh, bollocks." Simon shoved the fireman to the side and ran to the back of the building, dodging a half-dozen first responders, aware of the shouts, men pursuing him, not giving a damn.

The sectional door was open, beyond it a pall of smoke. Simon slowed, drew a breath, and in that instant the firefighters tackled him. One took him down at the knees, another more or less jumped on him. Simon hit the ground hard, wind knocked out of him. He lashed out blindly, a fist colliding with a helmet. Strong hands pinned him to the asphalt.

"Calm down, sir," said one.

"He's inside," said Simon.

"Just stop fighting."

Which only made Simon struggle all the more.

"Sir, please."

And then the pressure lessened. "I see him," said another voice. "He's coming out. I'll be damned. Come on, Trev."

One moment, they were on him. The next, the firefighters were up, running toward the shop. Simon raised his head. It was him. Harry.

Harry Mason staggered out of the building, face black with soot, hands thrust before him as if he couldn't see where he was walking. Not just soot on his face. Blood, too, running from his forehead and into his eyes. Mason collapsed before the firemen reached him.

Simon was at his side seconds afterward. He looked on as EMTs fitted an oxygen mask over Harry's face, rinsed his eyes with saline solution, then inspected the wound to his forehead. A wipe to clean away the blood. A bandage. All the while Mason's eyes remained on Simon.

"Can he talk?" asked Simon.

"I'm right here," said Harry, coughing. "What are you asking them for?"

"Make it quick," said the EMT. "We've got to get him to hospital. He's inhaled quite a bit of smoke."

Simon leaned closer. "Jesus, Harry, tough way of saying you need some time off."

"It was him," said Mason, a rasp. "He did it."

"Relax, Harry."

"Sent his bully boys. They surprised me, took the keys to the paint locker, then bashed me in the head. I heard them talking. Not proper English, it wasn't."

"You're sure?"

Mason closed his eyes, grimacing as a spasm shook his chest. He latched a hand on to Simon's arm. "It was him. It was the Russki. I know it."

"Blatt?"

"Recognized one of the bully boys from back when. Get him. Get the bastard."

Simon nodded as Mason coughed again, this time violently.

"Simon…give 'em to my boy."

"What, Harry?"

"The football tickets."

"Move away," said the EMT, seeing something Simon didn't.

"What is it?" asked Simon.

"The smoke. His lungs are burned. He can't get enough oxygen into his blood." She replaced the mask on Mason's face, called a colleague. "We're losing him. Alert the ER. Stat."

Simon stepped away as two more EMTs knelt by Harry's side. One ripped open his shirt. The second EMT administered CPR. "Get the paddles."

Simon could only look on. "Harry," he said. "Stay with me."

Five minutes later, Harry Mason was dead.

CHAPTER 31

London, England

It was the end of one life.

The shop was gone. The cars under his care, the two he'd bought on spec, his equipment, his flat, his possessions. All of it. Gone. He was broke, more or less.

None of it mattered.

Harry Mason was dead. Simon knew who did it. Harry had told him. *"Heard them talking. Not proper English, it wasn't."*

Night fell. The last of the fire trucks left. Finally, D'Art went home, too. Simon remained at the shop. He sat on the curb, legs stretched out, staring at the smoking wreckage and plotting his revenge.

Blatt. The man was going to pay.

Simon knew at that moment Boris Blatt was arguing to DCI Felicity Worth that he was no longer safe. That "devil," Riske, had compromised him. He had a list of all the people Blatt had testified against. Blatt had seen it with his own eyes. It was only a matter of time before his enemies exacted revenge. It was essential that he be moved to a newer, safer location. A place where Simon Riske, or anyone else, couldn't find him. And, oh yes, regarding the evidence Worth had requested implicating other Russian "beez-ness-men," Blatt might have turned up something. Rather a lot of it, in fact.

And Worth?

What choice did she have? The prospect of more high-profile arrests, headlines in the papers trumpeting the London police's sleuthing acumen, and the certainty of promotion for all involved were enough to tip the scales. There was only one answer she could give.

"Of course, Mr. Blatt. We're more than happy to oblige."

Out went Ditchfield. Goodbye, Somerset. In its place...*what?* A manor in the Cotswolds? A horse property in Sussex? Why stop there? A compound in Lyford Cay? A beachfront villa in Barbados? Take your pick, Boris. The British Crown boasted a surfeit of idyllic locations where they might tuck away a helpful informant. Within hours, Blatt would be long gone. This time, he wouldn't leave his registration behind in the glove box.

And so? Action, Simon decided, with a finality that scared him. Blatt wanted war. War he'd get. The time to settle scores had come. The Sicilians had it all wrong. Revenge was a dish best served hot and bloody, or not at all.

The end of one life.

But not the beginning of another.

Rather the resumption of an old one. A life cut short.

The back door was open.

Simon had called ahead, apologizing for the late hour. Arjit Singh stood by the stove, pouring himself a cup of hot chai. Sixteen years old, soon to return to Caltech, as a sophomore, he'd grown another inch since Simon had last seen him three months earlier.

"Tea?"

"Thank you," said Simon as Arjit handed him a mug.

"You smell like a chimney."

"My shop burned down."

"Dad told me. Bummer."

"Big bummer," said Simon.

"Dude, your eyes are really red. You okay?"

Nine months in the States and already talking like an American. Kids were chameleons. How long had it taken Simon to learn to speak French? To trade one identity for another? Six months after his father's death, he hadn't just learned a new language; he'd learned to become a new person. A Frenchman. And after that, something else entirely.

"Simon...you okay?"

"Not really," said Simon.

"I can give you some clothes."

"I may take you up on the offer." Simon sipped gratefully from the mug. "Oh, and by the way, I'm not here."

"I already told him that." Vikram Singh, Arjit's father, padded into the kitchen, wearing a Los Angeles Dodgers sweatshirt, boxer shorts, and slippers. Vikram Singh was a Sikh. Even at this late hour, his saffron-orange turban was in immaculate form. His beard, less so.

By trade, Vikram Singh was an electrical engineer, a graduate of the Indian Institutes of Technology, IIT. Upon immigrating to the UK, he'd accepted a position at MI5, where he'd risen to head their tech department. Surveillance, wiretapping, eavesdropping, anything that required an electronic advantage was his bailiwick. Twenty years earning a government wage was enough. After quitting, he set up shop at home to offer his services on a freelance basis. His second client was Simon Riske. His first was his former employer, Her Majesty's Security Service.

Singh loaded up a plate of cold samosas, naan, and chutney from the fridge. "You don't look so hot," he said.

"Your son informed me."

"Can you salvage anything?"

"I'm not keeping my fingers crossed."

"Cause?"

"Explosion."

"Accident?"

Simon shook his head. "Not hardly."

"Intentional, then?"

"An old friend."

Singh studied Simon for a moment. He knew how to read a man. He knew when to ask questions. As important, he knew when not to. He put down his plate, came to Simon, and patted him on the back. He could guess what was on Simon's mind. Yes, he would help.

"I'm going to need some privacy." Simon pronounced the last word in the English fashion. *Priv-a-cee.*

"How so?"

He explained that he needed something that could shut down all cellular communications within a one-hundred-square-meter radius.

"A jammer," said Vikram.

"Strong one."

"Want to listen in?"

"All calls diverted to me."

"Capture and kill."

"Something like that."

It was mandatory that the concerned parties not be able to contact the outside world. He didn't want anyone to interrupt his work.

"Not a problem," said Vikram.

Arjit made some notations on a pad of paper. "What do you think, Papa? Twelve band, a thousand watts?"

"You're teaching him the family trade?" said Simon.

"Summer job."

"Better than working in Starbucks," said Arjit.

"Can you give me a few hours?" said Vikram.

"I won't need it until tomorrow night. I have to pick up a few other things first."

"Anytime after three," said Vikram. "It may be a bit bigger than you expect. You won't be able to hide it inside a jacket pocket like the last one I gave you."

"Fit in a backpack?"

"With room to spare...for those 'other things.'"

Vikram Singh led Simon to the hall. "I don't like the look in your eye," he said. "I've seen it in others. The outcome wasn't positive."

"But there was an outcome."

"Simon..."

"Thanks, Vikram, but I know what I'm doing."

Vikram Singh studied him. "I'm sure you do."

Simon went upstairs with Arjit and returned wearing a hoodie, jeans, and basketball shoes. Now he was a Californian, too. Vikram stood at the back door.

"What's the bad news?" asked Simon, meaning *How much?*

"No bad news."

"Really?"

Vikram put a hand on his shoulder. "In India we are taught never to take from someone who has less."

"Thank you."

"I'm happy you came to me."

"Family."

CHAPTER 32

Barking, England

It was the east East End. Ten miles alongside the serpentine banks of the River Thames, past Hackney Wick, past Canary Wharf and East Ham, was a dull but dangerous patch of urban real estate called Crispe House, a twenty-story red-brick council building.

Simon heard them before he saw them. A loud, pulsing bass that rattled the car windows, an angry Eastern melody, a man rapping in a language he did not understand, the music all the more deafening because it was barely ten o'clock in the morning. He turned onto Gascoigne Road and there it was.

Crispe House. The only high-rise in miles.

A dozen men congregated in the courtyard. Young, bearded, braided gold chains around their necks, muscle tees and the muscles to do them justice, not a beer belly in sight. And of course tattoos. More ink than could be found on all of Fleet Street. The white Lambo and the gunmetal Mercedes G-Class confirmed he'd come to the right place. Not a bunch of thugs hanging out. Businessmen. Professionals.

Simon slowed the car. Officially, Crispe House belonged to the borough of Barking, as did the surrounding neighborhood. There were bus stops, traffic lights, and an athletic field across the way with a basketball court and soccer goals, all with nets intact. Then there was the absence of traffic. Where was everyone on a sunny weekday morning? His VW Golf was the last man standing. In fact, he was no longer in Greater London, or England, for that matter. He was in Albania. There was no better proof than the blood-red flags with silhouetted black double-headed eagles—one head facing east, one facing west—draped from windows of no less than six flats. This piece of territory belonged to the

Hellbanianz, the ethnic criminal organization that ran ninety percent of drugs into the English capital and points beyond.

Simon parked at the foot of the driveway. He left the car and walked slowly up the gradual slope. No one paid him the least attention. He was a stranger, a foreigner, not a *Shqipet*—an Albanian, and so, not worth their trouble. At least not yet. He'd traded Arjit Singh's hoodie and sweats for a black T-shirt, jeans, and work boots. A razor hadn't touched his face since the day before. If not an Albanian, then maybe a Slav, at least until they saw the color of his eyes.

"Hello," he shouted, hand raised in greeting. "I'm looking for someone. Maybe you can help."

"Who are you?"

"I'm looking for Agron."

A compact man broke off from the others and approached. Beard, chains, biceps the size of grapefruits. "Never heard of him."

"Agron Bexha. Your boss."

There was no mystery as to how Simon knew where to come. Agron Bexha, the undisputed head of the Hellbanianz, fancied himself a rapper and posted videos of his songs on social media. Fancy cars, big-breasted women in scant attire, piles of cash on white fur bedspreads…the usual classy fare.

"You police? You don't look like it." Russian accent without the charm.

"I'm American."

"Got a name?"

"Yep."

"Funny guy."

Simon held his ground as the others gathered round, moving closer, crowding him. A rugby scrum reeking of Drakkar Noir. "I need to see Agron." Simon patted his pants pocket. Inside was a wad of banknotes. Five thousand pounds. "I need to buy something."

"What you want?"

Not narcotics. The Hellbanianz's business was strictly volume. Bexha's gang brought heroin, cocaine, meth, and whatever else might be the drug du jour over on tankers from the continent. Bexha had ruled the docks for twenty years, and all of the police and MI5's best efforts hadn't changed a thing.

"Protection," said Simon.

"Like a pistol?" The man made the sign of a gun, a peashooter.

Simon shook his head. He pretended to hold a machine gun, a big one.

"Why you come here?"

"I saw Agron's video. Looks like you have a lot of them."

The man turned to his crew, discoursed in his native language. Laughs, a few retorts, still no consensus. Someone turned down the music. "So, you got cash?"

Simon nodded.

More Albanian banter. Finally, a nod, maybe a smile. Decision made. "Okay. You come."

Simon made his way through the crowd and followed the man into the building. A pat on the back as they crossed the lobby to show they were buddies. "I'm Luca."

"Simon."

As the elevator closed, three more men joined them, all taller than Simon. More buddies, even if none offered his name. Nothing he hadn't expected.

They rode to the thirteenth floor—*a sign?*—where Luca showed him into a dark, shabby apartment, shades drawn, the smell of sweat, weed, and other scents too tawdry to catalogue. This was not the VIP lounge.

"Sit. Please."

Simon found a spot on the couch that wasn't stained as badly as the rest. Two of Luca's friends took up position on either side. Nice and cozy.

"So," said Luca, grabbing a chair, turning it so he could lean on the back as he sat. "How much you got?"

"You're supposed to ask me what I want to buy first."

"What you want to buy, Mister America?"

"Captain America," said Simon.

Luca's smile faded. "What you want?"

"I need an AK-47," said Simon. "A Kalashnikov. Three clips. That's about a hundred rounds. If I need more than that, I'm in trouble."

"You have Kalashnikov before?"

"Long time ago. Twenty years."

"You? Bullshit. You never touch one."

"*A* for automatic. *K* for Kalashnikov, the name of the guy who designed it. A Russian, not an Albanian. Sorry. Takes 7.62-millimeter ammunition. Thirty rounds a clip. Muzzle velocity: seven hundred meters per second. You can't take down a Brinks truck without one."

"Brinks?" A name Luca knew. An expression of wild disbelief. "Where you do this?"

"Marseille," said Simon. "That's in France."

Luca considered this, then said something to the youngest of the group, the tallest kid, maybe twenty-one. Probably something along the lines of *"Twenty years ago? You weren't even a sparkle in your father's eye then."* Or not.

"I know where Marseille is," said Luca.

"Of course you do."

"But you're American. You say so."

"Long story."

"I don't like stories." Luca grimaced, patience officially worn out. "Money. Please."

"Don't I get to see the gun first?" said Simon. "And the clips?"

Luca massaged his forehead, eyes narrowed, a migraine. "You no buy anything. You give us your money. Maybe you even walk out of here."

"Says who?"

"Says me."

Events speeded up. A barked instruction. Hands grasped Simon's arms, lifting him to his feet. Luca stepped toward him, fist clenched, left shoulder down. He drew back his hand. The pressure on Simon's arms increased. They were strong. Simon would give them that. But he was strong himself. And he was angry. More than that. He was furious.

Simon shifted his weight to his right, twisting his torso, throwing both men off-balance. At the same moment, he lifted his left foot and drove it into the knee of the man to that side. The joint buckled, shearing cartilage, tearing ligaments. The kneecap dislocated. A scream. The grip on his left arm loosened. Man down. Luca's blow landed off target, glancing Simon's ribs. Simon drove his fist squarely into Luca's face, extending his arm to its fullest, crushing the Albanian's nose. Blood gushed as if from a faucet. Two down.

A flash of silver.

A knife, big enough to castrate a bull.

It was the youngest of the four, on his right. The tall one. A shout to warn off his friend, then lunging at Simon, the blade held before him. He was just a little too far away, Luca writhing on the floor between them. The point of the blade entered Simon's thigh, but only the tip. Pain. White-hot. There, then gone. Simon grasped the outstretched wrist, clutching it as tightly as he could, then tighter. The knife fell to the floor. Simon dropped to a knee, twisting the wrist violently. A snap, as crisp as a dry twig. The ulna? Then more, holding nothing back. A new sound. A boot on gravel. Spiral fracture.

"Fuck!" or the Albanian equivalent.

Simon scooped up the knife, spinning as he did so, a roundhouse kick, heel to jaw.

Down went tall boy. That makes three.

Simon turned to face the last man, knife extended, willing the man to come at him.

The man retreated, hands raised. Wise decision.

"Agron. Now."

Twenty minutes later, Simon left Crispe House. He carried a black duffel bag that appeared to be empty, more or less. Inside was an AK-47 assault rifle, cosmoline still on the barrel. Hardly new but in working condition. There was also a sound suppressor and five magazines of ammunition.

The white Lambo was Agron's. Simon had told him he'd tune it up for him next time he needed work done. Gratis, for his new best friend.

Simon was only limping a little.

CHAPTER 33

Chur, Switzerland

Anna stopped at a kiosk outside the bus station and purchased a cup of tea. It was eleven o'clock. The sun was shining in a royal-blue sky. A steady wind blew along the Rhine Valley, the air dry and crisp. South of the Alps, barely a hundred kilometers away, it was high summer. Here, on the range's northern flanks, she could taste autumn, still a month away. She crossed the tram tracks to a small park and headed to an empty bench at the rear corner, past a sandbox and a swing set and a statue of Johann Heinrich Pestalozzi. She sat sipping her tea, her hands enjoying the warmth.

Anna had a rule. Never underestimate the enemy. There was no upside in betting on an opponent's shortcomings. It was that mindset that had kept her awake night after night in São Paulo waiting for Os Cavalheiros. The right course of action was to assume they were every bit as capable as she. Or, in this case, far more.

Which meant they knew about Chatterbell. They knew she was keen to find the owner of the Volkswagen Polo with Graubünden plates. They also knew that she had a photograph showing at least one of the plotters who had killed her father, no matter how fuzzy the image.

Anna was a threat.

And so they were here.

A check of her phone. Still no word from Freddy Hold. She sent him a second message, stating that she was presently in Chur and asking if they might meet for an early lunch. To her surprise, her thread on Chatterbell asking for help with the photograph buzzed with activity. Three fellow sleuths had volunteered to clean up the image of the individual seated at the wheel of the VW. Thank you, Klaus, Vivek, and Yoshi. And this from Omnivision:

167 traffic cams in Lugano. Will find your VW on one.

Anna rose, uneasy at remaining in any one spot for long. Her eyes roamed the street, targeting a black Audi. But what model? All she remembered was the grill with four interlocking circles. A parade of cars passed by. None of them black. Against her will, she yawned. Sleep, if she could call it that, had come between the hours of two and five on a dewy hillside below the Castelgrande in Bellinzona. Not yet thirty and her bones ached like a person twice her age.

She wandered down a commercial street, boutiques and shops on either side. The last of her cash had gone for a train ticket and her tea. She had to rely on the e-pay function of her phone for anything further. Regardless, she needed a change of clothes, something to offer even a partial disguise. A five-foot-nine-inch blonde with biceps cut from stone and a side cut stuck out like a sore thumb. She entered the first clothing store she saw—a sporting goods store, thank God—and came out with a dark fleece, a matching ski cap, and a pair of glacier glasses. Now she was a mountaineer in search of a mountain. The cap had to go, and so, she realized, did her hair. She found a salon two blocks from the car dealership. She walked out ninety minutes later with just enough fuzz to cover a tennis ball and no more. Better, it was dyed brown. In place of the ski cap, she bought a baseball cap. *Go Yankees!* She caught sight of herself in a store window. There was still one thing. Back to the sporting goods store. Two rolls of elastic bandages and a deep breath, and she was her thirteen-year-old self.

For the umpteenth time, she checked her phone. Victory! A reply from Hold.

Happy to meet after work—6 p.m. Calanda Stübli. Augustinergasse.

No word about fulfilling her request regarding his client's identity. Still, why else would he be coming? Stupid question. He was thirty-something, apparently single, and not bad looking. And Anna was Anna. Never the prettiest but never lacking for attention.

Five hours to kill. She slipped her phone into her pants and started down the street. She couldn't stay in the city. *They were here.* She remembered their voices: calm, experienced, professional. They'd been inside strangers' homes before with the intent to do harm. They hadn't given up. Men like that never did. Every moment she remained on the street was another moment she remained exposed. An easy target. She had no doubt that they wanted her dead.

Nearby, a footbridge crossed a fast-moving stream and led to a residential district, a row of century-old brick-and-mortar apartment buildings with mansard roofs and scrolled metal balconies, set on the lower slopes of the mountains that surrounded the eastern half of the city. A hiking trail was visible, zigging and zagging up the forested hillside. No Audis there.

Twenty minutes later, Anna stood in the shade of an arolla pine, looking down at the rooftops of Chur.

They were here.

From a distance of no more than twenty meters, the men watched Anna cross the footbridge and proceed at a rushed pace up the block. They waited a proper amount of time before following. They were professionals, trained long ago in a city far away to trail others without being noticed. Surveillance was hardly their strong suit. They were assassins, first and foremost. *Ubitsya* and proud of the designation. Still, despite her attempts at disguise, her admirable vigilance, Anna Bildt was an amateur, and amateurs were easy game.

An incoming call drew one of the men's attention. *"Da?"* He listened to the instructions. *"Pozhaluysta. Da. Da.* Okay. See you soon."

"Well?"

"He is about to land."

CHAPTER 34

Tel Aviv, Israel

The SON Group
Transcript / Cellular Communication #898
Subject: S. Riske. Device: 0044–71–xxxx–xx89
Correspondent: DCI Felicity Worth / 0044–71–xxxx–xx77
Time: GMT 11:45. Date: 25-8-20XX
Duration: 3'23"

DCI Felicity Worth (FW): Simon, there you are. I heard what happened.

Simon Riske (SR): Yes, it was terrible.

FW: I'm talking about Blatt. You had no right to visit him. He called me in quite a state, going on about you threatening him with his trial transcripts. I'm not going to ask how they came to be in your possession. Some things I choose not to know. Now, listen. Boris Blatt is a critical component of Her Majesty's fight against money laundering and Eastern European organized crime. Even crucial.

SR: I understand.

FW: Do you?

SR: I needed a gearbox. It was crucial.

FW: I'm in no mood for your semantics, Riske. You're to leave Mr. Blatt alone.

SR: *Mr. Blatt?* Is that what you said? Why not just call him *tovarich?*

FW: Don't you raise your voice to me.

SR: He's a criminal. He kills people. At least three were mentioned by name in his indictment. Dead. Dead. Dead.

FW: It *was* you—

SR: He belongs in jail, not living like the Duke of Wellington. Have you seen his place? Of course you have.

FW: Henceforth, you will leave him alone. Do you understand?

SR: I understand.

FW: That's not what I'm asking and you know it. You are to have no further contact with him. No calls. No visits. Nothing. Boris Blatt no longer exists. Do I make myself clear?

SR: And Gerstmann?

FW: Why, you bastard! Forget you ever heard that name. Do I make myself clear?

SR: Crystal.

FW: Say it. Say you'll give me your word.

(Silence—twelve seconds.)

FW: Damn you, Simon.

SR: He burned my shop to the ground. I'm guessing he hoped I'd be in it. I lost everything. Because of him my friend is dead.

FW: I heard. I am sorry. But you don't know it was Blatt. He's under twenty-four-hour surveillance. He hasn't put a toe outside his estate.

SR: That is comforting.

FW: Don't, Simon. Don't you even think of it.

(Silence.)

FW: Where are you now?

(Silence.)

FW: Simon? Simon? Oh, damn.

END TRANSMISSION

CHAPTER 35

St. Moritz, Switzerland

Vadim piloted the Learjet low over the Maloja Pass, the wingtips practically clipping the peaks of the Alps. The sky provided a flawless blue canopy. Below, the azure crescent of Lake Silvaplana guided him to his destination. He descended rapidly, passing over Sils-Maria, leveling out five hundred feet above the lake as he reached the resort town of St. Moritz, the dovecote tower of Badrutt's Palace Hotel near enough to call out an order to Max, the barman.

He knew the area. For six years he'd attended the Lyceum Alpinum Zuoz, a preparatory academy for the rich and richer, farther down the valley. His mother had neither the time nor the inclination to parent. His father...well, Russian fathers were not well known for their child-rearing skills. What had Stalin, the "man of steel," said about his father, "Crazy Besso"? He knew the heel of his boot well enough to count the stitches. The best thing Vadim could say about his father was that he hardly knew him at all.

It wasn't until the age of eighteen that Vadim set foot in Russia. Against his mother's wishes, he enrolled in Moscow State University, the country's most prestigious institute, to study computer science. He flunked out after a semester. Ashamed, and admittedly at the end of a seven-day bender, he enlisted in the army, where he spent seven years in the infantry, never rising above the rank of sergeant.

Despite repeated efforts, he failed entrance to the Spetsnaz, the army's elite special forces. He was fit enough, no question. It was a matter of attitude. His record showed multiple instances of insubordination, dereliction of duty, and one count of striking an officer. End of story.

Instead, he chose a career in intelligence, not his father's KGB but his mother's GRU. Ten years of government service proved more than sufficient. At thirty-five, he said goodbye to Mother Russia and returned to Paris to work alongside his mother. He refused, however, to take her last name. He was not, nor ever would be, a Bettencourt. He was a son of Russia, even if Russia's most prominent son disavowed him. Vadim was enough.

The last of Lake Silvaplana slipped below him. He brought the jet in for a smooth landing. He deplaned immediately, leaving his copilot to handle the laborious landing and customs procedures. A helicopter waited across the tarmac, an Aérospatiale Écureuil, rotors a blur. The pilot stood beside the craft, waving for Vadim to hurry. Naturally, Vadim slowed his pace.

The flight to Chur lasted twelve minutes. A climb to fourteen thousand feet, a traverse of the Alps, then a vertiginous descent to the Rhine Valley. A short but adequate time to study the picture of Anna Bildt. He despised her at first sight. One of those who got up every morning eager to tear down the system, who disdained the rules—any rules—in favor of their own. More than that, he was angry at her. Not because of her actions. He would expect any child to do the same for a slain parent. He was angry because she had bested his men. She had made them appear unequal to the task, and thus, by extension, made him appear unequal. Worse—and the crime for which he would never forgive her—she had brought his mother into the equation. She had given Sylvie one more opportunity to look over her shoulder and offer him a disapproving glance. *"Mais, Vadim, pourquoi?"*

All of this left him seething when the helicopter touched down.

He found the men at the corner of Ringstrasse and the Sportplatzweg.

"Where is she?" he asked by way of greeting.

"Up there." Alec, a Georgian bumpkin, pointed to the mountainside.

"We can take her," said Pavel, who counted aggression as the first and only course of action.

"Definitely not," said Vadim. "Or not yet."

"Then what?"

"We take her to Shangri-la."

"What for?"

"A discussion." Vadim's clipped tone made clear he'd suffered enough questions. "We've got her phone. Grisha says she's meeting this fellow Hold at six."

Pavel knew Hold. He'd purchased the Volkswagen from him a week earlier. And so Hold knew Pavel, no longer as a customer but as a suspect in a capital crime that had been splashed in color photographs across all of Switzerland's newspapers.

"Where?" asked Pavel.

"Calanda Stübli," said Vadim, consulting the message from his younger brother.

"Before or after?"

"After," said Vadim.

CHAPTER 36

Too much to do. Too little time.

First, a pit stop at the clinic of Dr. Michelle Manley, Internal Medicine, 7 Harley Street.

"A nice puncture wound." Dr. Manley, seventy, a native of Jamaica, petite, officious, as dry as the Sahara, doctor to Anthony Riske thirty-odd years ago, and to Simon these last ten. He'd only known D'Artagnan Moore longer, though he wasn't sure if he trusted him so entirely. "Care to tell me about it?" she asked.

"Accident."

"Go on."

"I accidentally got too close to a knife."

"A rather big one from the look of it."

Simon offered no comment. The less Dr. Manley knew about it the better.

"I thought you'd put those days behind you," she said, eyes darting above the rim of her bifocals. She was his doctor. She'd seen the scars on his chest and back. She knew about his past.

"It isn't like that," said Simon. A lie. It was exactly like that.

"Isn't it?" And she knew it.

"Occupational hazard."

"One day, young man, you are going to tell me what that occupation is. I thought you fixed cars. Fancy ones."

"Among other things."

"Well, among other things, the knife missed your femoral artery by this much." Manley held out her hand, thumb and index finger separated by a razor's edge. "You have an angel on your shoulder."

Maybe a fallen one, thought Simon.

"I'd tell you to stay off it for a while," she continued, "but I sense you're keen on doing whatever it is you're doing."

Simon answered with a tight smile. "Keen" was one word. "Driven" was another. Better yet, "desperate." Every minute that passed was a minute Boris Blatt might use toward escaping, if he hadn't escaped already.

Ten stitches, a bandage, and two painkillers later, he was back on the street. But not before giving Michelle Manley a hug. "Thank you, and please, don't worry."

"Doctors don't worry. We're too busy for that."

"Thank you all the same."

She held him at arm's length. Her gaze could cut a diamond. "You look more and more like him, your father."

"I've never heard that."

"You have his…*commitment*."

From Harley Street to Covent Garden, 7 Tavistock Street, home of Charles H. Fox Ltd., purveyor of costumes, haberdashery, makeup, and wigs to London's theatrical establishment. It was this last item that especially interested Simon. In and out in ten minutes. Nothing custom-made required. Strictly off-the-shelf. He wasn't Sir Henry Irving and his audience wasn't Queen Victoria. This was a one-time performance.

A last question before leaving: "Do you by chance have uniforms?"

"But of course! What kind?"

A dash westward across the city.

Covent Garden to Southall. Fourteen miles. Forty-two minutes. At this time of day, some kind of record.

Simon arrived at Vikram Singh's a few minutes before three. "Am I early?"

"Perfect timing." Vikram Singh had exchanged last night's Dodgers sweatshirt and boxers for a three-piece chalk-stripe suit and a pearl-gray turban, or *dastār*, to match. "Come, let's take a look."

The two descended the stairs to the basement workshop. Smells of linseed oil and burnt solder filled the room. A raft of lights, as bright as an operating theater, illuminated a broad worktable.

"You've seen this before," said Singh, moving a compact rectangular stainless-steel case closer to them. "An IMSI catcher, but I prefer to call it a cell-site simulator, or CSS."

IMSI for "international mobile subscriber identity"—the unique code given to every mobile device.

"It does exactly what the name suggests. Turn it on and it pretends to be the nearest cell tower. Kind of shoves it out of the way and says, *Hey, look at me.* This one, though, goes a step further. It stops onward transmission of all calls in the area and, instead, directs them to a given number. Yours. Texts too."

"They've gotten smaller," said Simon.

"A marvel, if I may say so."

"Can Blatt detect it?" asked Simon, catching himself a moment too late. "I mean, can it be detected?"

The moment someone developed a tool to surreptitiously capture phone calls, someone else developed a "counter-tool" to let you know it.

"Not likely," said Singh.

Simon studied the machine's dials and switches and readouts, Singh explaining each in turn. A last look. Tutorial completed. "I do my best to make it idiotproof."

Simon closed the case. "This idiot thanks you."

Singh looked at him askance. "Battery life's four hours. Otherwise I would have had to add another lithium cell. Makes the whole thing rather clumsy."

"Should be fine." Simon hefted the case and climbed the stairs back to the kitchen.

"You've picked up a limp since last night," said Singh.

"Have I?"

Singh retrieved two bottles of mineral water from the fridge. He poured each into a glass, handing one to Simon. "Should I wish you good luck?"

"Probably not."

"By the way, what you said earlier…If it was a name, I didn't pick it up."

"I don't recall."

Singh finished his water and placed the glass in the sink. He accompanied Simon to the back door. It was a warm evening, humidity sky-high. There were balsam poplar trees in the neighborhood, the air rich with their scent. They walked down the block to where Simon had parked. Singh stood beside him as he unlocked the door and laid the stainless-steel case on the passenger seat.

"Thanks again," said Simon. "Quick work."

Singh stepped closer. "What you choose to do is none of my business, but in this case…" He sighed, manners warring with duty.

"Go ahead, Vikram."

"Whatever it is you're going to do…*don't.*"

Last but not least, transport.

The VW wouldn't do—not for what Simon had planned—the most obvious reason being he didn't want his car anywhere near Somerset, near Boris Blatt. There was another reason. Access and egress. Getting in and getting out. Actually, that was two reasons. And to think he'd earned an advanced degree in mathematics.

It was six: shift change. Simon stood across the street from the Wimbledon Police Station, the same station, or "nick," where he'd been booked for battery against Jack Hawley. If the uniform from Charles Fox wasn't a perfect match, it was close enough. Dark trousers. Crisp white shirt with epaulets. Peaked cap. Half hidden in the doorway of a fish-and-chips shop, he had a clear view of the station and the parking lot adjacent to it. Policing was a job like any other, meaning that officers of every rank were eager to go home the moment their workday ended. For thirty minutes he watched officers come and go, on foot and by car, torrent turning to drizzle to…well, nothing at all.

At six thirty, he crossed the street and skirted the fenced enclosure. He counted a dozen vehicles inside. Most were BMWs—sedans and smaller SUVs. There was an older Ford and a Vauxhall. All were painted silver or white and bore the Met's Battenburg livery, fluorescent yellow-and-blue checkered flashing designed to increase the vehicles' visibility in all weather conditions. Simon was interested, however, in the lone Range Rover parked in the far rear corner. The car was reserved for the rank of commander or higher and, even then, to be driven exclusively to and from high-profile crime scenes. He was hoping no bank robberies were planned in Wimbledon this summer's eve.

He continued past the lot, stopping at a corner to check his phone, tapping his foot as if expecting a call. He stayed there for a minute, one eye on the parking lot, hoping for a straggler. In that time, he attached a cord from his phone to a universal key fob. It didn't matter that he should in no way be in possession of a factory directory holding all Range Rover security codes. He highlighted the codes for model years 2018 to the present and hit SEND. Waiting for the codes to upload, he caught a streak of black, heard the gate rattle along its track. A Ford waited to exit. Upload complete, he put away the cord, dropped the phone into the pocket of his windcheater, and slid the fob into his trousers.

Simon timed his walk so that he passed the gate as the car turned left into traffic. A look to the rear of the station. No activity. Door closed. No faces in the windows.

He dashed into the lot, ducking low, snaking through the parked cars until he'd reached the far corner. The Range Rover was locked, as expected. He took an electric handsaw from his windcheater and inserted a metal blade. The "striker," or locking piston, on this particular vehicle was positioned thirty-seven inches from the bottom of the door. Sliding the blade into the doorjamb, he moved it higher until he felt a slim steel bar. The striker. Another look toward the station. No one. He turned the saw on. Metal on metal. High-pitched. Impossibly loud. Two seconds and he was through. He killed the saw. Silence. He opened the door. No alarm. Into the driver's seat.

Now it was a matter of speed.

He dropped the saw on the floor and placed the fob against the left-hand side of the steering column at a spot denoted (for this purpose) by three parallel lines. He counted to three and, with his right thumb, hit the starter button. The engine came to life. He sat up straight in case anyone was watching. An honest man had nothing to hide. Putting the car in gear, he drove slowly to the exit. Eyes dead ahead as he waited for the gate to slide open. A garden slug moved faster.

He turned left, away from the station.

Still not quite there.

He continued a few miles farther, out of Wimbledon and into Copse

Hill, a quiet residential district, where he pulled to the curb. A circuit of the car. Strips of transparent reflective tape on license plates, front and rear. The London Metropolitan Police were early adopters of automatic number-plate recognition (ANPR) technology. Fifteen thousand cameras positioned at strategic travel points across the country were capable of submitting fifty million "reads" a day. He'd worked a case not long ago in coordination with the Met using ANPR technology to track down a researcher for Big Pharma suspected of selling secrets to the Chinese. Guilty, it turned out. They'd caught him at Folkestone minutes before he boarded the car ferry for Calais.

And so Simon knew firsthand the accuracy and immediacy of the system. It was real-time and it worked. The reflective tape, however, screwed the whole thing up. Like trying to guess the color of a person's eyes through mirrored sunglasses.

One last matter and he could bounce.

He popped the rear hatch and went to work on the vehicle's LoJack transponder, the device that when activated would relay the car's GPS coordinates to appropriate authorities. A screwdriver to pop the sidewall. Needle-nose pliers to separate out the cables and snip the correct ones. Another moment to replace the sidewall and he was done.

Simon turned the car north. A stop at his own car to pick up his recent purchases, then back on the road. In twenty minutes, he was on the M4 motorway.

He was headed back to Bath.

To an unlovely residence called Ditchfield.

Already, his trigger finger was itchy.

Chapter 37

Freddy Hold was seated at a table when she arrived a few minutes past six.

"Anna," he called, standing and trumpeting her name as if they were long-lost friends.

A wave in return. A shy *"Grüezi,"* drowned out by the hum and bluster of the after-work crowd. It was called the Calanda "Stübli" for a reason. Wooden tables; arolla pine walls decorated with the horns of dozens of steinbock, large and small; black-and-white photographs of skiers and alpinists past and present. Of course, he had to kiss her when she arrived at his table.

"Can we speak English?" said Anna, pulling out a chair across the table, not wanting to sit on the banquette beside him.

Hold offered brief condolences, and for a few minutes they exchanged personal histories. Hold was a local, a ski instructor in Arosa, thirty kilometers up the Schanfigg Valley, during winters, and hoping to earn his mountain guide license. Selling cars was a temporary thing…and had been for ten years. At least he had a sense of humor, thought Anna. Not bad looking either. Black hair cut long, an angular face, broad forehead, brown eyes wizened by his time outdoors. And in shape.

Anna kept her story to the minimum, taking care not to mention anything about what had happened the night before. No one had tried to kill her. No one was following her. *They were not here.* She'd come to Chur to learn the identity of the man who'd bought the Volkswagen Polo. "Really," she said. "It's the only thing I can talk about."

"I remember him," said Hold. "He spoke German, but I couldn't place his accent. He wasn't Swiss, but he didn't sound as if he was from Germany either."

"Don't you need a passport to buy a car?"

"Greece. First one I'd seen. My boss thought there was something off about it. He's a major in the army. Counterespionage."

Switzerland. One of the few remaining countries with mandatory conscription. Maybe it wasn't such a bad idea after all.

"Did he look Greek?"

"Light hair. Blue eyes. Not exactly."

"But…"

"I'm a car salesman. He paid in cash. Nineteen thousand francs. I couldn't care less if he said he was Chinese."

"Name?"

"Georgiades, Paul."

A traditional alpine song played from the jukebox. Accordions and yodelers ran riot. Anna expected Heidi and Peter the Goatherd to wander in at any moment.

Hold leaned closer. With a look to either side, he slid an envelope across the table. "It's the most I can do."

Anna removed several sheets of paper and laid them on the table. Copies of Paul Georgiades's passport and his driver's license. The passport photo showed a man with long blond hair combed across his forehead. Tortoiseshell glasses. A week's worth of stubble, more red than blond. The driver's license photo showed a man with a crew cut, no glasses, no stubble, extremely pale. It took her a moment to conclude that it was the same man in both. And a moment longer to compare the photos against her own fleeting glimpses of the men who had assaulted her the night before. In truth, she wasn't sure.

"Does it help?" asked Hold.

"Give me a second."

Freeing her phone, Anna logged on to the Chatterbell website. The latest response to her thread asking for help enhancing the image of the man behind the wheel of the VW Polo had come from Herve866. At first glance, she was amazed. No longer was the pic a blurred collage of multicolored pixels. The driver's face was in focus, easy to make out. Blond hair, blue eyes, strong jaw, cleft chin. *Hello, Paul Georgiades.*

But not Paul Georgiades.

Herve866 had gone a step further. He'd run the enhanced picture through software made by a company called Clearview AI, a facial recognition tool normally available only to law enforcement personnel that compared the photo she'd posted against billions on the Internet.

Picture after picture, each with a different, if similar, name. Paul Demetrios, Peter Diamadis, Pavel Djordjevich—this last attached to a photograph of a Russian military identification card. God knew how the software had found that!

"It's him," she said, keeping the second part of her discovery secret. "Him" was Major Pavel Djordjevich of the Russian GRU. Too much information for a part-time car salesman. "May I keep these papers?"

"As long as you keep my name out of it."

"If I can," said Anna. "Sooner or later I'll have to go to the police."

Hold didn't like this, but he didn't stop her. On the heels of his triumph, he ordered a second beer for both of them. His generosity did not extend to offering her dinner. She supposed that she owed him. But when she invited him, he shook his head. "Dinner at my place. We can grill outside. Corn, peppers, potatoes. I'm a vegetarian."

To her surprise, Anna said yes. Hold excused himself to go to the lavatory. She checked her email. At the top of the list, the most recent, a message from an administrator at Chatterbell:

Urgent

Re: Thread "The Murder of Carl Bildt"

Dear Chatterbell member,

It has come to our attention that the above referenced thread has been accessed by a username and IP address associated with Russian military intelligence. We can offer no further advice but wish only to inform you of the occurrence. *Praemonitus, praemunitus.*

Hurriedly, she looked up these last words. Latin for "Forewarned is forearmed."

They were here.

Now she knew for certain.

Anna's eyes darted to the entry. The door was open, and she caught the blur of passing cars. Blue, silver, red. *Black.*

"What is it?" asked Hold when he returned. "Are you feeling all right?"

"Actually, I'm not." Anna regarded the earnest Swiss and realized she'd already involved him more than was right. "Can I take a rain check for dinner?"

"You're sure? If you need a place to stay...you don't have to worry."

Anna didn't worry about any man. She did, however, worry about the Russian GRU. "Thank you, but no. I have someplace I need to be."

"Now?"

"Yes," said Anna, sliding back her chair to stand. "Now."

"Let me give you a lift."

"No," said Anna as Hold began to rise. "That's not necessary."

"How far can it be?" asked Hold good-naturedly. "This is Chur. You can get across town and back in five minutes."

"No," said Anna, forcefully enough to silence the tables near them, draw several curious glances. "You've done enough already. Thank you, Freddy."

Finally, he sat down.

Anna walked to the door, peeked her head outside, looking left, then right. The street was calm, not a car to be seen, black or otherwise. She stepped outside, turning left, in the direction of the train station.

It was time to go to the police. A call to Inspector Tell—no relation to William—of the Swiss Federal Intelligence Service. She would inform him that she knew the identity of at least one of her father's assassins. Pavel Djordjevich, a major in the Russian GRU. Tell could take it from there.

Anna felt a stab of satisfaction. She'd done what she'd set out to—more, even. It was time for professionals to take over. She had no doubt that Tell was more qualified. But—there was always a "but"—was he as motivated? Look how far she'd come in the space of less than a week, and that didn't count escaping from secret agents. She had the name of one of the killers. The next step was to ID his accomplice.

Anna ducked into the doorway of a boutique. Phone in hand, she pulled up her thread on the Chatterbell website: 167 traffic cameras in Lugano. Surely, with a little more luck, she could track Major Pavel and his VW Polo and learn where he'd come from, and with whom he was working. All she needed was a picture of an accomplice, not even one in perfect focus. If Clearview AI software could ID Pavel, she had every right to believe it could successfully identify his buddy, too.

She resumed her course, faster now, invigorated. She couldn't stop, not when she was only beginning. Tell could wait.

"Anna!"

Him. The vegetarian car salesman. She kept walking. *Whatever you do, don't turn around.*

"Anna!"

"Didn't you hear me, Freddy? I'm—" Anna spun. Flaxen hair. Angular cheekbones. Not Freddy Hold. Pavel Djordjevich. He stood barely ten paces away. And yes, he was one of the men who'd broken into her house with the intention of killing her.

Anna ran. Ahead, a black Audi rounded the corner, accelerating rapidly. She stopped. She had nowhere to go. The Audi drew to the curb and halted beside her. The rear door opened from the inside.

"Get in," said Pavel.

She caught a glimpse of a man inside. Hulking shoulders, black hair, dead blue eyes, dressed in a suit. Pavel's boss. If she got in, she would not get out.

Anna turned and swung her fist, catching Pavel squarely on the jaw. Harder than she'd ever hit anyone before. Pavel looked as if he hadn't felt a thing. She on the other hand had fractured a knuckle.

"Miss Bildt, please," said the man in the back seat. "Don't make a fuss. We only want to have a chat."

"Yeah, right," she said.

"You! There! Stop!"

Anna turned her head. Freddy Hold was running toward them, shouting.

"No," said Anna. "Go back. Don't!"

There was a pop, then another, like firecrackers on Midsummer Eve. Freddy Hold fell headlong onto the pavement. The driver stood beside the car, outstretched arm resting on the open door. He turned the pistol on her. She knew him, too. Her second uninvited guest. "In," he said.

Anna looked at Hold. He was dead. She could tell by the clumsy way his arms were splayed.

Before she could react, a hand struck the nape of her neck. An axe chopping wood. Her knees faltered. As she collapsed, Pavel took hold of her and guided her into the back of the Audi.

And then they were moving, the world a blur.

They were here.

CHAPTER 38

Somerset, England

His calm took him by surprise.

A man setting out to end another's life should be apprehensive no matter his determination, his "commitment," as Dr. Manley had noted. His heart rate should be elevated, perspiration dampening his forehead. His palms should leave a track of sweat on the steering wheel, his fingers tapping compulsively. All these could be expected of a man contemplating a capital crime. *Should be expected.*

But no. Simon's pulse was rock steady, sixty beats per minute. His forehead was dry, as were his palms. His grip on the wheel as light as if he were taking a Sunday drive. His vision clearer than ever. He was doing what had to be done.

It was ten when he left the M4—the Bath, Stroud exit. And, like that, he was in the country. Rolling hills. Broad meadows. Wheat. Saffron. Rugged stone walls that looked as if they'd been built by Hadrian himself.

Driving instructions offered in an Englishwoman's firm, velvety voice came via the phone mounted on the dashboard. Not quite Emma Peel, but he could hope. She guided him down the A46 through Cold Ashton, Nimlet, Tadwick—towns as quaint as they sounded.

Five miles out came the first signs he was in enemy territory. Police cars tucked discreetly into lay-bys. He slowed as he approached the gatehouse at the entry to Ditchfield. Two unmarked sedans were parked across the street. A uniformed officer stood at the gates. Either Blatt had raised the alarm or Felicity Worth knew Simon better than she had a right to.

He continued past the main entrance, Emma Peel guiding him on a ten-mile loop, west, then south, then east, and finally north. An attack on the enemy's rear flank. He left the two-lane thoroughfare at the town of Ashwicke and turned sharply onto a narrow lane skirting an old water mill and thatched shed. Trees crowded in from both sides, branches scratching the sides of the car. The track dipped. The sound of rushing water filled the car. The temperature dropped five degrees in the blink of his eye. The Range Rover forded a stream, rocking back and forth. The smell of loam and rotting leaves. The road climbed and he was crossing a field as far as the eye could see, a waning moon providing just enough illumination. Without warning, he came to a gate, the fence to either side made from metal piping. A weatherworn sign indicated he had come to PROPERTY OF M. BLACKBURN. NO TRESPASSING. He stopped the car, got out, gripped the fence with both hands, and gave it a roughing up.

With apologies to M. Blackburn, he returned to the car, then nosed forward until it touched the gate. He pressed the accelerator until the gate gave way, not bursting open but falling flat in surrender. He continued another ten minutes, speed 30 kilometers per hour. Macadam gave way to a dirt track. He craned his neck out the window, hoping to see just a little better. Even so, he managed to drive over every last rut. Ahead, above the trees, a faint glow of light. A look at the map, his position on it. He killed the headlights. Ditchfield.

A hundred meters farther on, he stopped the car. He hauled the duffel bag from the back seat and set it on the ground. With care, he removed the Kalashnikov and inserted a cartridge, chambering a round, safety on. Like riding a bike. He stood, hefting the rifle to his shoulder, sighting the gun with his right eye. It felt good. Better than good.

Full circle, then.

Simon returned the rifle to the duffel, zipped it closed, then slung it onto a shoulder.

To work.

The first shot blew out the conservatory window, showering glass all over the magnificent parquet oak floor, the bullet lodging in the antique Gobelins tapestry depicting Louis XIV's coronation. In fact, Simon had no idea which room he was firing at, what the floor inside was made of, or whether there might be a Gobelins tapestry, a Gainsborough oil, or, perhaps, as a thank-you for all she'd done on his behalf, a picture of Queen Elizabeth II.

He lay in the tall grass beneath a stand of old-growth oaks, a shadow among shadows, fifty meters from the rear of Boris Blatt's country house. Lights burned from every room. Spots lit up the estate's stone walls, throwing a halo on the gravel pathways, topiaries, and neatly manicured lawns circling the grand home. No guards to be seen, but they were there, he hoped as frightened as Blatt. A look at the CSS—the cell-site simulator. Still no outgoing calls.

Simon continued firing, targeting one window, then the next, peppering the stone walls, basically trying to raise as much hell as possible. At the last minute, he'd attached the sound suppressor. The main road was two kilometers away. The report of a high-caliber weapon would carry that distance effortlessly.

Thirty rounds gone. Simon dropped the spent magazine and inserted a fresh one. Rising, he grabbed the duffel and circled to his left at a trot, remaining inside the line of trees until he was catty-corner to the front of the house. He dropped flat, raised the Kalashnikov, and recommenced firing. Window. Front door. Drainpipe. Gutter. He was taking apart Blatt's palace piece by piece. Even with the suppressor, the noise was deafening. The French had a better word for it. *Assourdissant.* Just saying it made you wince.

He looked at the CSS. "Come on, Boris. Give Aunt Felicity a call."

Still nothing.

Another magazine gone.

Suddenly, gunfire rang out from the house, clipping leaves and branches around him. The close ones sounded like bees zipping past. He spotted muzzle bursts at windows on an upper floor. He thumbed the weapon to full-auto and sprayed the building. Three seconds exhausted his ammunition. The return fire ceased.

Drop cartridge. Reload. Pick up bag. Run. Resettle. Fire.

The light on the CSS burned red. Outgoing call to a number in central London.

About time.

Simon answered in a working-class accent. "DCI Worth's office. Wallace speaking."

"Where is she? This is Gerstmann. It's an emergency."

"Not available, sir. Message?"

"This is Gerstmann…Oh damn it, this is Boris Blatt. Give me Worth."

"I'll pass along the message. I'm sure she'll be back to you shortly."

"Listen here. My house is under assault. They're trying to kill me. I don't know how many there are. Five or six. It sounds like an army."

"Shooting at you? Did I get that right, sir?" Simon fired off a dozen rounds, shattering another window. By now other calls were being made from inside Ditchfield, either with or without Blatt's knowledge. The CSS captured every one and made sure none was completed.

"Can't you hear it? She told me she put a half-dozen men out front. I need her to get me out of here."

"One second, sir. Let me see if I can raise her on another line."

"Hurry."

Simon covered the phone and waited half a minute. "Sir, DCI Worth asked me to tell you to remain calm and that we're sending a car to you presently. Can you be ready in ten minutes?"

"I'll be dead in ten."

"Stand fast. We're sending one of our commanders to get you. Coming in the back way. Don't bring anything with you. We'll get you to a safe place."

"Just hurry."

Simon ended the call, then closed the CSS and tossed it into the duffel. One last magazine. He fired several bursts, then ran back along his path through the woods. Over an ancient wooden fence that had last provided security during the reign of Queen Victoria, out of the trees, and across a shorn wheat field to the copse of alders where he'd left the Range Rover.

Backtracking was not an option. He had no intention of being seen by the police keeping watch on the main road. Inside the car, he returned the phone to the dashboard mount. No need for the maps app. He put on the wig and the officer's cap over it, pulling the brim low over his brow, realizing too late that women officers wore different caps. Didn't matter. Blatt wouldn't have time to note the error. Simon activated the four-wheel drive and steered across the field toward Blatt's automobile hangar, its pale metallic roof visible above the stand of trees. Another band of old-growth forest served as the unofficial boundary between Ditchfield and the adjacent estate. Slower now. A latticework of branches blotted out the moonlight. He stopped, allowing his eyes to adjust to the abrupt obscurity. No telling if the police had heard the shots fired by Blatt's men from inside the manor house. In any event, time was against him. He touched the accelerator. The car lurched over uneven ground. Boughs from a gorse bush thrust through the open window, stabbing his cheek. Directly ahead lay a fallen tree. He veered to the left, the car yawing violently, then saw a route through. A moment later, he emerged from the trees a hundred meters from Blatt's house. He rounded the far side of the hangar, accelerating once he regained the pavement, circling an ornate fountain and coming to a halt steps from the main entry to the house.

The doors opened immediately. Blatt, dressed in jeans and a sweater, rushed to the car. His bodyguards remained inside, two holding Uzi submachine guns at the ready. The front door of the Range Rover was locked. Blatt hadn't gone anywhere without a chauffeur in years. He opened the rear door, put a foot inside.

"Hello, Boris."

"'Bout time." The men's eyes met. Simon pulled off the cap and wig. The Russian froze. "You?"

"This is for Harry Mason." Simon turned and threw the barrel of the Kalashnikov over the seat, firing a burst into Blatt's chest. Four bullets. Maybe five. The Russian flew backward as if yanked by unseen hands.

Simon pushed his foot to the floor, leaving a patch of rubber. He was twenty meters away when he heard the bullets pinging off the rear.

He didn't look back.

Blatt was dead.

Simon had never felt more alive.

And he saw the lights in the rearview. Blue and white strobes. Far back, but no mistaking them. The police.

The real police.

CHAPTER 39

Somerset, England

Getaway.

Simon accelerated, spinning the wheel to the right, rounding the corner of the country house. Okay, his palms were sweaty now, his heart rate closer to a hundred than sixty. A last look in the mirror. A few of the police cars had slowed by the front doors, no doubt in response to the muzzle blast from the automatic weapons fire. But, to Simon's dismay, not all of them. Another sped past the doors, giving pursuit. Simon circled the hangar, searching for his earlier track, driving faster now, recklessly. He left the pavement and climbed a grass hillock, then down the other side. A moment later, headlights danced in his rearview. The police car was gaining ground. Just his luck. Some hotshot hell-bent on his first big bust.

Simon steered into the forest, visibility going from poor to worse. Without warning, an incline. There in front of him, a barrier. The fallen tree he'd gone around with such difficulty. He yanked the wheel to the left. The Range Rover tilted wildly, at least one tire leaving the ground. The nose dove further. Simon's head banged the roof. He braked. The vehicle landed back on all four tires. He pressed the gas. Up the other side. Lights once more in his rearview. Then a jarring thud, metal striking an immovable object. *So long, pal.*

Simon emerged from the forest and into the meadow.

The police car did not follow.

He abandoned the Range Rover behind the old watermill. Five minutes to wipe down the interior, then stash the cap, wig, and uniform inside the duffel along with the machine gun, the spent mags, and the rest of his gear. First things first. He had to lose the AK. If he knew to approach the Hellbanianz gang to obtain a weapon, so did the police. Agron Bexha wasn't that good of a friend.

Simon threw the duffel over a shoulder and set out. Somewhere a church tolled the eleven o'clock hour. He pulled the duffel tight across his chest and began to jog, keeping a hundred meters between him and the road, heading east. Late-night traffic was sparse. At the first sound of an engine, he dropped flat. In time, he reached a village. At the far end of the town, he spotted a Ford parked by itself at the end of an alley. No homes nearby. Streets deserted. No lights burning. He approached the car. A Taurus, twenty years old. He was inside a half minute later. Half a minute after that, he had the engine running. Headlights functional. Half a tank of gas. A pack of Player's in the cupholder if he was so inclined. A car thief's version of a hug and a pat on the back.

He made a three-point turn and followed the road out of town until it met the M4.

Midnight. A two-hour drive to London, and don't even think about driving a kilometer over the speed limit.

Two cars boosted in one day.

Enemy dispatched.

Officially on the run.

Just like old times.

Chapter 40

Paris, France

"There," gasped Sylvie Bettencourt, fingers wrapped around a thatch of her lover's hair. "Right there. Yes, oh yes."

His name was Claude and he was a professional, which was how Sylvie preferred things. He was a beautiful man, six feet tall, with swimmer's shoulders, wine-black eyes, and of course the other thing, built to match, though all she could see of him as she gazed down over her pale body was the top of his head.

Another gasp. Sylvie arched her back. She was more aroused than she could remember. If she let herself go on like this, she'd be done in five minutes. Claude was gifted, but not that gifted. There was something else fueling her ardor, making her burn like an insatiable teenager.

It was Riske. She'd seen and heard everything as broadcast by the phone mounted on the dashboard. His words as he killed Boris Blatt, the muzzle flash of the machine gun, the man's dying grunts. Watching, she'd felt the years roll back. Once again, she was an agent in the field. Doing what was required of her. Plotting, daring, killing. There was something intensely carnal about taking a life. Something wildly stimulating in, yes, that way.

"*Lentement*," said Sylvie. *Slowly*. Her hips bucked as another wave of pleasure washed across her body. She recalled his green eyes, the power of his gaze. He was not a beautiful man, and thank God for it. No smooth swimmer's chest for him. Her breath faltered. Her muscles tensed. It really was too much, a woman her age fantasizing so.

She didn't agree with Riske's actions, not one bit. There were better ways to even the tally. Still, she had the full measure of the man. That counted for something.

"Now," she commanded.

Claude slid atop her. She needed only several thrusts to climax. And as she came, it was Simon Riske peering down at her. Sneering, the bloody bastard.

"Enough," she said.

"But I'm not…" Claude continued his fevered motions.

Sylvie slapped him. "Finish yourself off in the bathroom."

Claude rose, all petulance and hurt. The male ego—was there a more fragile construct?

"There's a present for you on the entry table," she called after him, watching his perfectly formed rear disappear into the master bath. A thousand euros. Cash, of course. She had little doubt that unfriendly eyes scrutinized her every private account. What the boys in Moscow wouldn't do if they knew of her bedroom habits.

She rose from the bed, her body tingling, snatched her black silk robe, and tied it around her. She walked to the window and pulled back the drapes, but only a sliver. The Eiffel Tower, lit from top to bottom, was a stone's throw away. At the far end of the Champ de Mars, the dome of Les Invalides, lit warmly, a tribute to France's military might. Her gaze fell to the street below, to the shadows of the men loitering on the walkway in front of her building. Were they the same who'd followed her in New York? Did it matter?

Her phone rang. Who could it be at this time of night, she wondered angrily. She snatched it up, saw the number, felt a hole in her stomach open. Did he have eyes inside her house, too?

"Business hours end at seven," she said.

"I expected a warmer welcome." It was him. The Cellist.

"Then call your watchdogs off. I won't stand for it."

"You've been a naughty girl."

"Is that what Borzoi has told you?"

"It isn't the theft we mind so much as the carelessness."

"I don't know what you're talking about."

"The Persian in Beverly Hills told us everything. He even turned over the wire instructions you'd written on his business card. New York. Last month in Uruguay. Must I go on?"

"You must."

"You used to cover your tracks far more thoroughly. It makes me wonder what other mistakes you're making. I'm worried."

"Are you threatening me?"

"I wouldn't dream of it. I know how much you mean to Michael even after all these years."

"I do my job well."

"Unrivaled," said the Cellist. "I'll be the first to say so."

"What do you want, Sergei?"

"Tell me, Svetlana, what's left in your budget for the month?"

"Three hundred million, give or take."

"Plans?"

"A horse property in Andalusia. A building in Punta del Este. A Rembrandt up for private sale in Rotterdam."

"Michael loves his Rembrandts."

"Maybe he should look at them for once."

"I look at them for him."

"Then I couldn't be happier."

"He's away till the first week of September. I'll give you until then."

"I'm sorry. I don't understand."

"To pay back what you've taken. Let's choose a nice round number. Say, one hundred million dollars. Wire it to the general account. Tag it as 'expenses.'"

"Even if I had that much money, I wouldn't send it. This is blackmail."

"Then why don't we set a time and date now. Moscow's lovely in the fall. I'm sure Michael would enjoy hosting you at his dacha."

"Sergei, please. This is absurd."

"One hundred million," said the Cellist. "Oh, and Svetlana, *Indonesia . . . really?*"

The call ended.

Sylvie returned to the window. The figures on the street were no longer there. And no, she hadn't imagined them. Borzoi. The Cellist. The net was closing.

She caught a glimpse of herself in the window. A moment ago, she'd been romanticizing her past, reliving her days as an operative. Had she forgotten all she'd learned? She used to be relentless, remorseless, pitiless. And now? She was soft. The Cellist knew it.

No more.

Phone in hand, she scrolled through her contacts, stopping at the letter *S*. The SON Group. Tel Aviv, Israel.

Founded by General Zev Franck, pioneer of Israel's targeted assassination program, now run by his daughter, herself a former Mossad agent—a kindred spirit, Sylvie liked to think—the SON Group was known to law enforcement and intelligence agencies as a paradigm in electronic and digital surveillance. Ostensibly, the company's cutting-edge software was sold only to parties dedicated to tracking down terrorists and lawbreakers. A force for good, then. For the right price, however, other discreet parties might be accepted as clients.

"Yes. Good evening, Mrs. Bettencourt." A gravelly, unflappable female voice. Not a hint of surprise at being woken at two o'clock in the morning.

"Hello, Ms. Pine. I'm sorry to disturb you."

"How may we help?"

No pleasantries. No idle chatter. Sylvie wouldn't have it any other way. "I need to learn the current location of one of my associates." "Associates" meaning an individual who'd been targeted with the SON Group's malware.

"Our contract calls for level one penetration. Sound. Video, when possible. Geolocation is another matter."

"It's an emergency," said Sylvie.

"I respect your situation. However, providing you such information would alter our professional relationship. We prefer to remain a supplier, not an actor. Should anything happen to your associate, we would be in part responsible."

"I can assure you that nothing of the kind will occur."

"I believe you. Still—"

"In fact, it's a law enforcement matter."

"Oh?" The change in tone was immediate.

"The associate in question is wanted by the authorities. He is believed to have committed a homicide. You would, in fact, be helping the police."

"Your intention is to use this information to help local law enforcement apprehend a suspect?"

"Precisely."

"I see from your file that you are currently monitoring several associates. Which one are you interested in?"

Sylvie read off the number of Simon Riske's cellular phone, prefaced by the country code.

"An English number."

"I'd be advising the London police."

"We maintain excellent contacts with the Met. Would it be better if we reach out on your behalf…to preserve your anonymity?"

"I appreciate the offer," said Sylvie. "There are, however, a few wrinkles that I need to explain personally."

"I see," said Danni Pine. "Your request is unusual."

Sylvie could hear the "but" in her voice. An exception might be made.

"As I said, I can guarantee your firm's integrity will not come into question. No one will hear of the matter beyond you and I."

"Your word, Mrs. Bettencourt?"

"You have it."

"There will be an additional fee."

"But of course."

"One hundred thousand euros."

Sylvie bit back a rebuke. She had already paid five hundred thousand euros per "associate." Leave it to the Israelis to shake every last shekel loose. "I'll wire the money in the morning."

"Of course you will. I'm installing a piece of software on your phone that will allow you to track the location of your associate for the next twenty-four hours."

"Now?"

"Already done."

Sylvie watched as a new icon appeared on the screen. A globe. No title beneath it. "Just twenty-four hours?" she inquired.

"I'm sure you can contact the police in that time," said Danni Pine.

CHAPTER 41

What in God's name are you doing here?"

Simon opened his eyes. He lay on a leather divan in the living room of D'Artagnan Moore's home in Maida Vale, a leafy residential neighborhood in northwest London. A ray of sun peeked through the drapes. The antique Thomas Gardner clock above the fireplace read 5:55. Three hours of sleep was better than nothing.

"How'd you get in?" demanded Moore. "When...? Why? And what about my security system? Oh, to hell with it. I'll be in the kitchen."

"Coffee," called Simon as Moore left the room. "Black. Three sugars."

Simon wandered into the kitchen five minutes later. Two porcelain mugs brimming with coffee sat on the island. Moore stood at his range, frying up a dozen strips of bacon. "I'm waiting," he said, not bothering to look over his shoulder.

Simon picked up a mug and retreated to the table in the sun nook. "You remember what I used to do."

"I thought you were a pickpocket who stole the occasional car."

"The Artful Dodger, you mean."

"The French version," said Moore.

"Not hardly," said Simon. "You know it."

Moore placed the bacon on a pad of paper to dry, then removed a half-dozen eggs from the refrigerator and set them next to a mixing bowl. "I don't like to think about it. Doesn't match with the Simon Riske I know. There is such a thing as a doorbell. God forbid, you might have called."

"Not the best idea," said Simon.

190

"Because?"

"Because."

One-handed, Moore cracked the eggs, dropped them into the bowl, discarding the shells in the waste bin. "Scrambled all right?"

"Scramble away. Oh, and I'll help you install a better security system."

Moore whisked the eggs for a full minute, then poured them into a large heated frying pan. "Am I allowed to ask where you've been? Your clothes are filthy. Your face is scratched. You look like a wreck. And you smell to high heaven."

"No comment," said Simon.

"It's about the fire, isn't it?"

Simon eyed Moore from beneath a cautious brow. "Maybe some cheese in the eggs. Boursin? Oh, and chives."

"This isn't Claridge's," said Moore. All the same, he flung open the refrigerator door and peeked his head inside. "I have Irish cheddar. No chives."

"Sold."

Moore cut a fat slice of cheese, then chopped it into squares and dropped them into the pan, all the while tending to the eggs. "Last thing you said when I left was 'He's going to pay.'"

Simon looked at Moore, then past him. He was staring into Boris Blatt's eyes as he pulled the trigger.

"He did," said Simon, too quietly.

"Pardon me?"

"Listen, I'm not hungry," said Simon. "If I could use your shower."

"Guest bath, if you please. Throw your clothing in the wash while you're at it. And Simon?"

"Yeah, I know. I'm going to tell you everything."

Simon found D'Art glued to the television when he returned to the kitchen.

"Blatt was sixty-seven years old, a naturalized British citizen," said a news commentator. *"He immigrated to England in 2010, after making a career in the aluminum and precious metals sector and becoming known as one of the first oligarchs in the newly democratic Russia. After his conviction on charges of racketeering, he entered the Witness Protection program . . ."*

Simon refilled his cup of coffee, looking on as a helicopter, or probably a drone, flew over Ditchfield. He counted ten police cars in the country home's forecourt and a swarm of blue uniforms.

"Why?" asked D'Art.

"If I answer that question, I'll be making you an accessory."

"Damn it all, Simon. What have you done?"

"Restored order to the universe."

Moore's response was a scowl that could strip the paint off one of Simon's cars. "What am I to say to that?" He shook his head. "You didn't see the entire segment. That's not the half of it."

Simon picked up the remote and found another news channel. Same story, only worse.

"Police have given the name of Simon Riske as a person of interest."

A photograph taken from his driver's license filled the screen.

"Don't make a joke about it not being from your good side," said D'Art. "You're in deep trouble."

Simon checked his phone. Four calls from Felicity Worth. One from Vikram Singh. Another from his solicitor. An even dozen from Lucy Brown. And last, a call from Dr. Manley. Maybe doctors did worry about their patients. "They can't get me on this," he said, turning off the television.

"Sure about that, are you?" said Moore, with disdain. "You're farther down this road than I thought."

Simon didn't answer. The machine gun, the uniform, the wig, the cap, and the duffel bag were all residing comfortably at the bottom of the Thames a few kilometers upriver from The Compleat Angler, weighted down by a ten-kilo stone. Blatt's bodyguards wouldn't talk. If word leaked out that they had cooperated with the police, they'd never work again.

"D'Art, I need a place to lie low."

"A moment ago you were afraid of making me an accessory. Now I'm a member of your gang. What's next? Do I get a lovely tattoo like yours on my forearm?"

"D'Art..."

"You think this is going to blow over? This is murder, I believe with premeditation. Every policeman in London is looking for you. The only reason I'm not calling them myself is I don't want to lose my best investigator."

"Self-interest rears its ugly head."

"And that maybe Blatt deserved it—if not from you then someone else."

"An arbiter for justice."

"Sod off," said D'Art. "What the hell are you going to do?"

"There's a way out of this."

D'Art shot him a skeptical look as he put the dishes in the sink, ran hot water over them. All the while, he angrily mumbled a string of epithets, most of them about how someone could be so stupid.

"I had to do it," said Simon.

"You're going to tell me it was for Harry Mason."

"In part. Not all. It's about me. About the code."

Moore turned, wiping his hands on a towel. "'The code'?"

"A guy hits you, you hit him back harder. You don't just stand your ground. You take his."

"Correct me if I'm wrong, Simon, but didn't you start this? You and your quest for the holy gearbox?"

"He had something I needed. It was Blatt who started it."

"Because he wouldn't give you what you wanted? It was his property. He could damn well do what he wanted with it."

"He tried to make me look bad. He let the buyer know it was out there, but I'd failed to find it."

"He impugned your reputation…so you killed him. Fair enough."

"It was his way of getting even for what I'd done to him."

"He was pushing back."

"Damn straight. Making me look like a fuckup. I had to get the gearbox. Don't you see?"

"And so, 'the code.'"

"Yes," said Simon.

"He pushed back by torching your shop. You pushed back by shooting him dead." Moore put his head back and laughed, with outrage, not mirth. "What next?"

"Game over. He's dead."

"And you won. Congratulations. Your prize is a life sentence in one of Her Majesty's worst lockups."

"I did what I had to do."

Moore dropped the towel on the counter. "You really haven't left that world behind."

"D'Art, come on…"

"I don't know that I shouldn't be afraid of you."

Simon wanted to grab D'Art by the shoulders and shake some sense into him. How could he not understand? About some things there could be no gray area. No one fucked with Simon Riske. It came down to that. If he didn't have his honor—whatever that meant—he didn't have anything. He drew a breath, looking around him. At the professional chef's kitchen, the enormous flat-screen television on the wall, the Chagall prints. The comfortable life. Where was D'Art when he was fifteen? On the street dodging a rival gang's hitters? Chasing a deadbeat down a dark alley and beating him with a lead pipe until he came up with the vig? Simon thought not. D'Artagnan Russell McKenzie Moore was at Harrow in his tutor's chambers sipping sherry and opining about Sir Thomas More and his inflexible conscience. He hoped D'Art remembered that the sainted More'd had a code, too, and right or wrong, he'd died for it.

"You don't get it," said Simon.

"Don't I?"

Simon stood, came face-to-face with his friend. "That world doesn't leave you behind. Ever."

Moore looked at him for a long minute. Finally, he nodded. Simon wasn't sure if it was because at last he understood or he'd given up trying.

"About that place to lie low," said Moore. "I've got an idea."

CHAPTER 42

Royal Tunbridge Wells, England

The racing-green Bentley Continental swept along High Street in Royal Tunbridge Wells, top down, navigating traffic through the center of town.

"Came across it in the paper a while back," said Moore. "Foreclosure. Place has been empty for a year. To be auctioned off."

"You never mentioned it," said Simon.

"Didn't want to bring up any difficult memories." Moore glanced in his direction. "Should I have?"

"No," said Simon. "You were right not to, all things considered. In fact, thank you."

The car slowed. To the left was the Pantiles, a Georgian colonnade, long ago a popular walking street for Londoners and toffs, recently renovated to attract those same. Traffic thinned. Moore sped up. A minute later, they were on the far side of town, heading into the countryside. The sun was shining, the air rich with the scent of cut grass and hay. It was, Simon decided, a beautiful morning to be the most wanted man in England.

Moore turned left down a narrow lane, towering oak trees on either side providing a generous canopy. The road curved this way and that. There was the magnificent towering oak, centuries old, where he'd played Robin Hood with his chums (he was the Sheriff of Nottingham, of course), and the hedgerow where he'd dug a tunnel to hide in when in trouble with his father. Simon shifted in his seat, feeling more than a twinge of unease. Moore slowed and swung the car into a long driveway. At its end stood a rambling country house, red bricks and eaves and three chimneys, plenty of windows.

"Do you remember it?" asked Moore, bringing the Bentley to a stop, moving the gearshift into park.

"They've redone it," said Simon. "Used to be covered with wisteria, top to bottom. I think they've added a room."

"And it happened here?"

"The barn," said Simon. "It's around back."

"Maybe this was a bad idea."

"I'm fine."

"Sure?"

"Life," said Simon, putting his hand on D'Art's shoulder, meaning the good, the bad, and everything in between. No one got a free ride.

"I called the property agent," said Moore. "No viewings. Everything's virtual these days."

"You're sure?" Simon climbed out of the car and appraised the house. Different, yes, but the home of his youth.

"No one will see you here," said Moore. "Couldn't ask the man for a key. I figured you could find a way in, alarm notwithstanding."

"I guess you really do want one of these tattoos on your arm."

Moore laughed politely, then grew serious. "The police aren't going to stop looking for you."

Simon nodded.

"If you need an alibi…"

"That wouldn't be right."

"Against the code?"

"Something like that."

"So?"

"I'm working on it."

All houses have their secrets. Windows that stick unless you give the pane a knock. Panels in closets that lead to the attic. Hideouts in the basement. And Simon, circling his former home, knew where at least one such secret was hidden. He crossed the back lawn, head down, the barn a blur in the corner of his eye. He continued to a far corner of the house, trampling a fallow flower bed beneath the kitchen windows. At first, he couldn't see it. A thick coat of white paint covered the hatch set low on the wall, hardly above the ground. A second look. Yes, still there.

A smile. Yet, regret quickly took the place of joy. Part of him had hoped he wouldn't find it.

With the help of his Swiss Army knife, he cut through the paint, exposing the outline of the hatch, one meter square. A few thwacks with a stone freed the latch. He needed another half minute of yanking, pulling, and cursing before the hatch surrendered. The beam from his phone's light illuminated the cellar. The chute that had once sped coal to a storage bin had been removed even before Simon and his father had moved in. It was a short drop to the cellar floor, no more than ten feet.

Simon wiped the dust off his trousers and shone the light around the room. Tall beamed ceiling, concrete trusses, cobwebs. There wasn't much to see. A few discarded pieces of furniture, boxes coated with dust, a crate of Tang drink mix that might have been left by the Apollo astronauts themselves. Nothing that struck a memory.

He climbed the stairs to the kitchen one step at a time, testing each. The door was locked. No keyhole. A tumbler operated from the opposite side. Still, he yanked on the doorknob to little effect. He retreated to the cellar, scouring the floor for anything that might help. No crowbar, but a steel rod of indeterminate origin and strength, tapered to a sharp point.

Five minutes stabbing and digging at the doorjamb removed enough of the frame for him to pry the bolt free of it. The door swung open to reveal the back of an armoire. More shoving, like Sisyphus and his boulder. By the time he was able to squeeze into the kitchen, his shirt was soaked with perspiration.

And so, he thought, hands on his hips, smelling the air. Home.

Simon was not one for sentiment. It helped that there were only a few family snaps to pore over, also that he kept his past a secret to all but his closest friends. The fact was that he had little opportunity, and less inclination, to share teary, long-winded reminiscences about the good old days. But here, standing in this place, it was impossible not to succumb.

The house had been remodeled from top to bottom. The last occupants appeared to have been as enthusiastic in their spending as his father was. He'd never seen a refrigerator so big, a range with ten burners, or a walk-in freezer, which, he noted, still boasted enough food to victual a platoon, not to mention a forgotten case of Stolichnaya. A gift from Blatt's ghost?

He left the kitchen and made a tour of the downstairs: living room, den, study. With every step he expected to feel a jolt, to spot a long-lost possession that might trigger an avalanche of memories. He'd lived in the house from about the age of seven until twelve. Roughly five years that constituted his childhood. Happy years. Things changed drastically upon his move to France. There was no patina of fairy dust sprinkled over his time there.

But no, apart from the home's layout, nothing appeared familiar.

Still, he poked his head into every room, opening closets, peeking in corners. When he came to the front staircase, he charged up the steps two at a time, like the old days. He stopped on the second-floor landing and looked back, conjuring an image of the boy he'd been bounding up the stairs after him. Schoolboy attire. Gray slacks. Navy-blue blazer. Necktie askew. Hair a mess. Knees most likely scraped.

It was a bittersweet exercise. That boy had the world in front of him. A child of privilege, blissfully naive, spoiled even if he didn't know it yet—a child who hadn't learned to appreciate how extraordinary his ordinary life was.

Then, like that, it had all been pulled out from under him.

Instead of the boy, Simon saw men in blue uniforms coursing through the hallways, searching desks, rifling through drawers, and later taking those desks and dressers and, well, everything else away. Too clearly, he recalled the fear, the not knowing, the uncertainty that filled his stomach with ice and made his voice quiver when he spoke. No conjuring necessary. And the silence when he asked his father to explain what was happening, and more importantly, to an anxious twelve-year-old, what was coming next.

Simon advanced along the corridor until he reached his bedroom. A moment's inspection revealed it had been turned into some type of studio. An easel stood in the corner, a drop cloth balled up nearby. Nothing else, thank God. He closed the door, happy to have dodged that one. A sighting of *The Tower Treasure* or any of his old mysteries might have done him in.

And then he caught it.

A hint of bergamot, lemon, and some exotic spice he couldn't name. A grenade might as well have gone off in his head.

It was a smell, not an image, that blew open the floodgates.

He crossed the hall and opened the door to the master bedroom…*his father's bedroom*. Stronger now. He marched into the master bath, in its newest incarnation a temple of marble and glass. Oh yes, he knew that scent. It was his father's. Acqua di Parma.

He searched the medicine cabinet and the drawers. All were bare. A flight of imagination, then? No. He could taste the scent deep in his nostrils. Well, why not? Thousands of men wore the Italian cologne. Still, to Simon, it would forever belong to Anthony Riske. After all these years, he realized, it was all he had left of his father.

And so Simon came face-to-face with it. Had he expected otherwise? Of course he had, fool that he was.

A Sunday morning long ago.

Simon woke too early. Sunday was family day, the one day he spent with his father, from dawn till dusk. Of late, the time had grown in significance. Anthony Riske's business (Simon wasn't certain what exactly it was he did—something to do with metals and commodities) was growing, which meant that he was home later each evening and left earlier each morning. Simon rushed downstairs wearing his West Ham jersey, claret and blue. Like other twelve-year-olds, he was football mad—English football—and his father had surprised him with seats to the day's match against Chelsea. A proper London derby. From the start, then, a special day.

Sundays meant that Dad was in charge of breakfast. Pancakes, bacon (crispy, the American way!), muffins, orange juice—all to the accompaniment of Verdi or Rossini. "La donna è mobile" and all that. And so it wasn't just the absence of appetizing scents wafting up the back stairs that signaled something was amiss but the silence. Where was Pavarotti?

The kitchen was deserted, lights off, as still as midnight.

"Dad," Simon called.

No one answered.

Back up the stairs, down the hall, not running, not yet. The door to his father's bedroom was closed. It was never closed. Simon flung it open. The bed was empty, sheets turned back, barely slept in. A pack of Silk Cuts, a gold lighter, and a pouch of Fisherman's Friend mints—the heavy smoker's trinity—sat on the night table. The bathroom, too, was empty.

The first pangs of panic rose in his stomach.

Anthony Riske, forty years old, a stickler for schedules, a mostly benevolent taskmaster, stern but loving, steady, reliable...not one to leave Simon alone.

The search began in earnest.

A race through the house, Simon's voice anxious, then angry. "Dad? Dad! Where are you?"

But no matter how loudly or how often he yelled, no one answered.

Finally, there was only the barn to check.

He found his father hanging from a rafter, a coarse rope around his neck. There was no question but that he was dead. The eyes open far too wide, bulging, the tongue thrust out of an open mouth. Nevertheless, Simon had wrapped his arms around his father's legs and tried to lift him, if only to relieve the pressure for a moment. It was no good. Simon was a small boy for his age, not especially strong. Still he tried and he tried. What else was he to do?

CHAPTER 43

The monsignor was waiting as Simon pushed open the door and entered the barn for the first time since. He was a slight, raw-boned man—sixty, seventy, who could tell?—thinning gray hair, beard uncut in years, dressed in jailhouse dungarees. The face of a saint: torment and salvation warring in his blue eyes. His name was Paul Deschutes. Once he'd been Father Paul Deschutes, an ordained Jesuit priest, father to a flock in the French city of Montpellier. But that was before he fell away from God and into a life of crime, before he was sentenced to life imprisonment. Before he met Simon in a subterranean jail cell in a notorious penitentiary named Les Baumettes just outside Marseille.

"More than twenty-five years," said Simon. "I can't get over it."

"But you have. Look at you. You've put it behind you nicely."

"So you think."

"Everyone thinks."

And they did, the ones who knew. It was true. His most brilliant deception.

"He wouldn't leave without saying goodbye."

"Yet he did."

"No," said Simon. "I don't believe it."

"The police investigated. There was no one else."

"Sure they did," said Simon, not having it. The police, in his experience, were never to be trusted.

"He was in trouble with the authorities," said the monsignor. "He'd lost his business, his possessions. He faced time in prison."

"He was never charged."

"Because he was dead."

Simon gazed at the rafters. He saw him there for an instant, the body hanging where he'd found him, legs turning slowly. And his face...the pain, the terror.

A twelve-year-old never forgets.

"Can't you forgive him?"

"I don't need to," said Simon. "He didn't kill himself."

"So then what are you saying?"

Simon searched the monsignor's eyes, pleading for him to provide the answer. He saw nothing. He would have to find the answer himself.

"Simon...my son. You must let it go." A smile to lend succor. A priest's greatest gift. It did no good.

"He didn't leave a note."

"Simon..."

"If he loved me, he would have said goodbye."

Simon looked up, expecting an answer. Advice, counsel, something to ease the pain. The monsignor had fled.

The barn was empty.

It had been all along.

Chapter 44

Haute-Savoie, France

Anna opened her eyes.

A tall ceiling. Walls of rough stone. A woolen blanket pulled to her chin. Her head felt fuzzy, her mouth as dry as sandpaper. With effort, she sat up. She was alone in a spartan room. Light came from narrow windows high on the wall. And quiet. Anna could feel the stillness of the place.

She threw back the blanket and stood. She was naked. Her clothes, hastily folded, sat on a camp chair. Her bracelets were there, too. A bottle of mineral water rested on the nightstand. Thonon from Thonon-les-Bains, France. *France? What about Chur? What about Switzerland?* She knew she should feel terrified, but more than anything, she was thirsty. She opened the bottle and drank half down.

Better now.

Time to take stock of her situation.

She was alive. She was unharmed. She appeared to be in a safe environment. It was certainly clean. It was then she noticed the distinct scent of pine in the air. She could taste it. And dry...wherever she was, the air was very dry.

A dull throbbing pressed at her skull. Pavel and the axe he'd delivered to the back of her neck. Her last recollection was of hands latching on to her shoulder, thrusting her into the rear seat. Then a jab in the arm. And yes, there was a bruise below her shoulder. She remembered nothing after that.

Anna moved a chair nearer the window. She climbed up, then on tiptoes to see out. She gasped. Not from fear—quite the opposite.

Wonder. Mountains. A breathtaking alpine vista. All around her, craggy peaks rose into a cloudy sky, some dusted with snow. Nearer, a wooded meadow, a lake, the water a milky green.

The door was locked, as she'd expected. She dressed, then made her bed and sat on it, placing a pillow against the wall. Her phone was gone. She remembered the message from Chatterbell. The Russian GRU was monitoring the thread about her father's murder. *Praemonitus, praemunitus.* Forewarned is forearmed. She should have told Hold. He didn't deserve to die for her.

Time passed. An hour? Longer? She returned to the window over and over, hoping for some sun that might allow her to gauge the shadows. If anything, the day grew gloomier as it progressed. To her surprise, she saw a line of hikers emerge from the forest. All men, rucksacks on their backs, jogging at a trying clip. They reminded her of her own CrossFit club, the morning warm-up runs, four times around the block, before starting the WOD, the workout of the day. She watched them draw nearer. The casual style—shorts, T-shirts, some with long hair, beards—was a ruse. They were military. She knew it.

A voice called out. The men halted, dropped to the ground, and began doing push-ups. Ten, twenty…Anna lost count. The voice again. Another order. But what language? Not English, not German, not French. Russian, of course. Mountain climbers, then burpees. The leader calling cadence. Another command. The men removed their packs and broke ranks. Training was complete.

Anna almost didn't hear the door to her room open.

"Lunch."

It was Pavel, he of the iron hands and Teflon face.

"I haven't had breakfast," said Anna.

"Food's not bad," he said. "Roast chicken today."

"I'm vegan."

"Of course you are," said Pavel. He stepped inside the room. No workout gear for him. Blue twill trousers, black T-shirt. He tried on a smile. "How's your hand?"

"How's your face?"

"You throw a good punch."

"What are we? Friends? You killed Freddy Hold. You killed my father. You tried to kill me."

The smile left his face. "Follow me."

Pavel led Anna down a long, dim hallway, sconces every twenty paces, half of them working. Chipped paint hung off the walls like cobwebs. The carpet was clean but threadbare. Down a flight of stairs, across a wide lobby. She was in a hotel, or what had been one once years ago. There was a front desk but no concierge. No staff to be seen.

"Where are we?" she asked.

"The mountains."

"But where? France?" said Anna, thinking of her bottle of Thonon mineral water.

"Could be. Or Germany. Switzerland. Maybe the Pyrenees."

"No, we're in France."

Anna struggled to keep pace. The air was thinner here. The altitude six thousand feet at least.

"Enough questions, Anna Christina." And then Pavel lunged at her, as if on the attack, only to stop himself and laugh, before resuming their walk.

Anna calmed herself. It was not his actions, juvenile as they were, but the menace in his voice that sent a chill down her spine. He would kill her without a second thought.

A broad corridor led from the lobby. Through double doors and into the largest dining room she'd ever seen. Row after row of tables for four, all with pale green tablecloths. She counted twenty men, only a few women, seated. All eyes lifted to her but only for a moment. They had better things to think about.

Her lunch was an omelette aux fines herbes, pommes frites, and ratatouille. Yes, they were in France, thought Anna. Someone had forgotten to tell the chef they had a secret visitor. The altitude, the rugged, granite peaks, the snow even in summer. Anna guessed they were near Chamonix, not far from Mont Blanc.

She ate alone. Pavel sat nearby. The lingua franca was American-accented English. Anna knew better. There were too many men who looked a little too much like Pavel. The flaxen hair, razor-sharp cheek-bones, the sloe-eyed glances. She might as well be in Ivan the Terrible's mess hall. Somehow she had found herself in a camp of Russian soldiers or spies or something in between the two. Her only question was why they were pretending to be Americans. Not pretending, she thought, having a belated insight. Practicing.

"Miss Bildt." It was the man from the car, Pavel's boss.

"You are?"

"Vadim. We met briefly."

"I remember."

"How are you feeling?"

Anna put down her fork. "Are you serious?"

"Of course I am serious. Your welfare is my concern."

"What do you want?"

"To speak with you about your father."

"You should have asked him before you blew him up."

"No need," said Vadim. "We knew what he was up to. You, you're another story."

"You're the same as the police," said Anna. "I'll tell you what I told them. We never discussed his business. Look at me. Do I look like I care about banking? If he weren't my father, I never would've talked to him at all. People like him are ruining the world. They're responsible for killing off the fisheries, for ruining the atmosphere, for…Oh, forget it. So there. I told you. I can't help you, whatever it is you want. Can I go home now?"

"A fine performance, Miss Bildt," said Vadim. "We'll see if it holds up."

"It's the truth."

"That's what they all say."

"Fuck off."

"They say that, too." Vadim leaned closer. "Do you know what else they say?"

"No," said Anna, too defiantly.

"'Please stop,'" he whispered. "If you'll excuse me."

Anna lifted her fork. Her hand was shaking. Quickly, she put it down. It didn't matter. Her appetite was gone. She watched Vadim walk from the room. Pavel remained behind, her personal warden. She reminded herself that she'd been in prison before, and one a sight worse than this. No omelettes aux fines herbes in Brazil. She'd made it through then. She would make it through now.

Hers not to reason why. Hers not to do or die. Hers to get the hell out of here.

Escape.

CHAPTER 45

Royal Tunbridge Wells, England

The doorbell rang at two twenty in the afternoon.

Simon ignored it. A buyer coming to check the house without consulting the leasing agent. A second try, the chimes too loud for Simon's taste. If they had a key, they'd have entered by now. He moved to the landing at the top of the stairs. Through glass panes on either side of the door, he spied a woman's legs. High heels. A handbag. He considered calling D'Art, asking him what the hell was going on, when his phone rang. He checked the caller. A surprise, to say the least.

"Don't tell me," said Simon. "You need help installing the gearbox."

"I wouldn't know," said Sylvie Bettencourt. "3387 and I have parted ways."

"What next? Another Hockney? Any Van Goghs coming up for sale?"

"I'll be happy to tell you," she said, "if you'll just open the door."

"Pardon?"

"You're not inviting guests in?" said Sylvie playfully. Weren't they the best of friends? "I'm here."

"Where?"

"At your front door."

Simon kneeled to get a better look. "I don't have a front door. My shop burned down a few days ago."

"I know. Word spreads. I meant to say, I'm here...at the front door of the house in Tunbridge Wells. Excuse me, *Royal* Tunbridge Wells these days. A charming country home, red bricks, three chimneys. Come now, Simon. No need to keep up the charade. It's only me."

"And you want?"

"I have an offer for you."

"I told you in California. I'm my own boss."

"That was before you were wanted for murder."

Simon held the phone at his side. How far had word gotten? Blatt wasn't dead a full day. He considered his play. She was here. She knew he was wanted for Blatt's murder. It didn't matter how she'd found him. The only question was why she'd come.

A welcoming smile as he opened the door. "Come in."

Sylvie Bettencourt slipped past, closer than he would have liked. She was wearing a mint-green skirt and white cotton blouse, unbuttoned for effect. Her blond hair was, as usual, in perfect disarray. Her eyes, however, told a different story. Red rimmed and fatigued. No makeup could conceal the dark circles. "Did I barge in on your secret hideout?"

"Something like that."

"I'd have thought you kept a place in the city. A little boat on the Thames for assignations. A loft in a rougher part of town, say King's Cross." She stepped nearer, ran a hand along his shirt, made sure his collar was just so.

"Not my thing," said Simon, made uncomfortable by her display of familiarity. "You're the spy. Or you were."

"Yes, I was. See? I can tell the truth. Your turn."

"You're here. You mentioned something about me being wanted for murder. Seems as if you already know the truth."

"So much nicer when it comes from your mouth," said Sylvie. "Aren't you going to offer me something to drink?"

"As a matter of fact, I happen to have some vodka."

"Now, that is a coincidence."

Simon led the way to the kitchen, Sylvie close behind.

"Not what you'd expect from the outside," she said, taking in the modern décor, the Italian furnishings. "Très chic."

"The owners were forced to renovate when 'Royal' was added to the name of the town. City ordinance."

Sylvie set her purse on the kitchen island. "Marco Pierre White would feel right at home."

"I don't know him."

"Gordon Ramsay with a touch of class."

Simon grabbed a bottle of Stoli from the freezer and poured them each a drink, neat. "Cheers."

"*Za zdorovye.*" Sylvie made a tour of the kitchen, a hand to inspect the granite counters, a look into the cupboards. An expression of disappointment…or was it confusion?

"Something wrong?" asked Simon.

"Just fine," she answered.

"Feel free to tell me how you found me. Whenever you're ready."

Sylvie finished her drink with a flourish. "You must have some idea."

"Only one person knows I'm here. I can't imagine he'd tell you. Has to be my phone."

"I hope you'll accept my apologies."

"Malware?"

"Prior to Pebble Beach. I can't spend a hundred million dollars of my client's money without knowing a little something about the seller."

"Dez Hamilton was the seller."

"He was the owner. You were the seller. Him I didn't have to worry about. You I did."

"Have you cleaned out my bank accounts, too?"

"Please, Simon." He should know that she, for one, did not need to clear out anyone's accounts. "I rather think it's you who has some explaining to do."

"How much do you know?"

"Most of it."

Simon was well acquainted with malware. A powerful piece of spying software would effectively turn possession of his phone over to her. She could access his apps, read his emails, see his pictures (enjoy, Madame Bettencourt!), listen in on his phone calls, and, via a hot mic, be witness to every word he spoke aloud.

"I am sorry about Mr. Mason," she said, almost believably. "I know he was a friend."

"And Boris Blatt?"

"I'm not sorry about him at all."

"You knew him?"

"We had several run-ins over the years. He wasn't a spy, by the way. We'd never take a lout like him."

"I'd have thought he was a client."

"In a way, he was," said Sylvie. "Years ago. He didn't follow the rules. We kicked him out. Me, the government. England took him. Someone I know will want to thank you."

Simon finished his drink, then collected the glasses and placed them in the sink. Enough chitchat. "Have we come to the reason for your visit?"

"I'm getting you out of here. The country, I mean. I'm making sure the police don't get their hands on you."

"Because?"

"Because," said Sylvie. Reason enough.

"Patience isn't my strong suit," said Simon.

"Nor mine. I have a plane waiting. We'll be at the airstrip in an hour. In France an hour after that."

"Paris?"

"A rustic little cabin in the mountains not far from Chamonix. No prying eyes, I promise."

Simon didn't like the idea. "I'm not interested in going hiking, but thanks all the same."

"This isn't a vacation."

"Sylvie, this has gone far enough. I meant what I said about not working for someone else."

"I'm not sure you have a choice."

"Pardon me?"

"You're coming with me."

"I don't think so."

Sylvie took her phone from her purse. A moment to dredge up what she was looking for. Her eyes narrowed. A pleased expression as she handed him the phone.

"What is this?" he asked.

"History," she replied. "Yours."

Simon brought the screen closer. A video was playing. Night. Inside an automobile. The camera mounted on the dashboard. His car, or rather the London police's. Their dashboard, too, the phone placed there to give him directions. The car stopped moving. The rear door opened. Boris Blatt appeared. Words were exchanged, the volume too low to make them out. No worries, he thought acidly. It was the pictures that mattered. The barrel of a machine gun swung into view. Simon's face in profile illuminated by the dome lamp. A burst of fire point-blank into Blatt's chest.

Simon handed the phone back. No need to go any further.

"What do you want?"

"You, of course. Your skills."

"I get paid for my work," he said. "Generously."

"You'll earn every penny."

"I don't have my passport," he said.

"I'll get you a new one. With a new name. Your choice. You can choose your country, too. Within reason. Shall we?"

Simon hesitated. He was taking a big step. He remembered what he'd said to D'Art about not leaving that life. Until now, everything he'd done to obtain the gearbox for Dez Hamilton had been part of the job. Well, plus a little. Avenging Harry Mason was part of his code. There was no question about whether he'd done the right thing. What Sylvie Bettencourt was proposing, however, was something else entirely. He had no illusions about which side of the law she was on.

In the end, the decision was simple enough. She had a tape of him killing another man. He had no choice.

"Do I have time to get my jacket?"

CHAPTER 46

Royal Tunbridge Wells, England

He's in."

Nessa Kenyon watched from an upstairs window as the sedan pulled away, Simon seated in the rear next to Sylvie Bettencourt, an unknown man—most probably a GRU operative working out of the London embassy—at the wheel.

"I'll track him as long as I can," said Danni Pine, on the phone from her headquarters in the hills above Tel Aviv. "She won't let him keep his phone for long, not after using it to find him."

"Any more progress cracking hers?"

"Still grinding. We're stuck with a tertiary feed. The problem is, the people who work with me used to work with Grigori Novalev's bunch. He made sure he hardened his *matushka*'s phone."

"Tertiary," Kenyon knew, referred to apps that did not require a password to access. They included maps, texting, photos. Other more sensitive apps remained as yet impregnable. Bettencourt was well apprised of her digital vulnerabilities. All calls were made via WhatsApp and Telegram, encrypted end to end, thus promising unrivaled privacy. Emails and texts sent via Threema, similarly unhackable.

"They're headed to Chamonix," said Nessa.

"I'll mine her location data. If she's been anywhere near there in the past six months, I'll be able to pinpoint their probable destination. You don't have any personnel nearby?"

"FinCEN isn't the CIA. We're all about enforcement. Other people give us the clues, then we investigate. We subpoena documents. We issue arrest warrants. Mostly we fine banks for breaking the rules. We

213

don't put operatives in the field. As far as my bosses are concerned, I'm here to work with MI5 and the banking authorities."

"Your superiors don't know about Simon?"

"Just that he's helping us gather information about a suspect. A concerned citizen."

"And the rest?" asked Danni.

"Oh no," said Kenyon. "That wouldn't fly. We don't do vendettas."

"Come to Israel," said Danni Pine. "That's all we do."

"I'll buy you a coffee in Jerusalem when this is over," said Nessa. "I need to brush up on my biblical history."

"You're on," said Danni. "First let's make sure we get our boy back safe and sound. I don't think he knows quite what he's getting into."

"What do you mean?"

"Russians don't play nice."

"I don't think he cares," said Nessa.

It had started in Manhattan a year earlier. Too many properties were being purchased by foreign buyers whose identities were skillfully hidden behind a slew of holding companies. Not just apartments and condominiums but entire buildings. Forty million here. Sixty million there. Two hundred million. Three hundred. The sums were staggering, totaling over five billion dollars in the last year alone. And nary a family name to be found within a hundred miles.

Too often the funds were wired from banks in places like Liechtenstein, Greece, the Cayman Islands, and Cyprus. U.S. banks issued perfunctory suspicious activity reports, or SARs. The transactions were all very proper. All i's dotted and t's crossed. Never so much as a typo. Still, it was Kenyon's job to look beneath the surface.

She was asked to stand up a task force charged with finding out the buyers' true identities: names, nationalities, professions. Who were these guys? More importantly, how did they earn their money? They named it Task Force Lantern.

An early success revealed the money used to purchase an office tower in Chicago had come from a Ukrainian mobster, the subject of an Interpol Red Notice for the kidnapping and murder of five men. His son, working in the States with a green card, was arrested on charges of money laundering, wire fraud, and conspiracy. Nessa made him an offer.

Two years in the slammer or a one-way ticket home with all charges dropped. Repatriation was better than prosecution, even if the flight was economy class. The son named names. The first was Sylvie Bettencourt, "The Collector." A front for Russian money, he claimed. Connected at the highest level.

It sounded too good to be true. A leadoff homer. Nessa went to work. Yes, there was a Sylvie Bettencourt registered as a financial advisor in France with offices on the Avenue Charles Floquet. Yes, USCIS showed her traveling to and from the States frequently. A search of the web turned up photographs of her at auctions of fine art, automobiles, and real estate going back years. Nessa compiled a list of purchases Sylvie Bettencourt had made on behalf of clients, those that were public, at least, even if her clients' names were not. Four times in the past years she'd purchased classic or vintage automobiles at public auctions. She certainly wasn't trying to hide.

At the same time, Nessa reached out to her contacts in intelligence. CIA, FBI, MI6, France's DGSE, and a half dozen more. The silence was deafening. No one claimed to know the first thing about her. Some didn't respond at all. Maybe too deafening.

Kenyon didn't give up. A gangster lied as easily as he drew breath, but not when his son's freedom was on the line. She pressed the son, who pressed his father. *"Look deeper,"* they said. Bettencourt was once a spy. She'd worked out of the London embassy in the '90s. She was a superstar, until she wasn't. There was a rumor that she'd been formally expelled. Persona non grata and all that. If the name didn't ring a bell, a picture would.

Kenyon sent photographs of Bettencourt to her contacts, asking if anyone stationed in England thirty years earlier recognized her. Forget the name. Every spy had a half-dozen work names. Look at the face. Look at the figure. She wasn't someone you'd forget, not the horny old boys who'd manned the ramparts back in the day.

MI6 came back first. They knew Bettencourt as Susie Blackwell and Simone St. Claire. Identified as a commercial attaché working out of the London embassy in the 1990s, dates unspecified. No further details. The CIA replied next, offering the same Susie Blackwell, as well as Sylvia Barrington. Again, there was mention of her cover as a "commercial attaché," but then came something more. Bettencourt's real name was Svetlana Makarova. She was a trained covert agent attached to the GRU's First Directorate, which focused on the European Union, and she was later discovered to be a member of Unit 88611, aimed at covert activities and assassination with the goal of destabilizing Western governments. Last reported rank: lieutenant colonel. And this final flourish: suspected of murdering three men and one woman while in England. Hence, her expulsion and designation as persona non grata.

Nessa sent out the mandatory interagency request for all files on Svetlana Makarova, a.k.a. Susie Blackwell, a.k.a. Sylvia Barrington. Time passed. One month, then another. Finally, the files arrived, or rather, the invitation to review them at CIA headquarters in Langley, Virginia. On the appointed day, Nessa was shown to a carrel in the basement and given a dossier ten inches thick. They'd had Lieutenant Colonel Makarova in their sights for a good long while.

There were also tapes, the fruits of something called Operation Trench.

For sixteen hours over four days, Nessa listened to wiretapped recordings of Sylvie Bettencourt speaking to agents she was running across the United Kingdom, as well as to those she hoped to persuade to join the cause. The agents, or "Joes," and prospects all worked in the financial sector. Bankers, brokers, traders, merchants of one stripe or another.

The goal of her efforts was to move money from Russia—newly, rabidly capitalistic—into England, to use the international financial system to launder funds stolen by politicians, military officers, intelligence operatives, and politically connected businessmen during the first big grab following the dismantling of the Soviet Union.

It was from those tapes that Nessa came upon the idea of recruiting Simon Riske. How could she not after what she'd heard?

Her pitch went smoother than expected. All she had to do was play Simon the tape. He accepted as if it were the most natural thing in the world to chuck everything and go to work for the United States government. The question of putting himself in danger never came up. He would do it. Where did he sign?

Only then did she learn that restoring cars was not his sole profession. He had a side hustle, too. He was not a trained spook, exactly, but maybe something better. A man not bound by any rules. And he had that extra thing, the thing no one could teach. He was motivated.

It was Simon who had suggested taking the operation to the next level. No one inside FinCEN, or any other government agency, would have considered it. They were law enforcement, not intelligence. Even then, the play was too big, too audacious, too spectacularly arrogant. No one at Langley would have dared. Pull it off and your career was made. Blow it and, well…pack your bags and get on the next bus to Pismo Beach. For now, it was their little secret, just the three of them, and maybe a few others.

"Simon's gone silent," said Danni Pine. "They ditched the phone. If my map is accurate, they tossed it into a river."

"And Sylvie?"

"Not a peep."

"Do you think she has any idea Simon's working for us?"

"I think she's doing what she trained her entire life to do."

"What's that?"

"Be suspicious."

Part II

INSIDE

CHAPTER 47

Haute-Savoie, France

He was a prisoner.

Simon sat in the back of the Mercedes G-Class, Sylvie Bettencourt by his side, Vadim at the wheel. Simon never forgot a face, not when it was one to whom he owed a favor. Another Mercedes drove in front of them; a third came behind. He wasn't sure if the show was for him or for Sylvie, a measure of fear or respect.

The plane had landed at an airstrip outside the town of Annecy. From Annecy, the caravan drove into the mountains, past La Clusaz, Crest-Voland, the villages becoming smaller, less frequent, the road narrower, and the peaks taller, capped with snow. Conversation was scant. Sylvie had disappeared into her laptop five minutes after wheels-up. To judge by her expression, the manner in which her mouth twitched at regular intervals, something was wrong.

"That bad?" said Simon, at a rare time when she raised her head.

No response. A look to tell him to mind his own business. A few minutes later, she closed the laptop and slipped it into the briefcase at her feet. "I never thought it would be so difficult to spend money," she said.

"Sand through my fingers," said Simon.

"Did your friends at MI5 tell you what it is I do? Who I work for?"

"Nothing specific beyond the fact that you used to be a spy and they were keeping a close eye on you."

"And the woman your friend Cleak introduced you to…Kenyon from FinCEN? Anything?"

"Who?"

"Please," said Sylvie. "I applaud your diligence. Part of the reason you're here with me, instead of out there, running from the police."

"She may have said something about you laundering money coming out of Russia. They're eager to establish the identity of who's buying up so much real estate in the States. They've set up a task force. Lantern is the name. It didn't sound like she had much."

"She doesn't have anything," said Sylvie. "It's my job to make sure of it." A stern glare to drive home the point. "See her again?"

"No," said Simon. "But you know that already."

Sylvie's phone rang. She answered straightaway, as if expecting the call. The conversation was in Russian and heated. Simon turned his gaze out the window. His own Russian was fair, improved by a refresher course in the past six months, two hours via Zoom four nights a week with an instructor from the U.S. Embassy in London. And yes, he'd made sure his phone was stowed in a soundproof locker.

Sylvie's accountant, it seemed, was anxious about demands to forward records to someone referred to as "the Cellist." She, however, was adamant that he do no such thing. She ended the call with a traditional Anglo-Saxon expletive. No refresher course needed.

"Bad news?" asked Simon.

"I'm sure you caught every word," replied Sylvie, without rancor. Another of the skills she needed. "Does it bother you that I'm investing Russian money?"

"Why should it?" said Simon. "I was a private banker for a long while. First rule: 'Don't ask, don't judge.'"

"And the second?"

"Same as the first."

The car continued deeper into the mountains in the direction of Roches Merles, Chamonix, and Mont Blanc. Vadim left the highway and turned onto a macadam road that wound lazily up a gentle slope. Past cows and rolls of summer hay and wooden huts as old as the hills. Simon rolled down the window. The air was brisk and sharply scented, a welcome slap in the face.

And so here he was. *Inside.* Exactly where he'd wanted to be since Nessa Kenyon had contacted him saying she had some tapes she thought he should hear. Here he was, seated next to Svetlana Makarova, retired lieutenant colonel of the Russian GRU, First Directorate, founding member of Unit 88611, now using the name Sylvie Marie Bettencourt, and believed to run one of the biggest operations laundering ill-gotten gains coming out of the Russian Federation. He didn't give a damn where the money came from. Or, in truth, whether it was the fruit of illegal operations, wired from the account of a PEP—a politically exposed person, meaning someone who owed someone else a favor. "Favor" defined as a payoff: graft, extortion, bribery, all of the above. Let others solve those problems. Simon was interested in getting his hands on financial records that would implicate Sylvie Bettencourt in the crimes and ensure that she went to prison.

There was only one problem: he was heading to a retreat in the French Alps, not to her business headquarters in Paris. Already a misstep.

Men plan and the gods laugh.

The car slowed as the lead Mercedes turned onto a maintained dirt track. A hundred meters farther, the driver stopped and jumped out to open an imposing wooden gate blocking their path. Vadim drove through, not waiting for the others. The road climbed a steep grade before entering a pine forest. Switchbacks until they reached a false summit. The trees fell away. Ahead, an undulating meadow framed by towering granite peaks. Another gate, this one manned by a guard carrying a hunting rifle, the fence to either side topped with coiled barbed wire. The Mercedes might not give them away, but a Kalashnikov surely would.

Getting closer now. Simon sensed the anticipation in the car.

A speed run across the high valley. They passed a narrow lake, its water aquamarine from glacial runoff. A broad, sweeping turn to the right. Always climbing. Mountains closed in. The valley narrowed. Ahead, a dense band of clouds blocked the road. Visibility decreased to near zero. Vadim didn't slow. They were floating in a white void. Ten breathless seconds. The clouds dissipated. The world righted itself. Blue sky above. Ground below. And there, in front of them, like something out of a Gothic chiller, Sylvie's "rustic little cabin in the mountains."

Of course, there was nothing cabin-like about it. It was a belle époque castle. A once grand hotel cradled in a pavilion of gray rock. Five stories. A city block in length. Two fairy-tale turrets—Grimms', not Disney's—

the French flag flying from one, the Russian flag from the other. Too many rooms to count. But a fading palace, the cracks in the walls visible as they neared, wrought-iron balconies rusting and askew, the driveway riven with potholes, paint everywhere chipped and fading.

"Am I allowed to ask what this place is?" asked Simon.

"Once it was the finest hotel in the Haute-Savoie," said Sylvie. "It opened before the first war, the glory days of Europe's grand touring hotels. It closed in '39 and stayed that way for thirty years. The property was purchased by the PCF—the Parti Communiste Français—when Georges Marchais ran things. Twenty years ago, we took it off their hands, made it our own private retreat. Officially, it's called Relais des Alpes. We call it Shangri-la."

The imposing structure wasn't the only thing that had captured Simon's attention. Groups of men patrolled the grounds, most in hiking or workout attire. Women, too, but not many.

"Who are they?" he asked.

"Ours," said Sylvie. "Diplomats, intelligence officers, expats."

Simon looked closer. They appeared a fit bunch. Plenty of beards, hulking shoulders. Diplomats? He didn't think so. A summer camp for spies was more like it. "Where's the archery range?" he asked. "The arts-and-crafts shack?"

"There's a shooting range in the basement," said Sylvie, not missing a beat. "And quite a nice gym. If you need to brush up on your hand-to-hand skills, I'm told the instructor is excellent. His specialty is knives."

"Does the French government know?"

"They believe it's a recreational facility for our diplomats. Who's going to tell them different?"

Simon met her eyes. Not him.

Tires crunched on gravel as they came to a halt. Sylvie led the way inside, up a broad flight of stairs, through double doors. The lobby was immense, high ceilings, gold carpeting, elaborate woodwork, and all too empty. A woman stood behind the reception desk. Several keys rested on the counter. Sylvie was expected.

"We may be here a few days," she said to Simon, signing the paper-work. "You're free to do as you please. Hike, run, swim. There are a few mountain bikes lying around. I believe there's fitness gear in your room. You'll need new clothes. Tell Vadim what size you wear: shirts, jackets, slacks, shoes. If there is any particular brand you like, let him know. We'll send someone into town."

"Where am I going?"

"Someplace hot," said Sylvie, handing him one of the keys.

"You like keeping me guessing."

A smile to say of course she did. "You'll join me for dinner in, say, forty minutes?"

"Yes."

She picked up a key for herself—the old kind, attached to a slab of iron engraved with the room number. "I'm not going to regret bringing you along," she said. "Am I?"

"No."

"Good." She stepped closer and kissed him on each cheek. "Welcome."

The room was large and comfortable, if dated. Twin bed with a duvet folded neatly on top. Floral-patterned carpet. A desk, a low table, two chairs. A radiator beneath a window. It might have looked the same forty years ago.

"What does she want with me?" asked Simon as he opened the window.

Vadim leaned in the doorway, arms crossed. "You'll know when she tells you."

"Something about 'the Cellist'?"

Vadim's eyes locked on his. "Be careful what you say."

"Who is he?"

"Not a friend."

Simon gazed down at the courtyard as several persons emerged from a door and crossed the cobblestoned square. Two men following a woman. Immediately, he sensed something amiss. It was their bearing. Too stiff, too forced. He knew guards when he saw them.

The woman was tall and broad shouldered, her hair cut as short as an army recruit's. Before he could ask Vadim if she was one of them, the man behind her gave her a shove. It was hard enough to make her stumble and lose her footing. She turned and swung a fist at him. The man caught her forearm and twisted it violently toward the ground. When she cried out, he twisted it more, forcing her to bend double.

"Pavel!" Sylvie Bettencourt emerged from the doorway and walked toward the man. "Leave her."

The man—Pavel—pale, with flaxen hair as thick as straw and the build of a gymnast, released the woman's arm. "Try it again," he said. "And I'll hurt you. For real."

Flawless English with an American accent. But not an American. That Simon could see at first glance.

Sylvie exchanged a private word with the man, Pavel, scolding him, then gave her attention to the woman, speaking to her kindly and touching her cheek. The woman was not won over, turning her face away.

"I'm not your only guest," said Simon.

Vadim joined him at the window. "She's here under different circumstances."

"Oh?" Simon played it cool. What did he care about her?

"A nosy one," said Vadim. "Like you."

"Nosy about?"

"Her father." Vadim shook his head, laughed.

"Not a friend either?"

"Definitely not."

"What happened to him?"

A shrug. A hard look. What always happened to enemies? "I told her not to do this," said Vadim. "Bring you into the family. Trust you."

"And?"

"She doesn't listen. She likes people in trouble. She thinks she can control them."

"And you?"

"I think you know cars. Beyond that, not much. You can't fight worth shit." Vadim made a slow tour of the room. "You remind me of a guy I worked with back in the day. Yuri. Eighth Directorate. Foreign Technology. We carpooled together. Yuri was always bragging about how great he was, how his Joes had the most gold. American execs in Moscow. One was from 3M, another from McDonald's. Great, I told him. Just what we need: Post-its and Big Macs. But information is information. Maybe one of our bosses had a hard-on for French fries. Soon Yuri had a driver, then a bigger apartment, better suits. It was too much. I could sense it. I told my boss, 'Watch this guy. He's dirty.' He didn't want to know. Yuri's success was his success." Vadim sat on the bed, punched the duvet, bounced on the mattress. "Everyone thinks we Russians are so suspicious, always one step ahead. A nation of Spasskys and Kasparovs. It's the opposite. We believe everything." He stood, stepped closer to Simon. "Anyway, one day Yuri disappeared. Defected, if that's what they still call it. Never heard from again. Who knows what he gave the Americans in exchange for the recipe for 'secret sauce'?"

"I didn't ask to be here," said Simon. "It was Sylvie's idea."

"Sure it was."

"If you want to say something, go ahead."

Vadim leaned in, chin raised, reeking petulance. "Run," he whispered. "While you have a chance." He drew a pistol, a boxy Glock, and pointed it at Simon's forehead. "Bang."

He left a moment later.

Simon returned to the window. He studied the storehouse where the girl was imprisoned. He would have to do something about that.

Misstep number two.

CHAPTER 48

Haute-Savoie, France

Dinner was self-serve from the buffet: dark bread, herring, and endive salad.

"Not exactly the same cuisine as the last time we dined together," said Sylvie good-naturedly.

"I'm not so sure," said Simon, taking a bite of herring. "Just wait till the Michelin inspectors get here. I'd give it two stars."

"You're too kind."

The dining room was a vast, deserted expanse, a ghostly memorial to a bygone era with decorative pillars and trompe l'oeil frescoes of angels and cherubs gazing down from the heavens. Marx and Lenin would not approve. They might, however, sign off on the rickety tables and the orange plastic chairs.

"The people here—the campers—where are they off to when they leave?" he asked.

"Most return to administrative posts at embassies around the world. Attachés, secretaries, liaisons."

Simon speared an endive leaf. "They look more like they're off to poison an enemy of the state," he said. "Or throw someone out a window. A lot of people slip and fall from high floors in your country."

"I wouldn't know. It's been years since I worked for the government."

"And yet here we are. A perk for retired officers?"

"Something like that."

"What did you do?" asked Simon. "When you were an attaché?"

"Surely your friend Mr. Cleak at MI5 told you."

"As a matter of fact, no."

"It's confidential."

"Even after all these years?"

"More so."

Not too many questions, Simon reminded himself. A bite of herring. Salted butter on black bread. The finest in proletarian fare. "So how did you come to travel the world buying Ferraris and Hockneys?" he asked.

"I'd need a cold bottle of vodka and a tin of caviar to tell you the entire story."

Simon poured her a second glass of vin de table. "Have some of the local plonk. I'll settle for the highlights reel."

Sylvie swirled the wine in her Duralex glass. "Born Moscow 1960— oh, hell, 1956…I don't know why I care. A good state education, then off to a special school for special students. I was pretty. I was smart. And I had an ear for languages. We called it The Institute. Basically, it was a high school with a few special classes."

"Such as?"

"You expect me to say blackmail, seduction, assassination. I'm sorry. We concentrated on more mundane skills. Languages, etiquette, foreign political systems. Essentially, we were trained to pass ourselves off as being one of the enemy. English, French, American."

"A deep-cover operative? Is that what they call it?"

"Just a garden-variety spy. Remember, this was the seventies. The Cold War was burning white-hot. All the same, it was apparent that we were slipping behind. The socialist experiment was failing. Our masters didn't send us out to get military secrets. They wanted us to learn how everyone in the West was making so much money. And, if possible, to teach them how they could get their hands on it. They built replicas of cities in England and France and the U.S.—at least a city block—for us to live in. Stores with Western products, kiosks selling Western newspapers and periodicals, banks, pharmacies. Imagine our surprise when we went into a corner grocery and found the freezer stocked with bacon, butter, pizzas, and ice cream. Say the words 'Rocky Road' in Moscow and it was straight to the gulag. On the way home, I'd buy a copy of the *Herald Tribune* and *Paris Match,* with real English pounds. I'm surprised we didn't all hop the walls and make a run for it then and there."

"Why didn't you?"

"We were Russian." The very question was an insult.

"And from there?"

The excitement drained from Sylvie's face. "Nowhere. They kept us cooped up for years, as if they were afraid all that training had made us unreliable, disloyal. I didn't receive an overseas assignment until I was thirty. My first posting was to Paris, not as a spy but as a secretary. There I was, fluent in four languages, taught to spot a tail at fifty meters, a master of the dead drop, and all I did was take stenography eight hours a day and let my superiors pinch my ass."

"What happened?"

"Glasnost. Perestroika. Gorbachev. The eighties were one long glorious earthquake. One day I was a secretary, the next I was running agents at Renault and Crédit Lyonnais and Yves Saint Laurent."

"Saint Laurent?"

"One of the cutters was having an affair with a minister at the Élysée Palace. He gave us all the gossip about Mitterrand and his secret daughter. A randy old goat, that one."

"I didn't know," said Simon.

"Who did?" Sylvie finished a third glass of wine. "Now look, you've got me going on about myself."

Sylvie checked over her shoulder. The staff had stayed behind. They stood, arms crossed, glowering. Frenchmen, not Russians, God love them. "I think we're going to have to leave before they throw us out. Come. You can walk me to my room."

Sylvie rose, a little unsteadily. "I hope your radiator is working." Simon offered a hand. "A gentleman," she said.

Sylvie stopped at Vadim's table, saying a few words. He shook his head unhappily.

They rode an old Schindler elevator to the top floor. Simon held the door, as gentlemen do. The corridor was dark. She took his hand as they walked to her room.

"Get me a drink," said Sylvie once they'd stepped inside. "There, by the wall. Whatever you'd like. Cognac, brandy, vodka."

Simon poured them each two fingers of cognac. A suite for her, a spacious living area, the door to a bedroom closed. His eyes wandered the room, noting the windows—latch, not sash—looking for any other way in. Her purse and briefcase sat on a dining table. No sign of the laptop and too chancy to have a closer look.

Sylvie Bettencourt returned a few minutes later. Business attire was gone, replaced by cheetah-print pajama pants and a black cashmere sweater cut too low. She'd washed the makeup from her face and put her hair up in a ponytail.

"It's nice to have someone to talk to," she said, accepting the glass, sitting on one side of the sofa, her feet tucked beneath her. "Someone from outside."

Simon remained standing. "For now," he said.

"For now," said Sylvie. "Where were we? You wanted to know how I got into this line of work. One day I received a call. I think it was fifteen years ago. I was living in Zürich, working for one of the big Swiss houses. Private banking, like you. I'd left government service sometime before. One of my clients was a countryman, one of the new elite, worth a billion even then."

"An oligarch?"

"Almost but not quite. Of course, he is now."

"With your help?"

Sylvie looked at him archly, deciding whether or not she enjoyed the flattery. "He thought so. That's what counted."

"A call from?"

"Michael," she said with finality. "My boss." A hand raised high and swirled in a circle. "All of our boss here."

Simon required no further clarification. It was as he'd thought all along. There could be only one "Michael."

"Had you known him? On his way up? Even before?"

She gazed ruminatively at him. "If we're going to exchange personal stories, come sit." A pat on the couch too close for comfort.

Instead, Simon perched on the arm of the sofa. "Go on."

"No, I didn't know him. But he knew about me."

"He needed a private banker?"

"God no. He has a hundred of those. He has his own bank, for God's sake. He needed someone to find a place for all the money once it was in the bank. One place he couldn't keep it was Russia. He also knew better than to keep it exclusively in stocks and bonds and precious metals."

"And so 'the Lost Ferrari.'"

Sylvie nodded, sipped. "Too bad you aren't in the art world. We'd have run across each other earlier. Michael loves paintings. Old masters mostly. Rembrandt, Caravaggio, Rubens. Impressionists, less so. He has a rather Stalinist view of modern stuff."

"What about the Hockney?"

"My suggestion, not that he'll ever see it. No one will. Locked up in a free port. Geneva, I think. He has enough works socked away to give the Jeu de Paume a run for its money. The Hockney is a repository of value. Safer than the dollar, yen, or euro. Push comes to shove, someone's going to shell out good money for it. I mean, who knows what might happen to a man in his position?"

"So it's all insurance?"

"I think maybe that's what he tells himself. Me, I'd call it what it really is. Greed. Lucre. The exercise of raw power." Sylvie raised her glass, gave it a little shake. Simon obliged. Another splash of cognac for Madame Bettencourt. She took his arm when he returned and bade him sit beside her.

"How?" he asked, close but not too.

"Advisory fees. A surtax, as it were, for keeping order. He prefers ten percent, but he'll take five. Everyone pays. All the big players. Gas, timber, oil, metals. Straight across the board. No pay, no play."

"Extortion, then."

"The cost of doing business." Sylvie slid nearer, an arm draped across the back of the sofa, fingers suddenly stroking the nape of his neck. "And you?"

"And me."

"Do you know the cost of doing business, Mr. Riske?"

Simon regarded Sylvie. In the soft light, she looked like a woman half her age and twice as willing. She leaned forward, chin raised, eyes clear. She gazed at him frankly and in a fashion any man recognized. He leaned closer, entering her private space, their lips nearly touching. "I do."

"Well, then."

Simon ran a finger along her cheek. "After," he said.

She pressed her mouth against his, her lips moist.

"Sylvie," he whispered. "You won't respect me in the morning."

"A gentleman," she said. "Dammit."

He smiled.

She laughed.

Détente.

He paused at the door. "I still don't know why I'm here."

"Tomorrow."

His feet led him without thinking.

Minutes after leaving Sylvie, Simon traversed a hiking path through the forest at the rear of the hotel. It was after ten. A few men were out, smoking, huddled in tight knots, knocking back a beer or something stronger. Some looked his way. Some pretended not to. If anyone asked, he was out for a stroll before bed. He wasn't interested in sleeping. Not yet. Down the slope to his right was the storehouse where the woman was locked up. Who was she? What had she done? A fellow Russian spy who'd crossed Sylvie? If so, why had Sylvie spoken English to her? There was something about the way the men had treated her, something about the way she carried herself. She was in trouble. He had to assume her life was in jeopardy. Russians had only one way of settling matters. He didn't need to know more.

As he approached, he noted that the lights were out. He saw no sign of a guard, but that meant nothing. Somewhere there were cameras and a security shed. He continued on another hundred meters, before turning and retracing his steps.

Back in his room, he lay on his bed unable to sleep.

The woman.

He would have to get her out.

CHAPTER 49

The Internet

No one took notice of Anna Bildt's disappearance. Not a soul had witnessed her abduction off the streets of Chur. Police were concerned only about the mysterious shooting of a local salesman. A single by-stander, a shop clerk, had heard the gunshots. She had seen Freddy Hold fall and had run into the street to render aid. The woman offered only vague descriptions of the assailants—two men in dark clothing—and stated incorrectly that they had driven away in a silver sports car. She made no mention of a woman being forced against her will into the back seat of that, or any other, car.

Friends and family were also silent. Anna had no relations to inquire about her well-being. No aunts, uncles, grandparents, or siblings. Her friends in Copenhagen were used to her long absences. Those who called or texted knew not to expect a rapid reply. As for Hans-Peter Tell, he had forgotten her entirely. He didn't care for uncooperative parties.

To the outside world, Anna Bildt had not so much vanished as ceased to exist. Only in one place was her disappearance conspicuous, if not glaring. The net.

After posting more than two hundred times on the Chatterbell web-site in the days following her father's death—establishing the project file "The Murder of Carl Bildt," soliciting help to find the driver of the Volkswagen Polo, responding to every reply and offer of assistance, adding queries of her own—Anna had gone silent.

Yet even without her, the investigation continued and gathered steam. A single helper became two. Two became four. And so on. "The Murder of Carl Bildt" soon benefited from the attention of seventy individuals, and the number continued to grow. They were a varied lot. They came from Tunisia and Taiwan, Mexico and Madagascar, Singapore and Saudi Arabia. The vast majority, however, came from Western Europe and the United States. They had no connection to one another apart from a like desire to add one piece to a puzzle.

As the number of actors increased, so did their engagement. Some spent an hour, others two. Among them, however, was a kernel of enthusiasts who devoted their every waking moment to solving the mystery.

This is what they found:

After positively identifying Major Pavel Djordjevich of the Russian GRU as the man seated behind the wheel of the Volkswagen Polo minutes before the car exploded killing Carl Bildt, Chatterbell turned up additional photos of the man. And then the jackpot. Pavel Djordjevich, against every tenet of his training as a professional military intelligence officer, against every whit of common sense, kept an Instagram account under the name InternationalPaulD.

An examination of his recent postings included a photograph of the Zürich Airport with the tagline *"Grüezi, Schweiz!"*; a snap of Lake Lugano; and, uploaded less than twenty-four hours earlier, a picture of Djordjevich in the company of another man posing in front of an Italian restaurant in Bellinzona, their arms around the chef. "Best Pizza Ever!" read the tagline. "Grazie, Mario."

This last picture was quickly seized upon. The second man's face was isolated and fed into the Clearview AI software. Several hits came back. No military identification card but something as good. A picture posted on the Facebook page of the 166th Mobile Artillery Brigade, Sixth Division, of the Russian Armed Forces, taken six years earlier in the Eastern Ukraine province of Donetsk, identified Djordjevich's dining companion as Sergeant Alec Kosygin. Inputting the name brought a further trove of information. Pictures at a convention of intelligence agents in Moscow. An appearance on a Russian woman's Facebook page. More still.

A second cohort concentrated on traffic cams in and around Lugano. Another persuaded a member of the Swiss Federal Office of Transport to grant them access to all images recorded by cameras in the cantons of Ticino, Graubünden, St. Gallen, and Zürich. Over four days, ten analysts scoured more than sixty thousand archived photographs from one hundred thirty cameras. Their efforts allowed them to track the VW Polo from the bomb site in reverse chronological order as it passed the Lugano casino, the train station, the Lugano Nord exit from the A2, on and on, until a final photograph showed the car two blocks from the dealership in Chur.

Put together, the Chatterbell analysts had now established the identities of the men who had planned and carried out the cold-blooded murder of Carl Bildt, their presence at the scene of the crime, and their purchase of the automobile used as the murder weapon.

Chatterbell was a new kind of investigative entity, at once stateless and universal, an entity powered by curiosity, the desire to be of service, and the stronger desire to be part of something larger than oneself. Anna's old favorite, G. W. F. Hegel, might have seen it as the next evolution of the *Volksgeist,* the national spirit or collective ethos. He might have named it the *Cybergeist.*

Yet for all their work, none of the analysts remarked on Anna's failure to monitor their progress and congratulate them on their successes. Only one individual noticed Anna's silence and grew worried. His name was Alan Endicott, the founder of Chatterbell. It was Endicott and his staff who had alerted Anna to the interest of Russian intelligence. It was Endicott who then requested that Anna confirm she was safe and, when she did not, directed the attention of the Kantonspolizei Graubünden to the evidence gathered on his website, while adding his suspicion that Anna Christina Bildt herself might be the victim of foul play.

When he had finished, he made a phone call to the headquarters of the Swiss Nachrichtendienst des Bundes in Bern.

"I'd like to speak with Hans-Peter Tell," he said. "It concerns the murder of Carl Bildt."

CHAPTER 50

Haute-Savoie, France

Morning.

The sky had cleared. For the first time, Simon was able to view his surroundings. He took in the ring of mountains, the soaring limestone and granite spires. He remembered the drive once they'd entered the gate, up the mountain and across the meadow. The nearest highway was ten kilometers' distance. He'd be wise to appreciate his predicament.

It was after breakfast. A walk with Sylvie Bettencourt beside the lake. He had traded his own clothing for camp attire: shorts, T-shirt, a hoodie, and someone else's trainers, which almost fit. Vadim followed at a distance, a shoulder holster and pistol worn over his tracksuit. Maybe Sylvie didn't think he was such a gentleman after all.

"My work doesn't only involve asset acquisition," said Sylvie. "There's more to it. We…by that I mean my team…we monitor payments made by a subset of companies."

"Advisory fees," said Simon. "From Russian companies."

"Our job is to make sure our 'clients' are paying their fair share. We bill, we collect, and, if the monies are slow in coming, we do a little more."

"Protection." There. He'd said it. "Pay up or else."

Sylvie frowned at his choice of words but didn't correct him.

"Is that why I'm here?" asked Simon. "To be your muscle?"

"You're much too smart for that," said Sylvie. "Besides, if it came to that, I'd have already failed. No, that isn't why you're here."

"I'm listening."

She stopped by the water's edge. "After we receive the money," she went on, "we forward it to another party, where it's aggregated with other revenue streams."

"The Cellist," suggested Simon, remembering her heated conversation the day before.

Sylvie nodded, digging the toe of her boot into the mud. The water turned brown. "Yes, the Cellist. He's my problem."

"How so?"

"Skimming, padding, fiddling with the accounts."

"Tell Michael. It's not your problem."

"If only I could. You see, the man I'm referring to is Michael's closest friend. They grew up together. Went to school together. Attended Komsomol camp together. Practiced judo together. He introduced Michael to the woman who became his wife and the mother of his children. Michael went into intelligence. Sergei chose music."

"Sergei?"

"Obolensky," said Sylvie, walking along the lake's edge. "For twenty years he was the first cellist for the Moscow Philharmonic. Gifted, but no Rostropovich. Younger, more talented musicians came along. Sergei approached Michael. Could he do anything to help him keep his place? *After all, a man in his position . . .* Michael was happy to help. He guaranteed Sergei's seat in the orchestra for life. In return, he asked a favor. Mightn't he place some money in Sergei's account? Lots of it, in fact, in lots of accounts. There was no need to worry—he would take care of the details. This was fifteen years ago. Just after Michael's awakening."

"Awakening?"

"His 'road to Damascus' moment. Call it his 'Muscovite conversion.' Until then, he'd viewed himself as a defender of the Rodina. The last good man. His crusade was to stop the new class of businessmen from stripping the country of its resources."

"What changed his mind?"

"He realized he was on the wrong side of the equation. He could never stop them, not if he wanted a growing economy, jobs, prosperity, the love of his people. He needed their expertise. One day he decided to join them. He made them a simple proposition. Keep your companies, continue earning your billions, but show me the proper respect."

"'He prefers ten percent, but he'll take five,'" said Simon.

"As I said, he couldn't open accounts in his own name, so he asked Sergei if he might use his. Over time, the number of accounts multiplied. His advisors used banks all over the world. On paper, Sergei was a billionaire many times over, but of course the money wasn't his." Sylvie sighed, pushing a lock of hair out of her eyes. Disappointment clouded her features. "A year ago he called me to say he had discovered some discrepancies in my accounts. He claimed to have discovered differences between the costs of the assets I was buying and the amount I was paying for them. He accused me of inflating the price of an object—land, art, jewelry—and pocketing the difference. I denied it. I told him to check the books. I mean, it's all right there. You can see the amounts wired out of my accounts and the amounts on contracts. He said he had his own set of books. Which would Michael believe?"

"He threatened you?"

"Worse. He demanded I repay the difference to him."

"How much?"

"One hundred million, give or take."

Simon whistled long and low. "You didn't," he said. "I mean, you know…"

"Never," said Sylvie, as if a virgin defending her purity. "I know what happens to anyone who crosses the Kremlin. It's him. It's Obolensky. He's taking a few points off the top between the time I wire him the money and he passes it along. If anyone checks, he can point a finger at me."

"Do you know that?"

"A dangerous question," Sylvie responded, but her eyes said, *Oh yes, I know.*

"But Michael must take care of him," said Simon.

"Generously. He's given him shares worth tens of millions in the banks he controls, created a foundation for young musicians in his name in their hometown of St. Petersburg. The Cellist is doing just fine."

"But not fine enough?"

"Is anyone these days?"

"Why you?" asked Simon.

"We had a disagreement years ago. For some reason he begrudges me my position. My wealth. My status with Michael."

Simon nodded. An interesting story, to be sure. He would adjudge its veracity later, alone. Right now it was his job to be an attentive listener. "Do you have proof?"

A wind sprang up, chill and threatening. Sylvie turned toward him. "No," she said, her eyes meeting his. "Not yet."

Simon crossed his arms. Finally. The reason she'd spirited him out of England. To save her skin. Obtain proof party A was stealing from party B. As a financial sleuth, it was Simon's bread and butter. He'd done it a hundred times. On paper, it sounded easy enough, and Sylvie, with her cool demeanor and formidable personality, made it sound easier still.

"I watched you this last time," Sylvie continued. "I've seen what you're capable of. You managed to break into Scotland Yard to find Boris Blatt's sealed court testimony. You stole a vehicle from a police parking lot in Wimbledon. I won't bring up what you did to Boris Blatt."

"You've been paying attention."

"Call it 'due diligence.'"

"I prefer 'spying.'"

"It is," said Sylvie Bettencourt, "what it is."

They walked for a while without speaking, leaving the lakeside and passing through a glade of pine trees, navigating scree that had tumbled down the mountainside. Finally, the path ended. Before them, a sheer stone wall rose a thousand feet.

"If I say yes, what's in it for me?"

"I got you out of England," said Sylvie. "That's something. What I offered earlier: a new passport, a legend, money. A chance to start afresh."

Simon didn't recall any details about an offer. He did recall a threat. *Come with me or else.* "Money…Let's start there."

"How much do you want?"

Simon could already envision the parameters of the job. Breaking and entering. Some sort of computer work. There would be guards, a security system. And of course the unknowns.

"Five," he said.

"Five million dollars?"

"Pounds. I'm a UK resident."

"Done."

Sylvie shook Simon's hand firmly, looking him in the eye. *Deal.*

"And the video," said Simon. "Destroyed."

"Of course," said Sylvie, insulted.

"Where is he?" asked Simon. "Obolensky. Where does he live?"

"All over."

Ah yes, the unknowns. "I'm going to need more than that."

"He likes to visit properties purchased in Michael's name. One month in Sochi. A few weeks on Ibiza. Winter in Gstaad. Never in one place too long."

"That poses a problem."

"Yes and no," said Sylvie. "As I said, he's meticulous, if not obsessive. It's his practice, his 'duty,' as it were, as the custodian of Michael's wealth, to inspect all purchases made on his behalf. There's nothing I buy that he doesn't examine with his own two eyes."

"In person?"

"Always. He was the last one to have seen the Hockney watercolor I purchased earlier this year. I'm told he had a picture taken of him standing beside it."

"He inspects *everything*?" For once, Simon knew where Sylvie was leading.

"3387 arrived in Limassol, Cyprus, two days ago. We keep all the larger items at the free port there. The warehouse is ten times the size of Geneva's."

"And the gearbox?"

"FedExed from London the day we received it." Sylvie tucked a lock of hair behind her ear. An all-too-knowing smile. "He'll see that it's installed properly."

"So, Cyprus," said Simon.

"He'll show. It's just a matter of time."

"And then?"

"You do what Simon Riske does best."

"Be resourceful."

"Et voilà."

CHAPTER 51

Khimki, Russia

Panic in Moscow.

Panic in the drab industrial suburb of Khimki, on the tenth floor of the Tower. Alarms were sounding. Red alert. Battle stations. Fix bayonets!

Grigori "Grisha" Novalev sprang from his desk, toppling a mug of coffee as he snatched his laptop, and fled the office. Labored breathing as he rode the elevator to the ground floor.

"Lieutenant Novalev, a moment of your time."

Grisha passed General Markov, the unit's commanding officer, without a backward glance. *Go ahead, General. Fire me,* he railed silently. *Send me to Siberia. If I don't speak to my mother immediately, the consequences will be far worse.*

He charged through the doors and out onto the street. So many pedestrians! Who were all these people blocking his path at eleven on such a cold, rainy morning? Disaster was upon them. Not from I. I. Borzoi or any one of a dozen domestic foes but from Chatterbell, a ragtag assembly of wannabe secret agents, cops, do-gooders...he didn't know what to call them except "lethal."

He rounded the corner of Ulitsa Kirova, jogging intermittently, exhausted by the time he made it to Pushkin Park. Quiet. Privacy. At last! He found an empty table beneath a leafy pergola, a stone's throw from a statue of the great poet. He opened his laptop, set up a VPN, lighting a cigarette as he phoned his mother.

"Grisha? This is a surprise."

"Kill them," he said, jaw clenched. "Kill all of them."

"Pardon me?" said his *matushka*. "What do you mean? Who are you talking about?"

"Pavel. Alec. The girl. All of them."

"Grisha, what is wrong?"

"Do it!"

There. He'd said it. He drew on his cigarette, willing the nicotine to kick in, calm him down. If anything, his heart beat faster. It was freezing outside and he was sweating like a pig.

They executed traitors in the basement of the Lubyanka. A shot to the back of the head as they walked you to your cell. They said it was a relief, a respite from the torture.

There was a rumor circulating in the break room. One of their own—Kaminsky, a gifted infosec specialist working at a forward operating base in Donbass, Eastern Ukraine—had been caught giving a local girl gifts of wine and cheese. She was only seventeen but a member of the opposition. This man, Kaminsky, had been taken to a secret prison—the Batcave, they called it—inside an abandoned nuclear bunker and interrogated by someone known as "the Maniac." No, he wasn't making this up. Weeks later, Kaminsky was returned to Moscow, to a cell in the Lubyanka. They said he had no teeth, no fingernails, and no testicles.

And for what? Giving a teenager a bottle of wine? Trying to get laid? What would they do to someone caught stealing millions? *Billions?*

"Calm yourself. Do you hear?" said Sylvie. She'd been gone so long she spoke Russian with a French accent.

Grisha set down his cigarette. "Yes, *Matushka*."

"There now. Are you feeling better?"

"Yes," he lied.

"Tell me what's the matter."

For ten minutes Novalev related the advances made by Chatterbell in tracking down Carl Bildt's assassins. Positive identification of Pavel and Alec, full names, affiliation to the GRU. Photographic evidence showing the man driving the car used to house the bomb, including a picture taken less than two kilometers from the site of the attack exactly an hour before it. There was even a time stamp.

Worse, Pavel, that idiot, maintained accounts on various social media platforms and had for years. There, posted for all to see, was a picture of him and Alec with a chef in Bellinzona, not twenty miles from Lugano. Who knew what else might be found…*what was being found at this instant?*

"It's only a matter of time," he said in conclusion.

"What do you mean?"

"Vadim," he said. "If they have Pavel and Alec, they will surely find him, too. He supervised them in Switzerland. He accompanied them from Zürich to Lugano. I know how these things work. These people, these investigators, they've taken hold of the thread in their hands. All they must do now is pull it. Everything will unravel."

"I don't see how."

"Soon, I don't know when—today, tomorrow, next week—someone will discover a phone number. Pavel's. Alec's. They will dig up the call records from the service provider."

"But that's illegal," protested Sylvie.

"So what?" he barked. "They already know where Pavel and Alec were. They'll cross-check phone records in Chur at the time the car was purchased against call logs in Lugano when the bomb was detonated. I can't imagine too many people were in both those places at the critical time. From there, it's a hop to find Vadim's number. All they have to do is search for any other numbers that were also in both places."

"My God."

Grisha slowed, drew a breath. "And once they have his, they'll find yours. It's all there for the looking. Nothing ever disappears."

"I see," said Sylvie Bettencourt after a moment.

"I'm sorry," said Grisha. "I'm still upset. Anyway, where are we in all this?"

"I'm sending the American after the Cellist. Once we have his records, you will help me take what belongs to us, to our family."

"And the American, Riske, he believes you?"

"He has no choice."

"Forget the money. Tell him to kill Obolensky."

"Have you lost your mind?"

"Far from it."

"Michael would know or suspect. One is as bad as the other."

"He'd never harm you."

"Don't be naive."

"But Vadim is his—"

"I won't hear of it. Obolensky is the godfather to Michael's daughters. If any harm should come to him, the consequences would be unthinkable. The American is the answer to our problems. I know him."

"Do you?"

"What is that supposed to mean?"

Grisha had his suspicions. More a feeling than anything else. He'd received the same transcripts of Riske's conversations as his mother, had read the same articles in the newspapers. All well and good. He couldn't fault her conclusions. But Grisha was himself trained in subterfuge. Something was not quite right. Call it experience. Call it intuition. Call it being scared out of his wits. "Keep a close eye on him. That's all I am saying."

"He won't bother us when this is over. Vadim will see to it."

Vadim, his half brother, in all ways. Half his blood and half his brains. The worst solution to any problem. "And you think Riske doesn't know that?" Grigori Novalev drew a breath. "There's something else. My unit monitors Chatterbell closely. We have since the downing of Malaysia Airlines flight MH17, when the website identified the missile unit responsible for shooting down the airliner, even the commanding officer. He was executed, in case you're interested."

"I'm waiting."

"Yesterday a call was placed from their headquarters in England to the Swiss Federal Intelligence Service. I made a tape for you." Novalev cued the recording.

"Inspector Tell, this is Alan Endicott, director of Chatterbell. I have some information you may find useful. We've identified two men we believe with a high degree of certainty carried out the assassination of Carl Bildt last week. They are both either active or former agents of the Russian GRU."

"My God, this is wonderful news."

"They are Major Pavel Djordjevich and Sergeant Alec Kosygin. You can find the evidence as gathered on our website. May I send you their photographs?"

"Of course."

"One last matter. It concerns Anna Christina Bildt. We believe she is missing. Her safety may be compromised."

"Do you have any more details?"

"She was last seen in Chur. She had a meeting with a man named Frederick Hold. He worked at the car dealership where Pavel Djordjevich purchased the Volkswagen used to kill Carl Bildt. Hold was murdered two days ago. My guess is that these same two Russians were involved. Sadly, we have learned that Russian intelligence was following our investigation. I hope this will help."

"And these men? Do you know where they are?"

"We are working on it," said Endicott. "Believe me, we are working on it."

Novalev turned off the recording. "Now do you understand?"

"How long till they find us?" asked Sylvie Bettencourt.

"Days," said Grisha. "Maybe a week. Maybe they already have."

"This changes things," said Sylvie.

"What will you do?"

"I will protect our family."

CHAPTER 52

Limassol, Cyprus

Midafternoon in the eastern Mediterranean. It was hot and humid, with a fitful breeze, and the air at the port of Limassol on the southern coast of Cyprus was rank with the scents of diesel fuel and rotting fish. At three p.m., the port was bustling. Ships from Shanghai unloading rebar and cement. Bremen, delivering automobiles. Marseille, carrying wine, Champagne, and all manner of luxury goods La Belle France was known for. And, from Saudi Arabia, oil. The Republic of Cyprus was booming, and Nikos Christiades, driving his new BMW convertible along Harbor Road, knew that there was only one country to thank. They didn't call the island "Moscow on the Med" for nothing.

Christiades drove to the end of the loading zones, dodging the forklifts and trucks. He turned into a complex of warehouses, each a city block in length, tall enough to blot out the sun. Most belonged to one transport company or another. Maersk, Evergreen, MSC. After a mile, he crossed a set of railroad tracks and slowed as he approached a squat four-story building colored battleship gray, the letters *LFP* painted on the uppermost corner. He'd been coming to the building for seven years, and every day he told himself he'd never seen a prettier sight.

"LFP" stood for Limassol Free Port. A free port, in Cyprus or any other country, was a special economic zone where goods deemed to be "in transit" might be stored without being subjected to taxes, duties, or customs fees. A "tax-free" purgatory, as it were.

Nikos Papadokos Christiades, forty, slim, not quite handsome, a native Cypriot, trained as a lawyer at the University of Athens, had opened the Limassol Free Port in response to the demand from his Russian neighbors to the north for a safe entrepôt where they might keep their assets until such time as they wished to enjoy them. The LFP was the length of three football fields and contained ten bullion chambers for the storage of gold—primarily ingots—space for two million bottles of wine or spirits, and ten thousand fully secured, climate-controlled storerooms where clients could stash art, furniture, jewelry, and, ever more frequently, vintage automobiles. Fees ranged from one thousand dollars a month for the smallest rooms to fifty thousand dollars a month for spaces to house an automobile. Business, Nikos would be the first to tell you, had never been better. *Spasibo bolshoye.*

He parked in his designated space and took the elevator to his offices on the fourth floor. His secretary greeted him formally with a wink and a promise to bring him an espresso immediately. Once seated, he reviewed the day's arrivals. There was a shipment of antiquities from Cairo, something from a recently discovered burial chamber. A painting sent from London, a work by Monet. From the Water Lilies series. He didn't know it. And a Bugatti from Singapore. There were no names anywhere on the documents, apart from his own. The owners were listed as this holding company or that. Still, he knew the men behind them. Russian, Chinese, and Russian. Nearly all his clients hailed from authoritarian regimes. He guessed that it was not just taxes they were afraid of.

Christiades was particularly interested in the Bugatti, a 1935 Royale. He considered himself a connoisseur of fine automobiles, though he himself preferred sports cars. Earlier in the week, a car had arrived that had stolen his heart. A 1963 Ferrari GTO. The Lost Ferrari, it was called, purchased in a private sale for his very best client, Mr. Obolensky, and, by extension, an even more important client. Though, of course, Christiades knew nothing about this. Nothing at all.

At five, Christiades left for drinks at the Palm, his favorite taverna. Limassol was the country's second largest city, after Nicosia, but due to its location on the sunny southern coast, the center of the island's construction boom. Everywhere there were cranes rising into the sky, building offices, hotels, and condominiums. To encourage investment, the country's president had recently begun selling citizenships to wealthy foreigners, what he called "golden passports," for the price of one million dollars each. Already he'd sold more than a thousand, and the waiting list was growing longer by the day.

And so, as Nikos Christiades sat down at his preferred table, he was not surprised to see the daily specials listed in Greek, English, and Russian.

"Nikos, *allô*!"

He stood as his mistress arrived. Thirty, blond, svelte, with dazzling blue eyes. No Cypriot she. An ethnic Siberian from Kamchatka. They ordered drinks, Champagne for mademoiselle, a French 75 for the monsieur.

His phone rang as Oksana was telling him about her aunt, who required urgent surgery to remove a gallstone. The cost was five thousand dollars, far more than a Siberian widow could afford. "Please, Nikos, could you?"

A look at the caller. Christiades's expression turned to stone. "Sergei, a pleasure," he said. "To what do I owe the honor?"

"I understand 3387 has arrived."

"Excuse me?"

"The Ferrari. Red. Insured for one hundred million dollars."

"Of course. We have it in our most exclusive bay."

"And the gearbox? From London?"

"We did receive a second shipment. A large crate."

"I'll be flying in tomorrow. Find me a mechanic who knows his way around Italian cars."

"I'm sorry, Sergei, but the car must transit directly from ship to free port."

"Find me a mechanic who can install the gearbox," said Sergei Obolensky.

Well, then, mused Christiades, so much for the law. "Yes, sir."

"It shouldn't take long. A few hours at most. My plane lands at noon."

"It will be my pleasure to pick you up."

"Thank you, Nikos," said Sergei Obolensky. "And make the usual arrangements for my stay. You do remember?"

"The Midas Suite at the Amara."

A moment while the Russian cleared his throat. "And the other."

The call ended. Of course "the other." No visit to Cyprus was complete without it. Three women. Blond, brunette, and redhead. At Mustafa's on the northern side of the island. The Turkish side. Christiades shuddered to think.

"What is it, Nikos?" asked Svetlana. "Did I say something wrong?"

"No, my love. An important client. Would you excuse me? Just one more call."

Nikos Christiades left the table and stepped into the alley adjacent to the restaurant. Like any savvy businessman, he owned several phones. He chose the one he considered to be most secure, one that Sergei Obolensky knew nothing about, and dialed a number in France, in the City of Light.

"Nikos, lovely to hear from you."

The sound of her voice and already he could see La Tour Eiffel. "Madame Bettencourt."

"Sylvie—don't be foolish."

"Sylvie, some news that might interest you."

"I'm all ears."

Nikos Christiades hung up a few minutes later. One call and he had earned enough to pay for a poor Siberian woman's surgery.

"Waiter," he called as he retook his seat. "Another round!"

Now he just had to find a mechanic.

CHAPTER 53

Simon walked slowly back to his room, reviewing what he knew about the country. An island somewhere in the eastern Mediterranean, not far from Turkey and Lebanon. Nice beaches. Lots of history. There had been a civil war decades back—Greeks vs. Turks—after which the island was divided into north and south, a border running more or less along the middle. In 2004, the country joined the European Union. After that? The boom. Like anyone involved in finance, he knew that Russia had made Cyprus its own piggybank. The place was awash in rubles. It was a country of shady banks, corruptible officials, and flexible laws.

And a free port where Michael stored his valuables.

Simon shut the door to his room, wondering when he would be leaving. There was a suitcase on the bed that had not been there earlier. Inside it, he found the clothing he'd asked for: suits, dress shirts, slacks, jeans, and more. No swimsuits or suntan lotion. If only he'd known his destination earlier.

On the desk lay a manila envelope, his last name printed with a Sharpie in large block letters. Inside he found a Canadian passport, credit cards, a driver's license, and two thousand euros. The pictures on the pieces of identification had been taken from a photo he'd kept on his phone. Sylvie really had been watching him for a while. He didn't bother examining the passport. He could see right off that it was top quality. A blank stolen from an embassy.

He replaced the items in the envelope and walked to the window, directing his attention to the storeroom. A sturdy door. Transoms high on the wall. Not a storeroom, not quite a jail cell, but near enough. "The cooler," for better or worse. Who was the girl? What had she done? Not a Russian. Her English was fluent but accented. German maybe. He closed his eyes, trying to remember the words she'd spoken to Pavel. More likely Scandinavian. Norwegian. Swedish. Danish.

The words "Danske Bank" sprang to mind. The murder of the banker in Lugano last week had made front-page news. Simon didn't recall the man's name, only that his first thought upon seeing the photograph of the charred, mangled automobile had been *He knew too much, and he was about to spill the beans.* Swiss banks handled the money of too many nationalities to presume that a Russian had been the culprit. Suddenly, Vadim's words about the woman being nosy regarding her father made more sense.

He poured himself a glass of mineral water and dropped into a chair. He was guessing, nothing more. Best to leave it at that. He had come to take down Sylvie Bettencourt. His investigation was as important as the woman's, if indeed she was the banker's daughter. But—and here Simon kneaded his brow—he wasn't the one being held prisoner.

Voices echoed from the courtyard. Simon shot to his feet, looking on as two figures emerged from the ground floor. Vadim and Sylvie. They stopped near the storeroom—"the cooler," as he continued to think of it. A hushed, furious exchange followed. Sylvie pointed a finger at Vadim. Vadim shook his head, threw his arms wide. *Who, me?* The unjustly accused. Sylvie stormed past him down the hill, Vadim giving pursuit a moment later.

Simon tracked them down the drive and to a low-ceilinged building, a lodging of some type, where they disappeared inside.

No better time.

He picked up his room key, checked that his Swiss Army knife was in his pocket, and left the room. Down the hall to the elevators. He preferred the stairs, bounding up two at a time. Reaching the fifth-floor landing, he stopped. An eye to the elevator. The occupancy light was dark. The corridor to either side was vacant. He walked to the far end, stopping at the last door on the left. Room 521. Out came the knife. He freed the saw—slim and inflexible—and slid it into the keyhole. A second to find the tumblers. Another to position the blade. He turned the handle as he applied pressure. The tumblers fell, as loud as a judge's gavel.

Inside the vestibule, he closed the door behind him and locked it. A look at his watch. He started the chronograph. One hundred eighty seconds. Three minutes and he was out.

He crossed the living room. Sylvie's laptop sat on the desk, open a crack. He lifted the screen. The display lit up to a Sotheby's website. The automobile auction in London in a few days. It was there he'd first seen her. It had been the night Boris Blatt dropped twenty-five million dollars on a '64 Ferrari, not that Simon had stayed long enough to witness it. Anyway, he wasn't interested in the auction so much as the fact that Sylvie had failed to log out.

The keys were in the car and the motor running.

He knew well enough not to navigate away from the page. "Leave no trace" was the governing rule. He studied the icon bar running down the left-hand side of the screen, memorizing the programs she most frequently used. Word, Excel, and so on. Danni would need the information. He opened a new blade on the knife, this time the can opener, and only to ninety degrees. Next, he removed the toothpick. With care, he took hold of the can opener and yanked it up. A slim rectangular unit came free of the knife. A micro flash drive courtesy of the SON Group, headquartered in Tel Aviv, Israel. He inserted it into the USB port. *"Wait five seconds,"* he heard Danni instruct him. *"Three taps on the space bar. Wait another ten seconds."* Simon added five on top, just to be sure, though Danni would kill him for it. Ye of little faith.

Sylvie's computer was now infected with a very, very intelligent piece of malware. Diabolical, really. Every keystroke—past, present, and future—would be sent to a lab in Tel Aviv, allowing a team of computer scientists to remotely access all of the laptop's software, gifting them with usernames, passwords, everything necessary to read her mail, her texts, to break down every door, all without Sylvie's knowledge.

He replaced the flash drive in his knife, sure to pick up the toothpick as well. Only now did he turn his attention to Sylvie's browsing history. The first addresses concerned the Sotheby's auction, a list of cars to be sold. Three Ferraris, one of which he recognized and knew was going for eighty million, a Lamborghini, and a 1935 Rolls-Royce that had been driven by Winston Churchill. Sylvie wanted the Ferrari.

Below these, a new website: Chatterbell. He knew of it—a citizens' collective of investigative journalists. He scrolled down, following Sylvie's progress through the site. There it was. "The Murder of Carl Bildt." Next: "GRU agents identified." And finally: "Anna Christina Bildt Missing." Bildt was the banker killed in Lugano. The woman being held prisoner must be Anna Christina, his daughter.

Despite his curiosity, Simon didn't dare read the pages, even to see if there was a photograph of the woman. That would have to wait.

He continued scrolling, past stock quotes, past articles from *Le Monde* and *Der Spiegel,* back further still. Lo and behold, an article from *The Telegraph* two days earlier concerning Boris Blatt's shooting.

He checked his watch. Five minutes had passed. *Idiot.*

Simon left the laptop as he'd found it and ventured into the bedroom. There on the bed, her handbag. He peeked inside. A daily agenda, a passport…Indonesian, in the name of Suzanne van Vleet. No time remained to search further. He turned, anxious to leave. He heard a key in the lock. Voices in the hall.

Simon ran back into the bedroom, unlocked the door to the balcony, and stepped outside. A moment to close the door and make sure the handle was secured. A glance over the railing. Good news: there was a balcony directly below. Bad news: It was at least ten feet distant. There was no way he could reach it.

He looked back through the window. No one in the bedroom.

He opened the door, stepped inside.

"You can't be serious" came Vadim's voice from the salon. "You're overreacting."

"You heard what I told the residence manager," said Sylvie. "Clear the camp. Everyone out."

A family quarrel in the family language. Russian and heated.

Simon scanned the room. There was only one place he might hide. He dove for the floor, turned onto his back and slid beneath the bed, head turned, cheek scratching an aged horsehair mattress.

Hardly a second later, the door to the bedroom opened. A woman in low heels entered, followed by a pair of men's hiking boots.

"You know Grisha," said Vadim, plaintively. "Always so worried."

"Exactly," said Sylvie. "That's why I trust him."

The mattress sagged as Sylvie sat and removed her shoes. "And you,

Vadim, my eldest, always so careless, so sure of your place in the world. This, all of it, is because of you. It stops now."

"You can't be worried about some crazy website…They're nobodies."

"Nobodies?" Sylvie rose. The two left the bedroom. "See for yourself," she continued, standing at the desk, opening the laptop. "There…Nobodies who posted pictures of Pavel and Alec for all to see, names, ranks, who placed them in Lugano at the site of the bombing. Nobodies who have spoken to the Swiss police, told them that the girl is in trouble. I want to meet these 'nobodies.'"

"I'll take care of her," said Vadim.

"You certainly will," said Sylvie. "But not until I speak with her. I want to know what else she's been up to."

"I asked her. She said she knows nothing."

"Ah, now we can all rest easier," said Sylvie, in a theatrical voice. "Thank the Lord. Vadim Vladimirovich has spoken with Miss Bildt. The truth be known."

"Watch who you're talking to, Mother."

"Are you threatening me? Well, are you, Vadim?"

"Of course not. I'm sorry."

Sylvie returned to the bedroom. Simon saw her reach to the floor, pick up a pair of flat shoes. For a moment, her face was inches from his as she bent at the waist to put them on, adjust a strap around her heels. A look in his direction and it was over. She stood and he heard her mutter, "You wouldn't have the balls," before she returned to the salon.

"Wait until dark," she said. "Until everyone's left. I don't want anyone else seeing her. Take her up the mountain. See that she has an accident. Be creative."

"Yes, Mother."

"Make sure no one finds her body until next spring."

"And the others?"

"They work for you. Figure it out. And, Vadim, count yourself lucky you're his son."

Silence, the sound of the door opening and closing, a key locking the door.

Simon counted to a hundred, then slid from beneath the bed. Leaving through the hall was out—no way to relock the door. He stepped onto the balcony. Another look below. Possible? Maybe. Did he have a choice?

Over the railing. Both hands on the iron supports. He lowered himself as far as he could, feet dangling well above the railing below. A moment to take aim. He let go. His feet landed dead center on the top railing. For a second he had it, then he toppled backward, falling into space. He threw out an arm. His hand found the rail. He arrested his fall, his shoulder popping out of the socket, then popping back in.

It took everything in him not to scream. A pain so severe your body forbade you from remembering. He extended his other arm, grasped the railing. Somehow he pulled himself to safety.

Simon lay on his back, a hand covering his mouth, begging for the pain to subside. For the forgetting to begin. If he was whimpering, so what? Minutes passed. He concentrated on his breathing. The terrible throbbing eased. Finally, he stood. The balcony door was unlocked. A peek inside. The room was unoccupied.

He was back in his room a minute later.

CHAPTER 54

Haute-Savoie, France

It was like the old days.

A one-on-one with a Joe—either he worked for her or she was convincing him that he must. Sylvie had always found that persuasion worked more effectively than coercion, at least at the start. A smile, a cocktail, and, if necessary, a little more. Ideology never came into play. Not in London in the 1990s. It was all about money, power, and sex. Mix the three and surely somewhere they could find common ground, some mutually beneficial basis to work together. Sadly, she no longer possessed the same tools. Her pocketbook might be deeper, but it was those other things that had diminished, even if her willingness to use them hadn't.

Of course, Anna Christina Bildt wasn't a Joe. She was the opposite. Even so, the same methodology held true. Persuasion over confrontation. No need for intimidation, until there was the need for intimidation. She hoped it wouldn't come to that. And if it did, she had Vadim.

"So, Miss Bildt," Sylvie began. "I imagine you're curious as to why we went to the trouble of bringing you here."

The three of them were seated in an abandoned office in the basement of the hotel, Sylvie, Vadim, and Anna Bildt. It was an airless, confined space, with a chalkboard showing a duty roster from years past and a bulb hanging from a threadbare wire.

"I know why," said Anna.

"I'm not sure you do," said Sylvie. "Your father worked for me, in a manner of speaking. We were close for many years."

"I doubt that."

Sylvie regarded the woman seated before her. Stubborn, impetuous, headstrong. Not a chance of getting out of here in one piece and still playing it tough. It was almost like looking in the mirror, save that dreadful haircut. "So he mentioned me?"

"No," said Anna. "Never. We didn't speak about his work."

"Vadim told me you'd said as much. I'm having a difficult time believing him, or you. I'm trying to understand how on the one hand you say you barely spoke with him…you know nothing of his day-to-day affairs, are contemptuous of his work at the bank…and yet here you are, risking your life to find out what happened to him."

"He's my father."

"I didn't very much like my father either. I'm not sure I'd have done the same."

"Was he murdered?"

"He drank himself to death. The Russian equivalent."

"I'm only doing what any daughter would," said Anna.

Touché. Sylvie admired the woman's pluck, even if she disagreed with her every word. A person's responsibility was to themselves. Disobey that rule and pay the price. "You're a good girl," she said. "No one is doubting that. I'm sorry it's come to this. Let me explain. As I said, your father and I worked together for years. I relied on him. Maybe I gave him too much business. The authorities began asking questions. I know this because your father told me. We altered our arrangements. I was made to believe the authorities had lost interest. Fortunately, I discovered that your father was lying to me. He'd decided to cooperate, to provide them with evidence of his wrongdoing in exchange for immunity, a new life elsewhere. He left us no choice. And so…" Sylvie let her words trail off.

She poured them both a glass of mineral water.

"Anna," she said, after a companionable silence. "I need to know if your father shared his concerns with you."

"He did not."

A prim smile. A shake of the head. "He was a careful man. I am forced to believe that he made more than one copy of the evidence he was to give the authorities. A safety measure, if nothing else. Let me ask you again. Did your father provide you with any such materials? Papers, a computer disc, a flash drive, the password to a locker in the cloud?"

"No," said the Danish woman.

"Nothing?"

"Nothing."

Sylvie didn't believe her, perhaps because as a mother she couldn't imagine failing to say goodbye. "Not even a letter explaining his actions in case he was killed? It's the natural thing to do. You are, after all, his only child."

"His suitcases were packed and waiting for him in the front hall. That was the first I learned of his intentions."

"You fired a gun at Pavel. That doesn't sound like the actions of an innocent."

"I'd found the pistol in my father's desk."

"Along with the evidence he'd left behind for you..."

"There was no evidence," said Anna. "Pavel and the other one, they wanted to kill me. Of course I fired at them."

"Because you were expecting them."

"No!"

Sylvie turned and gave Vadim a look. She'd tried. "I have no choice but to presume that you're lying. It will be your job to convince me otherwise."

"I've told you the truth," said Anna.

"That," said Sylvie, "we are about to find out."

Anna Bildt convinced her.

It took an hour and two teeth. One finger was broken and, judging by the bruising of her torso, probably a few ribs. Not so bad, as these things go. In all that time, the woman never shed a tear or cried for mercy. Proof indeed. If only Sylvie's children were so strong.

Sylvie regarded the woman, lying supine on the floor, clothing torn, one eye swollen, the other staring at her. It seemed Carl Bildt hadn't left his daughter a note or, more importantly, evidence of his bad works. Well, then, one thing less to worry about.

CHAPTER 55

Tel Aviv, Israel

Ten p.m. The engineering lab was dark and, at first appearance, deserted. Flickers from the array of monitors lining every available surface—sixty-two and counting—cast ghostly shadows across the polished floor. In a far corner, two men sat on work stools, heads raised, eyes focused on the largest of the monitors. Both whispered urgently to themselves, rapt in concentration.

"All right, boys, what do we have?" asked Danni Pine, exiting the stairwell from her office on the top floor.

"Quiet," said one of the men, Dov.

The other, Isaac, shot her a venomous look, running his fingers across his lips. *Zip it.*

Both men were pale, unshaven, and, if you got too close, in need of a shower. In the spectral light, they might have been twins. They were no such thing, unless related by their devotion to computer science and all things digital. Dov Cohen and Isaac Gold were Danni's best software engineers, PhDs from MIT and Carnegie Mellon, respectively, veterans of the Israeli Defense Forces, and vice presidents of the SON Group, not that either gave two shekels about a title.

"What did you—?" Danni began, incensed, before regarding the screen. Any thought she had of upbraiding her employees vanished. She took up position between the two, placing a hand on a shoulder of each man.

"Two outs," said Dov. "Bottom of the ninth."

"Down by one," said Isaac.

"Man on second," said Dov.

Danni looked at the player standing at the plate. Number 8. "Come on, Braunie," she said. "You can do it."

Dov removed his earbuds and switched the sound to external speakers.

"The count is three and two to Braun. Kershaw winds up . . . Braun swings . . . and nails it . . . Going . . . going . . . Gone! Home run Milwaukee! And that ends it. A walk-off at the bottom of the ninth. Brewers sweep the Dodgers."

"Guess I brought him some luck," said Danni.

"Yeah, sure, boss," said Isaac.

Baseball had been an obsession Danni's entire life. Her father, retired General Zev Franck, had grown up playing the sport in Kibbutz Ben-Israel in the Galilee. His idol had been Sandy Koufax, the Hall of Fame pitcher of the Los Angeles Dodgers, and one of the few Jewish players in Major League Baseball. Danni had been watching and playing the game as long as she could remember. Like many Israelis, she enjoyed following the careers of Jewish players in the majors. Her favorite was Ryan Braun. If only she were a few years younger.

"Okay, then," she said. "Back to work. I ask you again, what have you got?"

On the primary monitor, Gold brought up a mirror image of the home screen of Sylvie Bettencourt's laptop. "Took a little longer than usual," he said. "There were a few obstacles in the OS we didn't expect. She's smart. She knows people are looking. She'd taken steps to harden the system."

"We're smarter," said Danni. "How much longer?"

Gold cleared his throat, looked sidelong at Cohen. "How long, Dov?"

"Two seconds."

"You're kidding me," said Danni. "I thought you were joking."

"Well," said Isaac. "It was really only 1.8665."

Danni had a problem believing her ears. A delay of two seconds in breaking an adversary's digital defenses was an eternity for a computer chip with dedicated neural network hardware capable of eleven trillion operations a second. "If word gets out..."

"I'm on it," said Isaac.

"We'll talk about this later," said Danni. "If you two boys are still working for me."

"Yes, boss."

"Okay, then," she said, pointing at the screen. "Impress me."

Isaac Gold double-clicked on the "Files" folder. Inside, second item from the top, was another folder, named "HCCH." "Holding Companies Switzerland," he said.

"'CH' stands for Confœderatio Helvetica," added Cohen.

"A fount of information," said Danni.

Gold opened the folder, revealing a list three pages long of holding companies, one hundred eighty-eight in all.

"Sort by date," said Danni. "Most recent first."

The most recent company listed was named New Regency IV. The file held all scanned copies of all documents pertaining to its establishment. Share capital of one hundred thousand Swiss francs. Purpose to hold one hundred percent of shares of the American Automobile Acquisition Corporation, founded this year, its president named as Mr. S. L. Obolensky, Russian citizen, aged seventy-one.

"Hold it here," said Danni. "Run a cross-check on that corporation."

Gold typed the words into the laptop's search bar. The name American Automobile Acquisition Corporation appeared in six documents, including two dealing with its founding. More interesting was the draft of a letter from Bettencourt addressed to "AAAC" requesting a transfer of $102 million to an account in her name at the Bank of Liechtenstein, Vaduz branch. Reason for transfer: "Purchase of 1963 Ferrari 250 GTO, chassis number 3387, from Desmond Hamilton, British citizen."

"Does she have an app for the Bank of Liechtenstein?"

Gold searched the apps folder. "I'm counting sixty-seven banking apps, and yes, she does have one for the Bank of Liechtenstein."

Sixty-seven, thought Danni. It's the mother lode. "Open it."

Gold double-clicked on the "BOL" icon. The username and password entered automatically. A list of recent transactions filled the screen. There it was. Top of the list was a debit in favor of Desmond Hamilton for $102 million. And wired into the account a few days earlier, a transfer from the American Automobile Acquisition Corporation's account at the Danske Bank, Lugano branch.

"Let's take a break," said Danni.

"But we're just getting started," protested Dov Cohen. "She has hundreds of accounts. And what about the holding companies?"

"If you're smart, you'll use this time to figure out why our software—the backbone of this company—took two seconds longer than normal to defeat some lousy Russian firewalls."

Danni left the lab and ran upstairs to her office. She dropped into her chair, already dialing Special Agent Nessa Kenyon.

"Danni…you okay?"

"We did it. Or rather, our boy did."

"*Simon did what?*…Hold on, I need a second to wake up."

Danni leaned forward and played with her collection of action figures: Moshe Dayan, Menachem Begin, Golda Meir. Not even seventy-five years ago, Israel was a dream fueled by rebels, seers, and madmen, or as they were called with hatred, "Zionists." Her grandfather had counted himself among their number, himself a refugee from Poland escaping yet another wave of pogroms. If only Dayan and Meir and Begin could see the economic powerhouse Israel had become. A country so formidable that its oldest enemy, the House of Saud, now recognized it as a state, even seeking it out as a partner. Danni was proud of the part, however small, her company had played.

"I'm back," said Nessa Kenyon.

"We've compromised Bettencourt's laptop," said Danni. "It has everything: bank accounts, holding companies, usernames, passwords, private correspondence. Basically, all paperwork and corresponding banking records for every purchase she's made in the last twenty years."

"Go on."

"It appears as if the holding companies are controlled by Sergei Obolensky. All the funds are wired from corporations with his name listed as either president or on the board of directors."

"It's a start."

"A start? You've got her. Direct ties to the closest friend of the Russian president."

"Maybe," said Nessa. "But it's not proof of tainted funds. We need another step."

"It's good to know who's sending Sylvie Bettencourt the money. Now we need to know who is sending it to Obolensky first."

CHAPTER 56

Haute-Savoie, France

*C*lear the camp."

Simon stood at the window, gazing at the parade of headlights and taillights coming and going from the hotel, the roar of engines shattering the alpine calm. For the past hour, the halls had shaken with footsteps, men calling to one another, doors slamming. He could see them filing down the path, suitcases in hand, rucksacks on their backs. It was an exodus en masse.

A rap on the door. Simon rushed to open it.

"Sylvie wants to speak with you," said Vadim.

"What's going on?"

"Ask her. Oh, and don't worry. You don't have to pack yet. You and me, we're leaving tomorrow. All right, then, shake tail."

The moment Simon entered the room, Sylvie Bettencourt said, "He's arriving tomorrow, flying into Paphos. His plane lands at noon."

Simon noted the travel bag by the door, her oversize purse next to it. "Obolensky?"

"Of course Obolensky. Who else would be flying into Cyprus?"

This was a new Sylvie, one he hadn't seen before. Curt, agitated, and, to judge by the way she was pacing the room, one step from a force 10 breakdown. She stopped long enough to pour herself a glass of scotch and drink half of it in a go. She caught Simon watching, then sighed and dropped onto the sofa. "Nikos Christiades, the man who owns the Limassol Free Port, will pick him up."

"A friend?"

"Ten thousand dollars' worth, at least in this case. Christiades booked him into the Amara Hotel. The Midas Suite. Appropriate. Obolensky instructed him to find a garage to switch out the gearbox."

"He doesn't plan on driving it?"

"He knows better. Our friend has other predilections he likes to indulge while on the island."

"Antiquities? Fresh fish?"

"I don't like to go into tawdry details."

"The more I know about his itinerary, the better."

"Women," said Sylvie. "A certain house of ill repute on the Turkish side of the island. Not the finest, from what I understand. Mr. Obolensky likes to dip his toe in the gutter."

"Married?"

"Almost fifty years."

"Happily?"

"A word with many definitions. They're together. That counts for something."

"Just the one night?"

"He doesn't tarry," said Sylvie. "Shall I book you and Vadim into the same hotel?"

"I work alone."

"Not this time." Sylvie finished the scotch. A defiant look his way. "And no, I don't trust you."

There came the sound of vehicles approaching, engines gearing down, doors opening and closing. Voices calling out. Sylvie pulled back a curtain. "The camp is shutting down."

"Is there a reason?" he asked, knowing all too well the answer.

"There is."

Simon rose and looked out the window. Passenger vans crowded the driveway. He counted approximately twenty men climbing into the vehicles. He didn't see Pavel or Alec among them. Another person was missing from his count. The woman.

"Your friend, Christiades, does he know where Obolensky is flying in from?"

"I told you. Obolensky keeps his whereabouts a secret."

Simon wasn't buying. A man of his stature. People talked. "But you must have friends in common?"

"I don't think Sergei would appreciate me taking an interest in his private life. Besides, why should I care? I do know that he likes to sail. During the summer, he's seen on the Côte d'Azur, the Amalfi Coast, Sardinia, Mallorca."

"That's a broad swath."

"Which is why you're going to follow him back to his home."

"Be resourceful."

"Exactly."

"Let's say I do. Let's say I find where he lives. It's sure to be guarded. Michael would have insisted."

"That hasn't stopped you before."

"Say I get inside. Then what? I'm not a hacker. Maybe I can mirror his hard drive, but no more. It will be encrypted. Without a password, it's worthless."

"I'm not interested in his computer," said Sylvie.

A surprise, but he'd grown to expect them. "What am I looking for, then?"

Sylvie stood at the side table, pouring herself another drink, wobbling oh so slightly on her feet. "Sergei Obolensky is a Luddite. He hates technology, just like he hates modern music. If he had a choice, we'd all be back in the court of Alexander the Second, listening to Tchaikovsky conduct his '1812 Overture.' He rarely carries a cellphone. He despises television. Does he use a computer? Of course. He has no choice. But he's also Russian, which means he's paranoid. He hears from all of Michael's advisors how vulnerable computers are, and how he must be sure to safeguard his information. This firewall, that encryption. Cover your camera, hide your keystrokes. He follows their advice, but in the end, he doesn't trust it. There's only one way to keep things safe. The old-fashioned way. Write down all important information and keep it hidden where only he can see it."

"Which is?"

"A little blue book."

"A blue book?" Simon said.

"A Moleskine, I believe."

"You've seen it?"

"Many is the time I've sat in my office as Sergei consults his book and we review our business together. I can see his long, slim fingers turning the pages now, reading out the account numbers, writing down the details of my latest purchase. If I'm going to find evidence of his wrongdoing, I need to see that book."

"And he keeps it close by?"

"At his home, I imagine, wherever that might be."

"You're sure?"

"You wouldn't be here if I wasn't," snapped Sylvie.

"And then?"

"Don't take it, God forbid. Photograph the contents. Put it back where you found it. Send me the information."

"Before anything happens to me...or the camera."

"That's what I'm paying you for."

"About that," said Simon. "I usually get half up front. Sometimes more."

"Are you usually wanted for murder?"

"I don't work for free," he said. "Under any circumstances."

"Give me an account number. I'll wire you a million."

"Now," said Simon.

"Shut up and give it to me."

Simon recited the routing number of a bank in the Cayman Islands, followed by his account number. He looked on as Sylvie logged on to her bank and made the transfer. Her phone buzzed, prompting her to type in a six-digit code to finalize the operation. Five minutes and it was done.

"I'll need some things," he said. "Electronics. You know. I have a colleague who usually helps me out."

"We have a contact in Limassol. He will be able to provide you with everything you need."

"I thought you said you'd left government service."

Sylvie drained her glass. "If only it were so easy. A little bit like that tattoo on your arm. 'The world doesn't leave you behind.' Isn't that what you said to your friend D'Art?"

Simon smiled uneasily. He didn't enjoy having his words quoted back to him.

"Get some rest. You'll leave with Vadim first thing in the morning."

"And you? Back to Paris?"

"I'll be doing what I always do," said Sylvie Bettencourt, picking up her bags, ducking into the corridor. "Going shopping."

To London, thought Simon. To buy another Ferrari.

The girl.

Simon did not return to his room. Instead, he took the stairs to the lobby, watching for a moment as the stragglers shouldered duffel bags and dragged suitcases to the front door. He looked for Vadim, for Pavel and Alec, didn't see them, then crossed the worn carpeting to the front desk. A pile of keys lay on the counter. No sign of the woman he'd seen earlier. Simon vaulted the desk. A horn blared outside. He froze. Someone shouted an angry response. Simon tried the door to the front office. The handle turned easily. A look across the lobby. No one.

Simon entered the office, closing the door behind him. A desk, a gooseneck lamp, a ledger. He spotted a key box on the wall. Locked, but not for long. The smallest blade from his knife, a paper clip straightened. Easy peasy.

Inside the key box, four rows of brass hooks. Beneath each a label, typed God knows when, surely before he was born. Simon ran a finger across them. "Salle de Conférence." "Cuisine." "Stockage Extérieur." "Générateur #2, Gauche." He took all of them. One, he hoped, would open the cooler.

"Can I help you?" the hotel manager asked as he left her office.

"Just leaving my key, but thank you," said Simon.

He passed through the front doors and down the steps, heading to his left, skirting the building.

Then he heard it.

A gunshot.

CHAPTER 57

Haute-Savoie, France

The storeroom door swung open. Pavel stepped inside. "Put on a jacket. We're going."

"Where?" asked Anna.

"Leaving."

"What...now? Where are you taking me?"

A sharp wind swept inside. Anna retreated a step. So the moment had come. Looking at Pavel, seeing the gun in his jacket, she wasn't scared so much as bewildered, the victim of some perverse irony. She had devoted her life to exposing crimes, denouncing autocrats, fighting for the disenfranchised, just hoping to help as much as one person could. She was under no illusions. She was no saint. She did it for herself as much as for anyone else. Now this. A captive for trying to unmask the murderer of a dishonest man. Someone who hadn't cared about autocrats, crime, or the disenfranchised, if he even had known what the word meant. The problem was that he was her father. Blood changed everything. But she wasn't ready to die for him. Not here, not at the hands of a Russian hood named Pavel.

"We're closing the camp," said Pavel. "Now come on."

Anna didn't budge. "Why?"

Pavel closed the door behind him. "Because of you," he said. "You and your friends on the net."

"Where are you taking me?"

"Annecy. We'll drop you at the train station."

"I don't believe you," said Anna.

"It doesn't matter what you believe. Get your things."

Play along, she thought. *It's your only chance.* Anna put on her jacket, found her cap, pulled it low over her ears. "Can you give me some money? I need a train ticket, something to eat, a place to stay. I have nothing."

"Later."

Anna stared at him. She recalled Alec shooting Freddy Hold, then turning the gun on her. She'd looked into his eyes. She'd seen nothing. Not in his eyes, not in Pavel's. There would be no "later."

Pavel put his arm across the doorway, barring her path. "Run and I'll shoot you."

"I get it." She slipped her hand into her pocket. Her fingers closed around the shiv she'd made for herself. A strut from the bedframe, sharpened as best she could.

"Let's go, then."

Pavel dropped his arm. As he did, Anna charged him, lowering her shoulder, knocking him against the wall. She jabbed the shiv into his side, once, twice. The blade barely entered his flesh, stymied by his jacket. He recoiled and she stabbed at his neck, missing, striking his face below the eye, the blade glancing off his cheek, laying open the skin to the bone. Pavel slid onto the floor, hands covering his wound.

Anna rushed out the door and moved to her left, toward the forest bordering the compound, into the trees, and up the mountain. Running was out of the question. Trying to walk fast was bad enough, the pain from her ribs hard to bear. Still, she tried.

She'd taken ten steps when she looked behind her. She caught a dark form on his hands and knees. Pavel. An instant later, a bullet struck a tree beside her, the report shattering the still air, more frightening still.

"Alec! Hurry!" she heard Pavel cry.

Anna ducked behind a tree, waiting a moment, then peeking out. Two men stood by the open storeroom. Light shown on Alec's face as he helped Pavel to his feet. No time to look any longer.

Ann broke from cover and lumbered up the hill, avoiding fallen branches, loose stones, reminding herself to zig and zag. But how when she was moving so slowly? She pumped her arms, trying to choose her steps wisely, too often stumbling. She was breathing too fast, panic winning out over discipline. The incline increased in severity. The trees were denser here. She settled into a forced march, constantly checking over her shoulder. It was too dark to see far. If there was a moon, clouds obscured it. She saw nothing behind her, no fleeting shadows at the edge of her vision, no signs of movement whatsoever. The slope eased. The trees fell away. Night enveloped her. A cloak of wind. One more step and then…*nothing*.

Anna froze, one foot touching the precipice. Darkness below. An abyss.

She jumped back, chest heaving, and bent double, hands on her knees. A trail followed the cliff's edge, a brown trail cut from moss and lichen running in both directions. Which way?

It was then she heard them. Men beating their way up the mountainside, speaking to one another in a foreign language, coming closer. She craned her neck, peering down the slope. A flash, an explosion of orange and blue. A bee whizzed past her ear. A gunshot.

Anna set off to her left, eyes locked on the band of dirt. Blackness, an infinite fall, to her right.

Faster, she urged herself.

The path narrowed. The slope to her left fell away, becoming a sheer vertical drop. Death to either side. Ahead, the trail dead-ended at a nearly vertical wall of jagged granite. Beyond it, she didn't know. She stopped, listened. There was only the wind, alternately fierce and shrieking, then still. There…*voices*. They were following. She climbed the rock crag, hand over hand, feet finding purchase on sharp edges. She moved mechanically, absence of choice besting a lifelong fear of heights. Her world narrowed down to the slab of rock in front of her. One step, then the next. Zen at ten thousand feet. Suddenly, she had reached the top. Below, maybe twenty meters, the trail resumed. Carefully, she climbed down, jumping the last few feet. She looked around her, aware that she was smiling crazily, mildly ecstatic. She set off again. The trail widened. The slope returned, scree and boulders. She began to jog. Finding a rhythm, she lengthened her stride. Another look behind her. Nothing. She continued for a few minutes before stopping. She'd done it. She'd lost them.

And now where to?

She scanned the dark for any lights. A village? A hut? There…she saw a grouping of yellow lights. Was that a car driving down a road?

The blow hit her below the knees. Her feet left the ground. For an instant, she saw the man rolling beneath her. Black hair. Weak jaw. Alec. She landed on her back, her breath leaving her. She placed a hand on the ground. Her fingers curled around a rock. She turned on her side, got to a knee.

Someone else struck her from behind, a boot to the center of the back. She fell onto her chest, her cheek slamming the scree, gravel filling her mouth. Pavel lifted her by the shoulders. Alec stood in front of her. He delivered a fist to the solar plexus, before Pavel shoved her to the ground.

Anna rolled onto her back, eyes gazing blurrily at the men towering over her.

"I told you," said Pavel, blood covering much of his face.

Anna saw the gun in his hand, hanging casually at his side. "You don't think I knew," she said. "What did you expect?"

"You brought this on yourself."

"You killed my father."

"He was going to the authorities," said Pavel. "He gave us no choice."

"Bankers are supposed to keep their mouths shut," said Alec.

"So you blew him up?" Anna let her head fall to the ground. She was exhausted. It was all too much and she wanted to rest.

"Not here," said Alec to Pavel. "We can't leave her."

"Makarova wants her to disappear. We're not going to carry her back to camp."

"Call Vadim," said Alec. "Ask him."

Pavel dialed a number on his phone. "No service." He returned his attention to Anna. "Stand up. Put them on."

A pair of flex-cuffs landed beside her. Anna picked them up and stood. "How? Can you help?"

Alec took the cuffs. "Put out your hands," he instructed.

Anna extended her arms. "Wrists up or down?"

"Down," said Alec, attaching one cuff. "Keep steady."

Anna shook her head. Suddenly, she was crying, despondent.

"Now she cries," said Pavel. "Once she drags us up here." He touched his cheek, wincing. "No one's going to find her here. What do you think?"

"Maybe," said Alec.

"We say she fell," said Pavel. "Back there. We couldn't do anything about it."

"You think?"

"Look at her. She's a wreck. We don't have any other choice."

Alec appeared uncertain.

Pavel raised the pistol, barely looking at her.

"No!" shouted Anna.

A gun fired. Pavel spun, eyes blinking. Another shot. He fell to his knees and toppled over. Alec dropped Anna's hands, turning toward the source of the fire. A man came out of the dark, arm extended, pistol pointed at her. Vadim. He looked at Alec, then moved his aim and fired. Alec fell to the ground. Vadim stood over him and fired again.

"Idiots," he said. "They posted on social media. Did you see?"

Anna couldn't find her voice. She nodded. She shook her head. Yes, they were idiots. No, she hadn't seen the post. Her ears were ringing. She couldn't take her eyes from the dead men.

"My brother tells me they won't stop—this online 'collective,' he called it. Chatterbell, yes?"

"That's how it works," said Anna. "We help each other."

"I must look at it." He pointed the gun at her. "And you, you'll keep at it, too, I suppose, until you have proof that I'm involved. More traffic pictures or links to my phone number, I don't know what else."

"For my father."

"But it can stop now," said Vadim. A reasonable suggestion. "The two who purchased the car, who made the bomb, planted it, detonated it…they're dead. Justice has been served, no?"

Anna stared at Vadim, affront winning out over fear. And Hold? Murdered in cold blood for trying to help her. What about him? She would tell the police what she saw. It was her duty. Justice had not been served, not even close. "It was the lady who ordered it done," she said. "Who is she?"

"Her, you won't get."

"They'll find you next. They'll put a name to a face, to a phone number. From there, who knows? It won't stop until it's over."

Vadim stared off. "Damn."

Then Anna saw it. There was someone else there, something behind

Vadim. She caught a shadow just beyond her vision, a person circling behind the Russian.

"Where will you go," said Anna. A statement, not a question. "The police have seen the proof. I may be dead, but so what?"

"Stop," said Vadim. "I've heard enough."

There it was again. A frisson of movement, closer now.

"They'll know you killed me. They'll find my body. They'll track you to the camp. You're already in enough trouble."

"She's right," said Simon Riske as he advanced out of the darkness.

CHAPTER 58

Haute-Savoie, France

Vadim spun, eyes wide, meeting Simon's fist, knuckles striking him beneath the jaw, the power of the blow staggering him, forcing him to a knee.

Simon followed the blow with another, a left struck downward to Vadim's cheek. The Russian toppled onto his back. Simon stepped on his wrist and freed the pistol. As Vadim struggled to stand, Simon spun the weapon so he held it by the barrel and lashed a blow to the temple. Vadim collapsed unconscious.

"You okay?" Simon asked the woman. He saw that her face was bruised, dried blood caked at the corner of her mouth.

"No," she said. "Not really."

Simon tucked the gun into his waistband. "Anna? Anna Bildt?" He offered his hand, but she made no move to take it. "I know who you are and why you're here," he said. "I'm sorry about your father."

"You're not with them?" she asked.

"Complicated question, but no."

"Who are you, then?"

"A friend."

"You speak American English," said Anna. "Like them."

"I'm an American."

"Sure you are." Finally, she took his hand and pulled herself to her feet. "Those two, they killed my father."

"Yes, I know."

"And another man, too. In Chur."

"They're not going to kill anyone else," said Simon. The wind picked

275

up, alternating erratically from benign current to banshee gale. "Can you walk?"

"I got up here, didn't I?"

"Dumb question."

Simon moved nearer to Alec and Pavel, kneeling by the bodies, checking for a pulse. None. He took each man's pistol, dropped the magazines, threw the pieces down the mountainside. Next, he put a hand to Vadim's neck. The pulse was slow and steady. An ox. Simon stood and slid his knife from his pocket. "Your hand."

Anna hesitated before stepping closer, her cuffed hand extended. Simon slipped the blade beneath the restraint, holding her forearm securely as he sawed through the tensile plastic.

"They're spies," said Anna. "Who are you?"

"I told you. A friend. My name's Simon."

"Nice to meet you, Simon. I think." Anna looked at the dead men, unfazed. "Now what?"

"Almost done." Simon returned to Vadim's side, patting him down, relieving him of his wallet and his phone. "Hold this," he said, tossing Anna the Russian's wallet. He turned his attention to the phone. Locked. "Step back," he said.

"Why?"

"Please."

Anna retreated a step.

Simon spotted a second set of cuffs on the ground next to Alec. He picked them up and turned Vadim on his side, wrenching his right arm behind his back, attaching one cuff, then yanking his left leg next to it and attaching the other to his ankle. Not quite hog-tied but close enough. He shook Vadim by the shoulder, then slapped his cheek. The Russian opened his eyes.

"Passcode," said Simon. "For the phone."

Vadim grimaced, aware of his predicament. He struggled against his bonds, then quickly thought the better of it. "I knew it," he said, spitting out a wad of blood and phlegm. "Had to be."

"I don't go in for murder," said Simon.

"It's none of your business."

"Actually, it is. Now tell me the passcode."

"Fuck you."

"No, fuck you!" Anna jumped forward and kicked Vadim in the ribs. "He's right. You're a murderer."

"Enough," said Simon, raising his hand. "Anna. Stop."

A last kick before she retreated, even then unwillingly.

Simon freed the pistol from his waistband, checked that a round was chambered, then placed the barrel against Vadim's forehead. "Passcode."

Vadim shook his head.

"Let's not play this game," said Simon. "It's your only way down this mountain."

"Yeb vas," said Vadim.

"Tough guy, eh?" Simon moved the pistol to the right and fired into the ground. "I didn't hear you."

Vadim squeezed his eyes closed.

Simon moved the pistol to the left, an inch from the Russian's ear, fired again, then placed the superheated barrel under Vadim's chin. "What's the code?"

"One, two, two, one," shouted Vadim, tears flowing from his eyes.

Why wasn't he surprised? Simon punched in the number. The home screen came to life. He was in. "A few more questions and we're done. Why does Sylvie really want the book?"

"He's stealing from her."

"Not what she told me," said Simon. "You need to synch your stories." He returned the gun to Vadim's forehead. "I've killed one Russian this week. I'll be happy to make it two."

Vadim bit his lower lip, mustering his courage. Simon pressed the barrel harder against him. "Why?"

Vadim exhaled loudly. Resistance over.

"Obolensky's accounts. She needs the information for Grisha."

"Who is…?"

"My half brother. In Moscow. Grigori Novalev. Unit 29155. He's a computer guy. You know, a hacker."

Suddenly, Sylvie's story made sense. She didn't need the notebook to check if the Cellist was falsifying records. She needed it to steal from him. No, thought Simon, catching himself, realizing he had not thought it all the way through. Not from Obolensky. She planned on stealing from Michael, who had parked his money in accounts registered in his best friend's name. Accounts listed in a blue Moleskine notebook.

The question was how much money? And how many accounts?

The answer was a lot. More than Simon dared imagine.

And so, the Indonesian passport. Escape to Bali after the deed was done.

Simon decided he needed to rethink his fees. Five million was far too low.

"You ready?" he said to Anna.

"What about him?" she asked.

"What about him?" said Simon, returning the pistol to his waistband. He activated the phone's flashlight function, directing the beam in the direction from which he'd come.

Vadim rolled this way and that, fighting to free himself from the cuffs. "You're a dead man," he said. "You know that?"

Simon put a foot on the man's chest. "I'm not the one all alone on a mountaintop in the middle of the freakin' French Alps."

"Sylvie will find you."

"Maybe," said Simon. "If and when she starts looking. I think I remember her saying something about you not contacting her until you'd gotten a new phone. Actually, I think it was an order."

Vadim's voice softened. The time for bravado had come and gone. "I'll freeze to death."

"Good," said Anna.

"Riske! Don't!"

"You heard her."

Simon started down the path, Anna close behind, as Vadim shouted his name.

The last stragglers had left the hotel. All lights were doused, save a few faltering lamps in the rear courtyard. The back entry remained unlocked. He led Anna through the dining room and into the kitchen, down a hallway to a small, enclosed room, a wooden table at the center, ten chairs around it. The staff dining room. Safe enough here. He turned on the lights. Anna dropped into the closest chair, her head falling to the table.

"I'll get some water, see if there's something to eat."

Anna said, "Thank you."

Simon ventured back into the kitchen, knowing well that there was little time to rest; they needed to make tracks. A look over his shoulder. No, he decided. She needed a break, even for a few minutes.

The walk down the mountain had been hard on her. Whatever adrenaline had fueled her escape had long since been used up. She'd told Simon what Vadim had done to her, and more than once he'd suppressed the urge to run back up the slope and put a bullet in Vadim's brain. God knows it would make things easier.

The refrigerator was stocked. He found a platter of roasted chicken, black bread, butter, and pickles. A tray to put it on. A bottle of mineral water, two glasses. When he returned, Anna was asleep. He set the plate in front of her, poured a glass of water.

"Be right back," he whispered.

Simon returned to the lobby, running up the main staircase to the third floor. First stop, his room. He gathered his new belongings, threw them into the suitcase, and carried it down the hall to Vadim's room. The door was unlocked. A travel bag like his sat in a chair. The keys to the Mercedes lay on the nightstand. He checked the drawers. Another pistol, several spare magazines. A phone with a lavender case. The pistol and ammo went out the window. He picked up the phone. The home screen lit up. Two messages. One from a Swiss number. The other from Denmark. Anna's phone, then. And still half charged.

A check of the travel bag. Dirty clothes. A toiletry kit. Inside it, several containers of prescription medications: Xanax, amphetamines, ketamine. He dumped the pills into the john and flushed. No PEDs allowed. He had to assume Vadim would find a way off the mountain.

When Simon returned to the dining room, Anna had woken up. The bread was gone and the pickles, but the chicken was untouched.

"You're not hungry?"

"I'm vegan."

"Not tonight," said Simon. "I need you strong." He placed her phone on the table. "Messages."

Anna glanced at the phone, but something was bothering her. "Who are you?" she asked. "Really."

"Someone doing the right thing," said Simon. "Like you."

"Then why are you with them? With Vadim and Pavel?"

"I can't say more. Not now."

"Simon Riske. Who isn't a Russian and isn't a spy but keeps company with Russian spies."

Simon nodded. It wouldn't serve her to know anything further.

Anna picked up the phone.

"Hey," said Simon as she typed in her passcode. "Stop."

"What?"

"You're dead."

"Pardon?"

Simon placed his hand over the phone. "No one can know you're alive. Not yet. Don't answer the messages. Don't call anyone. Don't post on Chatterbell. That's how they found you before."

"Okay. I get it," said Anna, displeased. She pulled the phone free, shielding it from him. "Do you mind?"

"Of course," he said. "I didn't mean to..."

Simon turned his chair away. He had a phone to look at, too. He punched in Vadim's passcode and, for the next minutes, made a cursory examination of his emails and phone records. Top of the list, a message to the fixed-base operator at Annecy Airport, instructing them to have his plane fueled and ready for a morning departure. There were several cryptic messages to Pavel and Alec, but Simon had no time to decipher them. He was pleased to discover that the phone was set up to pay electronically. Two clicks and anything his heart desired was his. Along with the money he'd found in Vadim's wallet, he was set.

On a lark, he checked the Photo app. Pictures of Sylvie, a mansion in a sunny locale, the Lost Ferrari, and of course several de rigueur shots of nude women. The last thumbnail—meaning the most recent photograph taken—caught his eye, if only because compared to the others it was so ordinary.

The thumbnail showed a navy-blue Volkswagen sedan parked on the side of a road. Europe, if he had to guess. Clay tile roofs. Stucco façades. Palm trees. Spain. Italy. Somewhere Mediterranean. Looking closer, he noted a time stamp in the lower right-hand corner: 0:33. Not a photo—a video clip. The hairs on the back of his neck stood up. *Could it be?* His eyes darted from the screen. Anna's head was bowed over her phone. Simon made sure the sound was muted, then hit PLAY.

The picture expanded to fill the screen. For a few seconds, nothing happened. The street remained quiet, traffic-free. Then a car entered the frame—a Beetle—coming to a halt at a stop sign. A moment later, a Maybach pulled up behind it, directly adjacent to the navy-blue sedan. It was hard to make out its driver. A head of sandy hair—that was about all. Strangely, the driver of the Beetle climbed out of his car and ran away, quickly out of frame. The Maybach began to back up, but only for a second. Less, even. A terrific flash of orange and black. A fireball enveloped the screen. The camera shook as debris flew in every direction. The lens steadied. The Maybach was a twisted, mangled wreck, engulfed in flame. Coils of ink-black smoke rose into the sky. The camera zoomed in until only the car filled the screen. Then closer still. There was something wedged into the windscreen, something awful, something Simon didn't want to see.

"What is it?" asked Anna.

Simon put down the phone. "Nothing."

"You look sick."

"Just tired." Simon tried a smile, failed miserably. "Anything important?"

"From my father's office," said Anna. "His secretary."

"If it's none of my business..."

"His attorney came by. He has a letter for me. Something from my father."

"I'm glad."

Anna appeared unmoved. One day she'd be happy, whatever it said. "He insists he give it to me in person."

"Do you know him?"

"His name is Aldo Rossi. They played tennis together. He's always trying to hit on me."

"When was it sent—the message, I mean?"

"This morning. I'll read it to you. 'Signor Rossi stopped by the office earlier. He has a letter for you from your father. He said it is very important. I asked him to leave it, but he insisted that he give it to you in person.'" Anna lowered the phone. "Are you sure I shouldn't answer him?"

"Too late now anyway."

"Sylvie," she said. "That's the woman. She was sure my father had made copies of whatever it was he was giving to the authorities."

"He didn't?"

"I don't know one way or the other. He didn't tell me and I didn't find anything."

"And that's what you told Sylvie."

Anna nodded, her eyes searching his own. "She let him beat me. She watched. It didn't bother her."

But Simon had no answer for her. He was responsible, too. "I should have gotten you out sooner."

"You saved my life." Anna wiped her eyes. Her shoulders gave a great heave. "And you? You're not afraid of them?"

"Sure I am," said Simon. "That's why I'm going to make sure they won't be around much longer to hurt you, me, or anyone else."

"Why do you want to stop them?"

"I have my reasons."

"That's all you're going to tell me?"

Simon pushed his chair back. "I think we should go."

Anna remained seated. "Where?"

"You? Lugano, if you feel safe. Your father's house. I'll drop you at the train station in Geneva. Sound okay?"

Anna nodded. "I can take care of myself from there. You do what you have to do."

"You're sure?"

"He's still up there, right?" Anna motioned toward the mountain.

"Should be there for a while."

"Then we're good," said Anna. "If I find anything out about, you know, if my father left behind something, I'll call you."

"Fair enough." Simon told her not to call Vadim's number—they had no way of knowing if it was compromised, and someone might be listening—and that he would send her the number from a new phone as soon as he purchased one.

Anna gave a thumbs-up. Her swagger was back.

"All right, then," said Simon. "Let's roll."

Chapter 59

Geneva, Switzerland

I need a plane," said Simon. "To Cyprus. Paphos International Airport."

"Of course, sir," replied the clerk, young, attentive, a pilot himself by the epaulets on his crisp white shirt. His name tag identified him as MATISSE. "When are you interested in traveling?"

"Five minutes ago," said Simon.

Matisse—first name or last—smiled. Surely monsieur was making a pleasantry.

"Really," said Simon.

The smile vanished from Matisse's face.

Six a.m. Geneva Airport. Terminal 3, for private aviation. A steady stream of men, women, and children, bags in tow, passed through the bright, modern building. It was August. Vacation time. The world was back at full speed and then some.

"I'm sorry," said Matisse, "but that's not possible. We require twenty-four hours notice."

Simon slid his passport across the counter, a thousand-euro note tucked inside, the denomination just visible. "Name of Hudson, Thomas. I'm sure my people called yesterday."

Matisse disappeared into a back room, the passport with him.

Simon turned, leaning his back against the counter. He'd been working his way through Vadim's phone, reading emails, texts, logging numbers from WhatsApp. Lots of interesting info to glean, nothing more than the American Express Black Card set up for electronic payment.

He put the phone away and studied his fellow devotees of private air travel. The women were attractive, maybe more than that. The men, less so, though well dressed, well scrubbed, robustly healthy. It was their luggage that caught his attention. No Samsonites here. TUMI, Vuitton, Longchamp. And their shoes: more Ferragamos than on the Via Montenapoleone. It was the accessories that gave the rich away. They might wear torn Levis and grotty T-shirts, but check their watches, their shoes, their purses, and their luggage. It was like some kind of chronic affliction. If ever they were caught without their Rolex, they'd perish instantly. Like a vampire stepping into sunlight. Try as he might, however, Simon couldn't hate them. In this world, it was good to be rich. Full stop. Why, then, did he fight it so?

"Mr. Hudson?" Matisse had reappeared, and in a considerably more helpful mood. "First, I must inform you that it is peak season, and of course you are asking for a priority reservation."

Simon nodded. *Of course.* This was the part Vikram Singh called "the bad news."

"We have only a heavy aircraft available. No midsize. No light. I can offer you a Bombardier business jet, a Global 5000. It seats thirteen, in case you have any friends. Two pilots and a steward, naturally. The good news is the flying time to Cyprus is considerably faster. Two hours fifty-seven minutes. And we are happy to pay all carbon offset fees."

"Naturally," said Simon, wondering if Matisse was going to add a Spanish guitar trio, or perhaps, this being Geneva, and Simon being single, the services of a "private secretary." Alas, no.

"The flight cost is forty-three thousand Swiss francs. Or about forty thousand euros. One way."

Unfazed, Simon accessed the phone's e-pay function. He wasn't sure if this counted as giving the credit card a trial by fire, but close enough. Matisse moved the electronic sensor next to the phone. Two clicks and a Hail Mary, mother of God.

"…should be ready in forty minutes," Matisse was saying. The first part had been drowned out by Simon's pounding heart.

"That's fine."

Matisse gave him the name of the captain, a woman and Swedish, and co-captain, male, Spaniard. The steward was male, too. Was Simon allowed to be disappointed? "You should be arriving at Paphos International Airport at 11:25 local time."

Matisse pointed to a lounge where monsieur could enjoy breakfast while waiting, perhaps a glass of Champagne, if so inclined.

Instead, Simon visited the kiosk, where he purchased a new phone and SIM card.

After setting it up, he walked outside, continuing a distance from the terminal. The number he dialed had an Israeli country code.

"Danni, it's Simon. I'm in Geneva."

"With Bettencourt?"

"Things went sideways. I'll tell you later. How'd it go?" he asked, meaning what had she found on Bettencourt's laptop.

"We own it, but it's not enough."

"How's that?"

"Kenyon needs to know who is sending her the money, proof that it is a bad actor. Right now we have holding companies, LLCs, but no names."

"I'm headed to Cyprus. I need anything you have on a man named Sergei Obolensky."

"The Cellist?"

"You know him?"

"Of course," said Danni matter-of-factly. "Anything specific?"

"Place of residence," said Simon. "Apparently he moves around."

"His name came up in the files we found on Sylvie's laptop," said Danni. "What's in Cyprus?"

"Who do you think?" said Simon. "Obolensky is our guy."

"Give me a day," said Danni.

Vadim's phone buzzed in his pocket. Simon looked at the screen. "American Express Travel Services." He ended the call with Danni and picked up. "Hello?"

"This is Audrey from American Express. We're calling to confirm your charges with Jet Aviation in Geneva, Switzerland."

"That's correct," said Simon. "I'm here now."

"In the amount of forty-three thousand Swiss francs."

"That sounds right."

"Thank you, sir. You may continue using the card as you like."

"One question," said Simon. "What's my card limit?"

"Black Cards have no preapproved spending limit, sir. We like to call our clients anytime we notice any unusual activity."

"I see. Listen, I'll be in Cyprus and some spots in the Mediterranean, most likely, over the next few days. Don't worry if you see charges from that area."

"Thank you. I'll be sure to make a note of it in your file so we won't need to disturb you again."

Simon ended the call. *No preapproved spending limit.*

No sweeter words.

Simon boarded the Bombardier business jet at 7:15 a.m. sharp. He had the plane to himself. No guitar trio, but a pair of noise-cancelling headphones and Vadim's playlist on Spotify. Surprisingly, he didn't have terrible taste in music. It was John Legend who played Simon to sleep.

He awoke as the wheels touched down on Cypriot soil. He had an hour until Obolensky arrived—if, that is, the man's plans hadn't changed. Upon deplaning, he cleared customs on the tarmac. The official barely glanced at his new passport. Simon rented a car—a Toyota Camry—purchased a pair of sunglasses and a hat, then made his way to the observation deck.

The view looked over the airport's two parallel runways. Beyond them, a flat plain, with modestly farmed, rustic homes here and there. He preferred the view behind him. The shores of the Mediterranean lay barely a quarter mile's distance, the ocean a succession of blues, light to dark.

A little after twelve, he spotted a BMW drive onto the tarmac and park not far from where he had disembarked. A tall, dapper man got out and walked to the customs office, hardly larger than a garden shed. A few moments later, both men emerged and returned to the BMW. Simon guessed the well-dressed man was Christiades, Sylvie Bettencourt's contact. Somewhere along the way, Christiades slipped the official a little something that went straight into the man's pocket. Obolensky's arrival would be a smooth one.

Simon spotted the plane a few minutes later, a dark private jet approaching from the west. The plane landed, braking quickly, and turned onto the apron. It was a monster, bigger even than the Bombardier Simon had taken from Geneva. He noted the Russian tricolor painted high on the tail as the aircraft came to a halt. *Welcome to Cyprus, comrade.*

The forward door opened outward. A blond woman in a captain's uniform descended first and greeted the customs official. Kisses all around. So they were friends. A moment later, a tall, bulky man filled the doorway.

Simon didn't need help recognizing Sergei Obolensky. He'd looked at plenty of photographs of the man already. Six foot three, seventy-one years of age, a heavy drinker's florid face framed by a thick head of unnaturally brown hair worn much too long. Dressed in a loose-fitting T-shirt, baggy jeans, and high-top basketball shoes, he looked more like an aging rocker than an accomplished classical musician.

Obolensky took the stairs with caution, one hand on the railing. The other hand carried a slim portfolio, more or less the size of a briefcase but a fraction of the width. No room for a blue Moleskine notebook in that. Once on the tarmac, he walked to Christiades. The men conversed while a single suitcase—a large leather duffel—was ferried to the car. Simon kept his eye on the plane's forward door, thinking it likely that Obolensky traveled with a bodyguard. But no. The co-pilot deplaned next, closing the door behind him.

Simon remained at his spot on the observation deck as Christiades drove away. His eyes followed the pilot as she crossed the tarmac and entered a building belonging to Athenos Aviation, a fixed-base operator that cared for private jets.

Simon hurried down the stairs and entered the building a few minutes later. The pilot stood at the front desk, making arrangements for the aircraft. "We're leaving in the morning," she said. "Do you need me to move it?"

"What time?"

"Wheels up by seven. Boss has a big day."

Simon helped himself to a cup of water from a dispenser at the end of the desk.

The agent craned his neck to see out the window. "You're fine," he said. "Fuel?"

"Five thousand liters ought to do it." She handed the agent a credit card. "I'll pick it up in the morning. And take a look at the front tire. It may need replacing."

"Where can I contact you? Usual place?"

"You know it."

"Nothing but the best, eh?"

The pilot winked at the agent. "Open checkbook."

"Saw you land," said Simon as she turned to leave. "Nasty crosswind. Where you in from?"

The pilot regarded Simon, her face turning to stone. She brushed past him without responding. He didn't follow. In case things didn't pan out with Obolensky, he had a tail number to track, plus the fact that wherever she was flying the next morning, she needed just two thousand gallons to get there. Private jets burned between three and five hundred gallons of fuel an hour. Take four hundred as an average, factor in a safety of twenty percent, and he could peg her destination as somewhere within a radius of four hours flying time. Two thousand miles, give or take. It was a start.

"Can I help you, sir?" asked the agent.

"Got everything I need," said Simon.

CHAPTER 60

Vadim awoke shivering. The relentless wind wrapped itself around his body, an ice-cold vice. It had rained during the night and his clothes were crusted with ice. He lay facedown, his free arm across his chest, his free leg drawn up as close to his belly as possible, his breath coming in bursts, as if he were drowning and desperately surfacing for air. He opened his eyes, surprised to be alive.

Despite his efforts, he had been unable to get to his feet. True, he had managed to roll a ways down the hill, but beyond that, nothing. The rocks he found were too blunt to cut through the sturdy plastic cuffs. He was not the most tenacious fighter. He was too much of a realist. He knew too well his limitations. How could he not? His mother had gloried in citing his shortcomings all his life.

But this? Vadim moaned, gazing up at the dawn sky. This was too much. Bested by a lesser adversary, failing to carry out the simplest of orders, allowing an untrained woman and a glorified auto mechanic to put his family in jeopardy. He didn't care so much about dying…but not dying like this. He would not let it stand.

Galvanized by his fury and humiliation, he mounted one last try.

He rolled onto his side. He placed his left, free arm flat on the ground, palm down. He brought his right, free leg forward, knee cocked to act as a lever to propel him to his feet. He counted to three and thrust himself upward.

And fell right back down, toppling to his side.

To his embarrassment, he began to cry, to shout for help—weak cries, hardly more than sobs. It was not his fault. It was Riske's. Vadim had warned his mother. So had Grisha. Don't trust the American. There's something about him. Beware. But no, she wouldn't listen. She never listened. Sylvie Bettencourt always knew best.

"Damn it!" he screamed at the top of his lungs.

His head fell back onto the hard earth, his well of self-pity run dry. So much for that.

"Allô?"

Vadim cocked an ear. A voice? A person?

Then again: *"Allô!"*

Vadim turned his head, squinted his eyes as a colorful shape came nearer. A mountain biker. Alone. No companions.

"Allô!" shouted Vadim. *"Au secours!"*

"J'arrive, monsieur!"

"Ici!"

Vadim wiped at his eyes, rubbed the snot off his upper lip. He was saved.

The biker bounced down the hillside. He was a young man, twenty at most, whippet thin, helmet, windbreaker. He unclipped and laid down his bike. Vadim mumbled a few words about a disagreement, being lost, nonsense mostly, as the biker sawed through the cuffs with a pocketknife.

The restraint broke. Vadim stretched his arm and leg. After a moment, he stood. The biker asked if he should call the police. Vadim said no, it wasn't necessary, but the man insisted, telling Vadim he needed medical care.

It was then that the man saw Alec and Pavel, lying ten meters up the hillside.

Vadim snatched the phone out of his hand and hit the man, one blow to the cheek. The biker fell. Vadim dropped to his knees and strangled him, thumbs finding the larynx, crushing it. It was done quickly. He stood, picking up the bike, watching from the corner of his eye as the man writhed and groped at his ruined neck. Vadim gave him five minutes.

He climbed onto the bike. It was damned difficult landing his shoes on the stamp-sized clips. He looked to his right, toward the path the girl had led them on last night. There was another way back to the hotel, a little longer but no need to do any climbing.

He pushed off and headed down the mountain.

*   *   *

The Mercedes was gone. Of course it was.

Vadim stormed through the back entry and ran up the stairs to his room. His pistol was gone, as was Anna Bildt's phone. He checked in his bag and found his laptop. He couldn't phone, but he could use his email. The most recent message was from American Express. Please rate your recent customer experience. He moved the cursor to the garbage icon, then stopped. He hadn't had a recent customer experience. He double-clicked on the message. We invite you to respond to a survey regarding your recent interaction with our Black Card customer service team. Screw the survey—he wanted to talk to someone.

Vadim used his computer to call the number listed and was informed that he had just spent over forty thousand Swiss francs to charter a plane from Geneva to Cyprus.

"It wasn't me," he said. "Cancel the card."

"I'm sorry, sir. Only the primary cardholder is permitted to cancel the card. If you'd like to report fraudulent activity…"

"No. I don't." Vadim caught sight of himself in the mirror. If Sylvie found out that Riske had escaped, that the girl was gone, she would kill him. Son or not. He'd failed her. He'd failed the family. There would be no reprieve. "Everything's fine. My mistake."

He remembered Riske asking about the blue book. He wanted it for himself, of course. And the girl? She'd already done her worst. No rush there. He'd circle back for her later, when he was done with Riske.

He showered and changed clothes, the hot water doing wonders for his swollen joints.

Vadim had one chance. Find Riske. Find the notebook. Get the job done, whatever the hell that meant. Downstairs. A beeline for the armory. He took a pistol, ammunition, then continued to the supply room at the end of the hall. He knew the combination to the safe. He counted ten packets of banknotes, ten thousand euros each. He took one packet, then decided, "What the hell?" and took them all. There were boxes of burner phones in one cabinet, SIM cards, bundled with an elastic band, next to them. One phone was enough. Then into the back room. The "secret sanctum." To the tall steel cabinet that held the crown jewels, its door ten centimeters thick, and with good reason. He opened it with care, ducking his head to see if it was still there. A smile. One thing Riske hadn't stolen.

A stainless-steel case, a little smaller than a shoebox, sat on the center shelf. But shoeboxes didn't sport the yellow and black trefoil indicating the presence of radioactive materials. Inside, a round container wrapped in a lead-lined cowl. He read the label. NOVICHOK. If he hadn't used it so often, he would be scared to death to be within ten feet of the stuff. Novichok, product of his country's finest weapons engineers: chemists, physicists, brains. A toxic nerve agent that slowed the heart and paralyzed the lungs. The smallest contact to the epidermis prompted immediate seizures. Ingestion led to a quick and painful death.

Vadim closed the case and took it with him.

He jogged past the space where the Mercedes had been parked. There was a truck in the maintenance shed, a Citroën, twenty years old. Beggars couldn't be choosers.

And so, Cyprus.

Wasn't there a proverb about not getting too close to a tiger before killing it?

Let Riske lead him to Obolensky.

CHAPTER 61

Lugano, Switzerland

We were worried," said Aldo Rossi, leading Anna Bildt into his spacious, wood-paneled office. "I've been trying to reach you for days. I went by your father's home to see if you were all right. The front door was ajar. Of course I went inside. There appeared to have been a struggle. Furniture was broken. Vases. I found bullet shells all over the floor, holes in the wall. Anna, please, tell me what happened."

Rossi was sixty, gray haired, and lean, his face as tan as a walnut dresser. He was a lawyer, so he was dressed in a suit. But this was Lugano, so his jacket was off, his tie loosened. Still, it was better than his tight tennis shorts and clinging Fila shirts.

"I'm sorry," said Anna. "I know you and Papa were close. I should have contacted you."

"Me? I would have thought the police—this man, Tell, who's leading the investigation."

"Tell? He couldn't find his dick if he tied a sign to it."

Rossi frowned. "There's the Anna I know."

"Did you think I'd changed?"

"Hoped, though I don't know why."

It was a few minutes before noon. In a concession to the weather, Rossi had his windows open. A warm breeze made the sheer curtains dance. The view looked onto the lake and Monte San Salvatore. Rossi wasn't just a lawyer but an accountant, fiduciary, and estate agent. If there was a deal to be done in Lugano—any kind of deal—there was a strong likelihood his fingerprints could be found on it.

Anna had come to Rossi's office on the Piazza della Riforma after stopping at her home. If Rossi had been there, he hadn't phoned the police.

There was no crime scene tape, no sign anyone had investigated anything. She'd showered and changed clothes, choosing her best pants and cleanest T-shirt for the meeting. Apart from her hair, she almost looked herself.

"Well," said Rossi. "I'm waiting."

"I had some unannounced visitors," said Anna. "The people who killed my father thought he might have left something behind. You know, something he'd planned to give to the police. I said he hadn't. We agreed to disagree."

"There was blood in the dining room," said Rossi.

"Not mine," said Anna.

"Thank God," said Rossi. "You shouldn't have been dragged into this. Carl would have been—"

"What?" protested Anna. "Carl couldn't have cared less if his actions hurt others. Or else he wouldn't have been doing whatever it is that got him killed. Money laundering, hiding this or that. I'm sure you know all about it."

"Anna!"

"Aldo!"

Rossi scowled. He was shocked, shocked. Captain Renault himself couldn't have done better.

"I've just undergone a crash course in the tactics of Russian organized crime," said Anna, rising, impatient after barely ten minutes. "That's who killed him. We've found them. Their names have been posted on the net and their pictures. Two of them are dead. Two others aren't. I've done what I can. Now I'm finished. All I want is my father's letter and to go back to Copenhagen."

"Of course you do," said Rossi. "I'm here to help in any way."

"Give it to me," said Anna, her hand extended. "The letter."

Rossi opened his top drawer, searched for something. "I imagine you'd like to discuss his will," he said with hope. "There's the house to begin with. Investments. There's an account at a bank in Zürich. You're a wealthy young woman."

Who requires a lawyer to manage her affairs, Anna added silently. "I need a few days, Aldo."

He shrugged, the gracious loser. "As you wish."

"The letter?"

Out came an envelope. White. Slim. An envelope like any other. Gravely, he rose and circled the desk, handing it to her as if she maybe didn't quite deserve it. Anna ran her thumb across the surface. Nothing bulky hidden inside. No secret flash drive. She studied her name, written in her father's unmistakable block script.

"Thank you," said Anna, folding the envelope and slipping it into her pocket.

"You're not going to read it?"

Anna paused by the door. "Goodbye, Aldo."

"Don't forget," he called.

"The will. Yes, I know."

Should I or shouldn't I?

Anna sat at the picnic table in her backyard, enjoying the shade given by the old Cinzano umbrella. She gazed across the meadow, the summer grass raked by a warm, comforting breeze. Closed her eyes and memories came flooding back. Why was it she remembered only the bad, not the good?

She turned the letter over in her hand, not entirely sure she wished to open it. She didn't want an apology. She was quite comfortable with her relationship with her father. His death, while shocking, had not provoked a spate of sympathy, no belated urge to revisit her opinion of him. Experience had made her wary of apologies. It was much easier to sin and beg forgiveness than not to sin at all.

An approaching vehicle marred the afternoon calm, someone noisily accelerating down the street. She turned her head. A black car and driving with abandon. She watched it come nearer. An Audi? Despite the sun, she was shaking. She stood, shielding her eyes. Was it him? Was it Vadim? Before she had time to think about it, the car swept past. Not an Audi. A BMW.

"I'm not scared," Anna shouted, rising to her tiptoes, throwing an Italian salute to show she meant it.

After a moment, she sat. As long as Vadim was out there, and Sylvie too, she would live in fear.

And so she picked up the envelope. She'd never wanted to be involved in her father's business. Yes, she'd looked for his killers, but she'd done so blindly. Out of duty, not even, really, out of love. In doing so, however, she'd crossed into unfamiliar territory. She'd ventured into his world. There was no going back.

Anna ran her nail beneath the flap—was it a bit loose or was it her imagination?—and removed the letter. As she'd guessed, a single page, and written on bank stationery. *Ah, Papa, it's the personal touches that count.*

Oh well, she thought, adding another layer to her armor. All for the better. Let's dispense with the sentimentality from the outset.

It read:

Dear Anna,

A man reaps what he sows. I won't apologize. We know each other too well for that. Still, I wish things had turned out differently between us. I had hoped that we could sail together once more.

If I might ask a favor. Go visit your mother. She loves you so much and always has something very special to give you, maybe even something that will make you think the better of me. Suddenly, I find that very important.

Papa

Anna spread the letter on the table, flattening the creases. She was confused. Her mother had died years ago when Anna was just fifteen. Why would he ask Anna to visit her? Had he been suffering from cognitive decline? Even a man with dementia would know if his wife was alive or not. He certainly didn't mean for Anna to visit her grave. Her mother had been cremated and her ashes spread in the North Sea. And what had he meant by saying that she had always given Anna something?

Anna reread the letter. The second time was no better. Her mood darkened. Was this one last jibe? Some nasty way to express his dissatisfaction with how she'd chosen to lead her life? And what about the tone? *"If I might ask a favor."* No matter how she tried, she could not imagine her father saying such a thing. Carl Bildt didn't ask for favors.

Carl Bildt said: "Anna, do this!" Part of her began to wonder if someone else might have written the note.

She grabbed the letter and went inside. She wasn't a drinker, at least not during the day. Still, she didn't hesitate to go directly to her father's study and pour herself a generous measure of aquavit from his sideboard. Aalborg—the expensive stuff. She savored the burn and poured herself a second. Maybe day drinking wasn't so bad.

"*Skål,* Papa! Thank you for ruining my life even when you're dead." She lifted the glass and saluted the large photograph of her father at the wheel of the *Serafina,* sailing the boat through rough seas. She moved closer to him, studying his mane of hair, those blue eyes. He was a handsome one—she'd give him that. "Oh, Papa, I didn't mean that. I love you. I do."

Anna put the glass to her lips and stopped cold. She was looking at one of the life preservers, one with the yacht's name stenciled on it. Serafina was her mother's name. *"Visit your mother,"* her father had written. Then: she *"always has something very special to give you, maybe even something that will make you think the better of me."*

Anna set down the glass as a wave of dizziness passed over her. She fell into her father's chair. He'd done it. Just as everyone had suspected. He'd left her proof. It was on the boat. On *Serafina.*

"That will make you think the better of me."

In a daze, Anna walked to the kitchen. She had to go there. Now. This minute.

She found her phone and punched in the words "Costa Smeralda."

The Emerald Coast.

CHAPTER 62

Limassol, Cyprus

Simon caught up with Christiades's BMW halfway to Limassol. Traffic along the coastal highway was modest and Christiades appeared in no mood to set any speed records. Simon kept a two-car distance, listening to the radio, tapping his hand to a series of Greek pop hits. The exit for the Amara Hotel came and went. Christiades continued another ten kilometers, exiting at the eastern edge of the city, winding his way through the hilly streets. Finally, he pulled into the lot of a car dealership, Cyprus Motorsport. Simon could see a dozen Alfa Romeos, Fiats, Ferraris, inside a modern, brightly lit showroom.

Simon followed the men after they entered the building and crossed the sales floor, waving to the salesmen as if he belonged there, continuing down a corridor to the mechanics' bay.

The only car in the garage was 3387. Next to it, on a dolly, was the gearbox Simon had taken from Boris Blatt. Several mechanics were working under the hood, removing the transmission. It was clear they were having a problem unscrewing it from the transverse mount.

"Excuse me," he said, stepping amongst them. "You're doing it all wrong. You have to go from the other side. Give me the wrench."

The mechanics looked at Simon, who was already taking off his jacket, rolling up his sleeves. He gave them a look. What the hell were they waiting for? Obolensky and Christiades stood alongside, arms crossed.

"Well," said Christiades. "Do as he says!"

One of the men handed Simon the wrench. He went to work, moving from screw to screw, eight in all. When he finished, he handed back the wrench.

"You know cars?" said Sergei Obolensky.

"I know Ferraris," said Simon.

"And this one?"

"A 1963 GTO. Looks like it came straight from the factory. Yours?"

"A friend's," said Obolensky. "I'm looking after it for him."

"Nice friend."

Obolensky didn't answer.

"This was a racer back in the day," said Simon. "Twenty-Four Hours of Le Mans, Sebring."

"Fast?"

"You're not a driver?"

"Me? As little as possible. I prefer to walk. Or to sail."

"Where?"

"Here and there. Spain. Italy. You?"

"I like dry land." Simon extended a hand. "Hudson. Thomas Hudson."

"Obolensky."

"Russia?"

"It shows?"

"Tell you what. I'll finish switching out the gearbox if you let me take you for a drive. You might like it more than sailing."

"Not a chance," said Obolensky.

"About the drive or about liking it more than sailing?"

"Both," said Obolensky.

"Well, then," said Simon. "Take good care of it. Be seeing you."

Obolensky was dressed casually for his adventure to the north side of the island: jeans, linen shirt, sweater draped over his shoulders. Simon's point of vantage was a gurgling fountain halfway between the Amara Hotel's grand entry and the elevator banks. His eyes followed Obolensky's spirited march across the marble floor. No bags, no accoutrements, as Sylvie might say. He'd left everything he'd brought with him in his hotel room. So much the better.

Obolensky slowed to place a call. Simon guessed it was to his driver, for a moment later a uniformed man rushed in. The two exchanged words. The driver rushed back out, Obolensky following.

Simon chose a diagonal course, crossing the Russian's path, allowing the Russian to spot him before turning his own head. *Why hello. You again?*

"Did you finish the work?" Simon called.

Obolensky had no choice but to answer. "In the morning."

"And then? A drive around the island?"

"To its new home in the free port."

Simon approached him. "A waste," he said, throwing his hands up.

"Not my decision."

"Are you free for dinner perhaps?" Simon asked. "My date canceled. Hudson's the name."

"I remember. Obolensky."

Simon extended his hand. The grip that met it was cold, damp, and weak. A dead fish. Simon maintained his normal pressure nonetheless. "I know a good place in Larnaca. Fantastic lamb. To die for."

Obolensky grimaced, wanting to free his hand, Simon not letting him. "I'm sorry, Mr. Hudson, but I have a prior commitment."

"You're sure?" And here, Simon placed his free hand on the Cellist's forearm, drawing him nearer.

"Quite."

Finally, Simon relaxed his grip. "Too bad," he said. "I hope I wasn't rude to ask."

"Not at all," said Obolensky, relieved to be free. "I wish you a pleasant evening."

"I'm sure you'll have more fun than me."

Simon left before Obolensky had a chance to answer. He walked to the far side of the lobby, sure not to look behind him, and found a seat at the bar of the Apollo Lounge. He ordered a KEO beer, the local brew, and some meze. When the bartender left, Simon opened his left hand and examined Obolensky's room key. Standard magnetic stripe. No need for a room number. Sylvie had already told him. The Midas Suite.

Simon checked his watch. Best to wait a while before venturing upstairs. He didn't want to interfere with the maid's turn-down service, and there was always a chance Obolensky might return unexpectedly. He enjoyed the beer, ordered a second.

His phone rang. Only one person had the number. "Anna?"

"Sardinia," she said. "It's in Sardinia. On *Serafina*."

"Slow down," said Simon. "What happened?"

"You were right. Everyone was. Papa left something for me." Anna paused to collect herself. She needed several minutes to explain how her father had left a clue for her in the letter passed along to her by Aldo Rossi. And that even if it had taken her a bit, she'd figured it out. "It's on his boat. The *Serafina*. He named it for my mother."

"And the boat's in Sardinia?"

"Porto Cervo."

"You know where exactly?"

"The yacht club. The Costa Smeralda."

"I need you to go there," said Simon. "I know it's a lot to ask."

"I'm on my way," said Anna.

"Excuse me? Already?"

"I'm in Genoa. Can't you hear all the noise? At the port. I have a ticket on the nine o'clock ferry. I'll be there in the morning."

"Anna, thank you."

"I'm not doing this for you," retorted Anna. "I'm doing it to get that bitch. To get Sylvie."

Simon said, "Good night." He pushed the beer aside.

Time to go to work.

As far as break-ins went, this one counted as the easiest of his career.

Simon pressed his back to the door of Sergei Obolensky's suite on the top floor of the Amara Hotel and remained unmoving, allowing his eyes to grow accustomed to the dark. Lights from the pool deck and the adjacent wings glimmered through the glass sliding doors. For a minute, he listened, ear tuned for the slightest disturbance. Satisfied he was alone, he crossed the living area and drew the curtains. He did the same in the master bedroom, continuing to the bathroom, snatching a towel from the rack before returning to the entry and laying the towel against the foot of the door. Only then did he turn on the lights and survey the room.

The Midas Suite lived up to its name. The living area was large enough to house a Grecian labyrinth with room for the Augean Stables left over. The décor was Late Mykonos Disco, everything white and cream and gold with plenty of mirrors and pillows and sofas you could disappear into. He inspected the room, lifting cushions, opening drawers, looking beneath sofas and chairs, his eyes seeking out the color blue in all its infinite shades: royal blue, powder blue, sky blue, cerulean, navy. There was no sign of any of them.

To the bedroom.

Simon stood in the doorway, studying the layout, taking a mental snapshot of everything in it. A chocolate truffle rested on the pillow; beside it, an order form for breakfast to hang on the doorknob; sheets turned down. A leather travel bag duffel sat on a luggage rack in one corner. The document portfolio Obolensky had carried off the plane, also leather, was on the desk. There were two books on the nightstand, one stacked neatly atop the other. The closet door peeked open an inch. A pair of tennis shoes were set neatly beside the dresser.

First, the leather duffel. Empty. Simon found the clothing folded and placed in the drawers. Briefs and socks in one; T-shirts and polos in another. No blue Moleskine to be found. Several linen shirts and a pair of slacks hung in the closet. Nothing in the pockets. Nothing on the shelf either. Bunched in a corner on the floor, dirty laundry. T-shirt, gym shorts, underwear, all damp with sweat.

A pair of jeans lay across the back of an easy chair. Again, Simon checked the pockets. A chewing gum wrapper. Dirol. A Russian brand. A receipt from an establishment named La Taverna in the amount of one hundred fifty euros and located on Via Vulpina, 07866—Olbia, Italy. In another pocket, a box of matches from Ristorante Mille Miglia, Porto Cervo, Italy. Simon typed both names into his phone. Both restaurants were located in Sardinia. The Costa Smeralda—Emerald Coast.

And Carl Bildt's boat, the *Serafina*. Also in Porto Cervo.

Simon returned the receipt and the matches to the pants pockets, as he'd found them, then arranged the jeans just so.

Both books on the night table were paperbacks. On top, a thriller by a popular American author. The sticker on the cover advertised TWO FOR ONE. The bookseller was Waterstones. Purchased in England, then. Most probably at Heathrow. The sales receipt tucked into the front cover proved him correct. Terminal 4. The date: one month earlier.

The second book was a German-language biography of Herbert von Karajan. The picture showed a fierce-eyed man with a thick head of gray hair. At first glance, a tyrant. Not someone Simon would care to work for. He read the back cover. Von Karajan had been a musician, like Obolensky, and director of the Berlin Philharmonic—a towering figure in his field. No receipt inside the cover but something better. An inscription. The book was a gift. One problem: the inscription was in Cyrillic and, to look at, penned hastily.

"To Sergei"…next words illegible…"my dearest friend"…again illegible…signed, name undecipherable. A dramatic looping scrawl taking up the bottom third of the page. An *M* perhaps, or a *W*. Or, thought Simon, a *V.* It was no good. Whoever had inscribed the book, he thought highly of himself.

Simon replaced the books precisely as he'd found them.

Into the bathroom. Marble, stainless steel, mirrors. A search of the drawers and medicine cabinet. No blue notebook. A toiletry bag sat beside the sink, unzipped. Toothpaste, toothbrush, cologne, moisturizer, razor and shaving cream, all arrayed neatly on a washcloth. Ten points for Obolensky. Simon did the same when he traveled. A look inside the bag. Several amber pharmaceutical vials. To regulate blood pressure, cholesterol, arthritis, mood. And, of course, the blue pill. He unzipped an interior compartment. *Well, well.* Another vial, this one glass and filled with a fine white powder. *Sergei, bad boy.*

Simon returned to the bedroom, remembering the leather portfolio as he was about to leave. It was too slim to hold a Moleskine notebook, barely the width of a fashion magazine. He undid the leather belt and buckle securing it. The case opened like an accordion file. Inside, a sheaf of papers. He slid them out and laid them on the desk. Sheet music, and transcribed by hand. Too many clefs for one instrument. A score? The title of the piece was "Concerto in B Flat Minor for Cello and String Quartet, 'Pathetique,'" by S. E. Obolensky.

The score ran to fifty pages. Impressive, thought Simon, who himself was not a musician and couldn't imagine the expertise and learning required. Hats off to Maestro Obolensky. He would have preferred to find the blue notebook that, contrary to Sylvie's counsel, he suspected the Cellist did not take with him everywhere he traveled.

With thumb and forefinger, Simon spread the carrier and replaced the score. As he did so, a piece of ivory card stock fell out. He turned it over. An invitation written in French and, thankfully, professionally printed in an easy-to-read font.

> You are cordially invited to attend the debut performance of the "Concerto in B Flat Minor, 'Pathetique'" by S. E. Obolensky
> Saturday, the 29th of August, 4 p.m.
> Villa Certosa, 07020—Olbia, Italy

And below that:

> Guests are requested to arrive no later than 3 p.m.
> Proof of identification necessary, as well as this invitation.

Simon noted that the space for the invitee's name had been left blank. The 29th was tomorrow. Olbia, he now knew, meant Sardinia.

Sardinia, where Carl Bildt kept his boat, the *Serafina*. And Obolensky a sailor, too. What were the chances?

And then he saw it, there at the bottom of the invitation:

> Sponsored by Danske Bank

CHAPTER 63

London, England

She should be enjoying it more. The sun was out. The view down the River Thames toward the Millennium Wheel, the Houses of Parliament, and Big Ben, exquisite. A pleasant southwesterly breeze cleansed the noxious London air. Even better, Vadim and Riske were in Cyprus close on Obolensky's tail and all other impediments eliminated. Everything was in its right place.

And beyond her control, mused Sylvie Bettencourt. Which was exactly why the old operative in her refused to celebrate.

Sylvie's eye wandered upriver to the ziggurat, the boxy, Orwellian headquarters of MI6, the British spy service, her erstwhile adversary. Had it been more than thirty years since she'd first stepped foot on British soil? A second secretary in the cultural affairs department of the Soviet Embassy. Well...so much as "cultural affairs" had to do with the identification, recruitment, and running of men and women willing and eager to undertake activities on her country's behalf. Not spying, so much. The world had changed. No one gave two whits for military and political secrets when your own country was falling apart...*had fallen apart*...and was simply seeking a means to survive. It was a matter of economic espionage. And, to be honest, not entirely in her country's best interest—certainly not as the embassy would define it. It was her job, as assigned by her GRU masters eager to strip what they could from the Soviet empire's still twitching carcass and establish avenues to get their spoils out. Legitimate avenues.

How she'd enjoyed the game. The discreet approaches, the initial nibbles, the less discreet wooing, and then "the ask." Will you or won't you? In the end, it was rarely about the money. It was about the

305

excitement, the involvement, the chance to be part of something bigger than themselves. To be "a player."

She thought of the girl, Anna Bildt, and her ragtag digital army, whatever they were called. Were they so different from Sylvie's own ragtag network? It was a fundamental human need to feel important. A need both Sylvie and Anna had exploited, if to different purposes.

How many had she seduced, quite often literally? Sylvie wondered. Six? Seven? An inordinately high number for a novice agent on her first foreign posting. There was Smithers, the oil man. Davies, in bottling, of all things. Evans, in foreign exchange. Through them, and their good offices, she'd brought out tens of millions of dollars, laundered them cleaner than clean, and seen to their legal introduction into the international financial system.

But she'd had her failures, too. Not many, but one so egregious, so spectacular as to overshadow her greatest success. It was not a story she cared to dredge up, but here, today, seeing the Union Jack whipping overhead, how could she not?

A simple enough mistake. She'd misread a man. She'd thought she had him in the palm of her hand, when in fact it was the other way around. It was he who drew too much out of her, made her lower her defenses, disobey her training. It was he who, in the end, persuaded her to tell the truth. The spy's cardinal sin. His weapon: honesty, emotion, romance. Did she dare call it love?

Things ended badly for both of them. She, declared persona non grata by the English government and expelled from the country, her career set afire. Worse for him.

And now, thought Sylvie, as she crossed Vauxhall Bridge and turned toward Battersea Power Station, she had a chance to remedy her life's most serious misstep. Once again, everything depended on a man she'd wooed and recruited. A man she believed she knew.

Could she have misread him, too?

Alastair Quince, director of Sotheby's automotive sales department, stood on the main stage of Battersea Park's Evolution London exposition center, directing the adjustment of a spotlight aimed at a black

Lamborghini Miura. "A little more to the right," he called to the stage-hand. "It needs to shine directly on the bonnet."

"Why, hello there, Alastair," said Sylvie, walking down the center aisle of the event hall.

"Hello there, beautiful," said Quince, jumping nimbly to the floor. He was tall and thin, the kind of man she'd imagined—until this moment—never left his house dressed in anything but a suit. "I didn't expect to see you until tomorrow evening."

"I was in town. I thought I'd take a look at my next gem a little early."

"It's out back," said Quince. "Follow me."

Quince led Sylvie behind the main stage to an assembly area packed with automobiles, all freshly washed and waxed.

"I hope you've received proof of funds," she said.

"Yesterday." Quince stopped, turning to face her. "Something wrong?"

"I'm sorry?"

"There's never been an issue before, has there?" he asked contritely. "You're one of our most treasured clients. Have we erred on our side?"

It was standard procedure for registered bidders to supply the auction house with a bank statement guaranteeing availability of funds no later than twenty-four hours before the event began. In this case, the Bank of Liechtenstein had provided said guarantee that Crystal Clan LLC of the Dutch Antilles—the company on whose behalf Sylvie would be bidding—had one hundred million dollars at their disposal.

Sylvie put a hand on his arm. "No, no, Alastair. Just some accounting issues on our end. New staff. You know how these things go."

Quince nodded eagerly, reassured that there had been no gaffe on his end. He didn't want any new staff replacing him.

They arrived at Lot 65, a 1957 Ferrari 335 S Scaglietti. Red, of course. Another sleek racing car, far sexier than 3387, at least to her eye. Her time with Simon Riske had left her convinced there was no wiser investment.

"What do you think she'll bring?" she asked.

"Who can tell?" said Quince. "Another 335 in awful condition, multiple owners, never raced, brought sixty-five last month in Dubai."

"That so?" Sylvie raised a brow, impressed, though of course, she already knew this. She also knew that the car had been certified as "factory new." And that the sixty-five-million-dollar sales price was deemed excessive by the automotive collecting community. She decided she'd go to sixty, no higher.

"Simon helping you with this one, too?" said Quince.

"In a manner of speaking," said Sylvie.

"Give him my best."

"I'm sure you'll see him before me." Sylvie checked her watch. A gasp. Late, as always. "I've got to run, Al."

"Till tomorrow evening," said Quince.

"Cheers," said Sylvie. A wave and she was gone.

Chapter 64

Costa Smeralda, Sardinia

Simon flew into the horizon, the rising sun at his back. At first, the island was a smudge. Slowly, it grew darker, the contours of its rugged hills growing visible. Its slopes carpeted with lowland scrub, the *macchia*. An ancient land.

The plane descended. The ocean grew lighter, shade by shade, as if refracted through a prism, each band neatly separated from the next. And in that water, boats, too many craft to count, sunlight flashing off their white hulls like so much fairy dust. Sloops, ketches, yachts, speedboats, and, of course, here and there, mega-yachts, the seaborne fortresses of the superrich.

The plane banked, over the island now. Below, amongst the verdant terrain and rolling hills, the red-tile roofs of the island's residents, villas small, large, and larger still. The plane descended, passing over the city of Olbia, then lower still until the wheels touched the runway.

Simon deplaned and walked to the immigration shed. Formalities were quickly seen to. A lone passenger. A private jet. One of Europe's rich and famous. "Welcome to Sardinia, sir. Enjoy your stay."

It was a cool morning, salt thick in the air, the Italian and EU flags atop the terminal snapping in a fitful breeze. Crossing the tarmac, Simon counted six jets with the Russian tricolor painted on their tail. Among them, far larger than the others, a Boeing business jet, essentially a 737, painted black with no other markings. Was the owner a man with a looping signature, Sergei's "dearest friend"?

At the rental counter, disappointment. The last car had only just been taken. Another early morning traveler. Simon's best efforts at charm, disbelief, and finally anger were for naught. Even the hint of a generous "sweetener" was ignored. Either the Sardinians had found religion or they truly had run out of cars.

So be it. Plan B.

Simon left the terminal, already behind schedule. The sun and flowering shrubs did little to ease his nerves. He spotted the sign for long-term parking. A crisp hundred-meter walk. No fence. Traffic at a minimum. He patrolled the aisles. Too new. Too old. Too clean. Too dirty. Finally, a white Simca LT. Ten years old. A healthy layer of dust and sea salt on the windscreen. Perfect.

A look over his shoulder. The coast was clear.

He snapped off the Simca's antenna, dropped it at his feet, flattened it with his heel, picked it up and fashioned a hook from the narrower end. Hardly perfect, but a "slim jim" nonetheless. A blade from his knife separated the seal from the driver's side window. In went the "slim jim." Door open.

The alarm sounded, surprisingly loud. Simon took note. He dove under the wheel, cut the appropriate wires. The alarm died. Sweet silence. A guard in a golf cart approached as he drove to the exit. Simon lowered the window, flashing his passport and the parking ticket (under the sunshade). *"Giorno!"* he called, very happy indeed to be back on the island.

"Giorno, signor," said the guard, just as happy to welcome him.

The ferry terminal in Olbia was a short drive north, around the port, to a long, narrow pier. The ferries, in from Genoa, Livorno, Civitavecchia, Piombino, arrived with the morning tide, ten-story behemoths, two hundred meters in length, each carrying thousands of passengers, hundreds of cars. It was seven a.m. The Moby ferry from Genoa was docking as Simon made his way to the end of the pier.

Despite the onrush of passengers, Anna Bildt was hard to miss. Simon raised a hand, moving to intercept her.

"You," said Anna, not entirely pleased.

"Me," said Simon.

It was a thirty-minute drive north to Porto Cervo on the Costa Smeralda. Simon's first time on the island, a rugged twin of Corsica. Foothills rose lazily from the winding coastline. A savage beauty tamed here and there by encampments of wealth, hotels, villas, small commercial enclaves.

"Well," said Anna, after they'd joined the highway. "I'm waiting. And don't say you were worried about me."

"Did your father like classical music?" asked Simon instead.

"What?"

"Classical music. Was he a fan?"

Anna shifted in her seat, confused. "It was all he listened to. Rachmaninoff, Tchaikovsky, Brahms. He liked the Romantics."

"What about the cello?"

"What about it?"

"A favorite?"

"Bach's prelude. The one from the movie—you know—about the British sailors, where the two guys play it, one with a violin, one with a cello. That was his favorite, the movie and the song. Now, mind telling me why?"

Simon handed Anna the invitation he'd found in Obolensky's room.

Anna read it aloud. "So?"

"Your father's bank is a sponsor. Do you know him…Obolensky, I mean?"

"Over the years, I met a lot of my father's friends at the yacht club. Is he a sailor?"

"Think so."

"Russian?"

"Oh yeah."

"I'd have to see him." Anna studied the invitation. "Are we going?"

"We are," said Simon.

"Am I allowed to ask why?"

"Sure." Simon nodded. "But first, I need to tell you the part that comes before."

"Is this a long story?"

"Getting to be," said Simon. "So there was an auction in California. Ever heard of Pebble Beach?"

He spent the remainder of the drive relating the events of past days. The sale of 3387 to Sylvie, the search for the gearbox, his run-in with Blatt parts one and two, leading to his eventual escape to the mountains with Sylvie Bettencourt. It was the whole story with nothing left out. "So you see," he said in closing, "we're both on the same errand."

"Now I understand," said Anna. "Why you were pleased that my father left me a note."

The Yacht Club Costa Smeralda presided over the island's largest natural harbor. The manager, Pietro Morandi, waited at the entry as Simon and Anna arrived. He was a compact, serious man dressed in white slacks and navy-blue blazer, with wavy black hair. He took Anna's hands as he addressed her, offering his sincerest condolences.

"He was only just here, your father," said Morandi. "Such a terrible world."

"He was here?" said Anna. "Recently?"

"Two days before."

"Sailing?"

"If only," said Morandi. "Then maybe none of this happen. Maintenance, I believe. I asked if he wanted to bring the *Serafina* inside the harbor for the season. I had his usual berth open. But no. He asked that I keep her moored at sea."

Simon and Anna traded looks. They'd come to the right place.

"Do you remember if he said anything else?" asked Anna.

Morandi shook his head. "Your father was a quiet man. I like this. And you? You are making a cruise today?"

"No," said Anna. "Maintenance."

Minutes later, Simon and Anna boarded a tender piloted by Morandi to take them to the *Serafina*.

"Call me when you wish to return," said Morandi. "Ten minutes and I am there."

The boat was a thirty-seven-foot Solaris, a racer, sleek hull, teak decks, a single mast, mainsail and jib, both furled. A combination lock secured the cabin. Anna entered the correct sequence. She removed the lock and opened the doors.

"Okay, then," she said. "We're here."

"Okay, then," said Simon.

Carl Bildt had visited the *Serafina* two days before his death. Simon hoped they were about to find out why.

CHAPTER 65

Porto Cervo, Sardinia

"Did you buy anything in Sardinia recently?" Vadim asked his mother.

"There you are," said Sylvie. "I was getting worried."

"Answer me."

Vadim stood on the curb of the Via della Marina, eyes glued to the tender carrying Riske and the Danish girl. The launch made its way to sea, beyond the harbor, finally stopping beside a sailboat. He could just see Riske and the woman board the boat before the launch returned to port. There were many boats moored nearby. No other, however, flew a red and white Danish flag atop its mainmast.

"Sardinia?" said Sylvie. "Of course. The Villa Certosa. Berlusconi's old place. Five years ago. Two hundred million. Euros, not dollars."

"He's here," said Vadim.

"I should have known," said Sylvie. "And Riske?"

"Like a lamb," said Vadim.

"A word?"

"He's indisposed at the moment."

"Nearby?"

"I can see him, yes."

"Everything all right?"

"Shipshape."

Vadim smiled to himself, more relief than congratulations. An email from American Express. A bribe to a clerk at the fixed-base operator in Paphos. And his good fortune to own a jet capable of flying at 600 knots an hour. But for those items, he'd be a dead man walking. Instead, he was one step away from regaining his mother's trust, now and forever.

Vadim kept his eye on the boat. It did not appear as if any effort was being made to put to sea. Why should there be? Riske and the girl hadn't come to Sardinia to make a pleasure cruise. They had come because Carl Bildt had left something of importance on his yacht. The girl had been lying.

Vadim admonished himself for not getting the information from the girl earlier, when he'd had the chance. He pledged not to make the same mistake twice.

And now both of them in the same place.

Vadim had a decision to make. Now or later? The answer came quickly.

"Don't let him out of your sight," said Sylvie.

"Promise," said Vadim, eyes on the *Serafina*.

"Go get our money," said Sylvie.

The call ended.

Vadim slid the phone into his pocket, adjusting the pistol in his waistband, making sure his untucked polo shirt hid it nicely. If Riske could find the blue notebook, so could he. It was at the Villa Certosa. What more did he need to know?

And so, thought Vadim as he made his way to the docks. Decision made.

Chapter 66

The *Serafina*'s cabin was surprisingly broad but low ceilinged, galley to the left, seating and dining area to the right, a wall of sophisticated navigation and communications equipment toward the bow.

"I'll search my bedroom," said Anna, angling her head to the fore. "You look in my dad's, aft."

Anna opened the door to her quarters. She had space to take one step before hitting the bed, the mattress shaped to fit the bow, skylight above the pillows. She began with the drawers, built beneath the bed. Some clothing: shorts, T-shirts, bathing suits, underwear. She ran a hand through them, then along the surfaces. Nothing. She turned her attention to the bed, looking beneath the mattress, then checking the pillows, the bedspread, the sheets. Nothing. She ran a hand along the shelves, looked through her desk, barely the size of a phone directory, then searched the bathroom.

"Anything?" called Simon from her father's bedroom.

"Don't think so," said Anna. "You?"

"Nada."

She joined him a few minutes later, helping search for whatever her father had left on his visit two days before his death. Finished with the stateroom, they moved on to the head, then the galley, checking drawers, appliances...well, *everything,* but to no avail. If her father had left something for her, he'd hidden it too well.

"Read it to me again," said Simon.

Anna read him the letter.

"Can you remember what your mother may have given you?" he asked.

"A soccer ball, boxing gloves, a gi for judo."

"Any of that stuff here?"

"No," said Anna. "It's all long gone. But maybe…"

"Maybe…" said Simon.

Anna dropped onto the bench around the table. "Mama died two weeks before my fifteenth birthday. She'd gotten me an iPod. It was engraved, 'Love forever, Mama.'" She lifted her eyes to Simon. "I didn't want it—I mean, every time I looked at it, I cried—so we ended up using it on the boat. We kept it plugged into the stereo so we could listen to music while we sailed."

"On this boat?"

"The *Oceana,* Dad's old boat. He bought the *Serafina* two years ago. I can't remember if we brought the iPod over. Maybe he did. I was in Denmark."

"And if it was here…," said Simon.

"The comm center," said Anna, pointing to the rack of gear built into the wall near the bow. She slid out from the table and moved fore to the cockpit designed for the navigator. Simon followed.

There was a satellite radar unit, a satellite phone, a depth finder, a GPS unit, and, at the bottom, an old-time Marantz amplifier. Anna opened a drawer below it. Inside were coils of wire, pliers, alligator clips, electronic bric-a-brac.

"See it?" asked Simon.

"No," said Anna, rummaging through the drawer. "Hold on."

A moment later, she lifted her hand, fingers clutching a matte-gray iPod, circa 2006. "It's dead," she said, pushing her thumb on the flywheel to power it up. "I mean, what does it matter? You can't store information on these."

"May I?" Simon examined the iPod, pressing the power button, confirming that the device's battery was dead. He put the iPod to his ear and shook it. Then again.

"What is it?" asked Anna. "Hear something?"

Simon shook his head. "He expected that others might come looking for it. You know, the same people who wanted him dead. He had to hide it somewhere they wouldn't think to look. Like you said, you can't store information on it."

Simon selected the slimmest blade from his Swiss Army knife and wedged open the case. He handed one half to Anna, then turned the other half upside down. Nothing fell out.

"Told you," said Anna.

Simon looked closer, gave the iPod a firm shake. A small, square-shaped object fell into his palm. He grasped it with thumb and forefinger. "Two gigs," he said, studying the miniature thumb drive. "Laptop?"

Anna was already opening her backpack. She placed the laptop on the dining table and inserted the thumb drive into the USB port. An icon appeared on the screen. It was titled: "For Anna."

"I was right," Anna whispered.

"Open it."

Anna double-clicked the icon. A directory appeared. Fifty items. Each was an account number. She opened the first. Customer information. Names, addresses, emails. Then more: transaction history, passwords, links to other accounts.

"It's her." Anna pointed at the screen. "Sylvie Bettencourt."

"Now we know why," said Simon.

"Is this what you were looking for?"

Simon nodded. Special Agent Nessa Kenyon of the United States Financial Crimes Enforcement Network was going to be very happy. "Mind if I send this to someone?"

"All yours," said Anna. "Put that monster away."

"Let's take a closer look." Simon sat at the table, pulled the laptop close. He spent several minutes examining the different accounts, digesting the information. He logged on to his email provider and tapped out a note to Nessa Kenyon. He allowed himself a moment's satisfaction. Yes, he thought, this is what we were looking for.

The boat swayed. A cloud passed overhead, blocking the sun. He raised his head from the screen. Anna was no longer at the table. Had she gone on deck?

"Anna," he called.

"Right here," she said, opening the door from the fore bathroom.

A look back at the stairs as a figure vaulted into the cabin. A man, landing heavily, off balance, a gun in his hand. Vadim.

No time to be surprised.

He wanted to kill them.

Simon was already moving, rising from the table, charging the Russian. He saw the pistol aimed at him. He dove to the ground as Vadim fired, rolling, colliding with the Russian's legs. He threw up a hand to arrest the pistol, the muzzle pointing at his head, grasped Vadim's wrist, forced the gun to one side. Another shot, deafening, the blast scalding his cheek. Simon drove his fist into Vadim's groin. A cry of pain. Vadim retreated a step. Still clutching Vadim's wrist, Simon rose, rapping the gun against the bulkhead…once, twice…the pistol falling to the floor.

Vadim struck Simon with his free hand, a glancing blow. Simon's grip weakened. Vadim shook loose. Off balance, Simon fell back. In that instant, Vadim opened the nearest drawer, snatched up a carving knife. He lunged at Simon, the blade slashing this way and that. Simon retreated, looking for something to defend himself with, anything, grabbing the laptop off the table, brandishing it as if it were a shield, parrying blow after blow.

"Get down," shouted Anna.

Simon ventured a glance over his shoulder. Anna was holding the pistol with both hands, eye down the barrel, aiming at Vadim. He turned too late as Vadim lunged, the knife avoiding the laptop, nicking Simon's shoulder, the pain white-hot. Simon dropped to a knee. Anna fired. Vadim halted his advance. His eyes narrowed and he made a guttural noise. It was unclear where the bullet had struck him. Vadim gasped. His body jerked spasmodically and the knife dropped from his hand. He groped at his pants, clawing frantically to remove something from his pocket. It was then that Simon saw the blood, a blossom on his hip, spreading rapidly. The bullet had struck an artery.

Vadim yanked a dark cloth package from his pocket. Inside it, half exposed, was a bottle. Whatever was inside poured over his hand, the liquid staining his pants, mixing with his blood. Spittle bubbled from his mouth. He began to shake. His eyes bulged from their sockets. A madman.

It was a nerve agent. Of course, thought Simon. A poison favored by the GRU. Used to kill off its enemies.

Vadim lunged at Simon, taking him in his arms, throwing him against the wall of electronics gear. He raised the broken bottle, struggling to bring it to Simon's face, the poison dripping onto Simon's clothing, onto his exposed forearm. The effect was instantaneous. A current traveled the length of his spine. His eyes watered. A foreign taste invaded his mouth.

Simon flung Vadim to the floor, the bottle sliding from his hands. The Russian was up as quickly, reeling against the bulkhead. Blood ran from his eyes. His mouth stood open, his tongue purple, grotesquely swollen. He staggered up the stairs, a terrible keening in his wake. There was a splash as Vadim fell into the sea.

"What is it?" asked Anna. "What did I do?"

"Stay back," said Simon, panicked. "Don't come near me."

He found a dishtowel in a drawer, scooped up the bottle, then hurried up the stairs and threw the bottle into the sea. He was sweating, his vision blurry, his eyes acutely sensitive to the sunlight. He dove into the ocean, pulling off his shirt, his shoes, his trousers, until he was naked, rubbing the water vigorously against his forearm, praying the poison would dissipate before his epidermis had absorbed too much.

He surfaced and sucked down a breath, unsure how he was feeling, other than frightened. Vadim floated nearby, facedown, unmoving. Simon treaded water, too weak to do more.

Suddenly, Vadim's body heaved, his arms flailed. Just once. He went quiet and sank below the surface.

Anna stood on deck. "Are you all right?"

Simon didn't answer. Time would tell.

CHAPTER 67

Porto Cervo, Sardinia

Simon climbed onto the boat, ordering Anna to keep at a distance. The tingling he'd experienced up and down his spine had vanished, as had his blurred vision and sensitivity to sunlight. For the moment, there were no other symptoms. If anything, he felt refreshed, the cool salt water a salve. He could only hope he'd been quick enough to clean the poison off his skin and that he hadn't taken any into his lungs. Doubtful on both counts. Anna threw him a towel, studying the scars on his chest and back, the tattoo on his arm. She made no comment—one of the few.

Simon went below and found a pair of shorts and a T-shirt among Carl Bildt's belongings. Too big, but what did he care?

"You're shaking," said Anna when he returned. "I'm sure there's a sweatshirt."

"Nah," said Simon. "It's not that." He wasn't cold. He was frightened.

"What the hell happened?" asked Anna.

"Poison," said Simon. "Some kind of nerve agent. My guess is Novichok. It's the GRU's preferred method of getting rid of their enemies. The bullet broke the bottle in his pocket. The poison must have entered his bloodstream directly. Ugly."

"Couldn't have happened to a nicer guy."

"Next time shoot him in the chest. Quicker that way for everyone."

"Next time kill him when you have the chance."

Simon thought about it. Probably not. He settled for hoping there wouldn't be a next time.

"Stay here. I need to clean up." He went below and washed down the floor with hot water and soap. It was all he could do for the time being. Afterward, he brought the laptop on deck and finished his message to

Nessa Kenyon, sending the contents of Carl Bildt's flash drive to a drop box, highlighting two files with Sylvie Bettencourt's account information. All the while, he was playing with just how Vadim had found them. He decided it didn't matter.

Anna called Morandi. The club manager was true to his word. Ten minutes later, he arrived with the motor launch. Ten minutes after that, Simon and Anna were back on dry land.

The first stop after leaving the yacht club was a pharmacy. Simon explained that he believed he'd been poisoned and that he required a shot of atropine. The mention of Novichok was enough. The pharmacist prepared a syringe and administered it himself. Simon felt better immediately. He didn't care if it was a placebo effect or not. He couldn't remember ever being more scared.

Suddenly, he was ravenous. They ate at a nearby café. Two plates of pasta for Simon. Nuts, fruit, and black bread for Anna. They paid the bill and Simon excused himself to place a call.

"Where are you?" asked Nessa Kenyon.

"Outside the Zegna boutique in Porto Cervo."

"Porto what?"

"Sardinia. Island south of Corsica."

"I know where it is. I thought we left you in France."

"Tell you about it later," said Simon. "Hey, did you get what you need?"

"I've only had a chance to check a few of them. If all the files are like these, there's more than enough to nail Sylvie Bettencourt."

"You're sure?"

"We charge her inside of ninety days, issue an arrest warrant, and press England or France to pick her up. With any luck, we'll have her extradited to the States inside of a year."

"A year?"

"If she doesn't fight it. Nightmare scenario, she flees to Russia. We ask Interpol to issue a Red Notice, then we confiscate her holdings in the United States. We give Switzerland the information and they do the same."

"Jail time?"

"Doubtful. Too rich. Too well connected."

"It's not enough," said Simon.

"Because of your work we stand to walk away with billions. In my book, that's a win. A big one."

"Congratulations," said Simon. "I'm happy for you."

"You don't sound too happy."

"I'm not in it for the money."

"Simon, please, we're grateful. Your country is grateful."

"It's not enough."

"It's what we set out to do," said Kenyon, an edge to her voice. The subtext was clear: *Don't mess this up.*

"Maybe."

"Come home. Let's celebrate. Uncle Sam will buy you dinner. You name the place."

Change of tactic. The carrot, not the stick. If anything, it only made him angrier. "Dinner? Are you serious?"

"Simon, I need you to calm down."

"Never calmer."

"Simon…"

"There's something I have to do first."

"What? You did it. You got what we needed to put a stop to one of the biggest money laundering operations in the world."

"Great," said Simon, teeth gritted.

"I don't like the tone of your voice."

"Must be the connection. Gotta run."

"Simon, don't go. We need to talk."

He ended the call. He found Anna sitting on a bench around the corner. "Feel like going shopping? You need a new dress."

CHAPTER 68

Villa Certosa, Sardinia

The Simca wouldn't do.

It was a Bentley Mulsanne Turbo—sky blue, a ragtop—that Simon steered onto the Strada Provinciale, heading south toward Porto Rotondo and the Villa Certosa. No need to steal one, though there were certainly plenty to be had on the streets. The local Eurocar agency was happy to rent him one. Cost: three thousand euros a day. Vadim's Black Card was happy to accept all charges.

Simon was dressed for an afternoon concert. A tan, summer-weight suit, linen shirt, Tod loafers. Anna looked chic in a lavender sundress and three-inch heels. He'd insisted. He wanted people's eyes on her, not him.

A thirty-minute drive south, a view to steal even the most jaded tourist's breath. A turn at Viale Rudalza. A tour of the Sardinian foothills. Eventually, a sharp turn onto the Via della Certosa. Signs of security began almost immediately. A car parked here and there on the side of the road, men wearing dark suits and dark sunglasses standing beside them, eyes trained on the road. Vigilant, make no mistake.

Simon rounded a turn. Ahead, a line of cars. He slowed. Anna tapped the invitation on her leg as a man approached. Security.

"No need to be nervous," said Simon, rolling down the window. "Your father sponsored this thing. You're royalty."

Anna wasn't buying it. "Our names aren't on the list."

The man greeted them in Italian, asking for their invitation. Anna leaned across Simon's lap, invitation in hand, one name recently added in model calligraphy. Miss Anna Christina Bildt.

"And him?" the security man asked.

"My fiancé," said Anna. "Thomas Hudson."

As requested, Simon and Anna handed over their identification.

"One minute." The guard walked to a knot of men, handed them the passports and invitation. A minute. The conversation among them grew animated. Another man returned, older, unsmiling. Was he waving at Anna?

"Anna, it's me," said the man. "Mario Cerruti. From the bank. Such a loss. My heartfelt condolences. I'm so glad you decided to attend in his place."

"Papa loved his music," said Anna.

"I'm not sure Mr. Obolensky is the equal of Brahms, but he was a client." Mario handed back the passports. "I told the others that Mr. Hudson was also a client. Enjoy."

Simon drove on. "You know him?"

"Never seen him in my life."

An attendant took their car. No ticket. The honor system. Simon followed the line of guests past the main house down a broad sloping lawn. The Villa Certosa—an impressive two-story home, rustic stone and clay tile, built in the style of an old Italian manor, with four wings situated around a central court—was off-limits.

Several dozen guests mingled beneath a sprawling open-air tent. Two bars, one at either side. Servers in white jackets offered hors d'oeuvres. Shrimp, caviar blinis, gravlax. Beyond the tent, closer to the sea, was an amphitheater carved out of the slope, looking like an amphitheater might have two thousand years ago. Six rows of white granite set in an arc overlooking a circular stage. Chairs had been arranged for the performance. The musicians tuned their instruments, arranged sheet music on stands, applied rosin to their bows.

And there, among them, Sergei Obolensky, impossible to miss with his shaggy, schoolboy's haircut, hulking shoulders, and hound dog's face. He'd dressed for his grand debut entirely in black. Black trousers, black open-necked shirt, black jacket. A smaller man stood next to him, his back to Simon. It appeared that Obolensky was showing the man something on his phone and making a big deal about it—3387, per chance? What other reason for his last-minute trip to Cyprus? Michael, if it was him, wanted to see proof of his latest purchase.

Simon helped himself to a flute of Champagne. With Anna on his arm, he made a casual circuit of the tent, eyes scanning the surroundings. It was evident that there was no way to get into the main house, not directly. It was too great a distance to approach without being noticed. Guards stood at every door. Others, no doubt, patrolled the grounds.

"Let me know how I can help," said Anna.

"You already have," said Simon.

"It was you who found the invitation."

"A man alone gets noticed. A couple doesn't."

"I'm your cover?"

"Something like that."

Anna appeared to like the assignment. "This place is enormous," she said. "How are you going to find it?"

"Working on it."

Simon had studied pictures of the villa on the flight in from Cyprus. Its sale by a past Italian prime minister had made the papers across Europe. It was here that the politician, formerly a billionaire media magnate, had consorted with an underage prostitute at some type of elaborately staged Roman orgy—recurring events that both Berlusconi insiders and the Italian public had referred to as "bunga bunga." Simon knew there were at least nine entrances to the ground floor including the front door. He also knew—as evidenced by his own eyes—that all were guarded. The ground floor was out.

One of the articles he'd read suggested the existence of a secret tunnel connecting the villa with a guesthouse, the better for the prime minister to whisk his paramours in and out. All well and good, thought Simon, but the only guesthouse he saw was at the far side of the estate, at least two hundred meters away. And yes, there was a guard there, too.

Which left the second story. Four terraces, too many windows to count, and six skylights. The terraces, he decided, for want of a better choice, were his way in. If, that is, he could reach them.

On the stage, the musicians took their places. A slew of guests left the tent to find their seats, first come, first served. It was three forty. Simon decided his absence would be more conspicuous once everyone was seated. He had twenty minutes and no idea what to do.

"Where's the loo?" asked Anna.

Simon searched the grounds. He observed a woman emerging from a low-slung brick structure not far from the villa—maybe a stable in an earlier time—and difficult to see due to the dense grove of olive trees and century-old oaks surrounding it. Another woman passed her, entering. Two men in white jackets stood on either side of a doorway leading inside.

"Up the hill," said Simon. "I'll go with you."

He set down his glass. Together they walked up the slope. Fifteen meters, more or less, separated the stable from the villa, the space dominated by the trees growing between the structures. Thick trunks, dense canopies, four or five seemingly growing as one.

Maybe, he thought. It just might do.

"I may be a while," he said in her ear, sure to keep a smile on his face. "Go back to the tent. Chill. If I'm not there by the time the concert starts, get the car and leave."

"I'm not leaving you," protested Anna.

"I'm sure it won't come to that. If it does…if something happens…you need to be far away."

Anna shook her head.

"This isn't your fight anymore," said Simon, squeezing her hand. "You did what your father wanted."

"And this is what I want."

"No," said Simon, more forcefully than he would have liked. "This time you need to think about yourself."

"Okay," said Anna.

"Promise?"

Anna nodded.

"Okay, then," said Simon. "See you in a few."

"Simon…" Anna put a hand behind his neck, drew him closer, and kissed him. "Good luck."

Simon entered the men's room. Two stalls against the far wall, both enclosed from floor to ceiling, both with open transom windows high on the wall. A communal urinal was to his left. He chose a stall, closed the door, locked it. Placing a foot against each wall, he climbed high enough to reach the transom. Even open, it was barely wide enough for him to reach an arm through. He unscrewed the hinges, removed the window, and set it on the ground. It was a simple matter to pull himself through the transom. Once on the roof, he lay flat on his belly.

The canopy of trees touched the far side of the stable roof. He crawled in the direction of the villa, until, concealed, he could climb into the thicket, selecting the sturdiest branch to stand upon, hands seeking out higher-placed limbs for balance. Step by step, he made his way, the foliage so dense he couldn't see the ground, or the villa, for that matter. He moved with care, threading himself over and around limbs and boughs, cautious not to draw attention to himself.

He reached the villa, hand brushing the coarse stone. A window was within reach, but not a window that opened. He wiped the sweat from his forehead. And now? To his right, maybe two meters, a terrace. He ducked under a branch, pulled himself onto another until he could extend an arm and grasp the cast-iron railing. His fingers touched metal—*finally!*—when the branch snapped. He dropped, losing his grip on the railing, barely latching on to a bough above him to arrest his fall. Swinging his feet, he landed a heel on the railing. Using it as an anchor, he inched himself closer.

Seconds later, he was standing on the terrace. The door was unlocked. He let himself in. A guest bedroom, unoccupied, as neatly made up as a five-star hotel. The décor was *Viva Las Vegas.* There was even a picture of Elvis on the wall. Obolensky hadn't gotten around to redecorating. Good news.

A moment to regroup. Simon shook loose his hands, brushed the dirt and twigs from his suit. A look in the mirror. No time for nerves. He was doing what he did best. In someone else's house, intent on taking something that didn't belong to him. He'd never felt more at home.

Simon had studied pictures of the villa's interior, too. He knew that the master bedroom overlooked the sea and that there was a media room with a screen that dropped from the ceiling. There was also a fitness room and sauna. And somewhere a two-story library-study with thousands of books and ladders on tracks to reach them. He'd start there. One problem. The library was on the ground floor.

Simon opened the door and peered out. He saw a wide hallway: ox-blood carpeting, paintings on the near wall, windows looking onto the courtyard on the other. No one in sight. Guards were outside, not in. All current residents and guests should be gathering for the concert, which was due to begin in—Simon checked his watch—thirteen minutes. If everyone was as prompt as their host had demanded, he should have the house to himself.

Simon closed the door and strolled down the hall, head high, step unbothered. Should someone ask, he was a guest of Mr. Obolensky. He had every right to be here.

Rooms to his right; some doors open, some closed. Bedrooms, as far as he could tell. At the end of the hall, a stairway descended—if he heard correctly—to an active kitchen. He turned left. Another long hall. He decided he didn't like large homes. If he wanted exercise, he'd take a walk outside.

Ahead, a door swung open. A woman stepped into the hall, looked at him, yanked on the hem of her dress. She was blond and angular, very pretty, her hair mussed. A man followed, balding, anything but angular, hurriedly buttoning his blazer and, a second too late, zipping up his fly.

"*Buon giorno,*" said Simon, a polite nod for the lady, a certain look for the man. He threw out an arm to indicate that please, they should go first.

"Hurry up," the man muttered in Russian. "Sergei will kill us if we're late."

"You always take so long," said the woman.

"Go, go."

Simon followed them down the main staircase and into the front hall. The couple knew their way. He trailed them past a living area and a dining room to a set of French doors giving on to the lawn. The couple exited. Simon did not. He'd spotted his destination not ten steps away. A pair of heavy wooden doors, more suited for a church, a black iron knocker on each. Beyond them, lit by the afternoon sun, books. Lots of them.

Simon entered the library and, with haste, closed the doors. No medieval padlock, just a simple bolt lock. Bookshelves took up three walls, floor to ceiling, a ladder running on a track beside each. A large mahogany desk held pride of place in the center of the room. A newspaper lay on it. *L'Unione Sarda,* the local rag. Honest to God letters sat in a tray, names and addresses handwritten in blue ink. Mira Obolensky in Prague. Dmitry Obolensky in St. Petersburg. His children? Handwritten letters from their father? Maybe Luddites weren't so bad.

Simon sat down. There was a folder holding a ream of musical staff paper, unused. A metronome used as a paperweight. A brass cup holding several pens. So far, no sign of a blue Moleskine notebook.

The desk had a lone pencil drawer. A keyhole lock. Simon had it open in ten seconds. Inside, a wallet, passport, receipts for the Amara Hotel. Nothing, however, from Obolensky's venture to the northern side of the island. Flesh was an all-cash business. He ran a hand inside the drawer. Nothing cached in a back corner.

He rose, replacing the chair. It was evident Obolensky treated the library as his office while visiting the island, maybe a practice room as well, a sanctuary. A place where he would feel comfortable keeping his most important possessions. He turned in a semicircle, asking himself where he would hide a book containing his most confidential information. With other books, of course.

His eyes surveyed the shelves, the hundreds of colorful spines. He looked closer. Most were older volumes, leather bound, titles embossed in gold leaf. *Il Gattopardo* by Tomasi di Lampedusa. The others also Italian. He selected one at random. He couldn't free it. He tried another before it came to him. The books were fakes, decorations, not books at all. He moved from shelf to shelf, tempted to laugh. A Potemkin library for the bunga bunga prime minister. He gave a last try. There had to be one real book. He tugged on another spine. Instead of a book, a desktop unfolded from the wall, and behind it, a concealed set of drawers, polished wood, brass knobs, the work of a master. He'd discovered an antique escritoire.

He opened the largest drawer. Bank statements. Dozens of them. Simon recognized the names. Swiss, French, German, and of course Scandinavian. *Danske Bank*. Still, no sign of a blue notebook.

He checked the smaller drawers, six to each side. Cash. Stacks of bound notes. Dollars, euros, Swiss francs, British pounds. Ten drawers in all. Simon opened each. No notebook.

A nook, top right, housed several books. New books, not leather bound, and yes, real. One name leapt out at him. *Herbert Von Karajan*. It was the biography he'd found at Obolensky's bedside the night before. But why was it here, hidden in the wall, and not by his bed?

With care, he removed it, noting its place. Too heavy for a paperback, he thought. Even one of large format. He set it on the writing surface and opened the cover. Again, he read the inscription, or what he could of it. *"To Sergei..."* Last night, he'd had no reason to examine the book. Today, however, was a different story.

Simon ran his thumbnail across the pages and opened the book to its middle. He always liked looking at the photographs first.

But there was no middle. The pages had been carved out to create a hollow cavity, a hiding place. First a Potemkin library. Now a Potemkin book. What better place to hide it?

Pale blue, if you wanted to know the exact color. The color of an autumnal sky.

Simon removed the notebook.

At that moment, the orchestra struck up a tune. He checked his watch. Four p.m. exactly.

Simon carried the book to the mahogany desk. He thumbed through the pages. He didn't see any notes about Sylvie stealing from the Cellist, or vice versa. Then again, he hadn't expected to.

He gave himself five minutes to photograph its contents. Fifty-six pages in all. Fifty-six pages of bank accounts, holding companies, passwords, law firms. He didn't care to estimate the wealth. It was too much for any man, no matter his rank or privilege. It was certainly too much for a thief.

Simon dropped the photos into a file and sent them to a number with a French country code, Paris city code: Sylvie Bettencourt. He typed in a line that she should transfer the rest of his fee immediately. Four million dollars, thank you. Somehow, he doubted he would be receiving it.

Simon replaced the notebook inside the biography of Herbert von Karajan, master of the Berlin Philharmonic. He then replaced the biography on the shelf, exactly as he'd found it.

Almost.

He inserted it one book to the right.

"He's obsessive," Sylvie had said.

Simon was counting on it.

*   *   *

"I told you to leave," he said to Anna, taking a seat on the granite beside her.

"You did it? Really?"

Simon nodded. The time for business was past. It was time to enjoy the concert.

Anna looked at him. "What if I say I never want to?"

Simon put his arm around her. Obolensky sat center stage, eyes to the heavens as he played a solo. "You know something…the music's not bad. Not bad at all."

"Shh!" The man in front of them turned, hands to his lips.

Michael.

CHAPTER 69

London, England

A glittering end to a glittering career.

Sylvie Marie Bettencourt swept into the exhibition hall of Evolution London on the bank of the River Thames at ten minutes before nine o'clock, greeting acquaintances, rivals, members of the Sotheby's staff with her practiced cool. A curt hello, a firm handshake, and on to the next. Smiles and chitchat were for afterward. Until Sylvie got what she came for, she was all business.

"Alastair," she said, greeting the Sotheby's auctioneer. "Any other serious bidders?"

"One or two," said Quince, as cagey as ever.

"No more?"

Quince leaned closer. "It's yours if you want it."

Sylvie bussed him on the cheek. "I want it."

The sole clue to her buoyant mood was her clothing. She'd chosen a black silk creation from Balenciaga—three thousand pounds at Harvey Nichols—that was cut too low on top, and too high on the bottom. She'd be lying if she said she didn't enjoy the looks cast her way. Admiring from the men. Damning from the women. The Brits always were such prudes.

Why not show off a bit? The Sotheby's automotive auction was the fanciest event on the calendar. Fairy lights strung from the ceiling accented the indigo spots. Attendants in black ties circulated with Champagne and canapés. All the heavy hitters were here: the sheikhs and billionaires, the aficionados and connoisseurs, the eager neophytes and seasoned collectors.

She entered the VIP lounge sponsored by Dom Pérignon, selected a few nibbles prepared by Nigella Lawson and Jamie Oliver. Quite good. It would be the last such affair she'd be attending for a long while.

Sylvie helped herself to a flute of DP. It was her custom to wait until an event's conclusion, but tonight was a night to break the rules. Maybe an hors d'oeuvre as well. A beef Wellington puff pastry with a dollop of horseradish. Divine. But just one.

The text from Simon Riske had arrived at three p.m. sharp. He'd done it. He'd found Sergei's sacred notebook. Her instinct to take Riske in from the cold, to make him part of the family, however briefly, had proven invaluable. She'd cast but a cursory glance at the information, enough to recognize Sergei's antique script—the man could have been a scribe in a monastery—as well as the names of all the right banks. That was enough. Without ado, she'd forwarded the information to Grisha.

"Go," she'd said. "Do your magic."

So he had.

Prior to entering the exhibition hall, Grisha had advised her of his progress. One hundred twenty-six billion dollars transferred to her account. He expected the figure to double before the end of the evening. *Two hundred billion dollars.* To whisper the sum was to grow intoxicated. *And hers!!* What was once Michael's now belonged to Svetlana Alexandrovna Makarova. A shopkeeper's daughter from Moscow was the richest woman in the world.

As for Grisha, he was currently on a plane out of Moscow.

As for Simon Riske, no such luck.

"Mr. Riske will not be returning to London," the message from Vadim had read, sent at 4:50 p.m. local time in Sardinia. (Thankfully, from a new phone.) No mention of details. That would come later when she could savor them. What mattered was that Vadim, her firstborn, had seen to it that Riske was no longer a bother.

That was that, then. *Marché conclu,* as they said. All that remained was to buy one last Ferrari, then…vanish.

The lights dimmed. Once, then twice. Sylvie made her way to her seat. Tenth row, center. She preferred to be a face in the crowd, eyes on her bidding paddle, not her. Her number this evening was 91. The music stopped. A woman announced that the auction would begin in five minutes. The rows filled up quickly. Sylvie was happy to see that the places to her right and left were vacant. She made a note to thank dear Alastair.

The first car on the block was a Lamborghini, estimated price three or four million dollars. Nothing to interest her. Upon its sale, the automobile was driven—slowly, very slowly—off the stage. A Rolls-Royce took its place—1935, black. She imagined Churchill seated in the back, touring London during the Blitz. A handsome car, but again, not for her. Michael was not a fan of the English.

A pause as the Rolls moved off stage. Sylvie used the break to send Vadim a message.

When are you arriving?

Soon, dearest Mama, came the response, instantaneously. Not at all like Vadim.

Sylvie smiled nervously. She wasn't accustomed to his sense of humor, either. Essentially, he didn't have one.

"Pardon me, ma'am." A small, florid man in a dark windbreaker took the seat next to her on her left. Older, seventy-ish, but spry. Maybe Irish. The man sat down, his head buried in the sales brochure, and she noticed the words EUROPEAN AUTOMOTIVE REPAIR AND RESTORATION embroidered on his jacket.

Sylvie leaned closer, a sour taste filling her mouth. That was the name of Simon Riske's shop. She had his business card. She was sure of it.

The man caught her staring. "Ma'am?"

"Nothing," said Sylvie. "I was just admiring your jacket."

"My job. Fixing up cars." The man smiled, covering his mouth as he coughed. "Bit of smoke in my lungs. Dreadful fire the other day."

It struck her that she'd seen him before. "Do we know each other?" Sylvie asked.

"I don't believe we've had the pleasure," said the man pleasantly. "Mason. Harry Mason. How do you do?"

"Mason...But you're—"

"Surprised?" The man seated directly in front of her had turned to address her. He was her age, give or take, lovely suit, sparse white hair, and dark, accusing eyes. Bodyguards flanked him to either side. He had an accent. A Russian one. "Hello, Lieutenant Colonel Makarova."

Sylvie expelled her breath. "Blatt?"

"How long has it been?" said Boris Blatt. "Ten years? Twenty? You didn't care for my offer to serve the Rodina."

"But I saw you…"

"What? Shot? Gunned down? Murdered? And you didn't phone the police? Shame on you."

Sylvie sunk in her chair, reeling. She'd seen it with her own eyes. Simon had leveled a machine gun at him and pulled the trigger from point-blank range. Blatt was a dead man. And Harry Mason, he'd died earlier the same day. Smoke inhalation.

"I'm alive, too," said Anna Bildt, taking the seat to Sylvie's right. "My father would have been cross with me if I'd let you kill me, too."

Sylvie recoiled in horror. The Danish girl had died on the mountain. Vadim had told her so.

"Excuse me," mumbled Sylvie, rising unsteadily, making her way to the aisle. She felt confused, nauseated, altogether overwhelmed. It was some kind of ruse. An elaborate deception. All of it. She saw it, but her mind remained paralyzed, too much in shock to put the pieces together.

Sylvie hurried to the rear of the hall. She needed quiet, calm. Instead, she saw Alastair Quince rushing toward her. "There's a problem," he said. "We just received a call from your bank. Your account no longer has funds available."

"That's not possible," said Sylvie. "My bank sent you a confirmation of available funds yesterday."

"And now they've rescinded it."

"My bank? You're certain?"

"Danske Bank. Lugano branch. A security officer phoned. He was extremely agitated. He asked that we detain you."

"Detain me?"

"Of course, we'd never do such a thing," said Quince. "However, we cannot allow you to bid."

"Give me a minute," said Sylvie. "I'm sure this is a clerical error."

"Hurry," said Quince. "We can't alter the schedule. Even for you."

Sylvie found a quiet spot shielded by a tall steel stanchion and logged on to her account. A minute ago, the balance had stood at one hundred billion dollars. She'd seen the figures. Frantically, she entered the passcode. It was a mistake, she told herself, a measure of confidence returning. No one called from a bank at nine o'clock in the evening.

Her finger hovered, trembling, over the ENTER key.

She did it.

Red numerals. A scream rose in her throat. Her balance stood at negative two million dollars. She doubled over, as breathless as if hit in the solar plexus.

Mason, Blatt, the girl, Carl Bildt's daughter. Now this. Suddenly the room was too hot. She felt dizzy. Fresh air. She needed fresh air. Surely there was an explanation.

Sylvie slid the phone into her purse, lifting her head, and walked straight into a man. She met his gaze. "You?"

"Hello, Sylvie," said Simon Riske. "Rough night?"

Sylvie forced a smile. "I'm fine, thank you."

"Are you?"

"Where's Vadim?" she asked, eyes darting over his shoulder. "Where's my son?"

"He won't be joining us."

Sylvie retreated a step, shaken. She knew exactly what he was saying. She gathered herself, swelling her chest. But all she could say was that she wanted to sit down.

Simon led her to a table. They sat. "You," she said again.

"Tunbridge Wells," said Simon. "You remembered it from thirty years ago before they changed the name…when you visited the house with my father."

"How…?"

"You looked in the cabinet where he kept the vodka."

"You're mistaken. I never—"

"You wanted to use his company to launder money. Even then, you were helping your government get assets out of the country. My father was a commodities trader. What could be more perfect? But he wouldn't play ball."

"This is preposterous. You're making it all up. Come now."

"Am I?" Simon signaled to a tall woman standing nearby. "Special

Agent Kenyon, meet Sylvie Bettencourt. Sylvie, meet Special Agent Kenyon of the United States Financial Crimes Enforcement Network. She has something to play you."

"Ms. Bettencourt." Nessa Kenyon stepped closer, phone in hand. "I think you'll recognize this."

Kenyon pressed PLAY and the three listened to a conversation between Lieutenant Colonel Svetlana Makarova and Anthony Riske made some twenty-eight years earlier, Makarova doing her best to persuade him to work on behalf of the newly democratic Russian Republic, offering him large sums if she might use his firm to launder money. Anthony Riske steadfastly refused.

Then another recording, this one in Russian between Lieutenant Colonel Makarova and her superior, in which she asks for permission to eliminate the uncooperative American. Permission granted.

"So you killed him," said Simon when the recording ended. "You made it look like suicide."

"He could name me as a spy," said Sylvie. "I had no choice. Don't expect me to apologize."

"Never."

Sylvie squared her shoulders, her eyes brighter. Yes, she was proud of what she'd done. "All this," she said. "For him?"

"He didn't leave a note. I've been looking ever since." Simon regarded Kenyon. "Thank you for allowing me to help."

Kenyon nodded, then turned and walked away.

"You missed your calling," said Sylvie. "You belong in my game."

"I'd say I found it."

"Tell me," she said with unexpected alacrity, one professional to another. "How?"

"I had to give you a reason to trust me. The best way was to make myself a mirror image of you."

Sylvie threw back her head, laughing bitterly, but at herself. "It worked. I wanted to believe."

"You needed me."

"I offered you a job in California. You turned me down."

"I was tempted. I knew you couldn't trust me yet. Not enough."

"And the Lost Ferrari—3387?"

"A fake. Harry and I did all the work. We have friends in Italy who went along."

"Dez Hamilton found the car on his property. It was pure chance."

"He didn't just happen to find it," said Simon. "Dez is a storyteller. Someone told him to go look."

"You?"

"A friend who works for Dez. I used to be in that game. Finance. I've got plenty of chits to collect."

"The same friend who told Dez you should be the one to restore it."

"Good bet."

"And the rest?" Sylvie demanded, sitting up. "Your factory? Blatt?"

Simon crossed his arms. He'd seen to it all cars under his stewardship had been moved from the premises before it was torched. He'd done his planning as thoroughly as Sylvie did hers. She didn't need all the answers. She sure as hell didn't deserve them.

"You destroyed his car," Sylvie continued. "It was worth fifty million dollars."

"You don't think I'd really do that to a Ferrari?"

"And all the while you made sure I could see or hear everything." Sylvie gasped and covered her mouth. A terrible look passed across her face. She'd cracked the code. "Her. Danni Pine. You know her. She's your friend."

Simon met Sylvie's gaze. No need to respond. Sylvie had answered her own question. He did, however, enjoy the moment.

"You sent me Obolensky's notebook knowing I would steal all the money," she continued. "And that you...*she*...would steal it back."

Sylvie was a clever one, thought Simon. He wondered if she'd gotten to the last part.

"And now?" she asked.

"The Americans will seek an arrest warrant for you. They'll ask the British government to pick you up and extradite you. You'll fight it."

"So I'm free to go?" Sylvie stood, amazed at her good fortune but still wary.

"Ask him," said Simon.

Sylvie looked to her right and left. She saw him approaching—that dreadful little man in his dreadful gray suit—and the color drained from her face.

"Good evening, Lieutenant Colonel," said I. I. Borzoi, retired prosecutor, right hand of Sergei Obolensky. "I, too, have some questions. Perhaps we might start with what you've done with the money you've stolen."

Three men formed a circle around Sylvie. Borzoi's men. The thugs who'd followed her in New York and staked out her apartment in Paris. It was them. She was sure of it.

"If you'll come with us," said Borzoi.

Sylvie stepped toward Simon. "Please. Help me. You know what they'll do."

Simon did. He retreated a step. He didn't want to be in the way.

One of the men took hold of Sylvie by the shoulders.

"I'll tell them it was you," she said. "You have the money. They'll find out."

"Probably."

Sylvie began to remonstrate, but words failed her. What did it matter who had the money, as long as Michael did not?

"Good night, Sylvie," said Simon.

The men led Sylvie Bettencourt out of the back of the building. To her credit, she did not fight them.

Simon watched until she was out of sight. And so it was over. He had done it. Revenge? Settling a score? Vengeance? Was it any of those things? No, he thought. A son's duty. That was all. He felt good. Very good, indeed.

Simon walked to the front of the hall. He found a seat next to Anna and Harry Mason. Nessa Kenyon joined them.

"What did we get?" asked Simon.

"Coming up on two hundred billion," whispered Kenyon. "We can't keep it. Not all, at least. They'll have a fit."

"Half?"

"Maybe a little more," said Kenyon. "And don't forget everything Sylvie purchased in the States. Ours."

"Not bad for a day's work," said Simon.

"We owe you," said Kenyon.

"No," said Simon. "Other way around."

"Gotta run," said Kenyon. "Lots to do."

"Goodbye, Nessa," said Simon.

A 1963 Ferrari GTO came up for bid. Racing Red. *Gran turismo omologato.* He still didn't know what the *o* word meant.

"How much you think?" asked Boris Blatt. "Twenty million?"

Simon took Anna by the hand. "Let's get out of here. I've got something to show you."

"Really?"

Simon laughed. "My new shop. It's a beaut."

ACKNOWLEDGMENTS

It seems barely a week ago that I finished *The Take,* the first novel featuring Simon Riske. In fact, it was 2017. In that time, I've been fortunate to rely on many professionals in the creation, editing, publication, and marketing of my works.

It all starts with my agent, Richard Pine of InkWell Management. He's the first to learn of my intentions for a story and the first to let me know what he thinks about them, good or bad. Either way, his support and encouragement are unwavering. The luckiest day of my career as an author was when he called to say he'd read the first pages of *Numbered Account,* my debut novel, and asked if he might represent me. That was sometime in May 1996. We haven't looked back since. My thanks also to his colleagues at InkWell: Eliza Rothstein, Claire Friedman, and William Callahan.

I'm blessed to have a terrific team at Mulholland Books / Little, Brown, led by my editor, Josh Kendall. His insight, imagination, and perpetual brilliance elevate my work to another level. My thanks also to Pam Brown, Liv Ryan, Kim Sheu, and Karen Landry.

In Los Angeles, I'd like to thank my new family at Brillstein Entertainment Partners: Amy Powell, Jon Liebman, and Kaleb Tuttle, as well as Marc Evans. There's a whole new world about to discover Simon Riske.

Finally, on the personal front, my gratitude to John Trivers and Liz Myers, two tremendously talented artists who allow this artist to escape the world for a month each year at their mountain hideaway and either begin or finish his latest work.

My love to my daughters, Noelle and Katja, who enrich my life and give it purpose. My love also to my mother, Babs Reich, ninety-two years old and going strong! Thanks to my brother, Bill, for our weekly "hikes" through the neighborhood. Good fun! And, finally, to Laura Kohani, to whom this book is dedicated. Words cannot express my appreciation for your love and support. You make life better in every way imaginable.

CHRISTOPHER REICH is the *New York Times* bestselling author of *The Take, Numbered Account, Rules of Deception, Rules of Vengeance, Rules of Betrayal,* and many other thrillers. His novel *The Patriots Club* won the International Thriller Writers Award for Best Novel in 2006. He lives in Encinitas, California.

MULHOLLAND BOOKS

You won't be able to put down these Mulholland books.

THE STOLEN HOURS *by Allen Eskens*

THE APOLLO MURDERS *by Chris Hadfield*

THE PLEDGE *by Kathleen Kent*

THE GOODBYE COAST *by Joe Ide*

LIKE A SISTER *by Kellye Garrett*

ONCE A THIEF *by Christopher Reich*

THE WHEEL OF DOLL *by Jonathan Ames*

Visit mulhollandbooks.com for
your daily suspense fix.